MR. SENSATIONAL

by

SERENITY WOODS

Copyright © 2017 Serenity Woods
All rights reserved.
ISBN: 1973778831
ISBN-13: 978-1973778837

DEDICATION

To Tony & Chris, my Kiwi boys.

CONTENTS

Chapter One 1
Chapter Two 8
Chapter Three 16
Chapter Four 21
Chapter Five 27
Chapter Six 33
Chapter Seven 38
Chapter Eight 43
Chapter Nine 49
Chapter Ten 54
Chapter Eleven 57
Chapter Twelve 63
Chapter Thirteen 69
Chapter Fourteen 76
Chapter Fifteen 79
Chapter Sixteen 87
Chapter Seventeen 93
Chapter Eighteen 100
Chapter Nineteen 105
Chapter Twenty 111
Chapter Twenty-One 117
Chapter Twenty-Two 122
Chapter Twenty-Three 128
Chapter Twenty-Four 134
Chapter Twenty-Five 139
Chapter Twenty-Six 144
Chapter Twenty-Seven 151
Chapter Twenty-Eight 155
Chapter Twenty-Nine 161
Chapter Thirty 167
Chapter Thirty-One 173
Chapter Thirty-Two 179
Chapter Thirty-Three 182
Chapter Thirty-Four 189
Chapter Thirty-Five 194
Chapter Thirty-Six 199

Chapter Thirty-Seven	205
Chapter Thirty-Eight	210
Chapter Thirty-Nine	215
Chapter Forty	221
Chapter Forty-One	226
Chapter Forty-Two	232
Chapter Forty-Three	238
Chapter Forty-Four	243
Chapter Forty-Five	249
Chapter Forty-Six	255
Chapter Forty-Seven	260
Chapter Forty-Eight	265
Chapter Forty-Nine	271
Chapter Fifty	276
Chapter Fifty-One	281
Chapter Fifty-Two	287
The Four Seasons	296
About The Author	302

Chapter One

"Sex," Coco said. "And lots of it."

She'd been looking out of the window as she spoke, but on glancing back at her friend, realized by Amy's startled look that she must have spoken louder than she'd meant to, and her voice had carried across the small coffee shop. The young barista foaming the milk behind the counter giggled, and the man leaning on the bar waiting for his latte looked up from his iPad and raised an eyebrow.

Coco's eyes widened with dismay. She'd spotted him as soon as she walked into *Bella's*. Although he was dressed much the same as the other early morning office workers in a dark suit and a long black coat to ward off the cool New Zealand air, something about him made him stand out from his surroundings. Maybe it was his height—he must have been at least six two. Or perhaps it was his dark hair, short and sleek at the back, longer and falling over his forehead at the front in a style that declared "I'm a naughty boy beneath this demure image—deal with it."

Yum, she'd thought as Amy had ushered her in out of the rain. Very tasty. But he hadn't looked up, busy concentrating on his Financial Times app or whatever had captured his attention so completely, and she'd torn her gaze away, her mind too full of her own busy day to dwell on the guy, however hot he might be.

Now, though, his eyes met hers and one corner of his mouth curved up.

"Classy," Amy said as they moved to the counter. She waved an apologetic hand at the man. "Sorry. I was asking her what she wanted for Christmas this year."

The man chuckled, put down his iPad, and accepted his latte from the barista. "Interesting request. Most women ask for perfume or jewelry." His deep, gravelly voice made the hairs rise on the back of Coco's neck.

She cleared her throat, mortified he'd overheard her words, and decided the only way out would be to make a joke of it. "Yes, well, that's what springs to mind when you sit on Santa's lap as a grown-up."

Amy snorted and started relating their order to the amused girl behind the counter. Coco couldn't tear her eyes away from the man's, though. Deep brown and warm with amusement, they crinkled at the edges as he smiled. He leaned forward conspiratorially and said in a low voice, "What I want to know is… have you been naughty or nice this year?"

She caught her breath. He smelled enticing, a mixture of manly body wash, hot muffins, and coffee, a mouth-wateringly morning smell. A vision shot through her head of him getting dressed, buttoning up the white shirt over tanned skin, hair ruffled from a night of passionate lovemaking…

She blinked, shocked at her train of thought. What the hell? Get a grip, Coco. His smile spread as if he'd read her mind, and she dropped her gaze, searching for something to say, a way to escape the conversation without embarrassing herself further.

Luckily, her gaze fell on his iPad, and what she saw there made her laugh out loud. Not the Financial Times, in fact not any newspaper app.

"Angry Birds?" She raised her eyes to his again. "Really?"

"What?" He gave her a mock-affronted look and tucked the iPad under his arm. "I'm up to level ten. It's addictive."

"I'm sure it is." She smiled. "Don't worry, your secret's safe with me."

He laughed and turned to go. As he passed her, he bent and whispered in her ear. "I hope Santa brings you everything you want for Christmas." His warm breath on her skin sent a shiver across her shoulder blades and down her back.

She watched him walk away, unable to stop her lips curving as he turned to push open the door and winked at her before letting it shut behind him.

"Yowza." Amy's wide eyes echoed her approval. "I wouldn't be disappointed to find one of those in my stocking."

Coco smiled wryly and accepted the cappuccino from the barista. "I wouldn't let a man like that anywhere near your stockings, Amy dear. He'd devour you in one gulp."

"One can only hope."

They both laughed and headed for the doorway.

"Shame you didn't find out where he worked," Amy said. "He was interested in you."

Coco opened the door and turned up the collar of her raincoat. It wasn't raining, but she was determined to stop the notoriously brisk Wellington wind from sliding its fingers down the neck of her shirt. She glanced up the street—he'd vanished, no doubt heading for one of the financial institutions downtown. She'd probably never see him again.

Squashing the answering ripple of disappointment, she frowned at Amy. "Don't exaggerate. I barely said two words to the man."

"Yes, but one of those words was 'sex'. His eyes lit up like the patient's nose in the game Operation."

She couldn't deny that—his eyes had definitely glimmered with interest. But it didn't make any difference. "That may be, but you know I'm not looking for anyone. Far too much on my mind at the moment."

Amy sent her a remonstrative look as they walked along the pavement. "You've always got too much on your mind. When was the last time you actually went on a date?"

"2010. But that's not the point. It's an important day today. I need to have my wits about me." *And I need to stop thinking about those brown eyes and that quirky smile.*

"True, this is probably the most important day of your life." Amy slurped her coffee. "So far, anyway. I hope you're prepared."

"Thanks. No pressure or anything." Coco's stomach continued to churn the way it had since she'd awoken that morning. Luckily, she had the coffee to settle it. *Thanks, Amy. Way to go to calm me down.*

Her best friend seemed oblivious to her nerves. "Absolutely there's pressure." She fell into step beside Coco as she started walking along Lambton Quay to their place of work. "It's not every day you get to become Queen of the Revolting Peasants at McAllister Dell."

"That's not my actual job title, you know."

"It should be. It suits you."

Coco sent her an amused look and followed it with an involuntary shiver. It was mid-December and they should really be heading toward a sultry New Zealand summer, but in Wellington, the capital city, it felt distinctly like early spring, and the fact that the sun hadn't yet woken up didn't help. The streets were shrouded in twilight, and the wet roads smelled of petrol and damp leaves. "Jeez, it's cold."

"Well, you would insist on getting to work at the crack of dawn instead of rolling in at five to nine like normal people."

"You didn't have to come in with me." Coco stepped carefully around the puddles in her high heels. The last thing she needed today was to slip, fall on her butt, and start the morning off looking like she was auditioning for *Singing in the Rain*.

"Oh, I'm not going to miss out on a chance to see Miss Stark at work. Especially when there's a new shipload of minions arriving today. I enjoy watching her cracking the whip, and I'm not going to get much chance over the next week." Amy was going on holiday the next day to visit her father up in the Bay of Islands.

"You know it freaks me out when you talk about me in the third person like that."

Amy shrugged. "Well, it's like you're two different people. I like Coco, she's warm, funny, and friendly. She's my best friend and I'd do anything for her. Veronica Stark—not so much. I'm glad I work in HR and don't have to deal with her. She scares the crap out of me."

Coco laughed and sipped her coffee. "You make her sound like a right old dragon."

"You know that's your nickname at the firm, right?"

Coco grinned. "Yeah. I kind of like it."

Amy rolled her eyes. "The crew arriving today doesn't know what's going to hit them. How many are coming again?"

"Not sure exactly. Half a dozen legal execs, several lawyers and, of course, Mr. Hotshot Fancy Pants himself."

"I hope you're not going to call him that to his face."

"Only if he annoys me." Which he had already, thought Coco, and he hadn't even set foot in the office yet.

"You should give him at least five minutes before you decide you're not going to like him," Amy scolded.

Coco said nothing. A sweep of uneasiness made her stomach flip again, and she wished she'd gone with her initial instinct and refused breakfast. But her mother had practically forced her to have a slice of toast, saying she needed to keep her strength up on such an important day.

"What's his real name again?" Amy asked.

"Felix Wilkinson. A.k.a. Fancy Pants."

Amy giggled. "What don't you like about him?"

"I've never met him. But he sounds like one of the young, flash, arrogant lawyers that are so annoying."

"Is he single?"

Coco sent her an exasperated look. Amy was desperate to get married, settle down, and have babies. Her job was just a convenient way for her to earn money to buy things to make herself prettier so she could attract a guy and achieve her dream. Coco didn't resent her for that, but a little part of her envied her best friend. What must it be like not to have the responsibilities piled on Coco's sometimes too-narrow shoulders?

She sighed, not wanting to think about the pressures and strains of life outside the office when such an important day loomed. Amy was right. She shouldn't judge Mr. Hotshot until she'd met him. But she couldn't shake the feeling that she was almost certainly going to hate his guts.

Part of it, she was sure, was the age-old competition between the Auckland and Wellington branches of McAllister Dell. The Wellington branch was the oldest and most prestigious, but for some reason Auckland had a tendency to grab the best young lawyers. Felix Wilkinson already had a reputation throughout the company of being a fantastic family lawyer, and it rankled amongst most of the Wellington partners that the Auckland branch had nabbed him. It did make sense that the person chosen to investigate the recent sexual harassment claim against one of the Wellington partners was from a different branch, but still, they could have got someone in from Christchurch or Dunedin, somewhere that didn't have the same rivalry.

But if she was honest with herself, that wasn't the main reason she was angry. The case was dredging up old memories and feelings about the accused partner—Peter Dell—she'd thought long buried. The guilt that had lain at the bottom of her stomach like sand on a riverbed was stirring up inside her, and nausea kept threatening to rise, together with uncharacteristic flutters of nerves.

She had to stomp on that before she walked through the doors. Veronica Stark did not get nervous. Veronica Stark did not have nerves. Or a heart, for that matter. She was a medical marvel. And the sooner she adopted her alter ego's persona, Coco thought as she took another swallow of coffee, the better.

"Poor Coco," Amy said, reaching out to squeeze her arm, obviously realizing Coco couldn't put her resentment into words. "It's a shame you have to deal with Mr. Hotshot on the day you take over the office."

Coco sighed. "Well I have practically been doing the job for three months, so it's no big deal really. It's kind of a relief that Mrs. Ingram's retired. At least I'll get paid for doing the job now."

"Youngest officer manager the firm has ever had," said Amy, shaking her head. "Who'd have thought it? I'm so proud of you."

"Yeah. Me too." Coco smiled.

"Why didn't they make you start on Monday?" Amy wondered.

Coco shrugged. "Something to do with the pay cycle starting on Fridays, plus yesterday was Mrs. Ingram's official last day. I wasn't going to argue—I was just pleased to be asked at all."

It was only another hundred yards or so until they reached the door to McAllister Dell, so she stopped in front of a shop window to check her appearance. There was no need to be nervous, she told herself as she took out her lipstick. This was just another day doing a job she loved. Still, her hand shook a little as she smoothed the lipstick over her lips. She always felt better once the lipstick was on.

Amy tried to coax her curly brown hair back into its clip and frowned as Coco ran a hand along the blonde locks that remained rolled into a tight bun.

"How come you don't have a hair out of place in this wind?" Amy asked resentfully.

"A shedload of hairspray."

"I know for a fact you don't use hairspray. I don't think Veronica's hair dare misbehave."

"Damn straight." Coco pulled her glasses out of her pocket and slid them onto her nose. She only needed them for reading, but she liked the professorial look they afforded her and tended to wear them most of the time in the office. "There. I hope they're ready for Miss Stark, because she's more than ready for them."

"Strength and honor," said Amy, putting her fist on her chest in a grand impersonation of Russell Crowe's Maximus.

"Don't make me laugh. You know Miss Stark doesn't smile."

"Oh yeah. I forgot."

Coco lifted her chin as they walked toward the large glass doors that marked the entrance to McAllister Dell's lobby. *I'm Veronica Stark*, she thought. She ran the office. And she wasn't going to let Peter Dell and Mr. Felix Fancy Pants ruin her special moment. No matter what the day threw at her, she'd take everything in her stride, the same as she usually did.

Chapter Two

Felix pushed through the glass doors of McAllister Dell's impressive building and walked up to the main reception desk. A young woman with dark hair cut in a neat bob smiled up at him from her seat and said, "Good morning. Can I help you?"

"Thank you, yes. Felix Wilkinson from the Auckland office to see Christopher McAllister. I believe he arrived yesterday?"

"Yes, sir. Mr. McAllister's working in the boardroom this morning—I'll give him a ring. If you'd like to take a seat."

Felix smiled at her and walked across to the waiting area. He sat in one of the plush leather chairs, put his briefcase on the polished oak table in front of him, and sat back to look around.

Uh-oh, was his first thought, although he maintained his calm appearance and made sure not to display his surprise and unease. He hadn't anticipated this. The Wellington offices of his law firm made him feel as if he'd travelled back sixty years or so to the nineteen fifties. They were a stark contrast to the swish, modern branch he originated from.

There, in Auckland, the offices were decorated with cream carpets, stylish chrome-and-glass furniture, and large, colorful abstract paintings on the walls. The huge windows overlooked the busy harbor of the City of Sails, and all the lawyers worked with the latest technology, with laptops and iPads, digital voice recorders, and with access to vast online libraries. Felix loved it. He'd been at the firm for five years, worked sixty to seventy hours most weeks, and was hoping to make partner soon. He hadn't been to the Wellington office before. He'd started work at the Bay of Islands branch because that was where his family came from, and he'd visited Christchurch, Dunedin, and Nelson, but both times he'd scheduled a visit to Wellington he'd had to cancel, once due to sickness, and the second time because his brother was getting married.

So this was his first visit, and unease bubbled in his stomach at his initial impression. Usually he wouldn't have thought twice about his surroundings—his head would have been working on the latest case, and he would've had his laptop out in seconds to save wasting time. But his reason for being in Wellington was to investigate the co-founder, Peter Dell, and for that he also needed to investigate the branch itself and its processes.

So far, it didn't bode well. The other co-founder of the firm, Christopher McAllister—now senior partner of the Auckland branch—had spent time developing policies on sexual harassment and other issues such as equal rights in the workplace and establishing generous maternity and paternity leave. The branch offered a good balance between male and female employees—okay, maybe not quite fifty-fifty, but a good sixty-forty, with an impressive percentage of minority groups represented. The branch's policies were reviewed regularly and updated accordingly.

From what Felix had read, the Wellington branch's policies hadn't been updated for years. And looking around the reception area, he thought he could understand why. From the dark red carpet to the old-fashioned flock wallpaper, from the polished oak table and chairs to the traditional, faded watercolors on the walls and the subtle but unmistakable stale smell of cigar smoke, the furnishings spoke of class and sophistication. They also stank of the old boys' network, of secret handshakes and deals made over after-dinner brandies in men's clubs, of the trophy wife at home and secret office affairs, and he didn't like it one bit. He'd been astonished to read the list of partners and see only one woman among them, with nearly all the females in the branch under thirty and working in the secretarial field.

The setup was unusual for an office in a capital city that was generally seen as modern and advanced, and he could only assume it was mainly due to the influence of the senior partner there, Peter Dell.

That did not bode well for his investigation.

He shifted uncomfortably in his chair. A week before, Christopher had called him into his office and explained that one of the young secretaries at the Wellington branch, Sasha De Langen, had accused Dell of improper sexual conduct, and by law they had to investigate the matter. Rob Drake, a lawyer in the Wellington branch, had interviewed Sasha and taken a written statement, but Christopher wanted a member of his branch unconnected with Peter Dell to carry out the hearing in the capital city.

Felix had been puzzled as to why Christopher had asked him when he had little experience with harassment issues—his expertise was in family law, with paternity suits, custody battles, and restraining orders. But Christopher had explained that was why he'd chosen him—Rob Drake had the harassment background, but Felix was good at understanding people and relationships, and he wanted his unbiased view of things.

Besides, it was pretty much a formality, Christopher had said. A misunderstanding that would be quickly cleared up and then they could all go back to normal.

But now, looking at the surroundings, Felix began to wonder. Maybe the story wasn't as simple as Christopher had implied?

"Felix!"

He turned to see his boss striding across the carpeted floor from the elevators. Ten years after co-founding the Wellington office in the eighties, Christopher McAllister had moved to Auckland to establish a branch there, and it was he who had hired Felix on his return to New Zealand after five years in the UK. Felix liked Christopher, who was pleasant, matter-of-fact, and of a similar build to himself, which was a good few inches over six feet and broad shouldered to boot. Felix hoped his own hair would mirror his boss's by the time he reached sixty—he'd much rather have Christopher's silvery white thatch than go bald.

He rose to shake Christopher's hand. "Morning."

"Flight okay?" asked his boss.

"Fine. Damn windy here though."

"Always is," said Christopher. "Makes your teeth ache in winter. Should be warming up by now. Fucking southerlies. Come on. I'll take you up to your office."

Felix picked up his briefcase and walked across the reception area, giving a parting smile to the young woman at the desk. She blushed prettily, and he chuckled to himself.

As usual, his first thought was that she wasn't as pretty as Lindsey. He sighed. It had been nearly eight years since Lindsey died—why did he always feel the need to compare other women to her? And, more importantly, would he ever meet anyone who exceeded the memory he had of her as the most beautiful girl on earth?

Unbidden, a vision formed in his head of the woman he'd met at the coffee shop before he'd visited the bank to get some cash out. He should have asked where she worked. Her bold statement about sex "and lots of it" had caught his attention, and her elegantly swept-up blonde hair and refined features had held it, along with her bright, intelligent eyes and her straight white teeth as she'd burst into laughter on seeing his Angry Birds app. Yes, she'd been a stunner, but he had to put her to the back of his mind. He'd probably never see her again, and besides, he had more pressing things to think about than getting laid.

"How's Peter?" Felix asked, following Christopher into the elevator.

Christopher shrugged and pressed the button for the fifth floor. "I suggested he take a two-week holiday until the investigation is over. Didn't want to suspend the man for such a trivial matter, but wanted him out of the picture, you know?"

Felix nodded, taking note of the word trivial. "But he's coming in this morning?"

"Yes, ten o'clock. Rob sent him a written notice setting out the allegations and stating he can bring a support person, that sort of thing. I wanted it all done properly." But his tone implied that he knew what the outcome was going to be. Felix frowned.

The elevator shuddered to a halt and the doors opened, and Felix followed Christopher out into another reception area much the same as the first, full of dark, earthy colors, mahogany and oak furniture, and dull watercolors that had probably been there since the founding of Wellington in the eighteen forties.

"This way," Christopher said, and led him through a maze of corridors. Felix felt a pang of homesickness for the spaciousness of the Auckland building. Thank God he was only there temporarily. He wouldn't want to work there on a permanent basis.

Christopher finally stopped outside an office and gestured for Felix to precede him. "This'll be yours for the duration of your stay."

Felix went in. It wasn't as bad as he'd feared—large windows overlooked the quay, and the harbor, although a dull gray in the early morning light, reminded him of home.

"Thought it would be a bit more familiar for you." Christopher smiled.

So, his boss was aware of the old-fashioned appearance of the Wellington branch? Interesting. Why had he never suggested to Peter Dell that they change it?

A long wooden desk stretched in front of the far window with a computer, notepads, pens and pencils, and several manila folders presumably holding the details of the case. To one side were four comfortable armchairs and a coffee table. In front of them stood a man who came forward now and held out his hand with a smile.

"This is Rob Drake," Christopher said. "He's an associate like yourself. Great guy, switched on, knows the branch inside out, as well as harassment law. He carried out the initial interview of Miss De Langen and put the file together for you. He'll be your right-hand man if you want anything."

The two men shook hands. Rob was about his own age, Felix thought—late twenties, a bit shorter than himself, with fluffy brown hair and large brown puppy dog eyes that the women in the office would no doubt be falling over themselves to stare into. But the eyes were intelligent, his handshake firm and confident, and Felix liked him immediately.

"Good to meet you," Rob said. "We've heard a lot about you down here, Mr. Oxford."

Felix smiled. He'd been given a scholarship to study law at Oxford University in England and had lived there for five years, the final two in London. His brothers still teased him when he unconsciously dropped Cockney phrases into the conversation. "All good things, I hope."

"Mostly." Rob grinned, and Felix laughed. He was relieved he had someone to help with the investigation. He'd quiz Rob about it when Christopher had gone.

"Right," his boss said. "I've got a few things to do before we meet Peter at ten and then hopefully I can be off out once it's all done and dusted. I'll leave Rob to show you around. Anything you need, just let Rob know, or Miss Stark, our office manager."

"You might want to put a crash helmet on for her induction meeting," Rob commented dryly.

"And hold onto your balls," Christopher said. "The Dragon has a tendency to emasculate most of the men around here."

"Her balls are bigger than mine," Rob said.

Christopher snorted and walked over to the door. "We're just teasing. Miss Stark's been here for ten years. Started on her seventeenth birthday. Hardest-working secretary I've ever known.

Top-class secretarial skills, and she runs this office with a rod of irony."

"You mean iron?" Felix asked.

"No." Christopher said. "You'll understand when you meet her."

"Jeez," Rob said, "is she only twenty-seven? I thought she was at least forty. Although she hasn't got the figure of a forty-year-old."

"Don't let her catch you talking like that." Christopher pointed his pen at him before opening the door. "She'll have you hung, drawn, and quartered before the end of the day." He winked and left.

"I'll take you over to her office now, if you like," Rob said, eyes twinkling. "Might as well get it over with."

Felix left his briefcase on the desk and followed him out of the office. "Is she really that terrifying?"

"Oh yeah." Rob rolled his eyes. "Scares me shitless. But Christopher was right—she's organized and efficient. She probably understands the law better than I do, and she knows this office inside out. She trained under Mrs. Ingram, who just left after a long illness. This is Miss Stark's official first day on the job, but she's run the office alone for the last three months, and she's been Mrs. Ingram's second in command for years. Very old school, you know? Traditional and bossy."

He turned at the end of the corridor and opened the door to the first semi-open-plan room Felix had seen, consisting of partitioned areas housing the legal secretaries—all women, he noticed—and others who he thought were probably the legal executives helping the solicitors with the day-to-day running of the firm.

Rob gestured to an office on the far side, and they crossed the workroom together. "Anything you want, she's your first port of call. So you need to get on her good side, right?"

"And how do I do that?"

"Do as you're told, don't answer back, don't make innuendo, and don't be cheeky."

"Right." Felix tried not to laugh. "Duly noted." He wasn't surprised, though. Most offices had a little Hitler who kept things running smoothly. They always looked the same: skinny and flat-chested with a face that looked like they'd been sucking lemons, a screechy voice, and absolutely no sense of humor. Although Christopher's description—and the lawyer's subsequent reference to her figure—had suggested maybe Miss Stark was different. And she was only twenty-seven, not late forties or fifties as most office managers were.

Interesting.

Rob paused outside the closed door that had *Miss V. Stark—Office Manager* on it. From inside came the distinct sound of someone being told off.

Rob pulled an *eek* face.

"Perhaps we should wait," Felix suggested.

"Absolutely."

Felix looked at the sign. "What does the V stand for?"

"Veronica," said Rob. "But don't call her that. She's very formal."

Felix raised an eyebrow, now thoroughly intrigued by the mysterious Miss Stark. He could hear her inside, chewing out what must be a younger secretary, judging by her tone.

"It's not good enough," she was saying. Her voice wasn't screechy at all, Felix noted. It was quite low, almost husky, and sent little fingers sliding down his spine. "These are silly mistakes, which mean you're not paying attention to your work. I know you're capable of better."

"Sorry, Miss Stark," came the miserable voice of a young woman.

"Sorry isn't good enough. The original letter's already gone to Mr. Hoyle for signing. Even if you'd made mistakes in your original shorthand, you should have had enough sense to transcribe them properly—it's basic common sense."

"Yes, Miss Stark."

"I mean, honestly, Sam. Or do you really not know the difference between a P-A-W-N shop and a P-O-R-N shop?"

Felix's eyes met Rob's, and they both stifled a laugh.

"Yes…I do, Miss Stark," stuttered the sorrowful Sam.

"Are you sure? Only you could've given our poor client a terrible reputation."

"I'm really sorry, Miss Stark. It won't happen again."

"Good."

Felix frowned. Hold on a minute. That voice rang a bell. It sounded like the girl from the coffee shop. He could distinctly remember the first words he'd heard her utter in that same husky voice. But that didn't make sense. Rob had described her like a straight-laced, uptight frump, and the coffee-shop beauty had not looked—and most certainly hadn't sounded—straight-laced.

"Are you practicing your shorthand every evening as I asked you to?" she continued. "Fifteen minutes while watching TV?"

"Um, yes, Miss Stark. Most nights."

"Every night, Sam. Without fail. I expect you to be a hundred words a minute by the end of the year. I'll be testing you myself."

"Yes, Miss Stark."

"Good. Off you go, then."

The door opened, and Felix and Rob stepped aside as the young secretary scurried out looking suitably ashamed. They peered around the door into the large office.

Chapter Three

Felix got his first sight of the inimitable Miss Stark, and immediately realized he'd guessed right—she was the gorgeous chick from *Bella's*.

Back then she'd been wearing a long raincoat, and he hadn't been able to get a good look at her figure, but the coat now hung on the back of the door, and he was able to peruse her at his leisure.

Tall in elegant black heels several inches high, she was slender but curvy, dressed in an extremely chic dark-gray business suit, the skirt a respectable one inch above her knees, the white shirt with only two buttons open at the neck and no sign of any cleavage on show. Her blonde hair was still coiled in a tight bun, and her make-up was simple and understated, apart from her lips, which were now a dark red. She also now wore glasses with a modern rectangular frame, and her whole appearance spoke of professionalism and efficiency.

He could see why others might think her cold and reserved. But the red lipstick was a dead giveaway and corroborated her statement in the shop. This woman desperately wanted to be kissed. She was gorgeous, and from that moment, watching her standing by her desk with hands on hips and those luscious red lips pursed, Felix wanted her.

It was a pity that the absolute last thing he could indulge in considering his reason for being at the branch was an office affair.

Rob knocked on the door, timidly enough to make Felix bite his lip so he didn't laugh.

She looked up at them over the top of her glasses. "Yes?" Her voice was crisp and said *Are you sure you want to bother me? I'm really not in a good mood.*

Her eyes met Felix's. They widened, and he was sure he heard her inhale sharply.

Rob said, "Sorry to interrupt you, Miss Stark, I know you're very busy, but I thought I'd bring Felix Wilkinson along to meet you. I'll leave you to it if that's okay. I've got lots to do." He winked at Felix and made a quick exit.

Felix watched him go before turning to see her studying him. She'd smothered her initial shock and replaced it with cool control.

"So you're the infamous Mr. Wilkinson." She beckoned him into the office and held out her hand. "Pleased to meet you."

"And you're the infamous Miss Stark," he said. They shook hands. She had a firm grip, and up close he could see her eyes were a startling green behind her glasses. "Very nice to meet you—again," he said, giving her a warm smile.

"Hmm." She didn't return the compliment, or the smile. "Please sit."

Felix lowered himself to the other seat in front of the desk, noting with amusement that she didn't join him but perched on the edge of her desk, looking down at him. A position to intimidate. Clearly, she was going to pretend their previous meeting—and her unfortunate admission to her friend—hadn't happened. Leaning back in his seat, he rested an ankle on the opposite knee and linked his fingers, adopting the most un-confrontational pose he could.

"I'm the office manager," she said, "and—"

"Yes," Felix interrupted, "I hear congratulations are in order."

She blinked. "Thank you." The icy stare said *Don't interrupt me again*. "Anyway, as I was saying, I'm in charge of those who aren't lawyers here—the word processor operators and the legal secretaries, the librarians and service clerks, and all the other litigation support staff. If you need something done, you come to me first, understand? I know everyone's workload and everyone's skills, and I can assign you the best person for the job."

Felix nodded. "Understood."

"In a minute, I'll show you where you put your general files for the typing pool, but I'll probably be assigning you your own secretaries as you're working on a special case."

Had he imagined it, or had there been an underlying hint of sarcasm on the word special? "Okay."

"Do you prefer a secretary with shorthand skills or do you use a digital recorder?"

He couldn't remember the last time he'd given dictation to a shorthand secretary. He really had travelled back forty years. Next thing she'd be asking him if he wanted a cigar. "I'm used to digital."

She nodded sharply. "Okay. I'll give you the abridged version of the general tour in a minute as you're only going to be here temporarily."

Okay, so now he definitely wasn't imagining it. She was annoyed with him, and he'd only just walked through the door. Was that because of their previous meeting? Because he'd seen behind the icy facade she wore in the office? "Sure," he said easily.

She crossed her arms. "Lastly, while you're here you should know that I expect a certain level of behavior from lawyers in the Wellington branch."

His eyebrows rose. "Oh?"

"Yes. There are a lot of young women here, both in the typing pool and throughout the rest of the office. I'm not stupid—I know relationships occur in the workplace, but I expect them to be discreet, and I expect you to use your common sense. I do not expect to come into work to find half a dozen twenty-somethings crying over their keyboards because you haven't returned their phone calls."

His eyebrows stayed somewhere around his hairline. "I see. I feel I should point out that it would be a bit crass to have an office affair considering I'm here to investigate allegations of sexual harassment."

She fixed him with her steely stare. "You may be a hotshot at the Auckland branch, Mr. Wilkinson, but while you're here in my office, I'm top dog. Got it?"

Felix met her green-eyed gaze and nodded. "You like to be on top. Check."

The words were out before he could stop himself, and he nearly groaned out loud. Great, Felix. Sexual innuendo. Hadn't he just mentioned he was there to investigate sexual harassment?

There was a stony silence for a good ten seconds.

She stared at Felix with a look that could have frozen lava, and then, very slowly, ran her gaze down to his feet and back up, taking in every inch of his appearance. Felix bore the appraisal, knowing he'd deserved it, but couldn't resist doing the same to her. He admired her sexy high heels, slim calves, and narrow waist, checked the hands that rested on her arms for a wedding ring, but didn't find one—and his gaze lingered on her generous, pert breasts before meeting her eyes again.

For the first time, a hint of smile curved her lips. "Are you going to be trouble?" she asked softly, tipping her head slightly at him.

Seeing the smile, he opted for humor. "I sincerely hope so."

To her credit, she gave a short, sharp laugh, pushed herself off her desk, and walked to the other side to shuffle some papers. "I'll show you around the office. Do you have any questions so far, Mr. Wilkinson?"

He got to his feet. "Yes, quite a few, but let's start with: what shall I call you?"

She glanced up at him over her the top of her glasses, a look he found so sexy that, if the door hadn't been open, he might have pushed her up against the desk and kissed her senseless. "Miss Stark will do just fine, thank you."

"I can't call you Veronica?"

"Nobody calls me Veronica."

He frowned at that, watching her tidy her desk and lean forward on it to check her emails. In spite of the fact that her white shirt was buttoned well above her cleavage, from his high vantage point he got a splendid view of her breasts encased in white lacy half-cups. Nice, he thought, before politely averting his gaze.

The phone on her desk rang, and she said, "Excuse me," before answering it. She listened for a moment then walked over to a filing cabinet and pulled out a manila file. Her back to him, she balanced it on top of the drawer and started to flip through it as she discussed the contents with the caller.

Felix took a few steps to the side of her desk and perused the items. At the edge nearest to him, she had a photograph in a frame, and he picked it up and scanned it quickly. It was of her with an older woman in a wheelchair. Her mother? The office manager's hair hung around her shoulders in golden waves, which made her look younger and softer. And he could just see that around her neck, she was wearing a gold chain with a word hanging from it. It said Coco.

Hmm.

He put the photo down and checked the rest of the desk. There were no little knickknacks that would suggest she was in a relationship, no small cuddly toys or love hearts or photos of a guy looking fondly at the camera. He walked back to the center of the room and waited for her to finish her call. She hung up the phone. "Sorry about that."

"No worries."

She looked blank briefly. "What were we talking about?"

"You asked me if I have any questions."

"Oh. Yes. Do you?"

"Yes. Why did I annoy you as soon as I walked in the room?"

She met his gaze, looking amused. "To be honest, you annoyed me before you got here."

"Because of the coffee shop?"

"Before then, actually."

"Wow. It takes some doing to annoy someone before they've even met you."

Her mouth twitched. "I'm not too fond of JAFAs."

"Just Another…Flipping Aucklander?" He smiled. "Actually, I was born in the Bay of Islands. But I get your point. I must say, I'm not too fond of Wellington myself. Far too windy."

She raised her eyebrows. "Well, you know what they say—Wellington blows, but Auckland sucks."

He laughed at that. After unbuttoning his jacket, not missing the way her eyes dipped to follow his movement, he slid his hands into the pockets of his pants and said, "Now, why don't you tell me the real reason I got up your nose before I even arrived here?"

Her eyes lifted to his and surveyed him coolly. "What makes you think that wasn't the real reason?"

"I'm trained to read the truth in people's eyes, Miss Stark. Quite clearly, you're withholding evidence." He leaned against the cabinet and studied her with the patient lawyer's stare he'd cultivated over the ten years he'd been studying the subject.

She blinked. "I…" She looked down at her desk and moved a file from one side to the other.

He frowned as an idea formed in his head. "Is it the case? Something to do with Peter Dell?"

Chapter Four

Coco studied him silently. This man had somehow welded the speech center of her brain into one large lump. She'd nearly passed out when she looked up from her desk and Rob had announced he was the Mr. Hotshot she'd been so dreading meeting. What were the chances? She'd been so certain he'd be slimy and obnoxious. True, he was as flash and confident as she'd expected, but his eyes were kind and gentle, and there was something in the way he looked at her that lit a fuse at the bottom of her spine and sent the flame firing up her central nervous system to explode somewhere behind her eyes, knocking out her ability to converse.

Was it just the way he looked? Most men looked good in suits, and his was a very good suit. Navy with a faint pinstripe, tailor-made from quality fabric, it was cut perfectly to fit his large frame, snug across his wide shoulders without being tight, the pants the perfect length for his long legs, not quite touching the ground over his stylish loafers. His light blue shirt brought attention to his brown eyes and dark hair, which continued to flop endearingly over his forehead. The subtle, darker blue tie complemented the suit and shirt perfectly. Had a woman dressed him? He wore a single gold signet ring on his right hand, but when she glanced at his left there was no sign of a wedding ring, although that didn't mean anything nowadays.

Not that she was interested, of course. Veronica Stark did not have time for this sort of thing. She moved more papers around on her desk, knowing perfectly well he was aware she was shuffling aimlessly. Would he push her, or change the subject? As a top lawyer, he'd be used to pressing the point and wheedling out answers.

"So, anyway," he said. His deep, gravelly voice was a big part of the reason why her brain was turning to mush. Talk about give a girl goose bumps.

His words implied a change of subject. Hoping that was the case, she made her voice crisp. "Yes?"

"What makes a senior partner say his office manager has 'top-class secretarial skills'? What does that constitute, exactly, in this day and age?"

She walked around the desk and studied him, arms folded. He had changed the subject. That won him a few points. "Are you checking my credentials?"

He smiled. "Just interested. Christopher was quite glowing when he talked about you."

"Oh." She blinked at the unexpected compliment. "Well. I have a typing speed of a hundred-and-twenty words per minute at ninety-eight percent accuracy, shorthand speed of a hundred-and-fifty words per minute at ninety-nine percent accuracy, advanced audio typing, up-to-date training in all Microsoft packages, various advanced secretarial courses, ten years of on-the-job training… anything else you'd like to know?"

His eyes widened. "That's pretty impressive."

She shrugged. "Actually those speeds were recorded a few years ago—I've probably dropped a little as I don't use it all day every day like I used to."

"You undersell yourself," he said. "There's more to doing your job than typing speed. I'm sure the key to being a good office manager is organizational skill, which is incredibly rare, as well as the ability to anticipate a man's needs before he knows what they are himself."

She met his gaze, wondering if he'd meant the words to have the double meaning that rang in her brain. Was he coming on to her? She was out of practice with the dating game. It was rare nowadays that men flirted with her—Miss Stark openly discouraged it, and it usually worked.

He blinked, and for a moment uncertainty flickered in his eyes before he dropped his gaze. She frowned, puzzled. The same look had crossed his face when he'd made the joke about being on top. Almost as if he'd flirted unintentionally and then regretted his words, which wouldn't be surprising considering his reason for being there.

She wasn't as naïve as she had been at seventeen. Over the ten years she'd worked at the office, she'd grown used to the way men and women interacted. In spite of her warning regarding relationships with the young secretaries, it was impossible to eliminate the occasional sexual banter. Light innuendo was a natural reaction when a person found another person attractive.

She cast her eye over his swept-back dark hair and smart suit as he studied his shoes. She'd called him Hotshot to Amy and had been certain he'd be flash and arrogant, but in actual fact he seemed nice. Young? Yes. Flash? A little, but his eyes were kind and the fact that he was there to investigate a case so close to her heart wasn't his fault.

And he found her attractive. She warmed from the toes up.

"Mr. Wilkinson…" she said softly.

His eyes came back to hers. "Call me Felix."

"Whatever you say, Mr. Wilkinson." She smiled. "Come on, let me show you around the office."

Keep professional, she told herself, heading for the door. It was her key phrase, one that had gotten her through many awkward situations. It was going to be a difficult day for many reasons, and the only way she was going to get through it was to try to keep her cool.

So she let Miss Stark show him around the workroom, indicating where to place his general work for the typing pool, but also introducing him to Maddy, the quick, efficient, and knowledgeable legal secretary who would probably be doing most of his work. Maddy was twenty-three, red-haired and pretty, and Coco watched Felix to see if his comments to Maddy were risqué, or if his eyes followed her as she walked away. He remained pleasant but professional, however, turning his gaze back to Coco to discuss Maddy's working hours rather than follow her butt in the tight skirt. Okay. Another point in his favor.

She walked him through the human resources department, trying not to laugh at the way Amy's eyes nearly fell out of her head as they were introduced.

"Goodness," Amy said. "What luck!"

Coco glared at her, but Felix just laughed and said, "Nice to meet you properly," before they walked on. Amy wasn't the only one eyeing him up, though, Coco thought as they continued their tour. Everywhere they went, he was met with simpering gazes, fluttering eyelashes, and reddening cheeks, and even the older women seemed to giggle girlishly as he walked past.

She might not have approved of their reaction to his presence, but she could understand it. As she walked beside him, she occasionally caught a whiff of his lovely aftershave, and she admired his crisp, well-ironed shirt, and clean-shaven jaw. He smelled and looked expensive. He'd be the type of man who showered regularly, who brushed his teeth twice a day and visited the hygienist, and he'd wear boxers or boxer-briefs, not Y-fronts. A clip in the shape of a pen held his tie flat against his shirt, and oh my God, were there cufflinks in his sleeves?

He was polite to everyone they met and held the door open for her as they walked back to the main workroom, and although he'd flirted with her, he hadn't been lecherous or overly intimate. She liked good manners. In fact, she liked everything about him. *Watch out*, her inner voice warned her. *Just be careful.*

She noticed that although he didn't speak much, he took in everything as they walked, his eyes scanning the offices and the people in them as if he were some spy recording details in a secret chip he'd had implanted in his retinas.

"Does it meet with your approval?" she asked eventually, wondering what he was thinking.

His warm brown gaze came back to rest on her. "Does what meet with my approval?"

"Whatever you're looking for."

He smiled. "I'm just trying to get a first impression of the branch. To see what the general atmosphere is like. Different workplaces have different sets of rules."

"McAllister Dell's rules and regulations are the same in all our offices," she pointed out.

"I don't mean the official rules. I mean the unofficial ones. It's about the people. Their age and social standing—their senses of humor. What may pass as acceptable physical contact or verbal banter here, for example, may not in Auckland and vice versa. In a sexual harassment case, it's imperative to establish what boundaries are usually considered acceptable in the employee's environment. If risqué banter is considered the norm, for example, it might put what's been perceived as an offensive comment into perspective as being a joke or a compliment rather than an actual advance."

Was he referring to the couple of sexual references he'd made, maybe trying to explain that he hadn't meant any offence? "I hadn't thought of that," she said. "I suppose we all have different acceptable boundaries."

"Yes, both personally and on a branch level."

"What are the other branches like?"

He tipped his head thoughtfully. "They're all quite different. Dunedin has a high proportion of lawyers who also play rugby, so there's quite a locker room feel to the place. Even with the women, jokes tend to be nearer the knuckle than, for example, in Christchurch. That office changed a lot after the earthquake. Obviously, the physical building was damaged and they had to move, but I think the employees grew closer as a result. It has more of a clique-y feel—harder to infiltrate, you know?"

She nodded and reached for the door handle at the same time that he did, and their hands bumped. He smiled and opened the door for her, and she walked through, trying to ignore the sensations skittering across her skin at the brush of his fingers.

"What about in Nelson?" she asked.

"Much more laid back, the same as the Bay of Islands, probably reflecting the warmer weather."

"And Auckland?"

A light came into his eyes. "Auckland's the best. Open, spacious offices. There are lots of women working there, and maybe because of that the place has a very respectful feel. Very modern and… I don't know, egalitarian, maybe. It feels as if it doesn't matter whether you're a man or a woman, Maori, Indian or white, gay or straight—everyone has an equal opportunity to rise high if they work hard and play fair." He smiled at her raised eyebrow. "I know I'm probably being idealistic and it's not like that at all, but that's how it feels."

He *was* being idealistic, but she liked that. He didn't sound like the kind of guy who took women for granted and used them before discarding them like some other people. His words made her feel that he'd made his previous flirtatious comments out of a genuine attraction to her.

"So is there much sexual innuendo in the Auckland office?" she asked, genuinely interested.

He shrugged. "Some. It would be indirect, if at all—general jokes or references to things said on TV shows, for example, rather than direct comments about another person's sexuality."

She had to ask. "So do you flirt with all the women you work with? Is that considered acceptable in Auckland?"

He stopped walking, and she turned to look up at him.

"Never," he said.

She blinked, startled. "You must have had office affairs, though."

"Never," he repeated. "I wouldn't do that. I couldn't. It would be so unprofessional."

Now she was confused. "You flirted with me, though, and you've only known me ten minutes. Is that because you don't work here—the normal rules don't apply? You're only going to be here five minutes so it doesn't matter what you say?"

"No." His lips curved. "But the first time I met you wasn't in the office. We met and interacted as man and woman, and that changed everything. That meeting was an irreversible chemical reaction, like burning wood to make a fire. We can try to cover it now and put the fire out, but the wood is already burned, and you can't undo that."

His analogy and the heat in his eyes sent her thermostat rising.

She remembered the first words he'd heard her say. *Sex, and lots of it*. Jeez. No wonder the guy was flirting with her.

Chapter Five

Felix hoped he'd made himself understood.

She looked puzzled, though, obviously thinking his words through as she walked across to the muffin cart which was surrounded by half a dozen people, including Rob Drake, choosing their mid-morning snack. Felix followed her across to it, hoping she believed him.

"Would you like to choose yourself something?" she asked. "The partners have an account that you are welcome to charge yours to, as you are a visitor. You can choose lunch from here too, if you like—they'll be back around midday."

He'd had breakfast some time ago and besides, he was always hungry, so he cast his eye over the assorted muffins. "Okay. I'll have one with a cup of Rosie later."

She raised an eyebrow. "A cup of what?"

"Ah...sorry. It's Cockney rhyming slang. Rosie Lee—tea. I spent a few years in London and it kind of rubbed off on me. Drives my family mad." He couldn't work out if the look she was giving him was admiring or if she thought he was crazy too, so he concentrated on choosing himself a chocolate-chip muffin, although he insisted on paying for it rather than charging it to the partners' account. No wonder their expenses were so high.

Next to him, she chewed her red lip before deciding on a bran and banana muffin.

"Do you buy lunch from here?" he asked.

She took a cup from the cooler by the cart and poured herself a glass of cold water. "No, I usually grab something in town."

He studied her profile, thinking how elegant she was, how beautiful. He loved the fact that everyone in the office thought she was cold and haughty. He felt like a medieval peasant who'd been allowed to see behind the rood screen in church, like Dorothy peering behind the wizard's curtain. Was he the only one who knew she wasn't like that inside?

One day, Felix knew he'd settle down—the memories of Lindsey and those nightmare days in London when he'd first heard of her death would eventually fade, and he'd be able to love again. But he wasn't there yet, and every time he slept with another woman, he was unable to shake off the feeling of guilt, as if he were cheating on her.

He'd remained single for the first year after she died, moving back to New Zealand under the gentle pressure of his parents, which in the end had been a good move, because he stopped seeing Lindsey around every corner and in every bar and restaurant he visited, and instead she just visited him at night, in his dreams.

He hadn't wanted to sleep with another woman, too full of guilt and unhappiness at his loss. But he'd also realised he couldn't stay single for the rest of his life. He'd only been twenty-two when she died, and she'd have laughed at the thought of him becoming a monk. He loved sex and had a high sex drive, and being celibate was not his natural state.

So he'd finally let his brother, Toby, arrange a date for him with a girl, and he'd gone out with her a few times and eventually they'd slept together, and after that it had been easier, although he'd still yet to give his heart to anyone. He wouldn't have called himself a womanizer. A serial monogamist, maybe—working his way through a succession of short-term relationships that usually lasted around four to six months before things grew too serious and he felt the urge to move on. But it had been almost a year since his last girlfriend—he'd been too busy concentrating on his work to worry about playing the dating game—and he felt out of practice.

However, the prim office manager's assurance that she was hoping for sex for Christmas made him want to make her wish come true. He'd spoken the truth—he wasn't a man who usually indulged in one-night stands and he'd been especially careful not to have affairs with the women he worked with. He respected women and thought flirting in the office put pressure on working relationships and was unfair to both sexes. But he was only human, and now he'd hopefully made it clear that he didn't normally flirt at the office he could possibly push things a little further.

"Perhaps you could show me a good place to eat?" he suggested.

She hesitated, watching Rob glancing up at them with alarm, as if Felix had asked Attila the Hun out for lunch. "Oh," she said breezily, "I often just go into the supermarket, not to a café or anything."

"Fine," he replied. "I could do with some supplies."

She sipped her water. "Supplies?"

"I'm staying in a hotel, but it's nice to be homely, and they don't have everything I need there. Their instant coffee is appalling." His eyes met hers as she took another sip. "And I love hot cocoa in bed."

She coughed into her cup. Rob stared, and the others at the cart turned and looked at them curiously, but Felix managed to keep a straight face, even though he was laughing inside. He'd guessed correctly—Coco was obviously her nickname.

"Everything all right?" Rob asked her.

"Fine." She wiped underneath her bottom lip delicately and met Felix's steady gaze. He could see her wondering whether his words were pure coincidence, or whether he did indeed know her name.

"Let's finish the tour," she said eventually. "Come on."

He followed her, allowing himself a secret grin.

She took him in to see the partners he hadn't yet met, and he was interested to see that they all spoke to her deferentially. She was obviously well-respected in the office.

She introduced him to Ted Hoyle, a bluff old lawyer who'd been there donkey's years, the same solicitor on whose letter the young typist had made the mistake. How would she react if the lawyer mentioned the slip-up? Would she lay the blame on Sam and drop her in it?

"Please to meet you." Ted shook Felix's hand, then turned to Coco. "I've just read the letter to Mrs. Parkinson. Are you aware of the error in it?"

"Yes, Mr. Hoyle," she said. "I do apologize."

"What if I hadn't picked it up? Mrs. Parkinson is one of our biggest clients, and it was quite an insulting mistake."

"Yes, Mr. Hoyle, I do understand. I had seen the error myself, but you are good to point it out in case I missed it."

"It's not good enough, Miss Stark."

"Absolutely it's not, Mr. Hoyle." Her calm voice soothed without being sycophantic.

"It was Sam, wasn't it?" Ted pressed. "I'm sure she took the dictation."

Felix knew the young secretary's initials would be in the reference at the top of the letter, indicating that it was she who had mistyped the phrase. Coco, however, smiled and said, "I'm not sure, Mr. Hoyle. Rest assured I'll find out and let them know their mistake."

Hoyle gave her a wry look. "You're sweet talking me. That's not the first potentially disastrous error Sam's made, and we both know it won't be her last."

"We're working on her accuracy, sir, and I'm sending her on a secretarial skills course next week. She's a good girl, Mr. Hoyle—she's just very young and trying a little too hard. She'll improve."

"Hmm." Hoyle looked both mollified and exasperated. He glanced at Felix. "You can never get your own way in this place. This one always manages to talk me out of whatever I want to do."

"I'm beginning to understand that," Felix said, amused and impressed by her loyalty.

"Thanks, Mr. Hoyle." She backed out of the office, and Felix—casting a last sympathetic grin at the old man—followed her.

"What?" she asked as they walked along the corridor and he drew alongside, casting glances at her.

"I can see why Christopher's impressed with you."

Clearly, she wasn't used to compliments. Her cheeks stained a faint pink, and her lids lowered over her green eyes.

They arrived at his new office, and she walked in. "And we're back where Christopher put you. One of the best views over the quay."

"It's lovely." He placed his muffin next to his briefcase, walked over to the window, and looked down at the ferry slowly making its way in after crossing the Cook Strait from the South Island.

She came to stand beside him. He could smell her subtle perfume, something sweet and flowery that stirred his senses. Her hair, although scraped tightly in its bun, shone in the early morning sunlight, and he had the feeling it would slip through his fingers like silk.

"You never told me what your first impressions of the Wellington branch are," she said.

He hesitated, not wanting to be rude. But he would have to discuss Peter Dell with her at some point, and being in charge of the secretaries, she would have a good insight into Dell's behavior toward the women of the office.

He glanced around the room. "It's very… old school. It reminds me of Oxford in many ways—which I loved, I hasten to say."

"You went to Oxford?" She blinked with surprise, her eyebrows raised.

He looked back out of the window, not seeing the water but instead remembering the beautiful buildings made out of the distinctive warm amber stone. "Yes. I won a scholarship there. It was so different from growing up in the Bay of Islands, I can't tell you. Every building was older than the Stone Store here, and I loved the traditional, antiquated feel of the place. As if I was just one of many, many lawyers who'd studied there in the past, along with famous statesmen and even kings and queens."

He glanced back at her. She was smiling.

"What?" he said, somewhat defensively.

"You're an old romantic," she teased.

He grinned. "Maybe." The grin faded at the memory of Lindsey lying in his bed in the flat in London, scattered in rose petals from the bouquet he'd bought her, telling him *You love romancing me, don't you?* His breath caught in his throat. How could it still hurt, after all these years?

Coco tipped her head, a frown narrowing her eyes. "Bad memories?"

He ran a hand through his hair, surprised at her astuteness. "A bit." He shook his head. He didn't want to talk about Lindsey. "Anyway, over there that old-fashioned, conventional atmosphere seemed right—Oxford couldn't be any other way, you know? But here..." He looked around again. "It feels outmoded. Outdated. Like maybe the partners are trying to cling hold of a time long gone."

"It's traditional," she agreed. "But I thought customers liked that. They expect lawyers to be conservative and old-school."

"Maybe some customers do—the older clientele who grew up in the fifties and sixties. But times are changing. We're dealing with the children of the seventies and eighties now, who have Kindles and widescreen TVs, and who've read John Grisham and watched Boston Legal. They understand the law better than their forebears did, and they have different expectations. They don't want deals to be done in the squash room and over long lunches—they want results as quickly and efficiently as possible with minimal cost."

Coco said nothing, her eyes thoughtful.

"Did you know Auckland's overheads are thirty percent less than Wellington's?" he asked.

That made her stare. "Truly?"

"And we have more office space."

She shook her head, puzzled. "So why, then? Is it much cheaper to rent in Auckland?"

"Not at all. But we are completely digitized. We do have paper files, but they are only for copies of essential documents. Everything is done online."

"What if there was a fire?"

"We back everything up on a daily basis. Our stationery costs are minimal. So are our expense accounts. We no longer take clients out for expensive lunches. Work is expected to be carried out in the office, or we go to the client's place of work, or we have online conferences."

Once again, she said nothing, but he could see her brain working behind her eyes like the engine inside a sleek sports car.

"So you don't like it here," she said eventually.

He shrugged. "I've only been here five minutes—I'm loath to make sweeping statements."

"It's a nice place to work."

"I'm sure it is." He studied her curiously. "Does it not bother you though—as a modern woman—that there are so few female lawyers and associates? And only one female partner?"

She looked bemused. "I've always believed it's wrong to give a woman a job just because she's a woman. The best person for a job should be the best person, otherwise it becomes tokenism."

"True. But do you think the best people have always got the positions here? Or do you think the partners have engineered it so it's male-heavy?"

She frowned. "Are you asking me off the record, or is this part of your investigation?"

He'd made her suspicious, and he didn't want to turn her into an enemy. He'd learned from being in court about the importance of timing, and how to change tack if the conversation wasn't going the way he wanted.

He patted down his suit. "No recording devices. Want me to strip and prove it?"

Chapter Six

Coco's eyes widened at the thought of this gorgeous lawyer stripping for her and gradually revealing the muscular, tanned body she was certain would be underneath. "Goodness." Her heart pounded, and for a moment her thoughts and emotions spun like a centrifuge. "That won't be necessary. I have to go. Please let me know if there's anything you require."

"Anything?" He was definitely teasing her now. She pursed her lips, and he laughed. "You're going to tell me off now, aren't you?"

"Mr. Wilkinson…"

"Call me Felix, please." He leaned on the desk, arms folded, smiling.

"Are you going to say that every time I call you Mr. Wilkinson?"

"Yes." He studied her, paused, and then said, "Are you married?"

She blinked, thrown by his comment. "Um, no. Hence the 'Miss'."

"Engaged?"

"No. But—"

"Living with anyone?"

She gave a frustrated sigh. "No."

"Gay?"

She rolled her eyes. "No. But, also, I never date anyone at the office." She made her voice firm. "We've discussed how unprofessional that is."

"True," he said. "Good job I don't work in Wellington, then." His eyes twinkled.

She glared at him. "I meant that I don't date anyone I work with. And that includes temporary staff."

"I can see Miss Stark is a woman of strict principles."

"Very," she agreed. His lips curved. Strict principles. Why did that make her think of handcuffs and erotic torture? Oh dear God, why did this man keep making her think about sex?

His gaze fell to her mouth again. "And is Coco as prim and proper as her counterpart?"

So his comment about the cocoa hadn't been a coincidence. She glared at him. "How did you know?"

"I saw your necklace in the photo on your desk."

He was observant, this one. She would have to be careful around him. Now she could see how he'd got his reputation, and exactly why he was such an excellent lawyer.

But now she was confused. He'd teased her and flirted with her, and then told her he never did that with women he worked with, which made her feel special, but she had no idea of his scruples—whether he was a man of his word, or whether he'd use any information he came up with to control her and turn it to his advantage, which he'd be used to doing in the courtroom. She needed to know. It suddenly felt very important to establish.

She bit her lip and raised her eyes to his. "Don't tell anyone my nickname," she said softly. There. She'd unzipped her fly, metaphorically speaking, and allowed him to see the vulnerable side of her, which she didn't do very often, especially at work. What would he do with it?

A frown flickered across his brow. For a moment he didn't speak, and she could imagine him processing his thoughts, weighing up the options. Although his astuteness made her uneasy, it also attracted her in equal measure. She liked clever men, liked the play of words, the fact that so much was going on beneath the surface of conversations. Suddenly she wished she could be in the hearing. She'd love to see what Felix made of Peter Dell.

He was still studying her, but now he pushed himself off the desk and walked toward her. Gosh he was tall, several inches taller than her, and she had her high heels on today. She had to look up to meet his warm brown eyes.

She'd half-expected to see them lit with sarcasm or interest as he calculated what he could do with the snippet of information he'd discovered she didn't want made common knowledge. But all his gaze held was kindness, such an unexpected emotion that she caught her breath.

"Don't worry. Your secret's safe with me." He smiled, his words echoing hers back in the coffee house.

She swallowed. "Thank you."

They were only inches apart. She could smell his aftershave again, such a manly, clean smell, and he was all width and breadth, with strong, powerful shoulders and big, gentle hands. Her heart raced, and when she moistened her lips his gaze dropped to her mouth.

He was going to kiss her—right there in the middle of the office where anyone could walk in, and God help her but she couldn't do anything about it. Her feet felt stuck to the floor, her body frozen. More than anything in the world she wanted to feel his lips on hers. It had been a lifetime since she'd been kissed, and she yearned for it, to be that close to another human being.

He didn't, though. His gaze roamed over her face and desire sparked in his eyes, but he didn't move.

"Come out for a drink with me tonight," he said instead, his voice husky.

A date? She blinked, her mind clearing. That was out of the question. For heaven's sake, he was investigating a case of sexual harassment. Maybe this was all a ploy to see if women from Wellington reacted to his flirtations. What the hell was she doing, talking like this with another member of staff?

She moved back and dropped her gaze, wrapping herself in Veronica's cool efficiency once again. "Sorry, Mr. Wilkinson, as I said, I don't date people at the office. Now, I need to get back to work. It's my first proper day on the job and I want to do well, get some things sorted. Please excuse me."

She stepped around him and walked out without looking back.

*

Felix turned to watch her leave and blew out a long, slow, frustrated breath. Man, that had been close. He'd been inches—fractions of an inch—from kissing her, which would, quite possibly, have been the absolute worst thing a lawyer investigating a charge of sexual harassment in the office could do to the office manager he'd only just met. She would have had every right to slap him, maybe even to march up to Christopher and tell him, and demand Felix be sent back to Auckland.

But somehow he didn't think she would have done that. Maybe afterward she would have regretted it, but at that moment, he was convinced she'd wanted him to kiss her.

He'd been so incredibly tempted to slip a hand behind to cup her head, another arm around her waist, and hold her tightly as he lowered his lips to hers. They would have been sticky from the red lipstick, and he would have smeared it slightly as he moved his lips across hers, tasting her. Maybe he'd have ended up with a lipstick kiss on his collar. The thought made him feel lightheaded.

He shook his head and walked back to the window. He had to start concentrating. This was a serious business, and filling his brain with thoughts of kissing and where that might lead to wasn't going to get him anything except a raging hard-on that nothing except some self-administration was going to get rid of.

Someone knocked at the door and he turned. Rob Drake stood in the doorway. The lawyer walked up to his desk, hands in his pockets. He looked amused.

"What?" Felix asked, already knowing what was coming.

"You do have a death wish don't you? Chatting up the Dragon?"

"I'm pretty sure her first name's Veronica."

Rob grinned. "I wouldn't go there. She'll eat you alive."

Chance'll be a fine thing. "What do you know about her?"

Rob shrugged. "What do you want to know? Christopher told you how good she was at her job."

"I meant personally."

"Is this part of the investigation?"

Felix huffed a sigh, knowing he shouldn't be asking about personal details and embarrassed because Rob was obviously as sharp as himself and had caught him out.

He gave Rob a wry smile and sat in one of the armchairs. "Fucking lawyers, we're as bad as psychologists, always answering a question with another question and avoiding the answer. Okay, cards on the table. I do like her. I'd like to know more about her. But yes, I'm also investigating the office and she's the office manager in charge of the secretary who's accused Dell of harassment. Did Sasha De Langen merely misconstrue something that other women would have regarded as okay? Because generally it's seen as acceptable? Miss Stark has already made it clear that I'm not supposed to dally with any of the girls while I'm here. It seems plain to me, but I want to know if she's as strict with the permanent staff—if she would have given Dell the same speech at some point. I need to know what's considered acceptable here and what's not—innuendo, physical contact, that sort of thing. I don't know the answer to these questions and you're supposed to be helping me."

It was a long speech, and he finished slightly breathless, only then realizing that actually, in spite of years spent in court developing ways to deal with people and get them to tell him what he wanted, he was actually a little nervous about this hearing, and about investigating his peers. He was flattered that Christopher had chosen him, but also aware that Christopher might have thought him expendable—what did it matter to his boss if the Wellington staff disliked Felix? Lawyers weren't exactly notorious for their altruism. He wanted to do this hearing properly and achieve the right outcome by upsetting as few people as possible. And some niggling sixth sense was beginning to tell him that wasn't going to happen.

He also now worried that he might have alienated his only ally, but Christopher had obviously chosen someone to help him who wasn't quick to take offence. Rob merely held up his hands in surrender, sat in one of the armchairs to the side, and put his feet on the coffee table. "All right. Let's get started. What do you want to know?"

Chapter Seven

Coco walked down the corridor, through the workroom, continued along the next corridor to the human-resources department, and threaded her way through the labyrinth of desks to Amy's nook in the corner. She occasionally took refuge here if she needed to get away from her desk, as few people knew of their friendship, and nobody would have thought to track her down there.

Amy was in the process of logging sick days onto the old and rather slow computer system. Coco thought briefly about Felix's intimation that their network was out of date and groaned silently. She'd come here to get away from him.

Her friend looked up and beamed when she saw who it was. "Hey you!" She patted the seat in the corner that Coco used as her thinking and hiding spot. "Can you believe that the annoying Mr. Hotshot Fancy Pants is actually Mr. Sexy Cool Dude from the coffee shop?"

"No." Coco sank into the seat and put her face in her hands. "What am I going to do?"

"Oh dear. What have you done?"

"Nothing! Nothing." Coco rubbed her nose. "I almost kissed him."

"I'm sorry, pardon?"

"It was nothing. He was just… nice." Her eyes met Amy's and she groaned at the leap of triumph in them. "Don't look so smug. Really, it was nothing."

"It doesn't sound like nothing. Where did you nearly kiss him?"

"On the mouth."

"Sweetie, I meant where in the building. Are you feeling okay?"

Coco touched her brow, not surprised to find it warm. "I think I may be coming down with something. And it was in his office. Not in the middle of the workroom or anything. He's found out my nickname. I asked him not to tell anyone and he said he won't." That one nice gesture brought a lump to her throat. He didn't know her from Adam, or Eve, or the snake for that matter. As far as he knew, she was the Dragon, the strict office manager who—if they were in a TV show—would be the one to know all the dirty secrets about the office and who, as a long-serving, devoted and loyal employee, would feel honor bound to cover them up. He was there to carry out an investigation, and he could have used that snippet of information to force her to tell him whatever he wanted.

But he hadn't. And his eyes had been kind.

"Oh…" Amy drew the word out, her face softening.

"What?" Coco blinked, heart still pounding from the memory of nearly having his firm lips touch hers.

Amy smiled. "Nothing. So what happened? He went to kiss you?"

"Yes. No. Sort of. Well, he looked like he was going to, but he didn't. And then he asked me out for a drink tonight."

"I hope you said, 'Absolutely, Mr. Fancy Pants, just tell me when and where and I'll be there.'"

"I said no, of course. And I walked out."

Amy sighed. "There really is no hope for you. He's young, obviously rich—did you see his watch? He didn't get that from the two-dollar shop. He's tall. He's smart. He's frickin' gorgeous. Seriously, girlfriend, I think your cheese has slid off your cracker."

"I can't," said Coco. "He's only here temporarily and then he'll go back to Auckland."

"So shag him senseless while he's here and then wave him goodbye. What have you got to lose?"

Coco closed her eyes and shook her head. "Amy…"

"Seriously, Coco. You don't have to sleep with the guy. I mean, I would but then that's me, but I know what you're like. You haven't been out in ages. I know you don't like leaving your mum, but she keeps telling you she wants you to have a life and this is the kind of thing she means. Just go out with him. Have a drink. Be sociable. Have a bit of fun, for God's sake. You're only twenty-seven, you work hard, and you deserve it."

Coco bit her lip and stared at the floor. This was exactly the argument she'd been having with her mother lately—minus the shagging part—almost on a daily basis. Eleanor Stark had got it into her head that it wasn't fair for a bright, pretty woman of Coco's age to be tied to a mother in a wheelchair.

Unbidden, her father's words the last time she'd seen him in hospital before he died rang in her head: "Promise me you'll always look after her, Coco. She's not a strong woman—she needs you. Promise me you won't ever leave her." It was a harsh instruction to a fourteen-year-old girl, one that had haunted her ever since. She already had to deal with the guilt of having someone else look after Eleanor during the day so she could earn enough money to keep them—and now Eleanor wanted to move into a respite home so her daughter could have a social life. Coco didn't want a social life at the expense of her mother's happiness. It was her responsibility to care for her mother, and she'd die rather than see her go into a home.

She stood, brushed down her skirt, adjusted her glasses, and blinked away the tears of self-pity. "I've got to get back to work."

Amy sighed, used to her friend's abrupt changes of persona. "Yes, Miss Stark."

Yes, she was Miss Stark in these offices, Coco thought as she walked away. She had her Veronica hat on now, and she wasn't going to let Coco out while she was at work.

*

"Multiple Sclerosis?" Felix raised an eyebrow as Rob described Coco's mother's condition. "That sucks."

"Yeah." Rob had brought his muffin with him and now proceeded to tuck into it. "I met her once in town. I get the feeling Miss Stark doesn't shop here much—maybe she usually goes out of town so she doesn't bump into anyone she knows. She's a very private person. Anyway, she was pushing her mother in a wheelchair. She introduced us out of politeness, but she wasn't happy about it."

"What did she look like?"

"The mother?"

"No, Miss Stark. Out of work clothes, I mean."

Rob smiled. "Softer. She doesn't wear glasses. And her hair was down."

Like in the photo. Felix wanted to meet that Coco. Very much.

But anyway, for now he had to get his head into gear because he had to read through the file before the hearing and it was already nearly nine. "Okay. So come on, give me your opinion. What do you think of Peter Dell?"

Rob sat back in his chair and linked his fingers. His face had taken on the lawyer's carefully guarded blankness that Felix knew he himself adopted in the courtroom. "Have you ever met him?" Rob asked.

Felix shook his head. "No real reason for that—he's only come up to Auckland once and I happened to be in the Bay of Islands branch at the time—I still work from there occasionally because my family live there. But no, we've just never bumped into one another, which I guess is kind of strange considering I've been here five years. I wondered whether that's why Christopher asked me to carry out the hearing. Because he wanted someone independent, who hadn't forged any opinions about the guy, you know?"

Rob shrugged. "Maybe. Although…did you get the feeling that McAllister considers there's even a case to be addressed here?"

Felix smiled wryly. "I did pick up on the fact that he called the case a trivial matter when I first arrived. Plus he said he hoped he could leave once it was done and dusted. I think he's expecting me to find Dell innocent." He tipped his head at his colleague. "Do you think Dell's innocent?"

Rob finished off his muffin and screwed up the paper bag into a ball. He threw it at the bin and missed, grumbled, and got up to put it in. "It's not our job as lawyers to decide whether the defendant is innocent or guilty, only to put the case to the jury."

"Yeah, well, I happen to be the jury on this occasion."

Rob sat back down. "And I'm not. I work with the guy—I'll give you the facts, but I don't want to pass judgement on him—at least not until after you've spoken to him and investigated, if you think it's necessary. Then I'll discuss what I think."

Felix said nothing. Had Dell appointed Rob, and he felt some kind of loyalty toward him? Or had Dell spoken to Rob and told him not to help Felix? He didn't think Rob looked like the kind of guy who'd cover up the truth, but you never knew. But then again, maybe Rob really was just trying to be fair and let Felix make up his own mind.

"Okay," Felix conceded, "so tell me this, then. As far as you know, did Dell have an affair with Sasha, the secretary who's accused him of sexual harassment?"

"Not as far as I know. But that doesn't mean anything. It's a big building."

"What about with other members of staff? Other secretaries?"

That made the corners of Rob's mouth curve up. He sighed and ran his hand through his hair. "I don't know for sure. I've never seen anything with my own eyes. I mean in that sense, what Miss Stark said to you was right—she does give each lawyer a talking to when they join the firm, and if she sees you 'dallying'—as you so gentlemanly put it—with any of the staff, she soon puts you in your place."

"But you've heard rumors?"

"Well, he markets himself as the perfect family man. Lives in a mansion, wife in pearls and twinsets, two perfect kids—the boy's a lawyer himself, just qualified, the girl's at university in Auckland. They hold dinner parties, donate to charity, you name it. And as I said, I've never seen evidence of any affairs, certainly not at the workplace. But it's just… the way he talks, you know? Sort of disrespectful to woman—he talks down to them. And the way the other partners talk to him. Innuendo. Sly remarks. Of course, that doesn't mean anything either way where Sasha's concerned—you'll see for yourself when you meet her that she's not exactly overt. I can't imagine him making a move on her. But if you're sitting here asking me, do I think it's absolutely a hundred percent impossible that he made unwelcome advances to her, I'd have to say no. There's reasonable doubt."

"A true lawyer's answer," Felix said. He smiled, but his stomach churned. He already knew he wasn't going to like Peter Dell. And that wasn't good when his boss was expecting Felix to find him innocent.

He sighed, stood, and stretched, then walked over to the desk. "I'll take a butcher's at the file now, I think."

Rob frowned, getting to his feet. "Butcher's?"

"Sorry. Butcher's hook—look. It's a London thing… never mind." Sometimes it was easier not to explain. "Will you come and get me when they're ready for me?"

"Sure."

"And where can I get a cup of…" He just stopped himself saying Rosie. "…tea?" That made him think of Coco's raised eyebrow, and he smiled.

"I'll get one of the secretaries to bring you one in," Rob said.

"No, I—" Felix gritted his teeth as Rob disappeared. In Auckland, all lawyers made or fetched their own tea and coffee. He liked it that way.

He opened the file and huffed another sigh. He'd be glad when the morning was over.

Chapter Eight

Coco couldn't concentrate. It wasn't surprising really, she thought—what with it being a strange mixture of a standard day on the job combined with the actual first official day as office manager, as well as the added pressure of knowing Peter Dell was about to go into his hearing. Of course the sudden ability of her brain to wander off course and start daydreaming had nothing to do with Mr. Hotshot and the way he'd nearly kissed her. She wasn't thinking about that at all.

She pushed away her keyboard and got to her feet. The monthly stationery order would have to wait. Her eyes wouldn't focus on the figures, and besides, she kept thinking about Felix's words, about how Auckland's overheads were so much lower than the Wellington branch's because they were mostly digital.

What could she do about that? She didn't dislike technology—she used the internet and email and shopped online and was proficient with lots of secretarial packages. But she didn't have a tablet, an MP3 player, or even a decent phone. She couldn't afford it. Technology had always seemed like a wonderful aid for the office, and she'd pushed for an update to the branch's computers a few years ago, and had hired a training consultant to explain to all the lawyers how to use digital voice recording. But it was difficult to be innovative when some of the more senior staff members were stuck in the Dark Ages. There was no way she'd ever get Ted Hoyle to use a Dictaphone, for example, not even an old-fashioned one with the tiny cassettes—he flatly refused to do anything except dictate to a secretary, and how could she fight that when he—and many others—were the ones who paid the bills? Change had to come from above, and she didn't have that kind of power.

And now she had a headache, so she decided she wasn't going to think about it for a while. She walked into the workroom and did a slow tour, checking out the place where the lawyers put their files for typing to make sure the legal secretaries weren't getting too far behind, ensuring all the printers had paper and were free of jams, briefly stopping to talk to some of the secretaries to see whether they had any queries, a circuit she did half a dozen times a day to the water cooler and back, just to keep an eye on things.

She noticed Sasha De Langen wasn't at her seat. Knowing she might have nipped to the bathroom, she said nothing for ten minutes, but when Sasha didn't appear, Coco walked through to the break room and found the young secretary standing at the window, lost in thought, a mug of tea in her hands.

"Sasha," Coco said softly. "Is everything okay?"

Sasha jumped and turned, looking startled. "Sorry, have I been too long? I was just thinking…"

"It's okay, there's no rush." Coco walked forward to stand beside her. "How are you feeling?" She glanced at Sasha's hand where she held the tea—the mug shook slightly, the liquid slopping up the sides.

Sasha looked back out of the window. Her long brown hair was drawn back into a ponytail, and she wore no makeup—her clear skin looked pale, as if bleached of color. "I feel a bit sick. I wonder what will happen when they find Mr. Dell innocent. Will I be sacked?"

"You've done nothing wrong," Coco said, a little sternly. "And anyway, what do you mean when? You mean if, surely?"

Sasha turned scornful eyes on her. "You really think the partners are going to find one of their own guilty?"

"Probably not, but it's not a partner who's running the investigation," she pointed out.

"I guess he'll want to talk to me, won't he? Mr. Wilkinson, I mean. Is that how it works?"

Coco thought one of the partners would have spoken to her about the process and cursed inwardly that she was the one who had to do it. She'd speak to the head of HR about that. But it wasn't fair to keep the girl on tenterhooks. "Yes, I would imagine so. First, he'll speak to Mr. Dell and inform him that he is investigating his conduct. He'll ask him whether he accepts or denies the allegations you've made, and give Mr. Dell the opportunity to explain his actions. After that, he'll decide whether he's satisfied with the answer Mr. Dell has given—if not, he'll go on to investigate further, and he'll talk to you, and me, amongst others, until he comes to a decision."

"So Mr. Dell may explain his way out of it, in which case Mr. Wilkinson might decide he doesn't need to talk to me." Sasha's voice dripped with bitterness.

"Maybe. Somehow, though, I don't think so." Coco thought of the way Felix had agreed not to tell anyone about her nickname. "Mr. Wilkinson is an esteemed lawyer, known for his fairness and decency. I think he'll want to hear your side of the story before he comes to a decision."

Sasha swallowed, then nibbled at a fingernail, and Coco felt a twinge of uneasiness. Although some of the young women on the secretarial staff were the same age as her or even older, and Sasha was probably only a couple of years younger, she was in charge of them all, and she should have made more of an effort to support Sasha. True, she had thought HR would explain more details about the hearing and what that meant for the secretary, but still, Coco knew she should have checked on her before this. They hadn't spoken privately since she'd heard the young secretary's allegations, partly because she was now semi-management and she wanted to be seen to be neutral, and partly because of the guilt that stirred inside her like a monster rising from the deep. She knew things—things that would have helped Sasha with her case. But she couldn't reveal them. And that ate her up as if she'd swallowed a cupful of devouring maggots along with her morning breakfast.

"I'd better get back to work," Sasha said.

"Probably best to keep occupied," Coco replied as kindly as she could. "Concentrate on other things."

"Yeah." Clearly, though, Sasha wasn't going to be able to think of anything else until she'd heard the verdict.

Sasha walked off, pouring her cool mug of tea in the sink as she left. Coco watched her go. At least the girl had had enough courage to come in that day. She could easily have pleaded sickness or taken the week off, as Peter had done.

Thinking of Peter made her stomach churn. She moved to the window and rested her forehead on it for a moment, closing her eyes and blocking out the view. How come, after all these years, she could still picture that scene in his office so clearly? Why had it haunted her so much?

She'd only been at the firm six months, fresh out of secretarial college, seventeen, naïve, and as innocent as they came. Christopher

McAllister had been in the process of setting up the Auckland office, coming and going between the two while he finalized details, leaving Peter to run the Wellington branch.

Peter had taken a liking to her from the beginning. Even in her naivety, Coco had sensed that. When he'd walked past her desk, he'd stopped to perch on it and ask how she was doing. He'd come over to sit with her in the break room sometimes. And he'd started asking her more than the others when he wanted to give dictation. He'd said it was because she was so quick at shorthand, and she'd half-believed him, although that hadn't explained the way he liked to watch her while she worked, and how his gaze had run up her figure, admiring her breasts and her legs. She hadn't been sure how it had made her feel. She'd never been on a date. Never even been kissed. It had been the first time a man had paid her any real attention, and in some ways, she'd been flattered. But she'd known he was married, and something about it hadn't felt right—he was thirty years older than her for a start.

So she'd tried not to think about it and had worked hard. She'd loved the job, and she'd known she was good at it. It had been difficult to get ahead because of dead man's shoes—or dead woman's, more likely, with the senior positions filled by older female staff who had looked likely to be there for donkey's years. But she hadn't let that deter her, and had practiced her shorthand and typing every night, taken every course going, and had generally worked her butt off.

Then one evening Peter asked her to help him finish a case he'd been working on. She'd stayed later than usual to finish some typing, and she'd gone into his office without thinking, even though there were only a few people left in the building. He'd talked for a while, made her some coffee, and hadn't seemed in a hurry to discuss the case. Eventually, she'd told him she should really be going because her mother would be waiting for her.

He'd sat beside her on the sofa to one side of his large office. He was still a good looking guy, and back then he'd been slim, athletic, with dark hair. He'd smelled good, and he was obviously rich. He'd sat too close to her and put an arm along the back of the sofa, and then he'd stroked her hair.

Coco had sat frozen, heart pounding. He'd talked softly, telling her she was beautiful, that he couldn't take his eyes off her, comments that had flattered her, made her glow. And when he kissed her, she didn't pull away.

Part of her had known it was wrong, but she'd been caught up in the moment, excited by the attention, by the newness of the sensations spiraling through her. She'd let him undo her blouse and slide it off her arms, take off her bra, and kiss her breasts. And then she'd let him make love to her.

It hadn't been quite like in the novels she'd read or the movies she'd watched. It had been awkward on the sofa, and he'd been heavy on top of her. He hadn't seemed to realize she was a virgin, and although she hadn't bled—years of cycling around the city had put paid to that—it hurt, and she didn't enjoy it.

Afterward, he'd kissed her again and told her she was pretty, and that she'd be rewarded for what she'd done. She'd gone home, straight to bed, and cried herself to sleep, full of shame. The next day, she'd wondered what to do. Should she go to work? Ring in sick? Or ring in and quit? But she had to work notice, so she couldn't really do that.

In the end, she'd decided she hadn't done anything wrong. Although she'd slept with him willingly, she was sensible enough to know she'd been taken advantage of and that what he'd done was wrong. So she'd gone to work—to find she'd been appointed to head of the typing pool.

It was never mentioned again. Peter never made another move on her, and she never said anything, too ashamed at her actions and too relieved at the extra income to make a fuss about receiving a promotion she didn't feel she deserved.

And that had been that. As the years went by she put it to the back of her mind, knowing she did a good job and that the promotion had been a good move on the company's part. And Peter kept his distance, was respectful, and treated her well.

Occasionally there was the odd rumor of him having an affair, but she ignored it and concentrated on her work. And she'd been happy—until this thing with Sasha blew up.

She knew Dell was guilty. He'd tried to do exactly the same thing to Sasha that he'd done to her, but Sasha—at twenty-three, six years older than Coco had been, and with six years more spirit—had refused, and now had to deal with the outcome.

Coco knew she should speak up about what happened all those years ago. She was in charge of the secretaries, and it was her responsibility to support them. But she liked her job. She needed her job. She didn't know what she'd do if she lost it—how would she cope? She could stay home and look after her mother instead of hiring a nurse during the day, but they still needed to eat, and she didn't want to rely on benefits. And in the current economic climate there just weren't that many jobs around.

So when Rob Drake had interviewed Sasha and taken her statement with Coco present, she'd kept quiet. Nobody suspected the cool Miss Stark would have been involved in anything like that.

But now here was Felix, asking questions and shining like Sir Galahad with self-righteousness. What would he think of her if she now admitted what she'd done all those years ago?

Chapter Nine

She checked her watch. Nine forty-five. Dell would be arriving soon, and then Felix would have to start the hearing. How was he getting on? Had he formed any opinions now he would have finished reading Sasha's statement?

She hovered in the hallway. Should she check on him, see if he needed anything? A pad of paper, maybe? Pens? Or perhaps there were other files he'd like to see?

She chewed her lip. She should run a mile, but she wanted to see him again. That, in itself, should have made her turn around and walk back to her room, but instead she found herself walking along to his office.

As she reached his door, she heard voices and paused in the doorway. Felix sat behind the desk, leaning back in his chair, tapping on his iPad. Rob sat in front of the desk, slightly turned toward her, his feet propped on the chair in front of him.

"…depends on his attitude," Felix was saying. "Regret goes a long way. It doesn't wipe out a crime, of course, but it's easier to forgive if someone's remorseful."

She hesitated, not wanting to interrupt, and turned to leave, but Rob looked up and saw her.

"Hey, Miss Stark. You need something?"

She turned back and gave them both a brief smile, noting that Felix put down the iPad and sat up in his chair at the sight of her. "I was just checking you have everything you need before you went into the hearing."

Felix glanced at Rob, who stood and grinned at him. "I'll let you know when Dell arrives," Rob said, and walked past her out of the office.

"Oh, you don't have to go…" But he'd gone. She looked back at Felix, who gestured to the chair Rob had vacated.

"He knows I have something important and confidential to ask you," Felix said.

"Oh?" Her stomach churned. She'd been dreading talking about Peter Dell, fearful of what this hearing might stir up.

Felix leaned forward on the desk, twirling a stylus between his fingers, and fixed his brown eyes on her. "Will you come to dinner with me tonight?"

Her nerves fled, and she glared at him. "I thought you were going to ask something professional."

"Whatever gave you that idea? Well, will you?"

"No. Thank you." She stood and smoothed down her skirt. "I don't date."

He leaned back in his chair and surveyed her, head tipped to one side. "What, never?"

Actually no, she thought, but she didn't want to get into that conversation. "Not with people I work with—I told you."

"But you're not married, engaged, seeing someone else, or gay."

Her lips twitched. "No."

"In that case, what have you got to lose? I promise not to tell anyone if you won't."

She looked at him over the top of her glasses, which usually struck fear into most of her work colleagues. Felix just raised an eyebrow, however, and his eyes gleamed, and she had the funny feeling she'd just turned him on.

"You're only here for a day," she said. "Won't you be going back to Auckland tomorrow?"

He shrugged. "Depends on my findings. I have a feeling I'm going to have to carry out a complete investigation." He grinned.

Her eyes widened. "You wouldn't do that—you wouldn't postpone a decision just so you can stay here and annoy me."

He laughed at that. "No, Miss Stark, I'm not that Machiavellian. But if I do stay here for a while, you're going to have to get used to me asking you on a daily basis—probably several times a day—for a date."

The thought of him being in her offices for more than a day made her a little dizzy. But that panicky excitement was dampened by the thought of poor Sasha having to wait for an outcome—one that she herself could hasten along, if only she had the courage to say something.

Felix leaned forward. "I've upset you. I'm sorry."

MR. SENSATIONAL

Once again, she was aware of his consideration, that he'd seen the slip in her mood. "No, no, it's not you. I was thinking of Sasha. She was very nervous this morning. It would be a shame for her to have to wait for a decision."

"Actually, it would probably mean the likelihood of a more favorable outcome for her. I may walk out of the hearing today having found Peter Dell innocent, but if I'm not satisfied with his explanation of his behavior, I will want to talk to Sasha and get her side of the story."

"And what if the partners pressure you to ignore the charges?" she said softly. It had been her worry all along. Part of her wanted Felix to find Peter guilty, as proof to herself that what he'd done all those years ago was wrong, maybe to finally assuage some of the guilt she'd carried with her since she was seventeen. But she couldn't see it happening. Surely Christopher and some of the other partners would put pressure on Felix to have a favorable outcome?

But Felix's eyes were clear, and his humor had vanished. "I do have a conscience, Miss Stark. I assure you, I'm here to find the truth."

She met his gaze and swallowed. His eyes bored into her as if he could see right through her, see what she was thinking.

"Someone told me you always know if people are telling the truth," she whispered. "In the court room, I mean. That you have an instinct for who's guilty and who's innocent. Is that true?"

"Oh," he said, not looking away. "If he's telling porkies, I'll know."

She blinked. "Porkies?"

He grinned. "Sorry. Pork pies. Lies."

"What..." She shook her head. "You baffle me."

"Hmm, likewise. You are a mystery, Miss Stark." He tapped the stylus on the table. "One I am determined to get to the bottom of. And I'm like an only child."

"Spoiled?" she suggested. "Badly behaved?"

His lips curved, but his eyes were so hot they sent a frisson running down her spine. "I always get what I want."

*

Felix watched Coco's eyes widen at his words. He grinned. He liked shocking her. She was obviously unused to flirting, but he sensed from the way her face flushed that she didn't entirely hate it.

"You're incorrigible," she said.

"Thank you."

"It wasn't a compliment."

He laughed. Behind her, Rob appeared in the doorway and nodded.

"Okay." Felix got to his feet. "It's time. Now, Miss Stark, I have something to put to you. I want you."

She gasped. "Mr. Wilkinson!"

"I haven't finished yet." He winked at Rob, who adopted an innocent face as she turned to give him an embarrassed look. "I was going to say 'I want you to do something for me.' I'd like you to attend the hearing."

She frowned. "Me? Why?"

"Officially? To take minutes, please. I could use a voice recorder, but this time I would actually prefer them done by shorthand and typed up."

"Any secretary could do that for you," she said.

"True, but firstly this is a delicate, confidential matter, and I don't think any of the other secretaries should be a witness to what's said in that room. And also unofficially, as far as I know, there are going to be six men in the room—me, Rob, Christopher, Peter, Hugh White from HR, and Jack Lawson, who's there as Peter's support. That seems a little unbalanced to me with regard to gender, and I'd like a woman in the room. I'd have asked the *only* female partner—" he didn't bother to hide the irony in his voice at the use of the word only, "—but she's in Christchurch today. So it would make sense for you to be there, as representative not only for the office staff and for Sasha De Langen, but for women in general."

She blinked. The request had clearly thrown her. "I… I have a lot to do…"

That surprised him. He thought she would have welcomed the opportunity to be there to defend both Sasha and the rights of women in the office.

"It is of course your decision." He smiled. "But I'd be grateful for the help."

She met his gaze, her eyes narrowing. He knew putting it like that would make it more difficult for her to refuse. "All right." She swallowed and smoothed her jacket down with her palms. She was nervous. He softened at that realization.

MR. SENSATIONAL

"Don't worry." He picked up the files on his desk and gathered them together in his briefcase. "It's not a trial. I doubt you'll have to say anything—I'm not going to call on you to give evidence, and I'm not expecting you to accuse or defend Peter Dell. It's more a case of providing a female influence in the room. Because of the nature of the accusation, I want to refrain from a 'guys all together' atmosphere. It's natural for members of the same sex to do that, but this should steer us away from those sorts of problems."

He didn't miss her twitch at the word sex, and he had to hide a smile. So maybe she was having trouble not thinking about the two of them in bed too? Every time he looked at her, he felt an urge to press his lips against hers, to slip off her jacket, unbutton her white shirt, and slide it down her arms and cup her breasts. To unpin her hair and see if it really did feel like silk in his fingers.

He stifled a groan and picked up his briefcase and iPad. He had to try to concentrate. There were more important matters at hand than the fact that he hadn't had sex for ages, and he didn't want to go into the boardroom with an erection.

"Ready?" he asked her.

She straightened her jacket—again—and nodded, so he walked to the door and stood to one side, gesturing for her to precede him. She did so, lowering her eyes and pressing herself up against the frame so she didn't have to touch him as she squeezed past. It didn't quite work—her breasts brushed his jacket and her hair came within inches of his lips, so close he could smell the coconut shampoo she'd used.

He sighed inwardly and followed her along the corridor, exchanging an amused glance with Rob, who appeared to be enjoying watching him flirt with the prim office manager. At least walking behind her, he could have a good look at her butt in the tight grey skirt.

She paused by a store cupboard to pick up a shorthand notepad and a pencil, then continued to the boardroom. She took a deep breath and knocked before opening the door. Felix and Rob followed her in.

Chapter Ten

It was a large room with splendid views over the harbor, decorated to impress and perhaps intimidate a little, thought Felix, with a long oak table running down the center surrounded by a dozen polished oak chairs. On the other three walls hung traditional oil paintings of New Zealand landscapes, and a coffee pot stood on a table in the far corner with cups and bowls of sugar and jugs of milk. The room smelled of beeswax polish, aftershave, and the faint smell of cigar smoke.

Christopher stood as they entered, as did Hugh White, the youngish head of Human Resources Felix had met on his tour. Jack Lawson, another partner in his late fifties, didn't rise, Felix noticed, and neither did the man in the room he hadn't met yet, although as he walked up to him, Peter Dell finally got to his feet, albeit reluctantly.

"You must be Mr. Dell," Felix said, holding out his hand. "I'm Felix Wilkinson."

Peter nodded, and they shook hands. "Good to meet you at last. I've heard a lot about you."

And I about you, thought Felix, taking the opportunity to size the man up for the first time.

He knew Peter, at fifty-eight, was a year younger than Christopher, but whereas his boss was ageing gracefully with his white hair, Peter was obviously trying to fight it with every last bone in his body.

True, the guy looked good—tallish, probably just under six foot, slim and he obviously worked out. Felix had half-expected a pot-bellied, leering, balding oaf with a stomach that hung over his belt, but the truth was far from it. Peter had dark hair, piercing blue eyes, sensuous lips, and he carried himself with a confidence that Felix knew would appeal to the ladies, although to himself it bordered on arrogance. The expensive suit he wore gave testament to the fact that the guy was wealthy and liked to show it.

Ultimately, there was nothing wrong with that. Felix himself liked his little luxuries and wasn't afraid to flaunt the fact that he was well off. And on the whole, Peter looked intelligent, shrewd and cool, not at all the bluff idiot Felix had somehow expected.

Still, as he released Peter's hand and stepped back, he had to stifle the urge to wipe his palm on his pants. *Slime ball* was the first phrase that jumped into his head. *He's guilty*, was the second, and although he annoyed himself with the immediate conclusion, he'd been right enough times in the past to not ignore his first impression.

Peter looked pointedly at Coco, who lowered her gaze and adjusted Felix's briefcase on the table so it sat squarely.

Hmm. Felix pulled out a chair opposite Peter. "I asked Miss Stark if she would attend to take minutes. I presume that's not a problem?" He didn't elaborate, knowing the other man would be furiously trying to assess the real reason he'd asked her to be there.

Peter met his gaze for a moment. His eyes were the color of a sky on an icy winter's day—strikingly blue but cold, and they sliced through Felix, heavy with disapproval and resentment. A lawyer's stare, meant to intimidate, with the weight of forty years of practice and seniority behind it. *Don't mess with me, boy*. Felix could almost hear the unspoken words.

He lowered his eyes, not wanting to antagonize the other man yet. *Careful*, he cautioned himself. He wasn't dealing with a witness here who, unused to the dramas of the courtroom, could be manipulated and handled like soft clay. Peter would know all the tricks of the trade, and in this sense Felix was acting naked, with nowhere to hide any aces.

Thinking of being naked made him think of Coco again, and he felt her presence at his side, calm and efficient, reassuring him. Was she intimidated by being with all these men? Did it bother her at all, working in the Wellington branch? He'd like to talk to her about it, get her point of view. If only he could convince her to go for a drink later. He wanted to get to know her better.

Concentrate, he told himself wryly. He glanced across at Christopher, who, like Peter, seemed confident and relaxed. Were they both expecting him to roll over and play along? Again, he remembered Christopher's description of the hearing as a trivial matter. They'd thought this was a formality, just a show for the other employees to prove the firm Took These Matters Seriously.

That puzzled him. He'd thought his boss would have realized he wasn't the type of man to carry out such a matter as a formality—that he would want to do it properly and find the truth. And he was surprised that Christopher himself would want it otherwise. But then the two men had established the firm together, he reminded himself. They were old friends, and this whole matter was more than a fleeting annoyance. The pride of the law firm was at stake, and even though he might not agree with his old friend's actions, Christopher wouldn't want to see the firm brought into disrepute over it.

For the first time, he understood what he was getting himself into and felt the first twinges of worry. Since Christopher asked him to chair the hearing, he'd hardly had time to go over the details, too busy with ensuring his current cases were up to date before flying to Wellington. He wished he'd given it more thought, maybe even passed it onto someone else. He loved working for McAllister Dell, and the last thing he wanted to do was put his job in jeopardy.

But then Peter smiled. "Of course Miss Stark is welcome. I have nothing to hide." He gestured for her to sit.

The atmosphere warmed a little, and Felix forced himself to release the breath he'd been holding and relax. Maybe he'd imagined that cold, intimidating look? Yes, he should trust his instincts, but it was important to keep an open mind too.

They all took a seat, Rob, Coco, and Felix on one side of the long table, Christopher, Hugh, Jack and Peter on the other.

Felix pulled his iPad toward him, clicked it on with the stylus, and unlocked it. He'd typed up a couple of sheets of notes using bullet points after reading through the files, and he glanced over them briefly, although he already knew what he was going to say.

Too late now, he thought, leaning forward, and resting his elbows on the polished oak table. Time to find the truth, the whole truth, and nothing but the truth.

Chapter Eleven

Coco risked another glance at Felix. It had been interesting watching his first meeting with Peter. She'd known Peter wouldn't want her—of all people—to be at the hearing, and had been prepared for him to complain. And she'd seen him stare down the new young lawyer, using that glare that had turned more men to stone than Medusa. She'd watched him use it on many occasions to intimidate other lawyers as well as clients and witnesses, to get them to bend to his will.

She wasn't surprised that Felix had flinched first. He appeared relaxed and in control, but sitting there facing the other older partners, he suddenly seemed very young. He must be nervous, she thought. Had he realized how much was at stake here?

He was leaning forward now, and he smiled, as if to reassure Peter they were all on the same side. "I'd like to officially start this hearing," he began. "I believe you were given notice of this disciplinary meeting, Mr. Dell, which stated that Mr. McAllister has asked me, as someone unfamiliar with the Wellington branch as well as with yourself, to carry out an investigation regarding the accusation made against you of sexual misconduct by Miss Sasha De Langen, a secretary at this branch."

Peter's gaze slid once more to Christopher's, but the other partner's eyes were fixed on the table in front of him, so Peter looked back at Felix. He nodded slowly. Coco wondered whether he'd expected a much more informal meeting, a "this is all a big mistake, isn't it?" on Felix's part with it ending in a handshake and them all laughing over the stupid young secretary as they talked about the latest rugby results.

It appeared that, if that was the case, he'd been sorely mistaken. Felix was the height of professionalism, and she could imagine him in court, crisp and smart in his expensive suit, charming the jury and making them feel as if his way was the only possible way the case could be presented.

"The purpose of this preliminary hearing," Felix continued, "is to establish the facts and for you to explain your side of things. If I believe after listening to what you have to say that there has been a misunderstanding, I'll bring this hearing to a close and there will be no further action. If, however, I'm not satisfied with your version of events, I am under obligation to carry out further investigation, and to speak directly to Miss De Langen and to other employees to try to establish things in more detail. Do you understand?"

Coco finished recording his words in shorthand and glanced up. Peter's lips were twisted as if amused and maybe annoyed at being treated like a common witness, but he just nodded again and leaned back in his chair, one arm hooked over the back, the height of relaxation.

Felix ran his stylus down the screen of his iPad. "Miss De Langen has stated in her written complaint that on the night of Monday, the fifth of December, she was working late to finish typing up a document relating to a family law case that had to be completed for the next day. Do you remember this case?"

Peter nodded. "It was a custody battle over two small children. I was going to court the next morning, and we didn't receive the diary of phone call logs that were essential for the case until late, and they needed to be typed up and included in the documentation."

"Did you ask Miss De Langen to stay behind and type them, or did Miss De Langen volunteer?"

Peter met Felix's gaze, cool as a cucumber that had been placed in the fridge for several hours. "I asked the room if there were any secretaries willing to stay late and work, and she was the only one who volunteered."

That was interesting, and was a mark in his favor. "What time was this?" Felix asked.

"She was just about to leave—it would have been around five thirty."

Felix scrolled down his pad. "How long did it take her to type the call logs?"

"About half an hour—there were a lot of them, and they needed to be in the format requested by the court."

"So she'd finished by six o'clock?"

Peter shifted in his chair. "It was probably a bit later than that. She brought the pages to me to check, which took about ten minutes, and I found some errors and asked her to correct them."

"So about six fifteen then?"

"About that, yes."

Felix looked back at his iPad. Coco noticed that he didn't nod—in fact he gave no sign of his feelings toward what Peter was saying, and made no attempt to put him at his ease.

"I'll read you Miss De Langen's statement, if that's okay," Felix said. He opened his briefcase and withdrew a manila file, opened it, and took out the top sheet of paper. He did all this quite calmly and methodically.

Peter watched, also with no emotion on his face. He had sat up, though. He no longer looked quite as relaxed as he had when Felix started.

Felix cleared his throat. "'I made the corrections to the file, reprinted them, and took them back in to Mr. Dell. He read them through and told me there was still something that needed to be changed. I asked which bit, and he suggested I come and stand beside him so he could point it out clearly. I walked around the desk and stood next to his chair, on the left-hand side. His left arm was hooked over the back of the chair, and as I leaned forward to look at the paper on his desk, he dropped his arm to rest on the arm of the chair, and I felt his hand brush the back of my skirt, near my left hip.'"

Felix paused and glanced up at Peter, and Coco did the same. He remained motionless, and merely raised an eyebrow. Next to him, Jack Lawson had a hint of a smile on his lips. Hugh White was frowning. Rob sat back in his chair, hands in his lap, watching Peter, his face carefully blank. Christopher's eyes met hers, then moved back to Felix.

Felix dropped his gaze and continued. "'I assumed the touch was an accident, a consequence of him dropping his arm to the chair. But as I continued to read, I felt his hand brush down my skirt and then rest on the inside of my right knee. I froze, the thought going through my head that maybe it was another mistake—maybe he was reaching for the drawer or something, but then I felt his hand slide up the inside of my thigh, and I realized it wasn't an accident. I said something, I can't remember what, something like "Get off" or "Stop it" and moved away."'

Felix stopped to pour himself a glass of water from the jug on the table. He took a sip, his eyes on the paper. Coco hesitated in her shorthand, wondering whether he was truly thirsty, or whether it was a technique to make Peter wait. Peter shifted in his seat, but made no other sign that he was bothered by the delay.

Felix put down his glass and continued. "'Mr. Dell stood up and faced me. He made no attempt to apologize. I asked him what he thought he was doing, and he said I'd been "asking for it" because I always wore short skirts and low-cut tops, and I'd been sending him the signs. I replied that I had no idea what he was talking about, and I was going to tell someone about what he'd done. He said that if I did that, he'd get me fired, and I'd never work in a law firm again in Wellington. I told him I didn't care. He then said that if I kept quiet, he'd speak to Miss Stark and get me a promotion. I said I didn't want that if it meant that he got off the hook, and I walked out. The next day, I filed my complaint."'

Felix put the paper on the table and leaned back in his chair, resting his elbows on the arms of the chair and linking his fingers in his lap. "That's Miss De Langen's statement. Maybe now you'd like to tell your side of the story?"

Peter and Jack Lawson exchanged a glance, and Jack leaned across the table to murmur something in Peter's ear. Peter's lips curved and he nodded and murmured something back before meeting Felix's gaze again.

Peter smiled. "I'd like to start by asking a question, if that's okay, Felix?"

Coco felt Felix stiffen at the lawyer's use of his first name when he'd been so careful to keep things on a formal basis, but he just nodded and said, "Okay."

"Do you think women find you attractive?"

Felix stared at him. "I beg your pardon?"

"As a man? Do you think women find you attractive?"

Felix picked up his stylus and played with it for a moment. Coco could imagine him pondering on where this was going, and wondered if he disliked the way Peter had turned the focus of the conversation onto him. "I have no idea."

Peter grinned. "Now you're being modest. Of course women find you attractive. You're young, smart, handsome, quite obviously rich." He gestured at Felix's watch. "All the things we're told in the *Men are from Mars, Women are from Venus* type books that women like."

Felix said nothing, continuing to hold the stylus at the tip, slide his fingers down until they met the table, and then flip the stylus over to start the process again, all the while watching the other man.

Peter continued. "Cosmopolitan did a survey once of the occupations which women find most sexy. Police officer and firefighter were up there, but do you know what was number five? Lawyer." He grinned. "We can't fight it, gentleman. Women are climbing over each other to get to us."

Jack guffawed. Hugh laughed. Christopher's lips curved, but he still didn't look up.

Rob ran a hand through his hair and glanced at Felix. Felix's face didn't change—in fact, she was sure his eyes grew a little harder.

Peter's smile turned wry at the lack of reaction from the man sitting opposite him, and he cleared his throat. "Anyway. It would surprise me if there's a single male lawyer in this firm who hasn't received unwelcome attention at some point in their career. Maybe not you two—" he gestured at Felix and Rob, "—as you're still young, and you're unattached, so if a woman did come on to you, it's unlikely you'd say no. But for those of us who've worked here a long time, deflecting unwanted advances is part of the job."

Felix tipped his head. "Is that so?"

"Unfortunately yes. As you know, law offices are filled with young women for whom a secretarial career is the most likely option if they're unable to go to university." He managed to make it sound derogatory, only a step up from being a waitress. Resentment bubbled in Coco's stomach, and she glanced up at Felix to see a frown on his forehead for the first time.

"That's certainly the case for the Wellington office," Felix said.

Peter's gaze turned steely at the implied criticism. "Strange as it may seem to you, we do not have male secretaries hammering on our doors for a job. It's a female-dominated profession, always has been, and I suspect probably always will be. Young women—it has to be said—are often looking for little more than a rich man to marry. And lawyers—especially partners, and extra especially senior partners—are a viable target."

It was an incredibly sexist statement, and yet as Coco thought about Amy, she knew she couldn't in all honesty call him a liar. She sometimes listened to the conversations of the young secretaries in the break room as she ate her lunch, and had to admit they often revolved around the men in the office.

She glanced up at Felix, who looked at her for the first time. He held her gaze as if trying to see what she was thinking. She looked into his eyes for a moment and then, slightly ashamed that she couldn't refute Peter's declaration, dropped her gaze.

Felix said nothing, but she had the feeling he was disappointed in her reaction. She swallowed and doodled in the margin of her pad, something she always told her secretaries not to do, and wished miserably that he hadn't asked her to join him. She didn't want to be part of this. Why hadn't she just said no when he asked?

Chapter Twelve

Felix saw the guilt flicker in Coco's eyes before she lowered her gaze. The competent and hardworking female members of the Auckland office proved that many of the young women of today thought of things other than finding themselves a rich husband, but the look on Coco's face suggested it might be otherwise in the Wellington office. Was that a concern for her? If so, why had she reached the age of twenty-seven and yet was still single?

He looked back at Peter, who was now almost openly smirking. He disliked the man more intensely with every passing minute, and he'd had enough of him taking charge of the hearing. He'd let Peter direct the conversation for a while out of interest to see what he'd say, but it was time to bring it back on track.

"We're not here to debate the marital aims of young women," he said flatly. "Miss De Langen has accused you of inappropriate sexual contact, and I'd like you to explain your side of things, please."

Peter's eyes narrowed, but he didn't argue. "As I said," he continued smoothly, "unwanted attention is something most of us have to deal with. It's not the first time, and I doubt it will be the last that a young secretary has tried to initiate a sexual relationship. She'd been showing her interest for weeks."

"How so? By wearing short skirts?"

Peter was too smart to go down that route. "Of course not. But the signs were there—we all know them. Leaning toward someone when you're talking to them, making eye contact, brushing against them. It was clear that she was interested."

"And you weren't?"

"I'm a married man," said Peter.

The two men studied each other.

"So you've never had an affair," Felix stated.

Peter held his gaze. "That's not the subject of this investigation."

"It's relevant background information to establish your behavior at the office," Felix countered. "But let me modify the question. Have you ever had an affair with anyone at the firm?"

"I love my wife," Peter said, a hint of anger in his voice.

"Of course you do," Felix replied. "And you wouldn't want her to know about any affairs you've had."

"I haven't had any affairs."

Felix nodded. "Okay." If that was the truth, Felix would eat his hat. "So what happened on the night in question?" he continued.

Peter shifted in his seat again. "It happened as she said, up until the moment she came to stand beside me at my desk. My arms were on the table, not where she said. I pointed out the mistake she hadn't corrected. She leaned forward, and brushed her breast against my arm."

"And you jumped up and moved away immediately," Felix said.

Peter's lips twisted. "No, Mr. Wilkinson, I did not."

"Why not?"

Peter hesitated. "I don't know. I'm not a monk. She's a pretty girl. And I was surprised."

"So even with all this attention you get all the time, you were surprised when you were alone in the office after hours and a pretty girl came on to you?"

Peter shifted again. It wasn't warm in the room, but sweat had started to bead on his forehead. And he'd shifted back to using formal surnames. He was sweating, and not just physically.

"I didn't say anything at first," Peter stated, "but that's not a crime. But she leaned right against me and ran a hand through my hair, and then she kissed my ear."

Coco lifted her head to look at him, and Felix glanced at her. Did she believe him?

"What did you do then?" he asked.

"Then I moved away. I stood and told her I was flattered, but that I wasn't interested. She turned angry, told me I'd been coming onto her. But I hadn't given her any encouragement."

"None?"

"No." Peter's hands bunched into fists on the table.

"You never touched her in the office?"

"No."

"You never made sexual jokes to her—never used innuendo?"

"I didn't encourage her," Peter said. Nice way to avoid the question.

"What happened then?"

"She told me she loved me. I told her that was ridiculous—that we hardly knew each other. She started to cry, then she told me she'd tell my wife. That made me angry because nothing had happened. I yelled at her and she ran out of the office."

"What did you yell?"

"I yelled that if she told my wife or anyone at the firm, I'd have her sacked." He glared at Felix. "I was angry. I hadn't done anything wrong. I know what devastation a sexual harassment suit can cause to the accused and his family, as well as his company. I've defended teachers who've been accused by their pupils, and it can ruin a man."

Felix glanced at Coco, hoping she was getting all this down. Her notepad was covered with the tiny lines and squiggles of shorthand, and she seemed to be keeping up with the conversation.

He wished he could be alone with her to discuss what Dell had just said. Did she believe him? Had she heard of any affairs, or of any other secretaries who'd experienced similar problems? He couldn't ask her in front of Dell—that would be unprofessional. If he wasn't happy with what Dell had said, he had to declare his intention to carry out a further investigation.

He looked over at Christopher, who'd spent most of the hearing with his gaze fixed on the table. His boss met his gaze, but Felix couldn't read anything into it. He didn't smile, though, and if Felix had to guess, he would have said Christopher was trying to tell him to brush away his concerns and dismiss the "trivial matter".

But could he do that? Did he really think Peter Dell was innocent of what Sasha had accused him?

He pushed his chair away from the table and stood, then walked over to the coffee pot in the corner and poured himself a cup. "Anyone else?" he asked the room.

Rob, Hugh, and Christopher said yes, Coco shook her head. Peter and Jack began a conversation and didn't even reply. Felix poured the cups and brought them over with the tray of milk and sugar, then took his place at the table.

He looked across at Coco as he waited for Peter and Jack to stop talking. She was still doodling on her notepad, eyes lowered. Her hair was so neat, tightly wrapped in its bun, not a hair out of place. The style might have made some women look harsh or severe, but it just emphasized her high cheekbones and fine features. She nibbled at her bottom lip as she doodled, lost in thought. What was she thinking?

Still waiting for Peter to finish his little chat, Felix tapped the notepad and she looked up, startled. He smiled. "I don't know how you make sense out of all those marks. It just looks like a load of nonsense."

She met his gaze, her cool green eyes shining like cat's eyes. Something simmered in their depths. Was it resentment? She didn't want to be in the room. She was hating every minute of this.

Why?

She looked at her notepad. "Each letter of the alphabet is represented by a symbol. Take your name, for example. The F is a long loop like this." She drew it on the pad. "The L is a long, curved line like the type of lowercase L you'd use in handwriting. And the X is just a lowercase x. Where the meaning is clear, we omit the vowels. And in this case join up the F and L, using a small line across the L to indicate the X, like this." She wrote his name in three short strokes.

"That's fascinating," he said. "I had no idea that was how it worked."

"It's pretty simple once you know the basics. The rest is practice."

"Every night, I seem to remember you saying."

"Without fail." She didn't smile. He wished he could say he was sorry for having asked her to join him in the room. Why was she uneasy? What did she know about Peter that he didn't?

The two men opposite him finally broke apart, and Peter leaned back in his chair, fingers linked. He looked less nervous, as if he couldn't imagine how Felix could possibly deny the story he'd related.

Felix looked at Hugh White, the HR manager. Hugh met his gaze and frowned. Felix looked at Rob, whose eyes were clear, almost challenging, as if to say *go on, what do you make of that?* Christopher was back to staring at the table. Jack and Peter bore similar slightly smug looks.

And then Peter glanced at Coco. Felix watched her raise her gaze to meet his. They exchanged a brief, unspoken communication before she lowered her eyes quickly. A smile touched Peter's lips.

And that made up Felix's mind.

"So let me just summarize what you told me." He poured milk into his coffee, added a sugar and stirred. "You're basically saying that Sasha is lying—that she made up the story of sexual harassment because you turned down her advances. At root, this is about revenge on her part—payback from a woman scorned."

Peter leaned his elbows on the arms of his chair and steepled his fingers. "Yes, that's exactly what I'm saying."

"You intimated this wasn't the first time you've refused a woman's advances."

Peter blinked slowly. "That's right."

"Have other women ever reacted in this way?"

"They've been upset. But no, they've never threatened me in this way."

Felix frowned. "I don't understand what Miss De Langen felt she had to gain by threatening you. She was unlikely to force you to have a relationship with her by threatening to tell your wife or someone at the office. In my experience—albeit limited, I accept—if a woman thinks a guy likes her and reacts to that effect, only to find out he doesn't, the likely result is embarrassment. I would have thought Miss De Langen would have been horrified if she'd genuinely thought she'd got it wrong—that she would more likely have made a speedy exit or even apologized. Not got angry. Not unless she'd been given reason to think you were interested."

Peter went still. Jack's eyes flicked to Felix and back to the man sitting beside him.

"I didn't encourage her," Peter said.

He met Felix's gaze, the same as he had when Felix had first walked into the room. This time, however, Felix didn't look away. He held the icy blue stare, content to wait, to prove that he was in control of this hearing, acting on his gut instinct that this man was guilty, that he'd intimidated Sasha, and tried to make her have a sexual relationship with him, and when she'd stood her ground and refused, he'd turned to blackmail. The woman had been upset enough to file a complaint. That in itself deserved further attention. Felix wasn't going to play along with the partners and pretend it was a trivial matter. He wasn't that type of man.

Peter continued to stare at him, his building anger evident in the way he clenched his fists once again. But Felix waited. And eventually Peter dropped his gaze.

Felix refused to let a smile of triumph touch his lips, but inside him the wave of relief made him feel almost light headed.

He finished off his coffee, closed the manila file and replaced it in his briefcase. "After some consideration," he said, "I've decided the matter needs further investigation. I propose that I stay here until the end of next week to interview other members of staff, consider my verdict over the following weekend, and give you an answer on the Monday. Is that acceptable?" He looked at Christopher, not Peter.

Christopher met his gaze, void of expression. Then he nodded.

Felix stood. "Thank you, everyone," he said. And he turned and left the room.

Chapter Thirteen

After the meeting, Christopher and Peter left the building, leaving behind a low murmur of rumor and speculation rumbling through the office like the earthquake tremors that occasionally plagued the capital.

Felix disappeared into his office and shut the door, and she left him to it, although she saw Christopher go in to say goodbye. What was the Auckland boss saying to him? Was he berating him for not brushing the case away as if it were the cobwebs in the dusty corners of the offices? Was he angry and worried about the reputation of the firm being brought into disrepute?

Rob Drake told her that Felix had asked for the rest of the day to read through some files and look up the procedure he was expected to follow, ready to start interviewing the next week.

Forget about him, she thought, and busied herself throughout the morning, casting her eye over that day's work generated by the secretaries, sorting out their hours for the following week, making sure everyone had been paid for the right number of hours, having a brief meeting with Accounts when she found two members of staff who hadn't, settling a dispute between two secretaries who weren't getting along, and generally ensuring that the office ran smoothly and without a hitch.

At lunchtime, as usual, she put on her coat, walked outside, and rang her mother on her mobile.

Nurse Rachel picked up the phone. "Hello?"

"Hi, Rachel, it's me."

"Hi, Coco. We were just talking about you."

"Oh. How is she today?"

"So so."

Eleanor Stark was currently in the middle of an attack that had started over a month ago, leading to problems with coordinating her arms and legs, incontinence, some trouble speaking, and bouts of dark depression at the thought that she was going to be that way for the rest of her life.

"I'll put her on," Rachel said.

The phone rustled and muffled voices sounded, and then Eleanor said, "Hi, love."

"Hi, Mum. How are you today?"

"I'm fine," Eleanor said, her standard response, her words slurring slightly. "Now, have you been thinking about our conversation this morning?"

Coco gritted her teeth. Eleanor had given her a speech as she ate her breakfast, something along the lines of "You're twenty-seven and should be out enjoying yourself, not looking after me." It was a recurring theme.

"No," Coco said.

"I want you to go out this evening. It's Friday night and I've asked Frances to come and stay with me for a few hours so you can socialize." Frances was Eleanor's best friend.

"I don't want to socialize," Coco said. "I thought we could have a marathon watch of *House*—four or five episodes until we fall asleep."

"That sounds lovely," Eleanor said softly. "But not tonight. Please, Coco. Do this for me."

Coco walked across the road to look at the harbor, her stomach churning. "Seriously, Mum, I haven't got anywhere to go. Amy's busy tonight, and I don't have any other friends."

"Then you should get some," snapped Eleanor. "There must be someone at work you can go for a drink with."

Coco hesitated as Felix's tall, smiling form jumped into her mind. She shook her head angrily. "It's my choice to look after you," she said, near to tears. "I wish you'd stop trying to push me away."

Eleanor ignored her. "Sort something out. Frances will be here from seven until at least ten, or whenever you get home."

She hung up.

Coco stared at the phone, then clipped it shut and slid it in her pocket. Eleanor had never hung up on her before.

It was a windy day in the capital city—no change there, she thought—and the breeze whipped the waves of Lambton Harbor into white horses. The ferry that crossed the Cook Strait from the North Island to the South—affectionately named the Vomit Comet—would be earning its nickname that day.

Depression settled over her. Eleanor meant well, and deep down Coco supposed she was right, but the truth was that she couldn't think of anyone to go for a drink with. She purposely maintained a professional relationship with everyone in the office, except for Amy, whom she'd known since secretarial college and who was unfortunately leaving for her holiday that evening. And Coco didn't want to get close to anyone else—didn't want to reveal that beneath the severe image of the office manager she worked so hard to project was a soft-hearted, passionate woman, too afraid of being hurt to open up and let anyone in.

Unbidden, Felix's brown eyes swam into her mind again, kind as he promised to keep her nickname a secret, and she sighed. He'd impressed her in the boardroom, and although his insistence on investigating the case could raise problems for her, nevertheless she was touched that he obviously felt Sasha's claims deserved to be considered.

But there was no point in going out with him. He would only be in Wellington a week at most—surely it was pointless to start a journey when she had to get off after one stop? And yet the thought of going out with him, of having a drink, getting to know him better, filled her with a warmth she couldn't shake.

Head bowed, she walked back through the streets to the building and rode the elevator to her floor. She left her coat in her office and checked with Rob. Felix was still in his room, he assured her, and hadn't appeared for lunch.

It was now one thirty, so she bought two different boxes of sandwiches from the cart, made two cups of tea, and went to his office. She knocked on the door, waited for him to say come in, and entered, finding him deep in contemplation, studying his iPad.

He looked up, and a smile spread across his face. "Hey."

"Hey." She walked in and put the mugs on his desk. "Thought you might like a cup of 'Rosie'."

He laughed, put down his stylus, and leaned back in the chair. "Thank you. That would be lovely."

"And I wondered if you were hungry. The cart leaves at two, and I didn't want you to miss out on lunch." She offered him both boxes.

He smiled and chose the chicken. "Will you join me?"

"If that's okay."

"Of course."

She moved the mugs to the coffee table, and he rose and walked around the desk to take the armchair across from her. They opened the boxes and began to eat the sandwiches.

She indicated the desk. "How's the investigation? Rob said you were going to take today to go through some files."

"Yeah." He picked at a bit of lettuce. "Actually, between you and me, I thought I'd take the afternoon to recover. I found the process a bit… hair raising."

He was confiding in her. Once again, she flushed with warmth, aware of the strange connection they'd made that, as he'd told her, they couldn't now undo. "You surprise me. You looked totally in control, especially at the end. I loved the way you stared Peter down."

He gave her a wry smile. "I'm sure he was wearing a syrup."

"Syrup?"

He grinned then. "Sorry. Syrup of figs—it's rhyming slang for wig. Toupee, you know. You can't tell me that black rug was real."

She rolled her eyes. "I need an English to Cockney dictionary just to talk to you."

"I know, I forget. I rented a house with a girl from Peckham for two years—it rubbed off on me."

She chewed her sandwich, studying him curiously. "Was she your girlfriend?"

He picked up his mug but didn't drink, staring instead out of the window. "Yes."

"Did she move back over here with you?"

"No." He sighed. "She died."

Coco inhaled. "Oh goodness. I'm so sorry."

He looked back at her, his eyes sad. "Thank you."

"Was she ill?"

"No. She went on holiday to Greece with some friends and went snorkeling. When she was younger she used to have asthma, but it hadn't been a problem for years so she didn't even think about it. But she had an attack—I think it was something to do with the pressure of the water—and they couldn't get her breathing again."

Coco put down her sandwich, filled with horror at the thought of losing someone at that age. "That's so awful."

"It was. Well, still is. It was seven years ago now, but I still have trouble moving on, you know? I've tried…" He gave a sheepish smile. "Quite a few times. But it's not easy."

Coco was only too aware of how a relationship could haunt you even after years had passed. Thinking about her ex, Michael, sent another wave of depression over her, and she pushed the second half of the sandwich away uneaten. Michael had effectively killed her hopes of another relationship by destroying her self-confidence to the extent that she was terrified of opening up to anyone again.

What was she doing here? Felix's intimation that he'd tried to move on implied that he slept around, and that was most definitely not the sort of man she was interested in. In fact, she didn't want a relationship with anyone, and certainly not Felix Hotshot Fancy Pants. She didn't want a social life at all. At twenty-seven surely she'd earned the right to live her life the way she wanted? She was going to go home that evening, change into her sweats, eat ice cream from the carton, and watch House in her bedroom, and her mother could lump it.

"I'd better go," she said, clicking the sandwich box shut.

Felix's eyebrows rose. "Already? You haven't finished your tea. Stay a moment."

"I'm very busy."

He ignored the comment. "Have you thought about my proposition? Would you come out for a drink with me tonight?"

Oh for God's sake… The world appeared to be conspiring against her. "No, thank you."

"Just one glass of wine. We can talk about anything you like—it doesn't have to be work."

"I… I'm busy."

"You look like you could do with a drink," he said.

She glared at him. "What's that supposed to mean?"

He blinked at her aggressive tone. "Just that you look like you need to relax."

"I'm perfectly relaxed."

"Yeah," he said, exasperation showing on his face for the first time, "with your hair wound tighter than a duck's arse and your shirt buttoned to your chin. You're totally chilled out."

Her cheeks burned. "I dress professionally! Do you think I should wear my skirts halfway up my thighs and my boobs out on display for all to see just to prove I'm not frigid?"

His lips twitched. "No. I didn't mean—"

She stood. "Just because my hair isn't tumbling around my shoulders and I'm not showing my belly-button piercing doesn't mean I'm straight-laced."

His eyebrows nearly shot through his hairline. "You have a belly-button piercing?"

Shit. She hadn't meant to say that. She'd had it done shortly after she left Michael in a fit of rebellion. "I... that's irrelevant. The point is that you don't know what I'm like inside—nobody does."

"Maybe not, but I'd like to find out," he said. "Come for a drink with me."

She was irritated now, though. He'd struck a nerve. "You're here for a week. You really think I'm so easy that I'll sleep with you after one drink?"

Now he looked amused. "Who said anything about sex?"

"So that hadn't entered your mind at all?"

He grinned. "I didn't say that."

"See. All men are the same."

His brow darkened at that comment and he also got to his feet, scrunching up his serviette and throwing it onto the coffee table in a ball. "That's unfair. I thought it would be nice to have a drink, to get to know each other. I know I'm only here temporarily, but I'm on my own, and I thought it would be a pleasant way to pass a few hours. Clearly, I was mistaken."

"So you were only looking for some intelligent conversation," she said in a sarcastic voice to cover her emotion. Tears pricked her eyes and resentment boiled as she remembered her mother's determination to get her to go out. That's what had pushed her to come into his office. What a mistake. "Yeah, right, Mr. I've-tried-to-move-on-quite-a-few-times. I bet you have. I bet you screw any girl who steps in your path and flutters her eyelashes at you. No, don't deny it—I saw the way all the women reacted to you today as I gave you the tour of the office." She batted her lashes. "'Why Mr. Wilkinson, of course I'll come sit on your knee and you can give me *dick*-tation.'" She took a step forward and said softly, "Well, if you were just looking for a good-time gal, you're talking to the wrong woman."

"Really." He put his hands on his hips. "If there's a woman out there more in need of a quick fuck than you, I've yet to meet her."

Chapter Fourteen

They stared at each other for a good ten seconds. Coco's chest heaved with indignation, as well as a strange excitement. The thought of a quick fuck with this gorgeous young lawyer made her head spin. Even the words—slightly shocking for a girl who rarely swore—made her aroused.

But then a shadow crossed his face, as if he'd been sitting in the sun and she'd leaned over him. He backed away, running a hand through his hair, his eyes widening.

"Shit," he said. "I'm sorry."

She blinked, taken aback by his apology, and blew out a breath. "It's okay."

"It's not okay." He spoke vehemently. "What the hell am I doing?" He spoke more to himself than her, she thought, seeing him staring across the room. "I'm doing exactly what Dell did to that secretary."

Coco's mouth fell open. "No," she said, but he wasn't listening.

"Maybe this was what happened between them. He thought she was interested and pushed too hard." He walked over to the window and stared out. "Jesus. I was so fucking self-righteous in there and here I am doing the exact same thing."

Suddenly all her anger fled, his obvious angst making her soften. "Felix, no…"

"I am." He turned to face her. "Why the hell did Christopher ask me to do this? I'm obviously unsuitable to judge whether a woman is willing or not."

"This is nothing like what's happening between Peter and Sasha," she assured him. How could he think that?

"Isn't it?" He glared at her. "How can I make a decision on what happened between them when I obviously can't control my own actions?" He looked puzzled. "It's so hard to read the signs sometimes—I can see how it would be easy to come onto a woman and make a move, only to realize you've read it wrong."

"It's not the same," she said again, moving closer to him. "You didn't misread the signs."

He either didn't hear her or didn't register the words. "What if she'd led him on for weeks, flirted with him, made him think he stood a chance, so he cultivated an opportunity to be alone with her, and at the last minute she changed her mind? At what point does it become his fault?"

"Felix." She waited for his eyes to focus on her, then reached up and touched his face. "You didn't misread the signs." Filled with a strange urge to comfort and reassure him, taking a deep breath, she raised herself on tiptoe and kissed him.

He froze, and for a brief moment she panicked and thought he was going to pull away and ask her what the hell she was doing. Gathering her courage, trying not to think that Rob or someone else might be standing in the doorway staring at them, she pressed her lips against his once, then again, lingering, willing him to respond, to understand.

And then his hand came up to cup her head, the other sliding around her waist, and he tightened his hold and responded, meeting the slow movement of her lips with kisses of his own, tentative, beautiful, soft kisses that took her breath away and made her want to cry.

She wanted it to go on forever, but after what could only have been fifteen seconds or so, he pulled back, dropped his hands, and slid them into the pockets of his pants. She moved back a little, and they studied each other, the afternoon sunshine sliding through the windows and across the desk in front of them.

"Sorry," she said, heart still pounding. God, he was gorgeous.

His eyes twinkled and his lips curved. "For what?"

"I don't know."

They both smiled.

"You didn't get the signs wrong," she whispered. "You mustn't think that. I can understand how difficult it must be for a guy, trying to decide whether a woman is interested or not. The problem is that sometimes the heart says yes but the brain says no. We want to, but for some reason we're telling ourselves we can't. And sometimes we need the guy to push a little—that feeling of being wanted is nice."

He listened thoughtfully and nodded.

"But that's very different from a guy refusing to take no for an answer. If I didn't want to go out with you, Felix, I wouldn't just have said no—it would have been very clear, in body language as well as verbal language. I believe that men like Peter read the signs as well as any other men, but they choose to ignore them. And in fact, they get off on it. They like showing a woman they're going to have them, regardless of what they want. They like the power. That's a million miles away from someone saying no but meaning yes, and I don't believe a man like you would ever confuse the two."

"Thank you," he said. "I hope that's the case anyway."

"Well, look, so there's no doubt, let me say, I'd like to go out for a drink with you tonight. But just for a drink, okay?"

His eyes creased at the edges as he smiled. "Okay."

"On one condition—that we don't talk about work. You take me out as Coco, not as Veronica Stark."

He nodded. "Agreed."

"Okay." She picked up their empty mugs, her heart pounding at the thought of going on a date. "I'll nip home and get changed, and meet you in town, shall I? Say, seven o'clock?"

"Sure. Can you recommend anywhere?"

"I don't get out much," she admitted, "but I've heard The Black Gull is nice, on the harbor front."

"Sounds good. I'll meet you there. Seven o'clock."

She hesitated, her heart continuing to race at the look in his eyes. Was she making the right decision?

It's just a drink, she told herself. *Don't get too excited.*

She smiled and left the office.

Chapter Fifteen

At just after seven, Felix leaned on the counter and sipped from the glass of Mac's Gold, scanning the bar to make sure he hadn't missed Coco's arrival. No, she wasn't there yet. Would she show up? He wouldn't be surprised if she didn't. Okay, she'd agreed to the date, but saying she'd be there and turning up were two different things.

He sighed. Perhaps it would be better if she didn't show up—he shouldn't be meeting her, not while he was carrying out the investigation. And yet what harm were they doing? They'd agreed not to talk about work—it wasn't as if he was going to quiz her about Dell, even if her summary of "men like Peter" had intrigued him. She spoke as if she had experience of what Sasha was going through, but surely that wasn't the case? Wouldn't she have told someone if Dell, or anyone else for that matter, had behaved inappropriately in the past? He couldn't imagine she was the type of woman to put up with unsuitable sexual contact, not after the speech she'd given him about how to behave with the secretaries.

A movement in the doorway caught his eye, and he turned, then stared as he saw her standing there, hesitating as she scanned the room looking for him. *Wow*, was his first thought, and at that moment he knew he'd been fooling himself by thinking he'd have preferred it if she hadn't shown up. It was a cool evening, spring continuing to blow its fresh breath across the city, and she wore jeans and a fashionable chocolate-brown jacket that she unzipped now to reveal a cream roll-neck sweater beneath. She wasn't wearing her glasses, and she'd uncurled her hair from the tight bun so it hung around her shoulders in waves, topping it with a trendy felt hat the same color as her jacket. She looked about five years younger in the casual clothing, all softness and curves, and a smile spread across his face so that by the time her gaze fell on him, he had to stop himself beaming like an idiot.

He raised a hand, and her face lit with relief before she made her way across to him. Had she worried he wouldn't be there?

"Hey." As she approached, he rested a hand on her upper arm, leaned forward, and kissed her cheek. "I'm glad you came."

"Me too," she said, although he wasn't sure if she meant she was pleased she'd come or relieved that he was there.

"What can I get you?"

She gestured to his glass. "Is that a Mac's Gold? I'll have the same, please."

He ordered one for her, paid, and indicated a table to one side of the bar. Because of the evening's coolness, the wood fire had been lit, and it crackled in the grate.

She walked before him to the seat, slipped off her jacket, and hung it over one of the chairs to one side, then slid onto the bench facing the fire.

"Mind if I join you?" he asked, pointing to the space beside her.

"Sure." She sipped her beer, her green eyes wide as he sat beside her, and she reached up and removed her hat, placing it on the table.

"Nice titfer," he said.

"Pardon?"

He grinned. "Sorry. Tit-for-tat. Hat."

She gave him a wry smile. "Okay, you're going to have to explain this rhyming thing. How does it work, exactly? And why do you bother using it?"

He settled back, aware of her subtle perfume, the swell of her breasts under the sweater, the fact that her legs were long from hip to knee, her thighs shapely beneath the jeans. She'd turned heads as she walked into the bar, but she hadn't noticed. He suspected she was well out of practice with the dating game. Why was that? Because of her mother?

"Okay," he said, "lesson number one in Cockney rhyming slang. Most rhymes consist of two or three words, and the last one rhymes with the original word. But only the first one or two words is used, like a code. So, like tit-for-tat referring to hat, we'd never say 'That's a nice tit-for-tat,' we'd say, 'that's a nice titfer.'"

She laughed. "I see. I think. So that's why a wig is a syrup—syrup of figs."

"That's right. You've got it."

"Tell me some more." Her eyes danced. "Give me a description of something using Cockney rhymes."

"All right." Naughtiness surged through him. "How about if I describe you?"

"Me?"

"Yes." He studied her mischievously, running his gaze down her. "I've already mentioned the titfer. I guess I have to say it looked very nice on your barnet."

"Barnet?"

"Your blonde barnet. Barnet Fair. Hair."

"Ha! Right."

"And it frames your boat lovely."

"Boat... oh, race?"

"Yup. Face." He smiled. "And you have beautiful green minces."

She frowned, trying to puzzle that one out. "Oh, mince pies? Eyes?"

"Yes! You're good at this. Now, let's start the other end—I know you're wearing Converses today but in your high heels you had very dainty plates."

"Plates of..." She thought about it. "Hmm..."

"Meat. Feet. And a nice pair of bacons."

She raised her eyebrows.

"Bacon and eggs, legs," he teased. "That one's not used as much as the others. Now, moving up..." He grinned. "I have to say you have a very nice aris."

"Why thank you. Explain please."

"This gets more complicated—it's a two-part rhyme. Aris stands for Aristotle, which means bottle. And bottle and glass means arse."

"Good grief, talk about convoluted." She smiled, a little shyly. "So you think I have a nice aris?"

"You have a beautiful aris. Almost as nice as your bristols." He smirked.

"I know I'm going to regret this, but...bristols?"

"Bristol City." He gestured to her breasts.

She giggled. "I love it. I'm going to learn Cockney and then we can speak code and nobody else will understand."

"Yes, that's kind of the point. It's a way to exclude strangers from the conversation."

"A bit like Morse code."

"Exactly."

"Okay, so what's the biggest compliment I could pay you in Cockney?"

He grinned. "Probably something about the size of my Hampton."

"Which is…"

"My Hampton Wick. You can guess that one. Leading to the famous phrase if you zip your pants up too quickly, 'Ouch, I've got my Hampton Court.'"

She laughed and took a long swig of her beer. "That cheered me up, thank you."

"No worries." It was good to see her smile. She'd swapped the red lipstick for a more muted shade, but her lips still looked soft and kissable, and she had a pretty smile.

"So how are you enjoying Wellington?" she asked, settling back.

"Oh, I like the city itself. I've been here a few times—just not to the offices. The city seems busier than I've seen it before though."

"That's because it's the premiere of that new movie on Sunday."

Of course—he'd forgotten about that. The movie, based on a bestselling Kiwi fantasy novel, was supposed to rival *The Lord of the Rings*, and everyone was talking about it.

"Are you going?"

She snorted. "There's no way I could get tickets. I wish I could go, though. I love those movies."

"Oh, you like fantasy?"

"Of course, and sci-fi."

So they proceeded to talk about what other movies they'd enjoyed, and Felix was surprised how much they had in common. They went on to talk about music, then moved onto food, then wine, and then a hundred different other subjects, the minutes flowing into hours until he looked at his watch and was surprised to see it had just gone nine.

"Jeez," she said when he told her the time. "It sure flies when you're having fun, doesn't it?"

He met her gaze and smiled. They were now drinking wine, and although he was far from drunk, he felt hazily relaxed, and sensed she felt the same from the way she'd curled up on the bench, tucking her legs under her. He sat with his legs stretched out, ankles crossed, arm along the back of the bench so it was almost—but not quite—around her.

They studied each other for a moment in companionable silence, and he felt as if, after swimming miles together down a deep river, for the first time they'd paused in their journey and were treading water, letting the silt settle beneath them.

She leaned her head on the bench and sipped her wine. "Tell me about the girl you knew in London."

That took him by surprise. It was the first personal subject she'd raised, and he hadn't expected it.

He ran a hand through his hair, unsure if he felt comfortable going into details. "I don't know that it's polite to talk about previous girlfriends when you're out on a date."

She smiled. "I don't mind. I'd like to know."

So he told her how he'd first met Lindsey when he was twenty and she was nineteen. She'd also been studying law, and they'd met at a party. Like him, she'd been there on a scholarship—she'd come from one of the roughest parts of London, and there was no way her parents would have been able to afford to send her to university, but she'd been so bright that she'd aced every exam she sat and the school had arranged for her to go to Oxford.

He described how beautiful she'd been, with her shining dark hair and the way she lit up a room with her smile. How he couldn't believe she'd fallen for him, and when she suggested they move in together, he'd taken a whole second to say yes.

They'd had two wonderful years, and they'd planned their futures together—talked about where they were going to live, how many kids they'd have. He'd thought he'd be with her forever.

And then she'd died. He told Coco about the moment when the phone had rung—he'd had a couple of mates around to watch the football, and all the while her parents were telling him the horrendous news, his mates were cheering in the background.

He tried to tell Coco how he felt when he heard the news, but at that point he had to stop.

She reached out and took his hand. "I'm so sorry."

He drew a long breath and let it out slowly. "It's not been easy."

"Of course it hasn't. You were in love, and she sounds lovely. She was a very lucky woman to have you feeling so strongly about her."

"I didn't sleep with anyone else for two years," he said, wanting to explain. "Part of me never wanted to sleep with anyone else ever again, but I'd moved back here and my family were worried about me. Toby—that's my youngest brother—fixed me up on a date, and I didn't want to go, but he bullied me into it, and I suppose I was glad he did, ultimately. I felt guilty for weeks afterward, but eventually I realized life has to go on."

She nodded. "I'm sure Lindsey wouldn't have wanted you to stay single."

"She would have laughed her head off at the thought of me being celibate," he said wryly. "I was pretty insatiable when I was younger."

Coco raised her eyebrows. "But not now?"

"Well, when I get the chance." He grinned.

"But you haven't met anyone else you want to share your life with?"

He met her gaze and smiled. "Not yet."

Her green eyes were clear, but he couldn't see through the glassy windows to her thoughts. What was she thinking? Was she aware of how attracted to her he was? He hadn't felt this comfortable in a woman's presence for a long time. Maybe it was just because he hadn't slept with anyone for a while, but every time he got near her, all his senses felt heightened.

He could smell her flowery perfume, something nice and light, making him think of summer. Her pale skin looked flawless, although she had a scattering of freckles across her nose. Her hair, now tumbling around her shoulders, looked like satin ribbons that would curl through his fingers. He wanted to kiss her again. The last time had only been a touch of lips, and he wanted to taste her, to press himself up against her, to possess her.

He sipped his Merlot. "So what about you?"

"What about me?" She twirled her glass in her fingers.

"Why are you still single at twenty-seven? You're beautiful, clever. I'm sure you could have any man you wanted."

"I don't think so." She lowered her eyes.

He studied her for a moment. "When was the last time you dated?"

She scratched at a mark on the glass. "I went out with a guy when I was twenty-one, and we dated for three years. I haven't been out with anyone since."

"You haven't been on a date for three years?" He stared at her.

She gave him a playful look. "Now you know how honored you are."

"I am. Jeez. Why not? Opportunity?"

She nibbled her bottom lip. "Not really. Well, yes, in a way—I stopped going out and socializing, so I don't tend to meet many men who aren't involved at the office."

He picked up on her words. "Why did you stop going out? Was this after you broke up with…"

"Michael. And yes." She fell silent. She obviously wasn't going to venture more details unless he prodded, but somehow he got the feeling she wanted to talk about it.

"What was he like?"

She continued to nibble her lip. Felix tried not to stare at it and think of something other than kissing her.

"He was nice enough," she said eventually. "He worked in finance. We met at church. I stopped going regularly when I was about fourteen after Dad died, but Mum goes every Sunday, and I met him when I was taking her there one week." She sighed. "Mum's parents were strict Catholics, and so's she. I went to a Catholic girls' school, and I was very, very shy. I didn't make many friends, and unfortunately I was one of those students who didn't rebel and go to parties and have a great time."

He returned her wry smile.

She continued, "I went to secretarial college for a year and then got the job at McAllister Dell. But I was still very shy. I didn't date anyone until I met Michael." She lowered her gaze, hiding her thoughts from him again. There was something she wasn't telling him, but he didn't have time to dwell on it because she was carrying on. "I was very naïve back then. We didn't have lessons on the facts of life at school and Mum would never talk about that sort of thing. I only knew what I'd picked up from the other girls, which wasn't much."

"Girls don't talk like guys, I guess," he said.

"They would sometimes, but I never really understood what they were saying. No frame of reference, you know? Anyway, I met Michael and we dated for a while. And eventually we slept together." She chewed her lip again.

Felix waited patiently for her to continue, sipping his wine. Eventually he prompted, "It wasn't what you expected?"

She looked across at the fire, the warm light playing across her pale face. "In the beginning, it was okay. I suppose it was how I thought it would be. It was only as time went by that things started going wrong. I guess that, well, we just weren't sexually compatible, you know?"

Felix filled with pity. He could imagine how difficult it had been for the virtuous Catholic schoolgirl who knew nothing about sex to deal with the demands of a guy who grew tired of the attractions of naivety and innocence. Now she looked embarrassed, and his heart went out to her.

"It's okay," he said, reaching out to squeeze her hand. "It happens. And there's nothing wrong with saying no if there are things your partner wants to do that you're not comfortable with. You shouldn't do anything you don't want to."

She looked back at him, and to his surprise a hint of mischievousness flittered across her face. "Um, I think you've got the wrong idea," she admitted. "It was me who wanted to be more adventurous in bed. That's where it all went wrong."

Chapter Sixteen

Coco couldn't help but giggle at the look on Felix's face. His eyes had widened, and now his lips gradually began to curve as he realized what she was saying.

"Hmm." He tipped his head and eyed her with newfound interest.

She sipped her wine, letting his imagination work for a while. She knew she should stop drinking, but for once she was enjoying being slightly tipsy and relaxed in a good-looking man's company.

Okay, she had to admit it—good-looking was rather underselling him at the moment. Felix Hotshot Fancy Pants was probably the most gorgeous guy she'd ever laid eyes on. When she'd walked into the bar and spotted him leaning on the counter, smiling as he waited for her to see him, she'd inhaled so quickly and deeply that her head had spun.

He wore jeans and a soft navy V-necked sweater over a white T-shirt that brought out how tanned his skin was compared to her pale complexion. He'd run his hands through his usually smoothed-down hair and now it looked ruffled and sexy. She'd thought he looked good in his suit—and a smart suit on a gorgeous guy took some beating—but the casual gear suited him, and he looked like a model for a clothing company.

She'd really enjoyed the last few hours. He'd listened attentively when she talked, not looked once at other women, even though one had walked past with a skirt up to her panties and her chest on display for all to see, and he genuinely seemed interested in what she had to say.

Now, however, she hesitated to relinquish more details, aware they were on the verge of stepping from the general conversation of friends to something more intimate. She'd never spoken about what happened with Michael, not with Amy, certainly not with her mother, and it didn't seem right to confess all to a guy she'd only just met.

And yet he leaned toward her, propping his head with a hand on the back of the seat, smelling good enough to eat—of fresh clothes and manly aftershave and that lovely warm muffin aroma that told her he'd nipped into *Bella's* again on the way to his hotel room. His chest was only inches from her arm—she could almost feel the heat from his body, maybe just an inch closer than a good friend would sit, telling her that he was enjoying the intimacy they were sharing. And he was looking at her with fascination, clearly wanting more information, and men so rarely looked at her that way that she couldn't keep silent.

She studied her glass, sobering a little as she remembered the details. "In the beginning, it was okay," she started. "Not magical, like you see in the movies, all ripping off each other's clothes and everything, but nice enough. Then, as the months started to go by, I began to realize that we weren't… um… progressing, shall we say."

She risked a glimpse up. His smile had faded, and his expression showed curiosity mixed with sympathy, as if he was trying very hard to understand. Up this close, she could see the slight hint of a five o'clock shadow—her fingers would scrape against it, should she touch his cheek.

"When you say 'we weren't progressing', do you mean emotionally or physically?"

"Both I suppose, although I meant more physically. It became clear that he wasn't really interested in sex." She frowned. "No, that's not strictly true. I think he was, but it was like… he thought there was something wrong with liking it, you know?"

Felix didn't say anything, a frown flickering on his brow.

"We always did missionary, and if we tried anything else, and he enjoyed it, he felt bad afterward. He'd withdraw from me emotionally. And I don't just mean the old 'I'm going to roll over and go to sleep', I mean he'd get up and walk off, and wouldn't speak to me for hours."

Felix's frown deepened. "You think that was something to do with his religion? That sex should be carried out to procreate rather than to enjoy, or something?"

"I don't think so." She couldn't quite believe she was discussing this with him, but he was so easy to talk to. Maybe that was why he made such a successful lawyer, because his clients found him easy to open up to. Or maybe she was just relieved to find someone willing to listen. "I've thought about it a lot over the last few years, and it wouldn't surprise me if he was abused when he was younger. He wouldn't discuss sex with me. It got worse and worse. I began to get frustrated—I think I sensed it was strange that not only would he not experiment, but he started to get angry with me if I suggested it. He made me feel..." Her cheeks grew warm. "Dirty. Like there was something wrong with me."

Felix's smile disappeared completely, his expression hardening. "That's incredible, in this day and age."

"I suppose." A wave of relief swept over her. He understood—he agreed. It wasn't her. "And because I couldn't talk about it to anyone, I put up with it for ages. I thought maybe there was something wrong with me, that I was perverted for wanting to try something different, for liking sex. I mean I'm not talking about swinging from the chandeliers or anything, but he wouldn't even..." She hesitated.

Felix studied her and then, to her surprise, reached up a hand to warm her cheek. "Wouldn't what? You can tell me."

She rested her cheek in his palm for a moment and closed her eyes, enjoying the human contact, the warmth of his hand on her skin. Then she opened her eyes, and he dropped his hand. "He didn't even like kissing. He'd turn his head away." She could hear her voice growing husky as emotion flooded her, so she stopped and took a big gulp of wine.

"Did he give you orgasms every time you had sex?" he asked.

She flushed warm. Orgasms? What a joke. Again, the height of pleasure had become something to be embarrassed and nervous about, until she'd hardly come at all.

But all she said was, "Occasionally. Very occasionally."

Felix released a long, slow breath, and she wondered what he was thinking.

"Are you wondering why I stayed with him so long?" she asked softly. He said nothing, and she knew she was right. "It's very difficult to explain. You must have had the same sort of thing in the past with your family law—where women continue to stay in abusive relationships. It's easy to think they're weak—that they don't value themselves, but it's not like that."

He shifted in his seat, moving a fraction closer to her. Now his arm where it lay along the back of the seat touched her shoulders, his thigh brushing hers. If anyone looked over, they'd think they were a couple. His presence comforted her. She felt safe in the circle of his arm, protected somehow. How different would her life have been if it had been Felix and not Michael whom she'd dated all those years ago?

"I'd like to understand," he said.

She looked down at his chest, concentrating on the weave of his sweater. "You think it's you," she said. "That you're at fault. Deep down, you're sure it's not you, but when someone constantly makes you feel that way, it's hard to fight it. With me, although I watched the odd movie where the woman made the first move and both the guy and girl seemed to enjoy sex, often in this world women are made to feel wrong for liking it. Or, alternatively, many women take the stand that there's something disgusting about liking sex, and they act superior, as if we should all feel the same. The rise of modern erotic romance novels has brought it more into the open—that many women enjoy sex and want to try other things and that it's okay to be like that. But there's no doubt that a good proportion of the female population look down on those who like reading erotic stories, insisting it's pornography, that it's demeaning to enjoy role-playing or being tied up or whatever—that it's somehow encouraging men to abuse their partners. Maybe that's the case, I don't know. All I know is, I don't feel like that, and eventually I knew I had to get out of that relationship."

It was a long speech, and she finished slightly breathless with the effort of trying to make him understand. "Sorry," she said.

"For what?"

"Rabbiting on."

He smiled. "You know where that comes from?"

"What?"

"Rabbiting. It's Cockney. Rabbit and pork—talk."

"I never knew that!"

He laughed. "Anyway, it's good. I meant what I said—I want to understand." He finished off his glass of wine, placed it on the table and considered her thoughtfully. "All relationships are about control to a certain extent, even friendships. The best are those where the control is equal, or where you can explore controlling each other in a safe environment by, as you say, using role-play or whatever. The problems come when one half gets off on controlling the other, and it takes over."

"I guess."

"All dating is a game. It's like being dancers, or ice skaters, circling one another. You look for the signs, hoping you don't misread them and get it all wrong. We've all done it. I had my face slapped at school."

She giggled. "Really?"

"I was sixteen. I chatted up this pretty girl, and I thought she was giving me all the signs, so I tried to kiss her. Turns out I was wrong. It's not easy."

"No, it's not." She smiled, and then bit her lip. She felt embarrassed about asking, about being so forward, but curiosity—and the several glasses of wine she'd had—prompted her to be brave. "So, what's your view on women and sex then? What do you like your girls to do in bed? Michael hated me taking the initiative. He disliked role-playing or talking dirty or swearing or anything like that. What do you think about it?"

Felix's lips curved. "Honestly?"

"Honestly."

"I love women taking the initiative. I don't think anything two people want to do in bed is wrong, providing it's consensual. I think pornography is in the eye of the beholder, so to speak—what's sexy for one person is pornographic for another, and I think it's a matter of luck almost, to find someone who feels the same way you do. I don't think there's anything wrong with looking at the naked body, and I think it's perfectly normal to get turned on watching other people having sex."

"Oh." If she could widen her eyes any more, her eyeballs would pop out.

"And I don't see why that should be any different for women than for men," he continued. "You've probably already worked out my view on that, but I believe in total equality. Are men stronger than women? Yes, and it's fun to explore that sometimes. Are there other differences in the sexes? Yes, although whether the majority are nature or nurture, it's hard to tell. But should women feel differently about sex than men? No, of course not! Why should they? Monogamy only came about when mankind developed farming, and ownership of land began to be passed to one's children—at that point it became important for a man to know the children he was giving his hard-earned land to were his own."

She raised her eyebrows. "I never thought of it like that."

He shrugged. "The last few thousand years have done a lot of damage to women and their place in society. That's one reason I enjoy doing what I do. I hope I can rectify that, even if it's only to a very tiny extent."

She nibbled her bottom lip. "So you think it's okay for women to suggest different things in bed, then?"

His warm brown eyes fixed her with a firm gaze. "Honey, let me just say, if you were my girlfriend, you could suggest anything you wanted, try any position you liked, swear as much as you felt necessary, and if you didn't have at least one—and hopefully two or three—orgasms every time we had sex, I'd be very, very, disappointed."

Chapter Seventeen

Coco couldn't look away. She felt as if he was looking deep into her soul, searching out all the feelings of frustration and guilt that hid in a dark corner of her psyche, and shining a torch on them, dispelling them.

Did he know she yearned for a man like him? That she hadn't even realized how much she desired it, but now he'd shown her a glimpse of what it would be like to be with him, she hungered for it so much she nearly climbed on top of him and smothered him in kisses?

His intense look faded, to be replaced slowly by amusement as she continued to stare, speechless. "Are you all right?"

She blinked and smiled wryly, but her heart continued to hammer. "I… um… are you for real? I didn't think men like you actually existed."

He laughed. "Sweetheart, I'm nothing special. Honestly—I'm not setting myself up as some kind of hero here. In the circles I mix in, most of the men I know feel the same. My brothers, my friends, they're all open-minded individuals who are very relaxed about women and sex."

"Really?" She couldn't imagine it.

"Do you read women's magazines?"

"Sometimes."

"Have you ever seen Faith Hillman's column? Well, she's Faith Thorne now, but she still calls herself Hillman in the magazine and on her blog."

Coco frowned. "Didn't she write about the Seven Sexy Sins?"

"That's the one."

"She married the guy she was exploring the Sins with, didn't she? Mr. Sinful?"

"Yeah. Rusty. And you know what they got up to! Well, they're good friends of mine."

Her eyebrows rose. "Seriously?"

"Yeah. Rusty went to school with my brother, Toby. He's just gotten married too, to a girl he met years ago on holiday. She got pregnant and he never knew, then back in February he was in Christchurch during the earthquake and who should be right in front of him when the earthquake struck but Esther and her son, Charlie?"

"Oh my God, that's amazing."

"I know. Anyway, long story short, second time around they got together permanently, but he's the same as me in his views on women. I think the majority of men—in this country anyway—are the same. You've just been very... unfortunate."

If only he knew the rest of the sorry tale.

She lowered her eyes, thinking over what he'd said. Was it true? Were most men open to women being more adventurous in the bedroom? She couldn't imagine it. What would it be like to have that kind of freedom? To be with someone who didn't frown if she made a tentative suggestion, but who laughed and said, "Absolutely," and proceeded to let her do whatever she wanted?

Felix's hand slid beneath her chin and he lifted it so her eyes met his again. "So, Miss Stark," he said in a teasing voice, stroking her skin with his thumb before dropping his hand again. "What kind of fantasies have you been indulging in? What would be your heart's desire, if you could do anything you wished?"

"I'm not Miss Stark," she whispered. "That's Veronica. Tonight, I'm just Coco."

His gaze softened. "Okay, Coco. I'm sorry."

"It's okay. It's difficult to explain how different I feel, out of the office. Like... I've escaped, I suppose."

He leaned his head on his hand again, just inches away from her now, and smiled. "So tell me your fantasies."

She looked up at him, heart racing at his nearness. Could she sit here and tell him the dreams she had, her secret, darkest desires? Usually, she would have said there was no way she could open up to an almost-stranger, but the wine had thawed her, and she was tired of shutting herself away.

"I suppose I dream most of escaping," she said.

"Physically, mentally, or emotionally?"

"All three. Physically mostly, I suppose. I haven't been on holiday for years, since Mum became confined to a wheelchair. She doesn't like being away from home, and I understand that. Occasionally, I've been away for a night, like when I went to Auckland on a secretarial refresher course, but that's unusual, and it's so much hassle to organize someone to come in and cover for me."

"It's quite a responsibility, and you're still young."

"I know." She shrugged. "I don't mind—I don't want her to go into a respite home. I know she'd hate it—she's very reclusive and hates being around strangers. It increases her stress levels, which makes her illness worse. But she keeps telling me she wants to go because she thinks I need to have a life of my own. It's causing a huge amount of friction between us at the moment." She bit her lip. She didn't want to talk about that because she knew she'd get upset.

"So someone looks after her during the day?"

"Yes, I pay for nurses to come in."

"And who's looking after her tonight?"

"Her best friend, Frances. She's very good—she occasionally fills in if ever I'm away, which isn't very often. And her daughter's about to have a baby, so she won't be around for much longer as she'll want to help out there."

He nodded and, to her surprise, reached out and picked up her hand. He turned it over and rubbed his thumb across her palm, a strangely intimate gesture that made her catch her breath and feel as if in that one small movement they'd crossed the threshold from friends to something more.

"So tell me where you dream about escaping," he said, continuing to stroke her hand, running his thumb lightly down her fingers, circling the base of her thumb, making her tingle all over.

She sighed, feeling in seventh heaven. "Somewhere hot and exotic. Bermuda, maybe, or Hawaii. I'd love to go to Hawaii."

"And what would you do in Hawaii?" His thumb brushed across the inside of her wrist. She hadn't known that area was so sensitive. Her nipples tightened, and she inhaled. His gaze dropped to her mouth, then returned to hers, growing warmer.

She moistened her lips with the tip of her tongue. "I don't know. Make love on the beach, I suppose. In the waves. Although I'd worry about getting sand where I shouldn't. Or being sunburned somewhere that doesn't usually see the light of day."

He chuckled. "Things like that don't happen in a fantasy."

"I suppose." She smiled. "I just think it would be wonderful, finding a secluded area, lying in the sun, and being kissed first by the sun, then by a man, all over…" She sighed.

"All over?" His eyes gleamed. "I presume oral sex is a part of this fantasy?"

"Oh yes…" she said breathlessly. "I'd love to try it."

He stopped stroking her hand and his eyes widened. "Oh, for fuck's sake, you're kidding me? He wouldn't even do that?"

"Felix, I was lucky he touched me down there at all." She could see him struggling with comprehension—that he was unable to believe there were men who were really like this. She smiled and stroked his hand in return. He was very idealistic, straight as a Roman road, maybe even a little self-righteous with his views, but she liked that.

He looked down at their hands and linked their fingers, stroking her palm again. She held her breath—seeing their fingers entwined seemed significant, as if he was trying to tell her something.

He smiled and released her hand, obviously trying to brush off his anger at what she'd told him. "Come on then, what else? What other fantasies do you have?"

She curled up beside him, conscious of the warmth of his arm almost around her shoulders. "Oh, gosh, where do I start?"

"You have a lot of fantasies?"

"Oh, all the time. Sometimes after watching TV programs, you know, like having sex outside in the park or something—I can't imagine what it must be like having that thrill that you might be discovered. Or in a limo."

He grinned. "You'd like to have sex in a limo?"

"Yes. After I won an Oscar for leading actress." She giggled.

"Where else?" He was back to stroking her hand.

She turned it over so he could brush her palm again, liking the frisson it sent up her body. "Um… in an igloo."

That made him laugh. "Jesus. I'd worry about frozen extremities."

"I'm serious. I find the Inuit fascinating. How do they do it? I'd love to go in an igloo. And have sex fully clothed. That would be fun."

He smiled and ran a finger up her arm, across her shoulder, and up her neck to her face. He brushed his thumb across her cheek. "What else?"

She felt in a wonderful tipsy, sleepy haze, alive with sensation, hairs rising all over her body. "Oh, I have all sorts of fantasies."

"Tell me about them."

"I can't." Her face grew warm. "They're private."

He lifted her chin again so she had to look into his eyes. "Come on, tell me."

She gave a little shake of her head, her face burning so much she knew she must be scarlet. "I couldn't."

"Okay, I'll try to guess." He grinned. "Does it involve… sex toys?"

She giggled. "No, although that would be fun."

"A particular position?"

"Hmm, not really. Although again, something other than missionary would be fun."

"Something more… forbidden?"

Gosh, her face could have been used as a beacon. "Maybe."

He thought about it. "Anal sex?"

"Felix!"

He looked amused. "What?"

She shook her head, shocked that he wasn't shocked. "Jeez."

"You don't think you'd enjoy that?"

"I… well I haven't… I couldn't imagine…" Her voice trailed off as he stifled a chuckle. "Do ordinary people really do that?"

"Didn't you read about Sin Six on Faith's blog? Eighteen percent of the population indulge, apparently." He grinned.

"Really? Eighteen percent?" She was stunned. Just how naïve was she?

"It's not that unusual," he said, confirming her thoughts.

"But…" Her mind spun with fascination as she tried to work out the mechanics. "Ooh. How does it… work?"

"Lubrication and lots of patience, to begin with anyway."

"You seem to know an awful lot about it," she observed.

"I read books," he said, although the gleam in his eyes told her he'd done more than read about it.

She fanned herself. "I think I need to lie down."

He laughed. "Okay, so if that's not your fantasy… Let me think. More than one partner?"

She went to deny it but couldn't lie outright, and instead just gave a reluctant, shy smile.

To her relief, he didn't make fun of her and he didn't laugh. "That's quite common too," he said.

"Really?"

"Christ, yeah. I imagine I have a harem."

She smiled. "You're a sheikh?"

"Yeah. I can pick and choose from all the women every night, depending on my mood. Quite often I pick more than one." He winked.

She looked at their hands, braver now he'd confessed. "I imagine I'm in one of those sex clubs. There's a room out the back, and men can hire it out for parties. I'm tied to a bed, and they get to use me any way they want…" Her face flamed again, so she stopped there. "You can imagine."

He drew in a long breath and blew it out slowly, the look on his face making her laugh. "I'm going to need a cold shower at this rate," he said, and when she glanced at his jeans, she saw the distinct outline of a very impressive erection. Her eyes returned to his, and he smiled ruefully. "Sorry."

"Don't be. I'm flattered. Surprised, though."

"Why?"

"That you're turned on by this. By talking about my fantasies."

"That's the fun part," he said, squeezing her fingers. "Sharing the imagination."

Their gazes met, and they studied each other for a long moment. She couldn't believe she'd been so open with him. She'd never talked about anything like that with anyone before. But he was so encouraging, and he made her feel… normal, maybe, for the first time in her life. It had been fun. It was a shame it would have to end.

She glanced up at the clock, shocked to see it was nearing ten. "Oh crap. I'm sorry, Felix, I really ought to get going."

"Okay. May I walk you home?"

"Sure." How lovely.

They rose and slid on their jackets, and she put on her hat.

They walked out into the cool night air. Luckily, it wasn't raining, and the sky was bright with a thousand, thousand stars.

Felix held out his hand and smiled at her. She took it shyly, and they began to walk.

"Thank you for a lovely evening," she said. "I really enjoyed myself."

"Me too. Most fun I've had a in a long time. In fact..." He glanced over at her. "Look, I don't want you to think I'm taking advantage of you, or that I'm assuming anything just because we've been for a drink and talked about sex. But I like you, and I have a feeling you like me. And therefore..." His eyes filled with a mischievous glint. "I have a proposition for you."

Chapter Eighteen

Her heart pounded. "Oh?"

He looked hesitant and impish at the same time. "Obviously, feel free to say no. But I'm here for a week, and I thought it might be fun if I helped you fulfil one or two of your exotic fantasies."

She slowed, then stopped, staring at him. "What?"

He shrugged. "I'm horrified to think you've reached the ripe old age of twenty-seven using the missionary position and nothing else. And without having oral sex!" His look of horror made her giggle. He sighed and continued, "I just thought you might enjoy exploring a few things together. No pressure, no commitment, nothing to worry about except having a bit of fun." His brows knitted together. "Please don't slap me."

Her lips twitched. "I promise I won't." She nibbled her bottom lip and glanced over. "You really want to have sex with me?"

Impatience and amusement crossed his face. "Of course I want to have sex with you, Coco. You're gorgeous."

The thought of having sex with a man she barely knew was exciting, thrilling, and more than a little scary too. "I don't know."

"You don't have to make your mind up now. Think about it."

"Okay."

They walked for a hundred yards or so in companionable silence. His hand was warm in hers, and he stroked her skin occasionally with his thumb.

She tried to act cool, as if men asked her every day to go to bed with them, but inside her mind worked furiously and she had difficulty in stopping her chest heaving with excitement.

Eventually, she couldn't keep quiet any longer. "When you said about helping me fulfil my fantasies, what did you mean by that?"

He'd been looking up at the stars, but now turned to look at her. "I thought it would be fun to make a few of your dreams come true." He smiled.

"I couldn't go anywhere," she said. "Away, I mean. It's a lovely thought, but I'm afraid I'm confined to Wellington." She wondered whether he'd look impatient and tell her to forget it. Talking about looking after one's mother must be a huge passion killer.

But he just shrugged and said, "I know. We wouldn't have to leave town. I have a few ideas." His eyes twinkled. "I wondered whether your mother's friend might be kind enough to stay over if you did have an evening out—until her daughter's baby was born anyway."

"I'm sure she would," Coco said, thinking that her mother would fill the room with song if she announced she had a date. "Where would we go?"

"The firm gave me a budget for accommodation while I'm in Wellington. I added a bit myself and I have a lovely hotel suite. I don't like roughing it." He grinned.

She smiled back and fell silent for a while, thinking. She couldn't do this. Could she? Surely agreeing to meet a man in his hotel room for sex made her a slut. Or did it? This was the twenty-first century, and she knew she often acted as if she lived in the eighteen forties. In books and movies, women often acted as if a good sex life was more than an option. They actively went looking for it, and were given the label of modern women who knew what they wanted and weren't worried about asking for it, rather than something derogatory.

She risked a glance over at him, taking in his height, the width of his shoulders, the way his skin looked brown against her pale hand. This wouldn't be a relationship. A week Monday, he'd be announcing his findings and returning to Auckland—there was no question of this developing into anything deeper. He was offering her something purely physical—an experiment, an adventure.

He met her gaze again and smiled, obviously realizing she needed time to think about this. She led him across the road and down past the bars of Cuba Street with their loud music and the tall heaters warming those sitting outside. It was strangely exciting to be out on a Friday night with a man—she hadn't dated in such a long time.

"Felix, what would happen if we see someone from the office?"

He thought about it. "I'm not a hundred percent sure, but I think we'd probably say hello."

She stuck her tongue out. "You know what I mean. Aren't you worried about being seen with me, considering you're investigating the case?"

He tipped his head from side to side as if weighing it up. "If someone asks, I wouldn't deny it. But I wouldn't volunteer the information either. You asked that we didn't talk about work, and we haven't. I'm out with Coco, not Miss Stark, as you pointed out."

"Yes, but wouldn't it be weird at work? If we slept together, I mean. You're going to have to interview me, aren't you? Don't you think it's a conflict of interests?"

"I don't, because what's happening with Sasha and Peter is completely unconnected to what's happening between the two of us. I don't see why we can't maintain a professional relationship in the office. Yes, you're Sasha's superior, but I don't see how things would change if we slept together."

Coco said nothing for a while. He had no idea about what had happened between her and Peter Dell, or that she was withholding information from him. Professionally, she should run a mile from this relationship.

But then again, she had no intention of revealing what had occurred when she was seventeen. She'd be open and honest about what she'd seen between Peter and Sasha, and anything else Felix wanted to know. But that little nugget of information would remain hidden deep within her.

And when it came down to it, surely what happened between her and Felix was their business and nobody else's?

Trying to ignore the fact that she was rearranging the details to suit herself, she led him down a side road and across to where she lived, a small, three-bedroomed Edwardian-style house with a tiny front garden surrounded by a waist-high wall.

"This is me," she said. She withdrew her hand and slid both hers into the pockets of her jacket, leaning against the wall.

He stood before her, only six inches away, just enough inside her personal space to feel intimate. She could smell his lovely manly clean smell still mixed with the aroma of muffins, which made her smile as she looked up into his brown eyes. Now she wore her Converses, he seemed a lot taller than her, and for maybe the first time in her life she felt enchanted by his masculinity and acutely aware of the sheer difference between their sexes.

"Thank you for walking me home," she whispered.

"You're welcome. I had a lovely evening."

"Me too," she said, and meant it. He'd been funny, entertaining, attentive, and warm. He'd made her feel as if she was the only woman in the bar, and that he'd had eyes for nobody but her.

"Will you think about it?" he asked.

She hesitated, because she was teetering on the verge of saying she'd already thought about it and she had her answer, but he must have worried that her delay meant she was about to refuse him, because he raised his right hand and stroked her cheek with his thumb.

"Before you say anything," he said huskily, "can I kiss you goodnight?"

She stared at him, heart pounding, so desperate to feel his lips on hers again that she could only nod, hoping he kissed her for at least as long as he had in the office, and didn't give her a peck on the cheek.

He didn't give her a peck on the cheek. Far from it. He kissed her like she'd never been kissed in her entire life.

First, his eyes lighting with relief as she nodded her consent, he raised his other hand to cup her left cheek, framing her face as his gaze caressed her features, her eyes, her nose and cheeks, her mouth. His gaze lingered there for a moment, and she tingled with anticipation, her lips parting as she inhaled. He smiled a little, and then he lowered his head and kissed her.

She closed her eyes, waiting almost breathlessly as he pressed his lips to hers in small, soft kisses, his mouth moving over hers with tenderness. He kissed across her mouth from right to left, then her top lip, then her bottom lip, so slowly it was as if he was afraid of moving too quickly and startling her, as if she were a deer he'd found in a forest glade.

She sighed, her nipples tightening and an ache beginning between her thighs, amazed at the response he was coaxing out of her with a simple kiss. As she sighed, her lips parted, and almost as if he felt it was an invitation, he brushed his tongue across her bottom lip.

Coco inhaled sharply, and he paused, lifting his head a little. He dropped his hands and rested them on her hips, his lips still only inches from hers, waiting for her reaction.

She studied his mouth, the hint of stubble on his chin. She took her hands out of her pockets and rested one on his chest, lifting the other to touch his face and brush the stubble. She ran her thumb across his mouth, following the curve as he smiled. And then she slipped it into his hair as he lowered his lips again.

This kiss was different—if the previous one had been a meal prepared with a pinch of Cajun spice, this one was a red-hot chili, with several jalapenos and a goodly amount of Tabasco to boot. As she sank her fingers into his thick, short hair, he wrapped his arms around her and pulled her tightly to him, covering her lips with his. He stroked his tongue into her mouth, and she groaned and returned it with a brush of her own, and that was it, fire licked up inside her, engulfing her, and suddenly she couldn't get enough of him. He overwhelmed all her senses—she was filled with the taste and smell of him, the hardness of his body pressed against hers, the way the short hair on the back of his head grew longer on the top, and she clenched her fingers in its softness. It wasn't anything like the kisses she'd had with Michael—that was like comparing a dull iron bar with a shining gold ring, or something bland and tasteless with rich, dark chocolate.

When he finally released her, they were both breathing heavily, and she couldn't stop her lips curving in pleasure and appreciation.

"Fucking hell," he said, lifting his head but keeping his arms around her. "You kiss like a goddess."

She flushed warm at the compliment. "And you're like Casanova. Gosh, you must have had a lot of practice."

"A man's only as good as the woman he's with," he said, and she thought how appropriate that comment was. With Michael, her world had been filled with pastels and muted shades, overcast and dull, the promise of what could be far off in the distance like a mirage that always turned out to be a figment of her imagination.

In one smooth kiss, Felix had turned her world into Technicolor, blazing into her universe like a comet, lighting up the dark corners inside her, making her shine. And it was then that she knew.

"Yes," she said.

He smiled. "Yes, what?"

"Yes, I'd like to have sex with you." She said it before she could change her mind. And as she said it, she didn't feel a flicker of doubt.

Chapter Nineteen

The following evening, Felix got out of the taxi and asked the driver to wait. Just across the path was the wall against which Coco had leaned the night before while they kissed, and he smiled. She'd been so tentative at first, and he'd felt as if he was handling something fragile, like cradling a butterfly in his large hands, afraid of crushing or frightening it. But then something had flipped an internal switch inside her, and without warning she'd returned his passion a hundred and ten percent, confirming his original thoughts that deep down she was a passionate being who'd been caged like a tiger for far too long.

He opened the gate and walked through and up the small path to her front door. He'd told her that he'd pick her up at seven. She'd been nervous about telling her mother that she was going out on another date, but he'd stopped himself from suggesting they make it the afternoon instead for several reasons—firstly he needed some time to get prepared, secondly as it was Saturday she'd have to ask Frances to cover for her anyway because she didn't hire nurses at the weekend, and thirdly... well, she needed to get out. She didn't say it and neither did he, but she'd clearly enjoyed being out and about the night before, and he thought that while he was in Wellington, he might as well give her a reason to get out of the house she was confined to most of the time.

He rang the bell and waited, wondering why he had butterflies. He felt like he was sixteen again, on a first date. Maybe it was because he'd gone to so much effort for her—quite why he had, he wasn't sure—or maybe the nerves were just excitement at the thought of spending more time with her.

The door opened, and he was surprised when his heart jumped at the sight of her standing there, smiling nervously.

"Hi," she said, slipping her hands in the pockets of her jeans. She wore a pretty green shirt a shade darker than her eyes, and her hair hung loose once again around her shoulders.

"Hi." From behind his back he produced a lei—a Hawaiian necklace of flowers—and placed it around her neck.

She laughed and fingered the paper flowers. "Why thank you—it's beautiful."

"Just to get you in the mood." He smiled, meeting her eyes. Once again, his heart leaped. She was excited and nervous too—he could see it in the rapid rise and fall of her chest, the flush in her cheeks. "Are you ready?"

She hesitated. "Um, one thing… I'm really sorry about this, I know it's the last thing guys want to do on a date, but I wondered, would you mind awfully…"

"Spit it out, Coco," he said, amused.

"Would you mind saying a quick hello to my mum?"

He chuckled. No doubt Coco had been getting the third degree from Eleanor Stark about where she was going and with whom. "Of course I don't mind—I'd like to meet her."

Coco walked backward to let him in, and led the way through to the living room. Felix looked around, noting the wide doorways for her mother's wheelchair access. Both the hallway and, as he walked in, the living room, were decorated in light shades but with vivid, colorful paintings and hangings on the walls—from scenes of exotic sites like Machu Piccu and the Egyptian Pyramids to Peruvian shawls and bright cushions. He made a mental note to ask her about them later.

Two women sat in the armchairs in front of the television, but he didn't have to ask which was Coco's mother. With the same blonde hair—albeit cut short in a manageable style—and the same green eyes, Eleanor Stark was like an older, paler version of her daughter. The ravaging effects of her disease had not been kind to her body, and she looked frail, but her eyes were bright, and she smiled as Felix approached.

"Good evening, Mrs. Stark," he said, and held out his hand.

"You must be Felix." She rested her hand in his. It felt like a tiny sparrow, all bones and no flesh, and he shook it gently. She smiled. "Coco's told me all about you."

"That's nice," he said, letting go of her hand, sure that Coco would have told her mother about five percent of the information she actually knew about him. "Likewise—it's lovely to meet you." He glanced across at the other woman. "You must be Frances—thank you so much for filling in for Coco tonight."

"Oh, you're very welcome." The woman looked flustered and blushed. He smiled, guessing that these two women didn't get to see many young men.

"Coco tells me you're taking her out to dinner tonight," said Eleanor. "Where are you going, anywhere nice?"

"A rather unusual Hawaiian restaurant," Felix said without batting an eyelid, gesturing at Coco's lei, conscious of her startled gaze.

"Hawaiian? That sounds different." Eleanor's eyes gleamed and she looked at her daughter. "You'll have to tell me all about it when you get back, love."

"Yes, Mum." Coco backed away hurriedly. "Anyway, we must be going. I'll see you later."

"Don't hurry back," Frances called as they left the house.

They managed to get out of the house and into the taxi before bursting into nervous laughter. Felix directed the taxi driver to his hotel, then turned to Coco and rolled his eyes. "That was a close one." He grinned. "Do you think she suspects?"

"Goodness, no. Although they did watch us kissing last night." She gave him an impish smile.

He pulled an *eek* face. "Oops."

"Apparently, we were lit up beautifully by the street lamp. She gave you nine out of ten for style."

He laughed. "Only nine?" Privately, he wondered if Eleanor was quite as prim as Coco thought she was. Her eyes had held a strange gleam when he told her about the Hawaiian restaurant, almost as if she didn't believe him. What had she thought of Michael? Had she had any inkling of why Coco broke up with him?

He reached out, took her hand, and gave her fingers a little squeeze. "Are you okay?"

She nibbled her bottom lip. "A bit nervous."

"Don't be. It's going to be fun. Are you dressed appropriately?" He raised an eyebrow.

She gave a wry smile. "Yes. I just hope my mother didn't spot the ties sticking out the top of my shirt." She dipped her head and indicated the back of her neck. The bow of her bikini ties was just visible.

Felix grinned. He'd told her before he left her the night before to wear a bikini under her clothes, knowing that would get her imagination whirring. Now, however, she looked nervous again, so he asked her about the colorful decorations in her home to try to take her mind off it.

"It looks as if you are well travelled," he said. "I thought you didn't go on holiday."

"Unfortunately, I don't," she admitted. "I buy them from all sorts of places, including second-hand shops. Mum and I watch a lot of travel shows—living vicariously, you know? And I try to get things that remind her of places we've seen."

"It's a good idea," he said. She certainly seemed very close to her mother. Their relationship had no doubt intensified once Coco decided after breaking up with her ex that she didn't want to get involved with another man. Would she ever be able to settle down with a guy and relinquish Eleanor's care to someone else? If she did meet a man, he would have to be very understanding about how he handled the matter of caring for her mother.

The taxi pulled up outside his hotel, he leaned forward and paid the driver, and they got out. Taking her hand, he led her into the bright foyer.

"Wow." She stared around her, eyes wide at the mirrors and marble pillars, the staff in their smart red uniforms. "I've never stayed somewhere like this."

"It's a nice place." He crossed the foyer and pressed the button to call the elevator. "And the suite's cool. Well, tonight it isn't." He grinned at her curious look but didn't elaborate. Let her puzzle for a bit.

The elevator dinged, and the doors slid open. He led her inside, slid his card in the slot, and pressed the button for his floor before pocketing the card again.

"Okay," he said as the doors slid shut and the elevator rose. "Time to get ready."

She turned startled eyes on him. "What?"

First, he slid off his jacket, then toed off his trainers and flicked off his socks. Then, trying not to chuckle as her eyes widened even farther, he unbuttoned his jeans and removed them to reveal his swim shorts. Finally, he grabbed a handful of his T-shirt and yanked it over his head, beginning to laugh as she squealed, "What are you doing?"

"Getting ready for our adventure." He gathered his clothes together in one arm as the lift dinged again, and when the doors opened, he grabbed her hand and led her along the corridor right to the end, to his rooms. At one point another couple passed them, eyebrows raised as they took in his appearance, but he just nodded and said, "Evening," and continued, lips twisting wryly.

He stopped outside the last door in the corridor and turned to look at her. "Ready?"

She swallowed, apparently not sure whether to be alarmed or amused. "Okay."

He swiped his card, opened the door, and stood back to let her enter.

He'd spent ages on the room, and now he followed her in nervously, unsure whether she would burst out laughing or think he was an idiot.

She did neither. She walked forward a few feet and then stood and stared, turning and looking around her, her mouth open.

It was a beautiful suite of rooms with elegant furnishings and a plush cream carpet, but most of it was invisible as he'd covered everything with yards of cloth he'd bought that afternoon.

He'd pushed back the sofa and chairs to the corner of the room and covered half of it with the quilt from the bedroom plus another quilt he'd found in the cupboard. Over the top of this he'd placed a golden-yellow flannelette sheet, giving the appearance of a beach of sun-kissed sand. He'd covered the other half of the room with several sheets of varying blue and green cloth, some made from cotton, some from shiny fabrics, and he'd scattered them with half a dozen soft toys in the shape of fish and turtles he'd found in the charity shops.

He'd set up his laptop on a table to one side of the room and linked it in with the data projector he'd borrowed from the office. Pressing a button, he projected a short movie he'd found online of a Hawaiian beach onto the opposite wall. Shearwaters and petrels hovered above the sea's surface looking for fish and crustaceans, and gulls cried above the sound of the waves. He'd set it to play in a loop, and the shift from end to beginning again was barely noticeable, making it feel as if the room really did look out onto the Pacific island.

His iPad played native Hawaiian folk music through the room's sound system, and he'd placed other items, including more leis, a large poster he'd found of palm trees, and various other toy animals, around the room.

He'd also turned the heating up to maximum before he left, and now the room was beautifully warm as if heated by the light of the "sun"—a giant yellow beach ball he'd found and hung in the corner.

She still hadn't said anything, and now he was really getting nervous that she was thinking there was something seriously wrong with him, so he gestured to the kitchen, where he'd laid out a selection of spirits and two glasses on the breakfast bar. "Can I fix you a cocktail? I promise not to make any crass jokes about a 'Sex on the Beach' or anything."

He watched her turn to him, and he half-expected her to start laughing. But to his surprise there were tears in her eyes, and as he stared, startled, one rolled down her cheek and she pressed her hand to her mouth.

Chapter Twenty

Coco bit her lip, trying to keep it together as Felix put his arms around her and hugged her tightly.

"What's the matter?" he said, stroking her hair. "Is it really that bad?"

She gave a little laugh and pushed back from him, wiping her face. "No, idiot. It's marvelous." She looked around the room, unable to believe what an atmosphere he'd created. "I can't believe you've gone to so much effort. For me." The tears threatened again, and she bit her lip.

He looked at her curiously. "Sweetheart, is it really so unbelievable to think someone might have wanted to spend time on you?"

"Yes. I only got one bunch of flowers from Michael in the three years we were together, and that was after an argument."

His eyes hardened. "I seriously want to punch that dude's teeth down his throat."

That made her laugh. She moved away and picked up one of the toy turtles and examined it as she tried to gather her wits, something she couldn't really do while he was touching her with no top on. "I can't imagine you punching anyone. You're like a very sexy teddy bear."

He smiled wryly. "Oh, I've knocked a few guys out in my time. One of them being my brother."

She giggled. "Toby?"

"No, actually this was my older brother, Matt. He beat me at cricket. I'm not a good loser."

"Remind me not to play Monopoly with you, then."

He smirked. "Oh, I hope we can find something more interesting to play than Monopoly."

Their gazes met. Her fingers tingled where they'd brushed his skin as he'd hugged her. He'd been warm, his chest covered with a scattering of brown hair, his defined muscles firm when her fingers had brushed against them of their own free will. He was tall, gorgeous, and kind, and he smelled divine.

And they were going to have sex.

It was quite possible she might faint from excitement before that.

He beckoned her toward the bar. "Come on, let me make you a drink. What do you like?"

She walked over and studied the miniatures he'd bought. Alcohol might be a good idea right about now. "To be perfectly honest, I have no idea. I usually drink wine or lager. I like coconut, though. And orange juice. Why don't you invent something for me?"

"Okay." He put some ice into a shaker and chose some bottles while he started telling her something he'd read online about Hawaii.

Coco half-listened, but knew she was perched on the edge of making a decision. She'd stayed awake until late, and then woken up early, thinking about whether she should go through with this. Right until the moment she walked through the hotel door, she was still debating whether she should turn around and go home. Because even though he'd kissed her—and the kiss had been amazing—she could still stop this. Could change her mind. But once they'd had sex, that was it—she wouldn't be able to undo it.

Her nerves hadn't disappeared, and she still had worries about working with him, but as she looked around the room and thought about the effort he'd gone to, and as she watched him at the bar, trying so hard to put her at ease as he talked about this and that, she took a deep breath and made up her mind.

Unbuttoning her shirt while he busied himself pouring the cocktails, she let it slip silently down her arms and threw it over a chair in the corner, and then took off her shoes and jeans and placed them on the chair too.

Then she leaned her butt on the back of the sofa where he'd pushed it up against the wall, shook back her hair, and did her best to look nonchalant in the bikini as he finally finished the cocktails and turned around with the glasses in his hands.

He saw her and stopped. His eyes widened, and he looked like a cartoon character who'd been hit in the face with a frying pan. "Holy... fucking... hell."

She looked down at herself. "What?" True, the bikini was quite tiny, and the triangles of the top barely seemed to cover her nipples. And the triangle at the bottom barely covered her mound. But she'd thought she looked pretty good in it. And she thought the silver barbell in her belly button was an attractive addition.

She looked back up and met his eyes, and then they both started laughing.

He came over and passed her one of the glasses, which came complete with a tiny paper umbrella and a stirrer. "I can safely say that is the most shocked I have ever been in my entire life." His gaze caressed her, lingering on her breasts before sliding down to her waist and hips.

"You like?" She turned slowly to give him a back view. By the time she faced him again, his answer was self-evident in the bulge that had appeared in his shorts, and she giggled. "Never mind."

He raised an eyebrow, picked up a tray with two pairs of sunglasses, and stepped onto the 'sand'. "You're surprised by my reaction? Honey, you're just lucky I didn't have a coronary."

She walked onto the yellow material, realizing then that he'd spread something soft underneath the gold cloth, because her feet sank into it like sand. "Ooh, this is nice."

He smiled and led her to the middle of the room. He sat, placed the tray just behind him, and put his drink on it. Then he lay down and stretched out, his feet just touching the "sea".

"Come on in," he said, lowering the sunglasses and putting his hands behind his head. "The water's lovely."

She laughed and sat beside him, put the cocktail on the tray, and slid her sunglasses on. Then she lay down. It was so warm in the room, it really did feel as if the sun was beating down on them.

"This is so wonderful, Felix, thank you so much."

"You're very welcome."

"I had no idea what you were going to do. I thought maybe you were going to show me Elvis's *Blue Hawaii* or something."

He laughed. "That would have been a lot easier."

She rolled onto her side and propped her head on her hand. "I mean it. I really appreciate what you've done. And oddly, it really does feel as if we're there." She looked over at the projection of the sea, at the birds diving into the turquoise water. If she concentrated, she could almost feel the salty spray on her face.

He sighed. "Well, it's the best I could do at such short notice. I'm sure if you manage to go there one day, you'll realize what a terrible job I did."

She smiled. "Well, I'm sure this will be the closest I'll get to the real thing so you don't have any worries." She reached over, retrieved her cocktail from the tray, and took a sip. "Ooh, that's lovely. What's in it?"

"Vodka, rum, orange juice, coconut, and some liqueur I can't remember the name of."

"Does it have a name?"

He rolled onto his side and propped himself up so he could retrieve his own drink. "I was thinking I'd call it 'Coco's Delight'."

She chuckled. "I love it."

He took a few swallows of his own drink and then lay the same way as her, head propped on a hand. "You really think you'll never get to the real Hawaii?"

"I doubt I'll ever travel." She stirred the cocktail. "Mum's condition may worsen, but it's not fatal. She's only fifty-five. I expect—and hope—for her to live for a good many years yet. And by the time I'm alone, I'll be too old to go travelling."

He frowned. "But surely you can get someone to look after her for a week while you take a break?"

She shrugged. "It'd be no fun going away on my own."

"You may meet someone, Coco. Fall in love?"

She met his gaze and smiled. "Seriously, Felix, I doubt there'll be a man willing to take on me and my mother. Why would they? I wouldn't, if it were the other way around. No, I fully expect to stay single for the rest of my life now. And that's okay, I've come to terms with that."

"Don't you want children?"

She met his brown eyes, surprised at the hitch inside her at his words. Emotion almost overwhelmed her for a moment, but she dropped her gaze and concentrated on sipping her drink before she answered. "Motherhood's not for me, not this lifetime." He frowned, and she got the impression he was going to press the matter, and she knew she had to turn the conversation away from herself. "What about you? Do you want to be a daddy?"

One side of his mouth curved up. "Lindsey and I used to talk about it. But after she died, like you, I decided that life wasn't for me. I spent six years determined to stay single for the rest of my life. But then Toby met Esther, and she'd had Charlie…"

"That's your nephew, I'm guessing. Is he lovely?"

"Matt has two kids and they're pretty cool. But Charlie... he's adorable. He's so like Toby, falls over his own feet, but watching Toby and him together..." He smiled ruefully. "I don't know. I guess I'm envious."

They fell silent for a moment. Coco sipped her drink, thinking that in some ways they were so different, and yet in many ways very similar, lost souls, thinking they were doing fine, but knowing deep down they were just papering over the cracks.

But it wasn't a night for those emotions. She wanted to wipe away the sadness in his eyes. They were supposed to be having fun.

She finished off her cocktail. "Okay, my turn to fix one. Drink up."

He swallowed the last mouthful and handed her the glass.

"How do I do it?" she asked as she walked to the bar.

"Add stuff. Shake it. Pour it in a glass." He lay down.

"Technical, then?" She laughed and made it up as she went along, poured the drinks out, and brought them back, and then started talking about a travel book she'd read recently. He listened and then joined in, and before long their mood had lifted and they were talking about all sorts of things, from history to movie stars to politics and everything else under the sun.

They had two more cocktails, and time passed, and gradually Coco relaxed, enjoying Felix's company—from his deep, melodic voice that soothed all her ragged corners, to his intelligent conversation, to the way his gaze frequently caressed her, running slowly up her body, as tender and sensuous as if it were his fingers.

And eventually, they reached the natural end of a topic, and she finished the last mouthful of her cocktail and placed the glass on the tray with a sigh.

"Another?" he said, preparing to get up.

"Not yet." She lay back, warm and at ease. She'd never felt so comfortable with a man—not even with Michael, whom she'd dated for so long.

Why was that? What was it about Felix she liked so much? Yes, he was gorgeous, but it was so much more than that. He was funny, sexy, and yet tender too. He teased her out of her shell as if coaxing a tiny animal toward him, gentle and kind. She'd only known him a few days, but she had to admit to herself she was already crazy about him.

He was watching her now, smiling, but his eyes were alight with more than just affection. He wanted her, but she could see he was trying to keep a tight hold on his desire, wanting to proceed at a pace that was best for her.

But what he didn't realize was that she wanted him too. More than she could say.

So she didn't say anything. She reached up a hand, slipped it behind his neck and pulled him down for a kiss.

Chapter Twenty-One

Coco threaded her fingers through the short hair on the back of Felix's head as their lips touched, and then ran her hand down the side of his neck, across his shoulders to his chest. The feel of his bare skin sent a thrill shooting through her, and his answering deep sigh that was almost a groan only intensified that thrill.

They were really going to do this. They were going to kiss and touch each other, and then he would move inside her. What position would they do it in? At that moment, she didn't care if it was missionary, because she knew instinctively it wasn't going to be anything like missionary with Michael. Things were already a thousand times hotter than they had been with her ex—like comparing a comet that had been hurtling through the atmosphere with a plain rock, and just the thought of taking this magnificent kiss any further got her heart racing.

He moved his mouth over hers with agonizing slowness, as if he was determined to make it last and savor every single piece of her, as if he was at a restaurant with a mouth-watering meal he didn't want to end. He kissed across her lips, touching his tongue there occasionally, and Coco gave in and let him proceed at his own pace, happily opening her mouth, and welcoming his tongue inside.

He tasted divine, of coconut and whisky and the taste that was just Felix, and she immersed herself in him, letting him overwhelm her senses until it seemed as if her whole world consisted of this room, this man, and the touch, taste, and smell of him. She ran her hand up his arm, admiring the contours of his muscles, so hard and defined compared to hers. His skin was warm and very slightly damp from the heat of the room, and she trailed her fingers down his chest, loving the curls of hair, his tight pecs, his flat nipples. She brushed them, and he raised his head to smile wryly at her, bringing his hand up to circle the tiny triangles of material on her breasts.

"Just so you know," he said, "the rule is that if you tease me, it gets returned threefold."

Excitement surged through her. "Ooh. Promises, promises."

He laughed and rolled away from her, stood, and went over to the light switch. He dimmed the lights and said with a grin, "The sun's setting," then pulled a chair from the dining table in the corner toward her. Leaving it a few feet away, he knelt and pulled her up, so they were kneeling and facing each other.

She held her breath, awestruck by his wide shoulders, the expanse of bare skin, and the way he just seemed to be so much bigger than her. She wanted to cover every inch of him with kisses, to taste him and feel the pulse of his heart beneath her lips, but she held back for the moment, too shy to take the initiative.

Instead, she enjoyed the sensations he was arousing in her as he skated his hands down her back and over her hips, then brought them back up to cup her breasts, brushing his thumbs across her nipples. He began to kiss her again, and she subsided into a spiral of hazy desire, raising her arms around his neck and pressing herself against him as the kiss gradually deepened and her pulse started to pound.

He slid his hands up her back and tugged at the ties at her neck. They unraveled and tumbled down her front, although the material clung to her breasts, refusing to reveal what lay beneath. Felix lifted his head, fixed his eyes on hers, and slowly pulled the ties down before dropping his gaze to caress her.

"Christ, you're beautiful." He cupped her breasts again, brushing her nipples with his thumbs, and the sensitive skin tightened and puckered. She inhaled and tipped back her head, closing her eyes, and that seemed to do something to him.

He pulled her toward him, falling backward onto the floor so she fell on top of him, and he slipped a hand behind her head and held her tightly while he captured her lips with his, delving his tongue into her mouth in a passionate kiss that left her breathless and aching.

"Felix," she gasped, not really sure why she exclaimed, but he didn't stop to let her speak. He pushed her upright so she sat astride him, and then, capturing her hands in his, he pulled them above his head until her breasts were on a level with his lips. His hot mouth fastened on a nipple, and she swore out loud as he brushed it with his tongue before sucking hard enough to make everything inside her tighten.

He murmured his approval, switching to her other nipple, and she could only sit there in blissful ecstasy as he did the same to that one, teasing the softening skin to a tight peak again before grazing it with his teeth and flicking the end with his tongue.

Coco began to think she could come just by him doing that, tantalizing and taunting her, swapping from one nipple to the other until they were both firm, wet buttons. She rocked her hips, not surprised to find him hard underneath her, and she felt a thrill deep inside when he grunted at the feel of her stroking up and down his length to arouse herself.

Then he lifted her and turned her onto her back, and she squealed in surprise, looking up at him with wide eyes. With deft hands, he peeled away her bikini bottoms, and then he stroked up her thighs to between her legs.

"Can I touch you?" he murmured, and she nodded hesitantly, suddenly shy, and opened her legs. Keeping his hot brown gaze on hers, he brushed up her thigh again, then touched his fingers between her legs and sank them into her. They slipped so easily through her flesh that she knew she must be swollen and moist, and she bit her lip as he slid his fingers deep inside her, eyes glowing with desire. She closed her eyes, her face burning at the obvious pleasure he was experiencing at exploring her. He kissed her eyelids, then her mouth again, and when he brought his fingers up to caress her clit and she gasped, he wasted no time in deepening the kiss again.

He stroked her for a while, and then finally raised his head to look at her. Still stroking her lightly, he said, his voice husky, "It's no good, I've got to taste you. Will you let me?"

She caught her breath. "You mean..."

"Yes, Coco, I want to go down on you and give you oral pleasure." He chuckled as her face burned again. Damn it. Must she blush all the time? "You're so adorable," he said and kissed her cheek.

He rolled onto his back, his head a foot in front of the chair he'd moved forward, and beckoned her. "Come here."

She pushed herself up and then hesitated. What did he want her to do? "I can't."

"Of course you can. Come here." He caught her hand and pulled her toward him. Hazy with drink and desire, she did as he bid, stopping as her knees reached his head.

"Put one knee here." He tapped the floor above his other shoulder.

She shook her head.

He held her gaze and raised his eyebrows. "Will you do as you're told?"

Her heart pounded. "Felix, I just can't."

He stroked her leg. "Honey, I'm not going to make you do anything you're uncomfortable doing. But I thought this was what you wanted—to try things you haven't been able to do before."

"I do…" And he was right of course. She was just so nervous about doing something wrong—of embarrassing herself, of looking stupid.

"You can lie down and I'll kiss you there," he said, "but from what I understand, this position is more pleasurable. You can control the pressure and guide me. I just want to give you pleasure, sweetheart."

Emotion washed over her at his generosity, and his face creased with sympathy as he obviously saw it gleam in her eyes.

"Aw," he said. "Come on. Make my day." He ran his hand up her thigh again. "I'm desperate to taste you, to bury my mouth in you. Please."

Her resistance melted at his gentle persuasion, and she gave in. "Okay."

He smiled and helped her position herself over him. "Lean on the chair," he said. "Get comfortable."

She did so, resting her arms on the seat as she straddled him, unable to believe she was really doing this.

And then he stroked his tongue through her. Coco nearly shot through the ceiling. The sensation of his warm, soft tongue buried in the heart of her was like nothing she'd ever experienced. The one time Michael had ventured down there, he'd given her a cursory lick before heading back up to climb on top of her, and she'd had to fantasize about what it would feel like to have a guy do what Felix was doing to her now.

But the fantasy didn't come anywhere near the reality. He brushed his tongue through her folds and slid it inside her, then proceeded to try various pressures and strokes before settling on low, slow licks and teasing nibbles that soon had her gasping with pleasure. And as if that wasn't enough, he raised his hands to stroke her breasts for a while before moving one hand beneath her to join with his tongue in exploring her.

Coco began to spiral out of control. He was just too good at this. He slowed his strokes, and she got the feeling he knew perfectly well how aroused she was and could control that arousal, drawing it out for her until she ached and begged him for release. And then he slid two fingers deep inside while he fastened his hot mouth on her clit, and everything tightened around him, her muscles pulsing around his fingers as she came in a glorious burst of ecstatic delight.

Chapter Twenty-Two

Felix watched Coco lift herself off him and collapse back onto the sand. She looked exhausted and sated, and he rolled onto his side to study her, smiling at her obvious bewilderment.

"Nice?" he asked.

She turned her wide, green eyes on him. "I can't believe you did that."

"And enjoyed it."

"Really?"

"Really. You smell and taste divine." He licked his fingers as proof as if he'd eaten fried chicken.

She swatted his arm. "Stop it—that's gross."

"It's not gross, it's perfectly normal, and you really need to widen your understanding of what's acceptable in bed. Or on the beach."

She shook her head, her expression showing a kind of puzzled wonderment. "I just can't believe it. You're so…" Her voice trailed off as she met his eyes.

He smiled. "So… what?"

"Amazing. Mr. Sensational, I'm going to call you."

He laughed and rolled back onto his back. "And now phase two. You're incredibly wet and swollen, and if I'm not inside you in five seconds, I'm going to explode." He pushed his swim shorts off and bunched up the duvet beneath his head to make himself comfortable. "Come here."

He'd forgotten she hadn't seen him naked before. She looked shocked at the ease with which he'd stripped off, and now stared at him with mouth open.

"What?" he said. "Did I forget to tell you this was a nudist beach?"

"Oh. My. God." Her lips curved. "Felix Wilkinson, you are such a sight for sore eyes."

He lifted his head and glanced at himself, then shrugged. "I guess if you haven't had any for a while it's not bad."

"Not bad? Are you kidding me? Felix, you're huge!"

He started laughing. "Thank you, but I'm really not—your ex must have been a small guy, that's all I can say. Now will you come here?" He patted his hip.

Her eyes widened even more, if that was possible. "On top?"

"On top. Come and ride me, cowgirl, hard as you like." He knew he should probably be a little less outspoken with his demands, but he'd had a few too many cocktails to control his mouth. Plus, she was such fun to tease. She looked shocked at almost everything said, and he was really enjoying her little gasps at his risqué comments.

She chewed her lip, and for a moment he thought she was going to refuse, but then she said, "Haven't you forgotten something?"

"Fuck. Condom." He reached for his jeans and fumbled in the pocket. "Sorry—I'm usually very responsible." He found it, dropped it, tried to tear off the top, and dropped it again.

She giggled and picked it up. "I think you're drunk."

"How much whisky did you put in that last glass?"

"I finished off the bottle," she said, tearing off the top of the packet.

"Jesus."

"I know. I've decided I like whisky." She removed the condom and held it out to him.

He put his hands behind his head. "Perhaps you'd be kind enough to do the honors, as I appear to be inebriated." Actually, he wasn't that drunk, but it was fun to pretend.

Again, he waited for her to refuse, but her lips curved, and she shuffled forward and straddled his legs. His heart rate increased. She was growing bolder, finding courage as time went by and he proved to her that there was nothing to be ashamed of, and he truly was enjoying playing with her.

She rolled the condom on him slowly, and he closed his eyes and blew out a long breath, swelling beneath her firm touch.

Without another word, she moved up to sit astride his hips, shifting so the tip of his erection sank a little into her softness.

He opened his eyes and admired her. She was slender without being skinny, her breasts high and full, her swollen nipples a pinky-brown color. Her skin gleamed in the dull light from the heat of the room. Lindsey had had a great body, but she'd been fairly short at five four, and he had to admit he liked Coco being tall. He didn't get neck ache when he kissed her, and he liked to slide his hands up from her knees to her hips, admiring her long slim thighs.

Thinking of Lindsey brought a brief flicker of guilt deep inside him. Would that ever go away, or would he always feel as if he was cheating on her?

Coco leaned over him, looking down at him. "Want me to stop?" she whispered.

She must have seen something cross his face. He met her gaze. Her green eyes were wide, clear and gentle. Did she understand that somehow pleasuring another woman didn't feel as unfaithful as being pleasured himself?

Oddly, she was the first girlfriend he'd ever discussed Lindsey with. Some of the others had known he'd been engaged and that his fiancée had died, but they'd seemed to assume that he wouldn't want to talk about her, and he hadn't really. So Lindsey had stayed hovering in the background, ever-present, and he'd always been conscious of her there. It hadn't stopped him having sex—he was only human after all. But always at the back of his mind was that worry that she was watching him, and in his mind he heard the words, *How could you?*

His family had said, "She wouldn't have wanted you to stay single," but how could they be sure of that? Yes, he knew she would have laughed at the thought of it, but if it were the other way around, for purely selfish reasons he wouldn't have wanted her to fall in love again. He would have wanted to be her first love and her last. If she'd gone into a nunnery, that would have been cool too.

But as much as he'd loved her, he didn't want to think of Lindsey now. The beautiful woman on top of him deserved all his attention.

And suddenly he realized maybe that was why he was feeling guilty. Because for the first time he was comparing Lindsey to someone else and finding her wanting. He hadn't thought that would ever happen, but perhaps enough time had finally passed for him to admit she wasn't perfect.

Or perhaps Coco really was that gorgeous.

She was still perched just above his hips, and as he moved, the tip of his erection pushed further into her moist warmth. He caught his breath. "No," he murmured. "Don't stop."

Coco brought her hand up to his face and caressed his cheek. Then she lowered her head and kissed him.

He let her move her lips across his and welcomed her tongue as she brushed it into his mouth. He ran his hands from her hips up the smooth sides of her body, cupped her breasts, and stroked his thumbs across her nipples. The soft skin puckered tightly, and she gave a low murmur of approval.

Then he dropped his hands back to her hips, held her, and pushed up.

She was still swollen and wet from her orgasm, and although she was tight, he slid into her easily. They both exclaimed, and she sat upright, widening her thighs. Bit by bit, she let him sink even deeper inside.

Felix's hands clenched into fists as he fought with himself not to move until she was ready, but it was so difficult when he was encased in such moist warmth. His hips gave an involuntary thrust, and she sighed, arched her spine, and dropped her head back.

Speechless with admiration, passion, and desire, he watched as she began to move on top of him. She rocked her hips, causing him to slide in and out of her, and although he would have liked to go harder and faster, he let her drive the pace, content to lie there and enjoy the view while she explored the sensation of having him inside her.

He played with her breasts, skated his fingers over her body, brushed her sexy piercing, then dropped his thumb between her legs and stroked her clit as she moved. She gasped and bit her lip, and he smiled, thoroughly enjoying himself, stretching out beneath her and continuing to circle his thumb through her warm, wet skin.

"Nice?" he asked, watching her eyelids flutter shut and then open again, her expression reflecting her growing arousal.

"It feels... wonderful." She stopped moving for a moment and experimentally tightened her internal muscles, making him groan. "I can feel you all the way up, Felix. Right to the top. It's an amazing feeling."

"I know," he agreed, struggling to keep control as she moved again, her slick walls sliding along his length. Heat built inside him, but he held on, wanting her to come first, sensing her climax wasn't far away when her eyes closed, her cheeks flushed, and she swelled beneath the regular rhythm of his thumb. He stroked her firmly, his fingers gliding over her swollen skin, running his other hand up to cup her breast and squeeze the tight nipple. And as she came, he thought there was possibly nothing more beautiful in the world than the sight of a woman in the midst of a climax, and at that moment he was pretty sure there was no woman more beautiful than Coco, with her silky blonde hair and her pale, curvy body, and her soft cries that proved the final straw in his efforts to hang on to his self-control.

The heat rushed up from his balls into her, and his hips jerked as his muscles pulsed exquisitely. "Fuck," he said through gritted teeth, eyes closed, unable to think about anything but the feel of her clamped around him, milking every last drop of fluid out of him for what felt like forever until he finally relaxed back into the softness of the sand, limp and exhausted.

He opened his eyes, and she was watching him, a small smile playing on her lips.

"Nice?" she said.

His lips twisted as he recognized his own words to her earlier. "Very nice, thank you."

"Oh God, thank *you*, Felix." She spoke vehemently, and leaned forward over him, looking intently into his eyes. "That was... well. I'm lost for words."

He stroked his hands up her sides, brought them forward to touch her breasts. "I'm glad you enjoyed it."

"I never realized it could be like that." Her green eyes considered him curiously. "No wonder everyone goes on about it so much. I never understood what the fuss was about before." She leaned forward and touched her lips to his. "I can't imagine what it must be like to be with someone and have sex like that whenever you want. I'd never be out of bed!"

He chuckled. "What a nice thought."

"How on earth are you single when you make love like a god? Are you in the Guinness Book of Records?"

He brushed a lock of hair from her cheek and tucked it behind her ear. "It's not always like that, honey."

"Really?"

He closed his eyes, not knowing what to say, and enjoyed the feel of her in his arms, the sensation of her close around him, warm and tight.

His thoughts and emotions spiraled, intermingling, entwining. Part of it was the alcohol, but part of it was the feelings she'd aroused in him. She'd started off shy and nervous but had blossomed under his touch, and her sheer joy in finding out that he enjoyed sex—that he didn't see anything wrong in that enjoyment, and that he was prepared to share his enthusiasm with her—had been refreshing and... well, rather a turn-on. He'd enjoyed himself more than he had in a long, long time.

She lifted herself off him, and he disposed of the condom, and then she curled up next to him, resting her head on his shoulder. They lay there and listened to the waves, warm and slick in the heat of the room, and Felix let his mind wander and dream about what it would be like to love another woman, and lie with her like this for the rest of his life.

Chapter Twenty-Three

Coco lay on the swing seat in her back garden and closed her eyes against the bright morning sunshine. The sun warmed her skin, and she couldn't help but smile as she thought of the previous night and the way Felix had turned up the heating in the bedroom to make it so sultry.

It had been a beautiful evening. Even now, her body tingled at the memory of the way his hands had stroked her skin, and how he'd so skillfully aroused her toward an orgasm that had blown her mind.

Obviously, the guy wasn't a virgin, and she'd known by his sexy, self-confident manner that he would be good in bed, but she hadn't expected him to be quite so good. Maybe because it was so far out of her frame of reference. She'd had orgasms before—mostly self-induced—and she'd had sex, but the stilted, awkward, slightly flat couplings she'd had with Michael weren't in the same league as the passionate, enthusiastic, fun lovemaking she'd had with Felix.

And yet he'd said *it's not always like that*. She'd pressed him for an explanation, but he hadn't elaborated and had grown quiet after that. Had he been thinking about Lindsey? She knew his ex had crossed his mind more than once that evening, but it hadn't bothered her. Michael had crossed her mind too, although she assumed it was in a slightly more detrimental way than how Felix had thought about his dead fiancée.

She'd wondered if she'd feel jealous at the thought of him missing Lindsey, but to her surprise she didn't—she just felt sad. It was no age to lose the one you love, and it had obviously taken him several years to get over her—if in fact he was over her. She suspected he wasn't. It would be natural for him to compare every woman he met to the woman he'd loved, and to find them lacking.

How did she compare to Lindsey? Coco had virtually no experience in bed worth shouting about, no real idea how to pleasure a man. No tricks of the trade or aces up her sleeve. And yet he'd seemed to have a good time. She'd gotten the impression he found her enthusiasm and enjoyment a turn-on, and that at least was something she'd been able to offer.

She sighed and opened her eyes to watch the clouds scudding across the azure sky. Summer was on its way, a time she usually loved. Christmas was looming, and she and Eleanor always made a big thing about the celebration, treating each other to goodies they found on the internet, buying nice food, Eleanor making colorful decorations that Coco would then hang around the room.

For the first time, however, she felt no enthusiasm about the coming festivities. Yes, she'd had a fantastic time the night before, but unfortunately what it had done was highlight her bleak future and show her what she was missing.

She'd curled up next to Felix for half an hour after they'd made love, comfortable in the circle of his arms, but it wasn't long before she'd thought of Frances trying to stay awake as she waited for her to return, and guilt had made her don her clothes and say she had to go. She'd offered to help him clean up, but he'd refused with a smile, the perfect gentleman, stroking her face before kissing her tenderly goodnight. They'd not mentioned work or seeing each other again, and she'd left feeling like Cinderella leaving the ball, certain she was returning to a life of drudgery and servitude.

That made her feel guilty, though. She didn't look after her mother out of duty—she did it because she wanted to, because she wanted to make sure Eleanor was loved and cared for. It wasn't a chore at all, and she hated herself for thinking like that, however briefly.

She'd known seeing Felix was a one-off, a brief adventure. What was the saying? Better to have loved and lost than never to have loved at all? Would she rather not have had the night before? Not have known his touch, or how it felt to be with a man who made her feel like a princess, as if she was the most precious thing in the world?

A tear rolled down her face and she bit her lip and closed her eyes again. Enough of that. She was not going to cry over Mr. Fancy Pants.

A bell sounded in the distance, and she sighed, wiped her face, and pushed herself up and off the swing seat. Entering the house, she went along to the bathroom and knocked on the door. "Ready, Mum?"

"Yes thanks, love."

She opened the door and went in. Eleanor sat on the shower seat. She'd washed and dried and wrapped herself in a white toweling bathrobe, but the effort had clearly worn her out, and she looked pale and tired.

"I wish you'd let me do more for you," Coco scolded. Eleanor leaned on the railing they had installed, and Coco supported her as she moved into her wheelchair.

"This is bad enough," Eleanor said, tight lipped. She sank into the seat with a groan.

"Are you in pain, Mum? Want me to get your meds?"

"I'll manage. If you could just take me to my room."

Coco pushed the chair silently through to the bedroom. At the back of the house, it looked onto the garden she'd made an effort to turn into a pleasant sitting area, with lots of flower borders, arching palms, and even a working fountain. Fantails fluttered on the bird table, pecking up seed, and sunlight slanted in through the open curtains across the bed, but Eleanor seemed oblivious to the beauty of the morning, too worn out from the exertion of showering.

Coco propped up the pillows and helped Eleanor into bed, and her mother lay back with relief, looking almost as white as the clean cotton pillowslips. Coco moved the chair to one side and poured her a glass of water from the jug on the stand, then smiled and made to leave, but Eleanor stretched out a hand.

"Stay a moment."

Coco paused, surprised. "Do you want something?"

Eleanor patted the bed next to her. "Come and sit down."

Coco did so, and took her mother's hand. "Are you okay?"

"I'm fine, darling. We didn't get much chance to talk last night—I was so tired. Did you have a nice evening?"

"Yes, thank you." Coco's cheeks grew warm, but she refused to look away.

"He seemed very nice."

"He is. He's very thoughtful and kind." She pictured the room with its beach and cocktail bar, and smiled.

Eleanor's lips curved in return. "And sexy?"

Coco's eyes widened. "Mum!"

Eleanor stroked Coco's hand. "Is there any chance it could turn into anything more serious?"

"No, Mum. He's only here for a week. He's working on a case, and he'll be leaving a week Monday."

"Where's he from?"

"The Auckland office." Coco hesitated. "He's investigating a case of sexual harassment at the Wellington branch. I shouldn't have seen him at all, really. I feel a bit guilty about it."

Eleanor shrugged. "No reason anyone should find out about it."

"I suppose."

"Are you seeing him again before he leaves?"

"I have no plans to." She was unable to stop the sweep of sadness that flowed over her.

"Perhaps you should call him and arrange something." Eleanor's thumb continued to stroke the back of her hand.

Coco sighed. "No, I don't think so. It's best we move on. It was fun, but there's no point in dragging it out."

"Sweetheart, men like that don't come along into our lives every day. You really should make the most of it while he's here."

Coco met her mother's gaze. Irritation bubbled inside her. "I know where this is going. But there's no chance of me falling in love and sailing off into the sunset."

Color flooded Eleanor's cheeks. "How do you know unless you allow things to develop?"

"Didn't you just hear me? He lives in Auckland!"

"So? People move, Coco."

She gritted her teeth. "Stop pushing. I'm not interested."

"Why are you so determined never to find a man?" Eleanor removed her hand, and her fingers clutched the duvet. "And why do you resent me so whenever I suggest it?"

"Because it's my business, and if I don't want to fall in love and settle down it's up to me, not you." Tears stung Coco's eyes. Why couldn't her mother leave it alone?

"But I don't understand. You're young—you deserve to have a husband and children."

"I don't want those things."

"I think you do but you're scared, and because you're scared you're refusing to allow yourself to explore the possibility." Eleanor's lips set in a thin line. "It's not about me pushing you. I know you look after me because you love me, but I don't want to be the reason you never find happiness."

"You're not the reason," Coco whispered, thinking of Michael.

"I've contacted the respite home," Eleanor announced. "Someone's coming around next week to talk to me about finding me a place."

Coco stared at her in horror. "Mum!"

Eleanor's face softened. "It's not a terrible place, love. These homes aren't like they used to be. There are proper care staff and nice rooms and places where you can go to socialize and mix with others your own age."

"You've always said you'd hate that," Coco snapped.

Eleanor ignored her. "It's nice of you to look after me, but you're not a trained nurse. What if something happened?"

"I'd ring an ambulance." Coco stood up. "For God's sake."

Eleanor struggled to push herself more upright in bed. "Did it ever cross your mind that what I want should form part of this decision?"

Hot tears scalded Coco's eyes. "It's not what you want, though, not really—it's what you think would be best for me, and that's not fair. I'm happy the way we are. We do all right, don't we?"

"We do fine, love. But you should have seen your face yesterday when you came in. You were glowing. You'd obviously had a lovely evening."

"I'd had sex. That's why I was glowing. That's all it was, Mum."

She waited for Eleanor to gasp, wanting to shock her. But to her surprise, her mother just raised an eyebrow and said, "I am a grown woman, love. I've had a child, and I'm not an innocent. I know young people don't wait until they get married anymore. Do you really think I assumed you were just having dinner?"

Words failed her. The two women stared at each other for a moment.

Eventually Eleanor bit her lip. "I know I've not always been the best mother to you. I had a very strict upbringing, and in the past, talking about things like this hasn't come easy to me. I don't know what went wrong between you and Michael, but I'm sure part of it was down to me, and I don't want to be the reason you don't find happiness."

"It wasn't you." Coco looked out at the fantails squabbling over the seed. "I'm not sure he was capable of love. For him that emotion was bound and gagged and only allowed to see daylight once a week.

He didn't understand. But Felix..." She hesitated. How could she explain the difference between the two men? She sighed and looked back at her mother. "I just wanted to see what I was missing, that's all."

A whisper of a smile passed over Eleanor's face. "Call him."

Coco opened her mouth to reply, and at that moment her mobile rang in the pocket of her jeans. She took it out, turned toward the garden again and said, "Hello?"

"It's me," Felix said. "Can we talk?"

Chapter Twenty-Four

Felix paced the floor of his hotel room as he waited for Coco to answer his question.

It had taken an hour of internal debating before he'd finally picked up his mobile and dialed her number. She'd given it to him when they were at the bar the first night in case he needed to change the time he picked her up for the Hawaiian evening, but she clearly hadn't expected him to call her after their rendezvous.

She'd left his room with a gentle kiss and a "Thank you for a lovely evening," but neither of them had mentioned meeting up again. He'd lain awake for hours telling himself it had been a one-off and she'd made it quite clear she wasn't in the zone for anything more. And he wasn't either. Was he? Of course not. He lived hundreds of miles away. He had no intention of moving to the old-fashioned Wellington branch, and Coco would never move away from her mother. It was just a fling—okay, a semi-nuclear brain-in-meltdown kind of fling, but a fling nonetheless. He'd had plenty of them and gone on to hardly give the girl a second thought. So why was the sexy secretary plaguing his mind so much?

In the background, he heard Coco mumble something, presumably to her mother, and then after a few seconds she said, "Hi."

"I hope I'm not interrupting you."

"No, no." There was the sound of a door opening and closing. "I was in with Mum, but I'm in the garden now."

"Everything all right?"

She blew out a breath. "Yes. We were just having a... discussion."

"Problems?"

She was quiet for a moment, and he imagined her turning her face up to the sun and closing her eyes, comforted by the warmth. "She's got someone from the respite home coming in next week to talk to her."

"Ah." He waited for her to elaborate, and when she didn't, he asked, "Are you okay?"

She fell silent again, and he wondered if she was crying. *Shit.* That wasn't the effect he'd meant to have.

"You want me to go?" he asked softly.

She cleared her throat. "No, I'm okay. But it's hard, you know? I wish she'd believe me when I say I want to look after her."

"I'm sure she does, honey. She just feels guilty that she's holding you back."

More silence. *Fuck.* He was really putting his foot in it.

"Why did you call?" she whispered.

"Ah… just checking on you."

"Felix…" She sounded amused.

He sighed. "I wondered whether you'd like to go to the Empire tonight."

This time she fell quiet out of shock. "You mean the first showing of the new movie?"

"Yep."

"But… Those tickets sold out the first day."

"I know someone." He shook his head as he thought of the palaver he'd gone through to find them. A couple who'd bought them seconds after they'd gone on sale had had to sell them when a relative died in America and they had to go to the funeral. Felix would have to pay them a small fortune, but it would be worth it if she agreed to go.

"You're joking."

"No."

"Oh my God, are you serious? You really have tickets?"

"Yes. Cross my heart! It's going to be quite an evening. There will be fans in costume and most people will be dressed up to some degree. I thought you might enjoy it."

"Oh my God!"

He laughed and then ran a hand through his hair. "The only problem is that it doesn't start until midnight. I'm not sure how easy that would be to organize for you. I'm so sorry I couldn't give you more notice, but I only found out I had them an hour ago."

"Oh, Felix. You're such a sweetie."

He scuffed the carpet with his toe. "I'm not. But I don't want to make things more difficult for you."

"It's okay, Frances told me last night she'd stay over if I wanted to go away. And Mum will be thrilled." She sounded wry.

"I thought I'd wear black tie for fun. Do you have a dress to wear, or would you like me to take you out and buy you something?"

"A la Pretty Woman?"

"Fuck, I wasn't implying—"

She laughed. "Felix, relax. It was a joke. No, I have something."

"Okay. I'll pick you up at eleven? I think it'll be worth getting there early to take in the atmosphere."

"Sure. I look forward to it."

He sighed with relief. "I'll see you then."

"Oh, Felix?"

"Yes?"

"Thank you."

He smiled and hung up.

Now he had to go and buy a fancy suit.

*

Felix rolled up in the taxi outside Coco's house just before eleven. It was dark, but the moon hung in the sky like a heavy Christmas bauble. He got out and fidgeted nervously with his bow tie. It had taken him half an hour to tie it, and he'd just begun to wish he'd bought a clip-on one when he finally got it sorted.

He had an evening suit back in his apartment in Auckland, but it was a couple of years old so he'd decided to buy another rather than hire one. Under the shop assistant's direction, he'd settled on a wool and mohair mix with what she assured him was grosgrain silk facing on the lapels that matched the braiding down the side of the pants and the bow tie. She'd advised a jacket without vents and with a peak lapel, and he had to admit it was a flattering cut. He'd also invested in a waistcoat, the scooped front showing off the pleats of his white shirt. Silver cufflinks completed the look.

Hopefully Coco would think he looked okay.

He knocked on the door and waited. Once again, he felt sixteen years old, as nervous as if it were a first date. Why did she make him feel this way? He hadn't had butterflies for years.

The door opened and she appeared. A smile hovered on her lips, but the words she'd been about to say faltered as she took in his appearance. Her gaze ran very slowly down him from head to toe before returning just as slowly.

Felix hardly noticed her appraisal, however, because he was too busy carrying out an appraisal of his own. She wore a plum-colored gown with an embroidered bodice and a skirt made out of some floaty material that fell to the floor in soft folds. She'd put up her hair in an elegant chignon, and had obviously taken time over her makeup. She looked divine. And she was his date.

She still hadn't said anything. Hoping she was thinking *Wow, you look pretty good* rather than *Oh my God what the hell are you wearing*, he smiled hesitantly and gestured to her dress. "You look fantastic."

She blinked, and a smile spread slowly across her face. "Oh, Felix, you look like a model."

He looked down at himself. "Plastic and without man parts?"

She laughed. "I swear you could easily have walked straight off an Italian catwalk."

Their gazes met, and heat shot through him at the desire in her eyes. He leaned forward, rested a hand on her hip, and touched his lips to her cheek.

She shivered beneath his touch, a movement so erotic he nearly pushed her up against the door and kissed her senseless. But she'd obviously taken time over her lipstick, and he didn't want to be reprimanded for kissing it off. Instead, he leaned on the doorjamb above her head and let his lips hover over hers, his thumb stroking her waist.

"I want you," he murmured.

"You've had me," she said, her lowered lashes dark against her pale face. She leaned back against the doorframe as if trying to move away from him, but she didn't push her hands against his chest.

He had to fight not to kiss her, to press his lips against her painted ones. They'd be sticky, he thought, and would peel away from his as he lifted his head. And... now he had an erection. "I want you again."

"Already?" She raised her eyes to his, and he caught his breath. They glowed with passion and excitement, green as two polished emeralds.

"I wanted you again five minutes after I'd had you."

It was the first time either of them had suggested they were interested in anything more than a one-night stand. Felix wasn't quite sure why he'd said it. Nothing had changed—he was still only going to be there a week, and their personal commitments wouldn't lend themselves to something more serious. But he couldn't help himself. Her perfume—something muskier than her normal flowery scent—wound around him, ensnaring him. Her breasts rose and fell with her rapid breaths. He wanted to drop his head and run his tongue over the swell of smooth, creamy flesh enticingly revealed by the low-cut neckline. He wanted to lift her skirts and plunge into her, lose himself in her.

"Oh," she said. Her eyes were filled with longing. But she swallowed and said, "Come on, let's not make this harder for ourselves."

He hesitated. Her words were at odds with her emotions—he could see that much. But he didn't want to pressure her.

He drew away reluctantly, dropping his arm so he could grasp her hand. "Of course, I'm sorry. Come on, we have a lovely evening planned. Are you ready?"

She nodded. "Frances is here. She's staying the night so it doesn't matter how late I am."

His heart hammered as he thought of what he had planned. If things went the way he hoped, she was definitely going to be later than she thought. But as yet he wasn't sure if she'd agree. Clearly her mind was at war with her heart, and he would just have to wait to see which won.

She picked up a small purse the same color as her dress and pulled the door closed behind her. They walked to the taxi, and he opened the door for her to get in.

"Your carriage awaits you, madam." He smiled as she slid into the seat. Then he walked around to the other side and got in, and the taxi slid into the waiting traffic.

Chapter Twenty-Five

It was only a short drive to the town center, but Coco's mind worked furiously every minute that passed as Felix's words whirled around her head. *I wanted you again five minutes after I'd had you.* Oh dear God. What was she supposed to say to something like that? She'd never been wanted in her life the way Felix seemed to want her, and his words and his desire, and the heated look in his eyes, eroded away at her stalwart intention to stay aloof.

But she mustn't sleep with him again. She knew that. Because although he was lovely, and sexy, and sweet, and… yes, okay, pretty much perfect, if she slept with him again she was in danger of falling for him, and that wouldn't end well, not with the situation at work, and not with him returning to Auckland the following week.

She was just out for the evening, to watch a nice movie with a friend. That was all.

Then he stroked his thumb across her palm where he was holding her hand. The innocuous gesture sent a frisson of desire through her. Her breath caught in her throat and her nipples tightened, and she cursed at herself for her foolishness. Why had she agreed to come out with him at all?

Still, she couldn't scold herself too much because as the taxi neared the center of town it became clear that they were going to have to park some distance away because of the crowds heading for the cinema. Felix paid the taxi driver, and they got out and began to weave their way through the people milling about. She was amused at the number dressed up as characters from the movie.

"I feel positively underdressed," she said as she passed someone in a full suit of armor.

He grinned. "Don't you think we look the part?"

"Well, you do." She'd nearly fainted when she opened the door and saw him standing there. She'd thought he'd looked good in a business suit, but in the black evening suit he really could have stepped out of a James Bond movie. As they walked, she was conscious of women glancing at him in approval, and she felt a swell of pride to think he was with her. Michael had been taller than her at six foot, but Felix topped him by several inches, and the smart lines of the suit emphasized his toned frame. Her gaze trailed down the pleats of his white shirt. Hold on a minute, was he wearing a waistcoat? Her mouth watered. A waistcoat and cufflinks. The man certainly knew how to dress.

He tucked her hand in the crook of his arm and they joined the queue. She'd been to the Empire Theatre dozens of times before and secretly preferred it to the multi screens in the town center. The Empire had one huge screen, and its foyer consisted of sweeping staircases, marble, and mirrors, with a bar decked out in flock wallpaper and mahogany furniture. It reminded her a little of McAllister Dell's Wellington offices, and she wondered what Felix would think of it considering his comments about it.

"How much did the tickets cost?" she wondered, thinking that they must have been expensive when they first went on sale, and that was before he obviously had to buy them through a second party who would no doubt have charged the Earth.

He smiled wryly. "Don't worry about it."

That meant they were expensive. She wondered how much. Hundreds? Thousands?

"You must really want to get in my panties," she said.

In front of them, a couple glanced over their shoulders and started laughing. Coco apologized, glanced up at a very amused Felix, and closed her eyes. "Jesus, did I say that out loud?"

"I honestly thought you'd enjoy the movie," he said.

Now she'd insulted him. "Oh God, I'm sorry," she murmured. "That sounded terribly ungrateful. I do really appreciate it."

"I'm not upset, Coco. And anyway, you're right." He bent lower to whisper in her ear. "I may not have bought the tickets to get in your panties, but I certainly wouldn't say no if the offer was there."

His warm breath on her skin sent a tingle through her and she shivered.

He put an arm around her and nuzzled her ear. "Do that again."

"Felix. Stop it." She pushed him away. "And please don't tell me we're sitting in the back row. I am not making out with you while this movie is on."

He laughed and dropped his hand to hold hers, and they moved forward into the foyer and up the stairs.

"Have you been here before?" she asked, catching sight of their reflections in the mirrors opposite the staircases. She had to admit they made quite a handsome couple.

"No."

"What do you think?"

He looked around as they reached the top of the stairs. To the right, the counter selling popcorn, ice creams, and soft drinks stretched away from them. To their left were a couple of bars with comfortable chairs and tables, manned by waiters in grey waistcoats with folded white napkins over their arms.

"I love it," he said, leading her over to one of the bars.

She raised her eyebrows. "You surprise me. I would have thought you'd have hated it considering how you feel about the Wellington office."

He frowned. "I don't hate the Wellington office—it's beautifully decorated. I just think it projects the wrong image. A place like this can afford to look like it's stepped out of the nineteen thirties, but a law office should reflect the world we live in, and that's a world of tablets, smartphones, and customers who know almost as much about the law as we do, or at least they think they do. They want to think we know everything there is to know about the law and that we're completely up to date with current legislation and findings. But the Wellington branch is stuck in a previous century, and that's not good for business."

He stopped at the bar. "What can I get you—a glass of wine?"

She nodded and asked for a Pinot Gris, and he ordered himself a Merlot, and they took their glasses over to the window as all the seats were taken. She thought about his words as they sipped their drinks. Was he right? Did the Wellington office project an air of archaic masculinity? She'd seen the data and knew that approximately forty percent of enquiries from their website were from women, but she was certain the percentage of female customers on their books was a lot smaller than that. Did that reflect the fact that they were projecting an outdated image and therefore putting off possible female clientele?

There wasn't much time for her to dwell on the matter, though, as the doors to the screen opened and people began heading toward it.

They took their glasses with them and liveried assistants showed them to their seats, two thirds of the way up and just off center.

"They're great seats," she said as they made themselves comfortable. Still feeling guilty about her earlier gaffe, she leaned toward him and whispered, "I do really appreciate it, you know."

His warm brown eyes lowered to her mouth, and she caught her breath as he brought up a hand to stroke her cheek. Then, to her surprise, he leaned forward and pressed his lips to hers. Just a light kiss, but it was enough to set her heart pounding at the nearness of him. Everything about him was perfect, from his brushed but just-ruffled-enough dark hair, to the five o'clock shadow on his jaw, to his sexy, obviously expensive and quality evening suit.

He lifted his head but didn't say anything, and she sipped her wine, feeling the sexual tension between them as if it were threads of silk drawing them together.

Could he feel it too? She thought maybe he could, because he didn't say much else as they waited for everyone to filter in and the film to start. He held her hand, though, and once the lights dimmed and the movie started, he laced his fingers through hers and kept them there, warming hers, a constant reminder of the predicament she would have to face when the evening ended.

It didn't stop her enjoying the film, however, which was as wonderful as everyone had said it would be, and the two and a half hours passed quickly, even though it was late. But she didn't feel tired—the atmosphere in the cinema was too exciting, with people cheering at certain points in the movie when they recognized scenes or characters from the book.

Eventually it finished, though, and everyone began making their way to the exit. It took them fifteen minutes to get from their seats to the foyer, and by the time they walked out onto the pavement her watch read nearly three a.m.

"I've had such a wonderful time," she said, slipping her arms around his waist. "Thank you so much, I really appreciate it."

"Oh, you're very welcome." He kissed the top of her head.

"I guess we're going to have trouble getting a taxi now?"

He rested his lips on the top of her head for a moment. Then he said, "Um, no."

"Oh?" She lifted her head to look at him.

He looked shifty. "I kind of arranged something."

"A taxi?"

"No…" He looked over her shoulder and signaled to someone. "Something slightly better than that."

She turned around, but couldn't see past the black limo waiting by the curbside. "Who are you waving to?" Then the penny dropped. A limo? The memory of their conversation in the bar rushed into her head. She'd told him she fantasized about having sex in a limo.

"I'm not expecting anything," he said, somewhat hastily. "I just thought it would be fun after such a nice evening." He cupped her face, apparently mistaking her speechlessness for anger. "Please don't be cross with me."

Cross? Her heart melted at the earnestness on his face, at his obvious wish to please her. She'd tried all evening to remain detached from him, to keep herself emotionally separate, but it had proved impossible. He was too nice, too gentlemanly, too damn sexy. He looked fantastic in his suit, and even though it was the middle of the night and she should really in bed, suddenly she wanted him more than anything in the world. "I'm not cross, sweetie."

He brushed his thumb across her cheek. "Really?"

"Of course not. Look what you've done for me. Organized a whole night out for a girl you hardly know with no real promise of her coming across. That's got to earn you some brownie points."

That made him smile. "I really don't expect anything…"

Could he not see how much she wanted him? The warmth from his hand spread through her, firing her desire. She glanced at the limo. Was it possible to have sex in there? What about the driver, would he be able to see what they were doing?

Eager to find out, she grasped Felix's hand and led him toward the waiting car. "Come on, I've always wanted to see inside one of these."

Chapter Twenty-Six

Felix had a quick word with the driver, confirming what he'd requested when he rang to book the limo, and then the driver opened the door and gestured for Coco to enter.

Felix followed her. He'd had a quick look on the internet at pictures of the inside, but nothing could prepare him for the reality.

"Jesus." Coco moved across to one of the seats, then sat and stared around her. "This is…" She shook her head. "Words fail me."

Felix had to agree with her as he sat opposite. The inside of the limo was nothing like he'd ever seen before.

The car stretched away from them, and could easily have accommodated twelve people on the curving fawn leather seats. His shoes sank into the plush chocolate-brown carpet. A mixture of carefully placed spotlights and fairy lights set into the ceiling and a narrow fluorescent yellow strip that ran along the edge of all the seats gave the interior a gentle glow. Folksy jazz played softly out of the speakers to the side. On one side, a bar half-filled the wall, lined with a dozen wine glasses and a dozen tumblers with a couple of decanters full of spirits. A bottle of champagne sat cooling in a bucket of ice.

The driver closed the door behind them.

Felix and Coco stared at each other and then started laughing.

"This must have cost you an absolute fortune," she said, looking up at the lights and fingering the smooth seats.

"Actually, it wasn't as bad as you might think. They had a special on." He grinned and gestured at the ice bucket. "I know we've got to be at work in about five hours. But would you like a glass of champagne?"

"I'd love one." She smiled as he raised an eyebrow. "Oh come on, this is like a dream. I don't care that I've got to work tomorrow—I'm not going to waste a second of this." She sighed. "It's a shame it's only five minutes to my house!"

"Oh… you needn't worry about that." He took off the foil and the wire casing on the bottle. "I've hired it for an hour. The chauffeur's going to drive north along the coast for half an hour before he heads back." He gave her a mischievous grin, hoping she wouldn't mind.

Her lips curved. "I see." They both glanced toward the driver's end as the engine started and the limo pulled smoothly away. "Can he see us?"

"No. There is a window up there, but there's also a screen you can slide across. You talk to him via the phone." He pointed at the receiver on the wall along from her seat. "So… we're all alone." He popped the cork.

Letting her digest that for a moment, he poured two glasses of the champagne, settled the bottle back in the bucket, and passed her one of the glasses. Then he moved to sit beside her. "Cheers." He held up his glass.

She raised hers slowly and clinked it against his. "Cheers. And thank you, Felix, for a lovely evening." She sipped the champagne and murmured her approval.

"You're very welcome. And it's not over yet." He didn't want to push her. She'd made it clear that the night at his hotel was supposed to be a one-off, and Lord knew after all the hassle at work he didn't want to talk her into doing something she really didn't want to do.

But equally, she'd stated this was one of her fantasies. She was dressed like a goddess, so beautiful it took his breath away. And she was looking at his mouth and moistening her lips with the tip of her tongue as if she was desperate for him to kiss her.

So he did. He moved closer, his arm along the back of the seat, until their hips touched and he could feel the heat from her body pressed against him from thigh to shoulder. He waited for her to look up at him, and he gave her a gentle smile. And then he bent his head and let his lips hover an inch from hers, relieved when she moved the final inch to meet him.

She tasted sweet, of the chocolate he'd gone to get for her in the cinema mixed with the champagne, a heady mix. Her lips were soft, still slightly sticky from the remnants of her lipstick, and he enjoyed the way his own peeled from hers as he moved them across, planting soft kisses from one corner of her mouth to the other before moving to her cheeks and around to her ear.

She sighed and tipped her head so he could access her neck, and he ran his tongue down to fasten his mouth over where the beat of her pulse flickered under the skin. He sucked, and she moaned and softened against him, bringing up a hand to slide into his hair as she kissed him again.

Whether it was tiredness or the alcohol or he was just drunk on her, he didn't know, but he felt as if he were in a dream, the sexy music and the lowered lighting combining with the feel of the woman in his arms to make his senses spiral and his head spin.

He kissed her for ages, taking his time, and they sipped champagne before their lips met again to taste each other slowly, erotically, tongues sliding, teeth occasionally grazing, exploring each other and making the blood thunder through Felix's veins.

Outside, through the darkened windows, he could just see moonlight glinting off the waves of the harbor to the right as they headed north. He wished he'd told the driver to go to Auckland. He could easily have sat there with Coco in his arms all night.

After a while, even though it was a cool night, he grew warm in the heat of the car as his internal thermostat rose. He pulled back from her for a moment, put down his glass, undid the buttons of his jacket, and slid it off. He threw it onto the opposite seat and turned back to her.

She slid her hand down his waistcoat. "Jesus, Felix. You look so sexy in this."

"Thank you."

She touched his bow tie. "And not a hint of elastic in sight!"

"This took me half an hour to tie, I'll have you know."

She giggled and her eyes met his. They were filled with longing, and with the hazy desire that currently also swirled inside him.

"Are you sure the driver can't see or hear us?" she whispered.

He shook his head, heart pounding. "These cars are made for privacy."

She put down her glass and nibbled her bottom lip. "Do you want to know a secret?"

His lips curved. "Sure."

"I'm not wearing any underwear."

He stared at her. "Really?"

Her green eyes were wide, challenging. "See for yourself if you don't believe me."

He studied her for a moment. She didn't look away. She was growing bolder, he thought. The knowledge that she'd purposely chosen not to wear panties pleased and excited him. She'd gone out with him tonight expecting something to happen. And that gave him courage.

"You naughty girl." He tightened his arm around her shoulders, pulling her to him, then placed his other hand on her knee and began to pull her skirt up slowly. "You've gone commando all evening? With all those people in the audience?"

"I know—I'm so wicked." She giggled. "That's what you've done to me, Felix. You've corrupted me."

He grinned and continued to hitch up her dress until he found the hem. Moving his hand underneath, he rested his palm on her warm thigh. She inhaled, and he bent his head and brushed his lips against hers while moving his hand up. Her knees seemed to move apart involuntarily as he reached the top of her thighs. He touched his fingers between her legs and found not cloth but velvet skin.

He *tsked*, stroking up to the flat of her belly before returning down. "A Brazilian?" he murmured, still brushing his lips against hers in small kisses. "Very adventurous."

"You like?"

She wanted to please him. That made him glow.

"What do you think?" He took her hand and moved it into his lap. Her fingers found his erection and stroked along the length.

"Oh. Something tells me you like it very much." She ran her tongue across his bottom lip before grazing her teeth on it.

He swelled under her hand, turned on more than he could say by her newfound bravery. Cupping the back of her head, he kissed her properly, sliding the fingers of his other hand down between her legs and into the heart of her. She was already swollen, the skin slippery, enabling his fingers to glide inside her. He groaned, and she sighed and parted her legs farther, and he plunged his tongue into her mouth, his fingers inside her mimicking the movement of his tongue. Bringing his fingers up coated with her arousal, he explored the folds of her skin and circled her clit. Lifting his head, he watched her as he stroked the tiny button, rewarded when she gave a long moan and moved her hips to push herself against him.

He would have been happy to bring her to orgasm there and then, but after a few more strokes she pushed his hand away. Her cheeks were flushed, her eyes half-lidded with desire.

To his surprise, she rose from the seat, moved across and sat astride him, knees resting on the leather either side. "I presume you have a condom," she whispered, kissing around his jaw to his ear.

Felix put a hand in his pocket and pulled out his wallet, fumbled inside, and threw one onto the seat.

"Good." She kissed him, then lifted her head and brushed his tie. "Can we keep our clothes on?"

He understood—not only did they both find each other sexy in their evening wear, but stripping naked in the car might be a step too far. He nodded. "Absolutely. You look fabulous in that dress." And he meant it. The plum color brought out the flush in her skin, and the sheen of the material made her glow.

She smiled shyly and dropped her hands to his waist to explore the button of his fly. Unpopping it, she slid down the zipper and stroked him through his silky boxers.

He closed his eyes and tipped his head back on the seat, enjoying her gentle touch, enjoying the whole evening, this slow exploration of each other, this beautiful woman in his arms. There were a hundred and one things he wanted to do to her, with her, but he was content for the moment to let her proceed at her own pace, to let her develop and explore her sexuality at a rate that she felt comfortable with.

After a while, she slipped a finger into the elastic around his waist, pulled the boxers down, and released his erection, which sprang up, desperate for some action. He opened his eyes and looked into hers.

"Show me how to touch you," she whispered.

Surprised, he was nevertheless happy to comply. He picked up her hand and murmured, "Lick your palm."

Her eyes widened, but she did so, running her tongue from her wrist to the tops of her fingers. Then he closed her hand around him and moved it up and down, long strokes from base to tip, her slick palm sliding around him.

He moved his hand away and watched as she continued to arouse him, apparently fascinated by the process. "Did you never do this for your ex?" he asked, puzzled.

"He didn't like me touching him." She didn't raise her eyes, but continued to study what her hand was doing, pausing for a moment to examine the head of his erection, exploring the bumps and ridges with her thumb.

Felix closed his eyes again, his arms stretched out along the seat, reveling in her touch. She was like a virgin, and the process of educating her, of enjoying her process of discovery, was a wondrous thing.

Eventually, though, he couldn't bear her touch anymore—he was going to come in her hand, and he wasn't sure if she was quite ready for that. Besides which, he wanted to bury himself inside her.

He pulled her hand away, ignoring her complaint, ripped the foil off the condom and rolled it on, then pushed up her skirts and lifted her on top of him.

"You're very demanding," she said, moving her hips until his tip parted her soft folds.

"Is that a complaint?" He held her hips and pushed up. She sank onto him, making them both gasp.

"Jeez. No, no, no."

He laughed and brought her head down to kiss her, and she began to move on top of him, rocking her hips so he slid in and out of her velvet sheath. He moved his hands around her back, found the zipper of the bodice of her dress, and undid it six inches. He slid the straps off her shoulders, and the material fell to her waist, exposing her breasts.

Felix groaned and covered a nipple with his mouth, sucking and groaning again as her tender skin contracted to a peak beneath his tongue. She moaned in return and arched against him, and he did the same to the other nipple until they were both wet and tight. Then he kissed her, continuing to play with her breasts while she thrust slowly on top of him, her slow regular movements driving him insane.

After only a few minutes, however, she lifted her head and kissed his cheeks, then his nose. Still moving, she said, "Felix…"

His eyes fluttered open, and he saw her studying him curiously.

"Mmm?"

"How do you make love to your other girls?"

He had not expected her to say that. "What?"

She kissed his ear. "I mean, I know you're being gentle with me, and I really appreciate it. But when you're with other women, are you the same? Or are you more…" Her voice trailed off, unable to put her feelings into words.

He put his hands on her hips, stilling her movements, and looked into her eyes. Her words had surprised him, but he suddenly he realized he'd been thinking about their relationship—such as it was—all wrong. Coco thought of their time together as an adventure. She wasn't thinking any further than tonight, and she fully expected not to sleep with him again. She'd told him that she was the one who'd wanted more in a physical sense with her ex, and although he had needed to be gentle at first, she was trying to tell him it wasn't enough.

She swallowed, obviously nervous she'd said too much.

He stroked her face. "There aren't that many other girls, but don't worry." He kissed her. "I know what you want."

She didn't say anything, but her chest rose and fell quickly.

"You don't want to make love," he said.

She blinked and her mouth fell open. "Oh! I do, I…"

"No, you don't." He moved his arm around her waist and gripped her tightly, then moved forward and turned to lower her onto the carpet on her back, still inside her. She squealed, but he ignored the exclamation, knelt over her, gripped her hands, and pinned them above her head so she lay powerless beneath him. "You want to be fucked."

Chapter Twenty-Seven

Coco stared up at Felix. His eyes blazed, and his words made her heart thunder, but she couldn't tell if he was angry or turned on. Had she upset him? He seemed to have gotten the wrong idea—she certainly wasn't saying she didn't appreciate his gentle manner, or that she wasn't enjoying himself.

But she had felt he was holding back, and she'd regretted that. He was obviously afraid of hurting or frightening her by letting his passion free, and she wanted a hundred percent of him, not a watered-down version.

And that's what he'd picked up on. He'd understood, and he was offering her the part of him she'd known existed behind his gentlemanly manner. She'd asked him, and she couldn't now take her question back.

And deep down, she didn't want to.

You want to be fucked, he'd said, and he was right.

"Yes," she whispered.

His lips curved. He found her desire a turn-on, and the heat in his eyes was passion, not anger.

Still he didn't move, but he pushed his hips forward, burying himself in her, forcing her to accept all of him. She'd never felt so stretched, so full—she could feel his thick, hard length all the way up, right to the top. She couldn't take any more, surely? He wasn't a small man, but she hadn't realized last time how gentle he'd been, letting her guide the pace.

She gasped, tugging automatically at her hands, but he refused to free them, using his weight to pin her there. She was totally at his mercy—he could do whatever he wanted with her and she'd be powerless to stop him.

Jeez, that was sexy.

And so was the man leaning over her, supporting himself on powerful arms, hot as sin in his white shirt and black tie. His eyes fixed on hers, he moved his hips slightly from side to side, making sure there was no more of him left to bury inside her, and she groaned, finally understanding why they called it screwing.

Satisfied she'd taken all of him, he pulled his hips back until he was almost out of her, and then he thrust forward.

Coco gasped, arching against him, eyes wide at his challenging stare.

"Are you sure?" he said silkily. "You think you can take it hard and fast?"

She said nothing, bewildered by this other Felix, even though she'd been suspicious he existed. Taking her silence as acquiescence, he moved again, and again, setting a punishing pace with hard, deep thrusts that soon had her panting and moaning in equal measure.

He dropped to one elbow above her and kissed her deeply, thrusting his tongue into her mouth and then planting hot kisses down her neck to her breast. He sucked her nipple firmly enough to make her squeal, then raised himself to kiss her again.

"Are you enjoying this?" he murmured, nibbling her earlobe.

"Um, yes..."

"I thought so." He bit the lobe harder. "You're very wet."

"Felix!"

"What?" He kissed her. "It's a good thing. Makes for less friction."

He was naughty, this Felix, and it excited and aroused her in equal measure. She waited for him to thrust again, but to her disappointment he pulled out, holding carefully onto the condom.

"Oh." She pouted.

He grinned and pulled her up onto her knees. He kissed her, then he made a circular motion in the air with his finger. "Turn around."

She stared. "Huh?"

He kissed her nose. "I want to fuck you from behind, sweetheart. Turn around and lean on the seat."

Her heart raced. Michael had never once taken her from behind, as if the position was somehow dirty and forbidden, too base and animal for decent people to indulge in. The thought that Felix didn't think it was forbidden—in fact, he obviously enjoyed it and was going to take pleasure in doing it—thrilled her.

She turned around, and he moved so he knelt between her legs, and then he pushed her down so she leaned on the leather seat in front of her. He lifted her skirts so they hung over her waist, baring her ass to his view.

Then he slapped her butt, and she jumped and squeaked, "Ow!"

He laughed. "Come on, Coco. You must have had one of your exotic fantasies about a bit of mild BDSM, right?"

"Goodness, no!"

"Liar. I don't believe you, with your active imagination." He rubbed his hand over her butt cheek where he'd slapped, caressing what she was sure would be an imprint of his fingers. "I'm not into pain, but there's something sexy about a little chastisement."

She leaned her forehead on her arms. She wasn't going to make it out of the car without dissolving into an orgasmic heap.

He moved his hand from her butt cheek around her waist and then beneath to stroke her. He laughed as he obviously found her even wetter than before, and he plunged his fingers into her, sliding them through her slippery folds. "Wow."

"Felix…"

"Jesus. You're wetter than October."

"Felix! Why do you like embarrassing me?"

He leaned forward and kissed her back as he continued to stroke her. "I don't mean to embarrass you. But talking dirty is sexy and it's something you have to get used to if you go to bed with me. And later I'm going to make you do it back, so you'd better start picking up some tips."

Later? He wanted to sleep with her again. Oh hell, what was she getting herself into?

But it was too late to worry about it now because he was moving behind her and she could feel his hand guiding his erection into her.

"Widen your legs, sweetheart," he said.

She complied, unable to believe she was being so wanton, and he pressed into her folds. Then, before she could prepare herself, he slid right inside her.

She gasped, and he held the position, hands on her hips, waiting for her to adjust.

"This way feels deeper," he said huskily. He moved his hand underneath. "The man presses against the woman's G-spot here, in this position. It's supposed to be the easiest way for a woman to achieve an orgasm without clitoral stimulation."

"Oh," she said faintly. "I don't think there's any worry about that."

He chuckled, returned his hand to her hip, pulled almost out of her and pushed forward again. She moaned as he filled her, feeling him so deep inside, she couldn't believe she'd actually accepted all of him.

"Okay?" he said.

"Yes," she whispered. *I'm so okay, you'll never know.*

"Good. I'm going to fuck you hard now, so get prepared."

Before she could reply, he thrust again, harder this time, and he quickly set a rapid pace, his hips meeting hers with a sharp smack as he plunged deeper and deeper inside her. She clutched hold of the seat, gasping when her nipples brushed against the cool leather, closing her eyes as her internal sensations gradually overwhelmed her external senses.

All she was aware of was the slide of him through her slick center, the sound of his guttural grunts as he thrust, the warmth of his hands on her butt as he continued to stroke her. At first he leaned forward and brushed her nipples, or dipped his hand beneath her to rub her swollen skin, but before long his fingers were digging into her hips and she knew he was close to coming because she was too. There was no way to avoid it—this was just too hot, too sexy, and she couldn't have held back to save her life.

He thrust harder, and she opened her legs as wide as she could for him as the sensations began to build inside her, the exquisite tightening of her muscles that announced the arrival of her climax. She'd never felt such a long build up, a long, slow contracting that made her gasp as he pounded into her, and then suddenly it swept over her in a rush and she cried out with the force of it. He exclaimed loudly and shuddered, swelling inside her, and she pushed back, clenching around him. He dropped back onto his heels, bringing her with him, holding her tightly. Impaled upon him, all she could do was wait for the pulsing of her muscles to finish, conscious of the warmth of his arms and the fact that he was placing kisses along her shoulder and up her neck as he whispered gentle and tender endearments into her ear.

Chapter Twenty-Eight

The following morning, Felix took a long swig of his coffee, swallowed, and sighed. He'd hoped the triple-shot latte would help him keep his eyes open until lunchtime, having managed only three hours sleep after returning to his hotel room. In spite of the late hour, he'd lain awake for a while, his mind playing over the events of the night before, pictures slipping through his mind like a slideshow of Coco beneath him and kneeling before him, and sitting back on him with her back arched in sublime pleasure.

He'd had a fabulous evening, although he was puzzled as to quite why he'd so enjoyed himself. He'd been to the cinema before. Slept with women before. True, the midnight premiere in the Empire had been a bit different and the movie had been great, but he knew it was more than that. Coco had proved to be fun company, and they'd talked for hours about nothing in particular. She was intelligent and amusing, and even though they'd carefully steered clear of any topic connected with work, they'd still found plenty to discuss.

And then of course they'd followed it with the session in the limo, and that had blown Felix's mind. Although initially he'd felt a strange pang of disappointment that all she was looking for was sex, that had quickly disappeared as her enthusiasm for his passionate lovemaking had overwhelmed him.

And yet afterward, he'd drawn her into his arms and she'd curled up on the seat as the car slowly made its way back south along the coast to Wellington, and he'd watched the moonlight playing on the water, filled with more than the usual brief pleasure he felt after sex. He felt content, and had to admit to more than a tiny rush of affection for the girl dozing lightly in his arms.

But same as the night before, they'd parted without any talk of meeting up, and therefore he'd lain awake wondering whether he should ask her out again, and what her answer would be. Half of him hadn't been sure she would go to the cinema with him, but she had. Would she turn him down now, after all the fun they'd had together?

He blinked and focused on the iPad lying on the desk in front of him. He was supposed to be reading over his notes ready for interviewing Sasha De Langen at ten o'clock, not daydreaming about Coco with her silky blonde hair and red lips, and the way she liked to thread her fingers through his hair when she kissed him…

Someone cleared their throat in the doorway. He lifted his head and for a moment thought he'd conjured her up out of his dreams. Then he realized it was Miss Stark standing before him, not Coco. She'd pulled her hair back into its tight bun again and donned her glasses, and she wore a black suit today with a pencil skirt and a white blouse beneath the jacket. Her lips were a bright pinky-red. He got a hard-on just looking at them.

She cleared her throat again, her arms crossed over her breasts where she clutched a clipboard. "Good morning, Mr. Wilkinson."

He grinned. "Good morning, Miss Stark. How are you today? Did you have a nice weekend?"

He thought he saw a faint glimmer of amusement in her eyes. "Yes, thank you. You?"

"Most amusing," he said. "I didn't get much sleep though. There was some bird outside that kept me up all night."

She looked at the floor, struggling between laughter and embarrassment, and he chuckled to himself. She walked into the room to stand before his desk and said, "If you were that bothered about sleep, maybe you should have told the bird to go away."

"Oh, I would never have done that." He leaned back in his chair and surveyed her with a smile. "She sang beautifully."

She met his gaze, and for a brief moment they just studied each other.

His stomach did a strange flip. But he didn't have time to analyze it because at that moment Rob Drake appeared in the doorway.

"Hey, Miss Stark," he said, walking into the room.

"Good morning, Mr. Drake."

He glanced around the room. "No Sasha yet?"

"She'll be along in a moment," Coco said. "She's asked me to be present, if that's okay with you. I therefore thought I could combine it with taking minutes." She turned her cool green eyes onto Felix.

He hesitated. He'd planned to question Sasha alone, hoping that with nobody else there to answer for her, he'd be able to get a better idea of whether she was telling the truth. He didn't know Coco well enough to know how defensive she'd be of her secretaries. Certainly, she'd stood up for the unfortunate Sam.

She was looking at the floor, but as his gaze slid to her she raised her eyes, and to his surprise he saw uncertainty and maybe even a little resentment in their depths. Sasha had asked her to be there, and she'd felt as if she had to accept. That interested him. Why didn't she want to be present? Because of what had happened the night before? But then he remembered the look Coco had exchanged with Peter Dell on Friday at the disciplinary meeting. There was an undercurrent here he couldn't define.

He shifted uneasily. He had to remember he was here to do a job. That had to take precedence over his desire to get the office manager in the sack again.

"Of course I don't mind if Sasha wants you here." It would be good to have her taking minutes anyway—he'd thought he'd have to rely on his own note taking, which was always distracting when he was trying to interview. He stood and gestured for them both to take a seat in the chairs surrounding the coffee table. "Whatever will put her at ease."

Coco sank gracefully into one of the chairs and crossed her legs. He couldn't stop himself glancing at her tight pencil skirt. What was that faint ripple beneath the fabric at the top of her thighs? Dear God, was she wearing stockings? Now he was going to have real trouble concentrating.

He forced his gaze away, picked up his iPad, and walked around his desk. He wasn't even going to look at her. He was going to focus all his attention on Sasha, when she eventually arrived.

Luckily, at that moment she appeared at the doorway. At least he presumed it was her. A slender young woman of medium height with straight dark hair, she was pretty in an intense, serious, bookish way. Like Coco, she had glasses, and she wore long pants and a shirt she'd buttoned up to her neck, as if frightened of encouraging any male attention. Which he guessed she was, if she had in fact told the truth about Peter Dell. She was biting her lip, and she looked as if a loud noise would make her jump through the roof.

She stood on the threshold, her shoulders hunched toward her ears and her hands jammed in her pockets, so he walked over to her, smiled, and held out his hand.

"You must be Sasha—very pleased to meet you. I'm Felix Wilkinson."

"Hello, Mr. Wilkinson." She shook his hand—a good, firm grip, then looked up and met his eyes. He corrected his initial impression of her. She might be nervous, but this girl was no walkover.

Her challenging glare made his back stiffen. *We're not all like Peter Dell*, he wanted to say on impulse, but he bit his tongue and forced a smile on his face.

"Yes," she said, "I'm Sasha."

"Please, call me Felix." He ignored Coco's frown and gestured for Sasha to sit beside her. "Miss Stark said you requested she be here."

"Yes." Sasha glanced at Coco, then looked back at him. "If that's okay."

"Of course." He took the seat opposite her and rested the iPad on his knee. "Would you like a drink of anything before we start?"

"No, I'm fine, thank you."

He glanced at Coco, but she was looking at the floor and didn't look up. He couldn't worry about what was going through her mind now. He had to concentrate on the matter at hand—even if her skirt had ridden an inch up her beautiful thighs.

Jesus, he really was no better than Dell. He dragged his gaze away and focused on Sasha. "Obviously, you know why we're here. You've made an accusation of sexual harassment against Peter Dell, and when this happens, it's company policy to carry out an investigation. I've been asked because I'm from the Auckland office and I have never met either you or Peter Dell, and therefore I can offer a fair and unbiased opinion."

"Yes," Sasha said, although she looked highly skeptical.

Felix held her gaze firmly, determined that she believe he would be open minded and impartial. "I assure you, Sasha, I'm here to try and uncover the truth. I have no agenda, and I promise to be thorough in my investigation with all parties concerned."

"Okay."

"I'm sure you're aware by now that Peter has denied your allegations."

"Yes." She frowned.

"I asked him about the events of the night in question, Monday, the fifth of December. I know you've already given Rob here a statement, but if you wouldn't mind, I'd now like you to describe in your own words what happened that night."

Sasha nodded. "Okay."

So she told him, and her story reflected pretty much word for word what she'd declared in her statement. Dell had asked her to stay behind to finish typing a diary of phone call logs ready for a case that was appearing in court the next day. She typed them, took them to his office and waited while he read them. Then he called her over to his desk, ostensibly to point out a couple of mistakes she'd missed, but when she leaned forward to look at the document, his hand brushed her hip. She thought it was a mistake, but then he put his hand on the inside of her knee and slid it upward.

At this point Sasha stopped and blinked a few times. There was no other sign that she was upset, but she looked fixedly at the ground, and Felix got the impression she was trying to keep her emotions in check.

"Would you like a glass of water?" he asked kindly.

Without looking up, she nodded, and he glanced at Rob, who got up quickly to fetch a cup from the cooler in the corridor and brought it back. Felix tapped on his iPad for a minute or two to give her time to calm herself as she sipped the water.

Was her emotion genuine? Or was this all an act put on for him? He found it difficult to believe, but he was astute enough to realize that if she'd made it all up in the beginning, she was certainly a good enough actress to be able to carry it through. Or even if she really was worried and nervous now, that didn't mean she was entirely innocent.

He glanced at Coco. She'd been taking minutes as he talked, her pencil moving gracefully across the paper in the usual indecipherable squiggles of shorthand, but now she lifted her gaze to his. He gave her a small smile. One hovered briefly on her lips before she dropped her eyes to her notepad again.

He flicked a brief look at Sasha, who was staring into her cup, then glanced at Rob and raised his eyebrows in query to his colleague. Rob gave a no idea shrug.

Felix frowned, the weight of the decision bearing down on him for the first time. In the big scheme of things, it was a tiny matter—there were no lives at stake, no governments about to crumble or children at risk. And yet he couldn't dismiss it as inconsequential. If

Sasha truly had been sexually harassed, she'd been through a traumatic experience and either way it could affect her and her relationships with other people for a long, long time. If he found Dell innocent and he really was guilty, it would undermine her faith in justice and make it very difficult for her to trust in men again. Equally, if he believed her and found Dell guilty and he was in fact innocent, he would be destroying a good man's career, as well as damaging the reputation of his own firm. It was not a light decision to make, and he cursed Christopher McAllister for putting him in this position.

Still, he'd taken the role and there was nothing more to be done. He sighed and said to Sasha, "Shall we continue or do you need more time?"

Chapter Twenty-Nine

Sasha put her cup on the table. "No, carry on. I'm sorry, it's just..." She rubbed her nose, and her shoulders slumped as if she'd finally released all the tension from her system and let down her guard. "I'm not normally a wuss. But it's difficult to stand up for myself against the image of McAllister Dell, you know? I like and respect Mr. McAllister, and I liked Mr. Dell well enough up until that point. He was nice—he talked to me whereas a lot of the older partners act as if you're invisible."

"Truly?" Felix was astonished at her comment, as well as surprised at the way she'd suddenly opened up. Even Rob looked startled. He'd told Felix that getting a statement out of her had been like getting blood out of a stone. But maybe she'd decided this was her opportunity to put things straight.

Sasha gave a humorless laugh. "Oh yes. They'll walk straight by me and not even say good morning. So it was nice whenever the senior partners took the time to talk. Mr. McAllister always asked about my cat. Mr. Dell always asked what I'd done at the weekend. Sometimes he'd sit on the edge of my desk. He'd ask if I'd been out, and with whom, and he'd tease me about having a boyfriend." Her cheeks flushed.

"Did he do that often?"

She shrugged. "Most weeks, after the weekend. But I didn't think anything of it. It's something most women have to put up with, especially from older men."

Felix studied his iPad, but he wasn't reading. He puzzled over Sasha's words. Was it true? Did men usually tease women about who they were dating? It wasn't something he would have dreamed of doing, but of course he had seen it happen. How insensitive.

He looked up to see Coco watching him. Her lips curved very slightly in one corner, as if she could sense his confusion. Was she amused by his confusion or by his naivety?

He ran a hand through his hair and cleared his throat. "How did you feel when Mr. Dell asked you to stay late that night?"

"I wasn't worried," Sasha said. "I'd worked late before for Mr. McAllister and for Mr. Hoyle. Plus, we get paid overtime and I needed the money, so I was happy to do it."

"Did Mr. Dell ask you to stay late," Rob interjected, "or did you offer? This is quite important, Sasha."

"He asked me," she said immediately. "He came up to my desk and told me that I was one of the best secretaries in the office. I remember feeling flattered by that." Her expression darkened. "Pathetic, eh?"

"It's understandable," said Felix. Dell had told him that he'd posed a question to the room and Sasha had volunteered. Felix was going to have to ask the other secretaries in the office if they could remember exactly what happened.

"I remember thinking it was odd, though," Sasha said without being prompted.

"Why?"

"The call logs had already been sent to us in a pdf file. That document would have been perfectly acceptable to submit, but Mr. Dell insisted that they needed to be retyped. It didn't make sense at the time, but I just assumed he was being a perfectionist—he's a bit like that."

Felix noted that down. He'd check to see if there had been an original file later. Coco should be able to tell by the date of the file on the computer. "So you did the typing for him and took a copy of the document to his office?"

"Yes."

"Why didn't you just email him a copy or tell him where the file was saved?"

"We don't do that here," she said. "The older lawyers like everything in hard copy."

"We like to destroy at least two rainforests every year," Rob said dryly. Coco sent him a glare, and he dropped his gaze.

Felix stifled a smile. "Okay, so you took him a copy. He read it and mentioned some errors."

"Yes."

"Did you walk over to his desk to look at them, or did he call you over?"

"He called me over. I didn't think anything of it until he pointed out the error—I'd already told him I hadn't lined one of the columns up right. I wondered why he was telling me something I already knew."

Felix nodded and read her statement. "And then he brushed your hip."

"Yes."

His eyes met Coco's as her pencil paused on the paper. Now they were coming to the crunch. "You didn't think there was anything wrong with this?"

Sasha hesitated. "Initially it was a fleeting touch. I thought it was an accident. It happens, you know? You lean forward and misjudge the distance."

"But then he touched your knee?"

"Yes. The inside."

"And you still thought it was an accident?" He couldn't stop a hint of doubt creeping into his voice.

Her eyes hardened. "You have to understand, all this happened in the space of seconds. We're adults in a working relationship—I'm not going to jump up at the first sign of physical contact and yell rape, Mr. Wilkinson."

"I apologize if I offended you," he said, stifling irritation at her resentfulness. "But I have to get the details clear. Peter touched the inside of your knee, and initially you didn't do anything?"

"I thought maybe he was reaching for the drawer or something."

Felix frowned. "Was it possible he took your lack of reaction as acquiescence—that he thought you approved of the touch?"

"I…" Her voice tailed off and she looked confused.

Felix hesitated. Dell had told him Sasha had touched him first, but even if that wasn't the case, he could have been trying to cover his embarrassment at making a move on a girl when he thought she was interested. It was no excuse for lying, but it was a hard world out there for both sexes, and he wasn't about to ruin a man's career because Dell had misunderstood what he thought were obvious signs.

He thought of Coco—how he'd flirted with her, then worried he'd got it wrong, before she finally kissed him. He sighed. "The point I'm trying to make, Sasha, is that sometimes it's difficult for both sexes to distinguish between flirting and genuine interest. I need to establish whether what happened here was a misunderstanding—whether there was any reason that Peter may have thought you were interested in him."

"There wasn't," she said flatly.

"You told me that he often stopped by your desk to talk to you."

"Occasionally, not often."

"When he did, you talked about what happened at the weekend. About your boyfriends?"

Her cheeks flushed. "He asked me. I never offered any information."

"But you answered him?"

"Yes, I suppose so."

"In what way would you answer him? With a flat 'no'? Would you turn away or tell him not to be so personal?"

Her cheeks grew redder. "No, of course not. I was always polite. I'd tell him I'd had a nice weekend, and that I'd spent it on my own."

She'd grown defensive, so Felix decided to change tack. "What result are you looking for from this case, Sasha? If Peter is found guilty, what would you expect to happen to him?"

"I'd expect him to be sacked, of course," she said. "How could he continue to work when he might try it on again with other women?"

"That's quite a harsh outcome considering nothing happened between you."

"Something did happen," she snapped. "I was assaulted."

"I didn't mean to imply that what happened hasn't had an effect on you," he said, wishing he'd chosen his words more carefully.

"Well, it has." Her lip trembled.

He decided to change tack again. "Do you think you have a good sense of humor?"

Her gaze flicked to Coco, as if asking for help as to the change of direction. Coco gave her a small smile and a slight shrug.

"I suppose," Sasha said.

"Do you ever discuss sex with your workmates—men or women?"

She glared at him. "No, never."

"Ever tell sexual jokes? 'That's what she said' comments?"

She huffed a sigh. "No more than anyone else."

"So you have done that?"

She narrowed her eyes. "Maybe once or twice," she said.

"Is it possible that Peter Dell overheard these jokes?"

"I suppose…" She glared again. The look in her eyes almost made him squirm, but he refused to be intimidated, his own irritation rising at her aggressive manner.

He gestured at her. "What about your clothing. I see today you're wearing a long-sleeved shirt and pants. Do you ever wear a skirt?"

"Of course."

"What type?"

The corner of her mouth curved. "You really want to discuss fashion, Mr. Wilkinson?"

Her smart comment didn't amuse him. He didn't smile, but merely raised an eyebrow. "Do you ever wear short skirts?"

She met his gaze for a moment. He could see that she wanted to lie, but that she also knew he'd know if she was. "Occasionally," she said eventually. "They're not short short, only an inch or so above the knee."

"And what about your tops? Do you always wear shirts?"

"Not all the time." Her eyes were like icicles, her speech clipped and sharp.

Unusually, he lost his temper. He was trying to solve this case—a case that he hadn't wanted to take on in the first place and that he was wishing he'd refused—and instead of helping him understand what had happened, she was insinuating that his questions were unfair, and casting him in the same mold as Peter Dell, which lit his fuse.

He leaned forward, a movement that he knew she'd interpret as confrontational, especially considering he was taller and bigger than she was. "The urge to draw the attention of the opposite sex occurs on a biological level, not a conscious one. It's part of human nature. The fact is that women often dress to attract attention—by wearing low-cut tops, undoing an extra button, and buying fabrics that are vaguely transparent. Don't you agree?"

Coco lifted her head and stared at him.

Sasha stiffened and froze. Then she stood, very slowly, every bone in her body showing her indignation. "I could come to work naked, Mr. Wilkinson, and I still wouldn't be 'asking for it', as Mr. Dell so politely put it. I'm insulted and appalled that you are intimating that anything I've done or worn could have justified the way Mr. Dell touched me. I did not court his attention, nor did I want it, hence my complaint."

And she walked out of the room.

Chapter Thirty

"Nice," Coco said wryly.

Felix put his head in his hands and said, "Fuck."

Rob cleared his throat. "I'll just go and make sure she's okay." He left the room.

Coco sat silently and watched Felix. She sensed he was unused to losing his temper. For some reason, Sasha had pushed all his buttons. Was that because Coco was in the room? Or just that the case had just touched a nerve since their relationship began?

Eventually he lifted his head and ran his hands through his hair, sat back in his chair and looked at her.

"Sorry," he said.

She raised an eyebrow. "I don't think it's me you should be apologizing to."

He looked out of the window mutely. Suddenly he looked very young and unsure of himself, his hair sticking up at the front, and she felt a wave of affection for him, in spite of her initial anger at his insensitive words. Obviously, he thought of himself as a champion for everyone regardless of their gender, race or color. He'd shocked himself with his comments to Sasha, and she supposed he felt even worse knowing Coco had overhead it.

She ran her gaze down him, unable to stop herself remembering how he'd been in the limo—dressed to kill in his tux, so commanding and possessive, knowing exactly what she wanted. And yet he'd held her so tenderly afterward, asking her if she was okay, making sure he hadn't hurt her. He'd stroked her hair, kissed her, and murmured endearments until they eventually arrived at her house. And then he'd let her go reluctantly, telling her what a wonderful time he'd had. She'd hardly had a wink of sleep, and she guessed he hadn't either.

But she mustn't let her affection for him stand in the way of the fact that he'd just been incredibly insensitive and rude to poor Sasha, who was already suffering from the stress of the situation. She didn't know Sasha well, but the very fact that the girl had asked her to be there proved to Coco that Sasha had been nervous, even though she often came across as hostile and devil-may-care.

"Do you really think she was 'asking for it' because she occasionally wore a skirt above her knees?" she asked, curious as to whether he'd given the notion even a fraction of a thought.

"Of course not." He stood and walked over to the window, hands behind his back. "I was just trying to establish whether Dell might have thought she was dressing provocatively for him." He turned to look at her, frustration showing in his frown and the pained look in his eyes. "It's hard sometimes, Coco, to know. Beneath our attempt at civilization, we're all chemicals and hormones and electrical impulses, governed by our biological urge to reproduce."

She remembered the way he'd reacted before, when he'd suddenly realized he'd pushed her in a way that he'd obviously thought Dell might have pushed Sasha. She understood, but that still didn't excuse what Dell had done. "I know what you're saying, but nowadays we're supposed to have the ability to control our base feelings, aren't we? Isn't that what being civilized is all about?"

"Yes, but it's not that easy." He gestured to her clothing. "For instance, I know you're wearing stockings and that you have a white lacy bra on beneath your blouse." She felt her cheeks grow warm—how had he known that? "You paint your lips red and you spray on perfume." She opened her mouth to protest, but he held up a hand. "I know you do this for yourself as much as anything. But I defy anyone to say they take care over their appearance and don't get a kick from the attention it draws from the opposite sex. Men too—I'm including myself in this. I wear nice suits and use product in my hair and splash on cologne because I know I look smart, and I feel good when women look at me with admiration. It may be shallow, but at least I admit it."

"Maybe you're right," she admitted. "We all like to be admired. But that's not really the issue here."

"I know. Just because I want to look good doesn't give permission for any woman to march up and run her hands through my hair—I get that." He paced the room, frowning. "I do understand Sasha's comment, that even if she walked in naked, she wouldn't be 'asking for it'. But equally, if a woman flirts with a man, wears a low-cut top and bends forward to give him a view down her cleavage, crosses her legs, flutters her eyelashes, moistens her lips, blushes, gives him all the signs that we have to look for if we have any hope of finding a partner to share our lives with… If she does all that, the man is going to make a move. It's in our nature. And it seems incredibly unfair for the woman to then act outraged." He ended breathless, stiff and indignant.

Coco thought about it, trying to imagine how she would feel if she were in a man's shoes. "I happen to agree. It's true that even in this day and age, the man is usually the one to make the first move. And I can only guess how nerve-racking that must be. It's a fine line for both sexes, I think. As you say, we all dress to attract attention because it makes us feel good to be admired, and it's unfair to then protest when we receive that attention."

Then she thought about Peter, about what had happened all those years ago. "But that's not the same as 'asking for it'. I concur that if Sasha flirted with Peter, if she did all those things you mention, then it would be hypocritical for her to cry that he'd assaulted her. But I guess the point here is: did she send him those signs? Does she occasionally wear short skirts? Yes. Does she wear lipstick, style her hair, wear perfume, and try to dress nicely? Yes. But does she unbutton her shirt every time he passes by? Does she make sexual innuendo, flirt, moisten her lips, giggle, and generally encourage him? No, I don't believe she does, and I'm sure when you get around to talking to other members of staff, they'll say she doesn't either. And if you come to the conclusion that she doesn't do that, and has never done that where Dell is concerned, I'm sure you'll understand just why she feels so incensed at your semi-accusation that she 'asked for it'."

Felix studied her, his face expressionless, for a while, blinking occasionally. What was he thinking? Was he about to shout at her for being so confrontational? For disagreeing with him?

Then, to her surprise, his lips slowly curved, and he came forward to sit opposite her. "Thank you," he said, tipping his head, and fixing his warm brown eyes on her.

She raised her eyebrows. "What for?"

"For being honest with me. For fronting up to me. I'm glad you challenge me. I do my best, but sometimes it's hard to see things from the other side."

She shrugged self-consciously under his admiring gaze. "I haven't always been so brave." And maybe if she had, Sasha wouldn't be in this position, she thought sadly. "It's something I've had to work on."

His gaze flicked over to the door before coming back to rest on her. "Obviously, after last night's escapades, tonight we need a good night's sleep." He winked, and chuckled as she looked down, embarrassed. "But tomorrow, would you like to do something again? Maybe fulfil another of your exotic fantasies?" His eyes gleamed.

She hesitated. She should say no. She'd had her fun, and indulging repeatedly was never going to end well.

But he was so gorgeous, and she couldn't shake the memory of him turning her over, whispering erotic things in her ear as he thrust in and out of her so forcefully. He was like a drug, and she was very quickly becoming addicted to him.

"I shouldn't," she said.

"I know." The look in his eyes told her he understood and felt the same. He knew this was a bad idea—that they were getting hooked, but he felt as compelled to see her again as she did him, and that finally convinced her.

"Okay," she whispered.

A look of relief crossed his face. "Thanks, treacle," he said.

"Treacle?"

"Sorry. Treacle tart—sweetheart." He winked at her, his good humor restored, and turned back to his iPad, but his gaze burned into her butt as she left the room.

*

She thought about his look of relief a lot over the next two days, while he continued his interviews of the partners and other lawyers. Sasha had gone home after the interview and then phoned in sick the next day, and Felix had left her alone, saying it was easier to carry out the investigation without her there anyway, and he'd speak to her later in the week once he had a clearer picture of events.

Coco had never given much thought before to how men felt about asking women out. Of course nowadays it was considered perfectly acceptable for a woman to ask a guy out on a date, but she couldn't ever imagine doing so herself. How scary would that be, though? Trying to work out if the guy in question was interested? Plucking up the courage to make the move, knowing she would have to act all nonchalant if he turned her down? Having to face him after that, knowing he knew she thought he was attractive?

The strange dance the sexes carried out was complex and confusing, and it was no surprise the occasional problem like the one with Sasha occurred. But still, Coco wasn't convinced that was the case here. Knowing what she knew about Peter Dell suggested to her that Sasha probably hadn't given him any signs at all—he'd taken a liking to her and had decided he would try to seduce her, convinced she wouldn't dare turn down a senior partner, possibly hoping to make her an offer of promotion or something to persuade her to accept his advances. He disgusted her, and she was disgusted with herself for not being able to tell Felix the truth about what had happened to herself in the past.

But she couldn't, and there was no point in torturing herself over what was done. She had to move on and hope that Felix was smart enough to understand the truth and make the right decision.

She didn't see much of him for the rest of Monday or Tuesday. He remained confined to his office with the door shut most of the time as he and Rob interviewed the partners and associates, and she purposely kept out of the way. Luckily, she was busy, and the time went quickly.

Monday evening proved hard work, with Eleanor giving her yet another lecture about her private life and trying to convince Coco that moving into a home was a positive thing. It was like a war of attrition, as if her mother was trying to wear her down gradually, eroding her love and patience like the sea erodes rock. The same thing happened Tuesday when she got home from work. She told Eleanor she was going out with Felix again, and Eleanor became so gleeful that Coco nearly told her she wasn't going.

"I knew you'd see sense eventually," Eleanor said, rubbing her hands together.

Coco stood up and smacked the paper she'd been reading on the table. "Stop it. This is nothing, Mum, just a brief distraction. It doesn't mean anything. Stop acting as if I've found the love of my life and I'm getting married in the morning."

"It's not just a dalliance," Eleanor said, her face glowing with more color than Coco had seen it in decades. "I know you, sweetheart. There's more to this than a quick fling."

Hot tears scalded Coco's eyes, but she blinked them away and glared at her mother. "Felix is here for precisely six more days, then he moves to the other end of the island."

"You could always move with him." Eleanor winked and giggled like a teenage girl.

Coco left the room. She hated doing that—walking away, because it seemed unfair when Eleanor's mobility was so strictly limited, but sometimes she needed the space and it was a relief that Eleanor couldn't follow her.

She went into her room and started to get dressed. She knew she should tell Felix she'd changed her mind, text him not to come around, but she couldn't bring herself to do it. Eleanor was wrong, and he was only a distraction. But it was a nice distraction all the same.

Chapter Thirty-One

Felix rang the doorbell and waited for Coco to answer. He leaned on the doorjamb, a little tired, wondering if he was being sensible planning an intense sex session while he was so busy with the case.

He'd spent the rest of Monday and most of Tuesday talking to the partners and other lawyers in the firm about Peter Dell. Unsurprisingly, Dell's colleagues had little criticism of the senior partner's behavior. No, they didn't know anything about him making advances on Sasha De Langen, or indeed any other women at the firm. No, as far as they knew he had never had an affair. Yes, sometimes he made mildly sexual jokes, but didn't everyone? No, they were unaware of any member of the firm being upset by anything Peter had ever said. In fact, he was the life and soul of the party, liked by everyone, including all the women.

He had no way of knowing whether the lawyers were covering for Dell, or whether they were telling the truth. But certainly, apart from Sasha's statement, he had no evidence as yet that Dell had behaved inappropriately to anyone in the office.

Coco opened the door, and his heart immediately lifted, so much so that he knew he'd done the right thing arranging to see her again. For a moment, she looked briefly distressed, although she brightened as she saw him, and giggled when she saw what he was wearing.

"How many layers?" He stepped back to let her out of the door and ran his gaze down her, taking in the pants and boots, the woolly hat, and the thick coat whose bulk indicated more clothing underneath.

"Um, seven, I think. I'm just glad it's not a hot day or I'd look a right dork."

He laughed and took her hand, noticing that she didn't go back inside to say goodbye to her mother. But perhaps she'd already said goodbye.

As they walked to the car, he wondered whether Sasha's case was playing on Coco's mind. He hadn't spoken to her much over the last two days, and he'd had no way to gauge what she was thinking. He'd texted her a couple of times, just a small joke or a smiley face, and she'd returned it each time, so she couldn't be that mad at him. Plus, she hadn't rung or texted to cancel their evening. Still, he noted the droop of her shoulders, the sadness in her eyes as she got into the waiting taxi, moving awkwardly with all the clothing. Perhaps it was her mother, then.

He got in and directed the taxi to the hotel, then turned to her and smiled. "Any idea what we're up to this evening?"

For the first time, humor lit her eyes. "I have a few ideas."

He grinned. "I meant which scenario."

"Oh." She giggled. "Well, I'm presuming it's the igloo one, although I have no idea what you've come up with for that. I'm guessing we're not on our way to the airport to Reykjavik though."

"Nope. I've brought Reykjavik to Wellington tonight." He smiled and took her hand again, soft in its woolen mitten. He couldn't help himself asking, "Are you okay?"

She waved the other hand, and her eyes took on a glassy sheen. "Just family stuff. Mum's driving me nuts. I nearly yelled at her tonight, and I've never done that before. I had to walk out of the room." She bit her lip and looked out of the window.

"Do you want to talk about it?"

She shook her head without turning around.

He frowned. He wasn't her boyfriend. He wasn't even her friend really, not in the confidante sense of the word. Their relationship was purely physical, and there was absolutely no reason she should confide in him or open up to him.

And yet as his gaze caressed her profile, her straight, slightly pert nose, her pale, clear skin, her long slender neck, he felt a sweep of affection for her and an urge to comfort her, to take her in his arms and make everything right.

He cleared his throat. This wouldn't do at all. He was growing soft in his old age.

He lifted her hand, slid off her glove, and raised her hand to his lips. She looked back, watching as he planted a kiss on her knuckles, then on her fingers, then turned her hand over and kissed her palm. He lowered her hand, but continued to rub his thumb across, stroking the sensitive skin inside her wrist.

"I'm glad to see you're well wrapped up, anyway," he said, deciding distraction was probably the best course of action. "It's going to be cold where we're going."

A hint of a smile touched her lips, and she ran her gaze down him. "You look good. If a little bulky."

He grinned. "You can have fun peeling the layers off later."

She met his gaze and he held it, hoping his eyes were telling her how much he was looking forward to this. Over the last two days, he'd talked and smiled and jotted down notes and puzzled over Sasha and her case, but every time he was alone, pictures of Coco had flooded his mind, and he'd had to struggle to pull himself back to reality.

The journey to his hotel took no time at all, but it was still too long, and he thrust the money into the taxi driver's hand before leading Coco through the doors of the hotel and across the foyer.

"What's the hurry?" she complained, smiling nevertheless. "You can't wait to get me naked?"

He led her to the elevators and pressed the button. "Oh, getting you naked is going to take a very long time tonight. But I can't wait to kiss you. I dreamed about it practically all night last night."

The doors slid open, and he pulled her inside, pressed the button for his floor, and then before the doors were completely shut, he pushed her up against the wall and his lips were on hers.

He hadn't been joking—he'd dreamed about her all night. And not just kissing—about the slide of his hand up her pale thigh, the softness of her nipples on his tongue, the sound of her sighs as she came, clenching around him. He grew hard just thinking about it, although there was no way she was going to notice through all the layers of clothing.

Her lips were soft, and he forced himself to kiss her slowly, wanting to make the evening last and to enjoy every minute with her. He pulled her hat from her head and threaded a hand into her hair, which felt like slippery silk ribbon in his fingers, and cupped her head while he moved his lips across hers and stroked his tongue into her mouth. She moaned and raised her arms around his neck, and he reveled in the blissful feeling of her in his arms, so welcoming, so yielding.

By the time the elevator doors slid open, he was ready to rip off her clothes and do her right there, but he just sighed, took her hand,

and led her to his door, smiling at the sight of her, with her lipstick kissed off and her hair all ruffled as she jammed her hat back onto her head.

He stopped outside, holding the door handle. "Are you ready?"

"I have absolutely no idea what to expect," she said, eyes wide.

He grinned, and opened the door. Coco stepped inside, and gasped.

He tried to look at it with fresh eyes, which was difficult as he'd spent the previous evening, some of lunch, and the past two hours working on it. He'd visited the local supermarket and asked for any spare cardboard boxes they had going, flattened them and managed to smuggle them into his room, then reassembled them. He'd moved the furniture back against the walls again, covered the carpet with a white sheet, and stuck the boxes together in the shape of an igloo in the center of the room—nowhere near as big as a real igloo, but big enough so they could get inside it. He'd covered the igloo with another white sheet and stapled it on, and he had to admit it offered a pretty good representation of the real thing. That evening, he'd plugged in his laptop and projected onto the wall a scene of a vast tundra where it was snowing heavily, and the speakers played the sound of a swirling snowstorm. He'd turned on the air conditioning to its lowest setting, and then finished the scene by adding a blue circle of paper to one side of the igloo. A large, stuffed toy seal sat solemnly staring into the fishing hole.

Coco burst out laughing. "Oh my God, Felix, you are certifiable."

"I can't believe the temperature. It's taters in here." He shut the door behind him. His breath wasn't quite frosting before his face, but the room was decidedly icy.

"Taters?"

"Sorry. That's an old one. Potatoes in the mold—cold."

She gave him a wry look and walked over to the igloo and began inspecting it while he made them a drink—a glass of mulled wine made from red wine warmed with slices of orange and lemon and cinnamon sticks. He'd left it in the saucepan on the tiny stove, and it was still warm enough to make his insides glow.

He gave her a glass, and she tasted some. "Yum," she said, and licked her lips.

"Yeah, not bad. My mum's recipe."

"I wasn't talking about the wine." Her gaze raked him, and then she giggled.

Felix grinned, put an arm around her and pulled her close. "Have I cheered you up?"

"You always cheer me up." She looked up at him, resting one hand on his chest. "I mean it."

"Thank you." He felt surprisingly pleased by her comment.

Holding her head, he kissed her, enjoying the warmth of the wine on her tongue, alcohol and excitement beginning to thread through his veins, the anticipation of the evening ahead almost too much to bear.

She raised her free arm around his neck and slid her fingers through his hair, and they kissed for a while, slowly and languorously. He could tell by the hungry way she responded to him, and the pure delight she took in it, that she'd been telling the truth when she'd said her ex hadn't enjoyed it. Felix couldn't understand it. Who didn't enjoy kissing? For a start, it was like preparing a canvas before applying the oil paints—necessary to get the best finished product.

However, foreplay was also a task he'd never considered a burden but more of a pleasurable pastime. It had become clear to him in his teens that women took a lot longer than men did to get turned on. His mates had sometimes complained about it, expressing impatience with the laborious process of arousing a girl. Felix had never understood that approach. Hell, what wasn't fun about kissing, licking, and touching? The whole process was so enjoyable, why wouldn't he want to spend as long as he could leading up to the denouement, which could easily be over in minutes, if not seconds, if the girl was really hot?

So he'd thrown himself into the task of exploring what women found satisfying as he grew in experience. He learned quickly that every girl was different. Some liked using their tongue when they kissed, others didn't. Most liked their nipples paid attention to, but occasionally one flinched, so he learned to take it slow before launching right in. He'd yet to find a woman who didn't like receiving oral sex, but not all liked to give it, and that was fine. He preferred it if they did, though.

That was one area Lindsey hadn't been so keen on. Felix didn't like to think about it because he preferred to think of her as perfect, but it was the one area on which they hadn't quite seen eye to eye.

She'd gone down on him because she loved him and she knew he enjoyed it, but he'd been able to tell that she didn't enjoy it much. She'd licked around him as if he were a melting ice lolly, but had disliked taking him far inside her mouth with an obvious fear of gagging, and on the few occasions he'd lost control and come, she'd been careful to move back out of the way. It had puzzled him at the time, because in most other ways she was very open about sex and willing to try almost anything. He knew not to take it to heart though, because other girls before and after her had reacted in a similar way—some refusing to let him come in their mouth, others relenting but then spitting quietly into a tissue afterward. He didn't complain, but he'd always felt strangely hurt afterward, as if he was somehow disgusting.

So he thought he knew how Coco felt about sex considering what her ex had been like, and it sounded as if Michael been a hell of a lot worse in general than Lindsey had been in just one aspect. He wanted to continue to prove to Coco that nothing she wanted to do was revolting or repulsive, and that where he was concerned, everything was on the table.

Including them, if she so desired.

Chapter Thirty-Two

Coco leaned back against the kitchen counter and let Felix kiss her senseless. Jeez, he was so good at it. How had she lived without this all her life? How was she going to live without it once he'd gone? No, she wasn't going to think about that. Wasn't going to think about how bereft she would be once he'd left and there were no more secret assignations to look forward to, to brighten her day.

Once the thought had entered her head, though, it was difficult to stop it, and Felix must have sensed the lapse in her passion because he lifted his head and stroked her cheek. "What's the matter?"

She shook her head and smiled. "I'm eager to get inside. You've done such a wonderful job here—you're absolutely amazing."

"Yeah. Mr. Sensational. I remember." He smiled.

She meant it—she could hardly believe it was the same room in which she'd lain on the beach and watched the ocean. For a start, it was freezing, and the snowy vista he'd projected onto the wall mysteriously added to the cold so that she really felt as if she were standing in Siberia somewhere, the wind howling the snowflakes around her. The igloo was delightful—it even had the little tunnel to protect the doorway she'd seen in photographs. And as for the stuffed toy seal...

The tears came without her prompting, and she had to blink quickly to stop them falling. Felix obviously saw them, though, because his lips curved even as a frown crossed his brow, and he put his arms around her and pulled her close. "What's up with you? This doesn't look like how Miss Stark would normally react." He kissed her forehead. "You really are two different people, aren't you?"

"She keeps her emotions very well hidden," Coco mumbled. She laid her cheek on his chest. He wore so many layers that she couldn't hear the thump of his heart, but it was comforting all the same.

He tightened his arms around her, and they stood there like that for a moment. She could almost feel the cold snowflakes touching her face—was tempted to stick out her tongue and catch them on there, let them dissolve on its warmth.

She liked him. There, she'd thought it, and the world hadn't crumbled. She liked him a lot, and she was going to miss him when he went. But that was okay. It didn't mean she should leave right now, or not see him again, or even tell him. She'd admitted it to herself, and now she could bury it deep inside her like an artifact, and maybe one day she'd be able to excavate it and look at it again, admire it like a treasure, something pretty she could keep close to her heart as she grew old and gray, alone.

"Jeez," she said out loud, "what the hell is in that wine?"

"A splash of brandy. Or two," he admitted. "Why?"

She shook her head and pulled back a little to look up at him. "I'm growing maudlin and I've only had one glass."

His face creased. "That was not the intention I had at all—it was supposed to be relaxing." He let his arms fall and took her hand. "Come on. Let's go inside—I'm sure that will cheer you up."

She didn't want him to think she wasn't having a good time, so she brightened her smile and kissed his cheek before letting him lead her across to the tunnel into the igloo. It was only one box deep and wouldn't have given much protection against the roaring wind and snow, but it looked good.

She dropped to her knees and crawled inside. Then she sat back on her heels and stared in delight.

The ceiling wasn't high, maybe a foot above her head where she was kneeling, but it was surprisingly spacious, bigger than a lot of tents. Felix had brought one of the bed mattresses into the room and built the igloo around it, and he'd covered the mattress in a couple of duvets and pillows before finally throwing a large square of faux fur over the top to give a rustic look.

To the side of the 'bed' he'd placed a tray with a bowl of Kiwi chocolate fish, and he put their glasses and a jug of the mulled wine he'd brought in with him onto it. The light from a small lamp filled the room with a warm glow, and although the cool air still made her unwilling to strip off, it felt cozier than the arctic conditions of the living room.

She burst out laughing when she saw what he'd hung from one of the walls—the large head of a toy reindeer, looking for all the world like a stuffed deer from a hunting cabin.

He pushed the duvets to one side, sat on the bed and smiled at her. "What do you think?"

She crawled over to him, pressed him onto his back and sat astride him. "I think you're marvelous, Felix Wilkinson, and I think you deserve a rather excellent shag this evening for all your hard work."

He laughed and ran his hands up her. "Well, that wasn't the only reason I did it all, but I wouldn't say no."

She leaned forward and kissed him, and felt his hand slide into her hair to cup her head. He liked to hold her firmly while he kissed her, as if afraid she might move away, but there was little chance of that happening. He kissed like a king, his lips warm and firm, moving across hers with a slowness that made her heart race and an ache begin between her thighs. His tongue brushed into her mouth, sweet with wine, and she did the same, shy at first as always, but growing with confidence as he murmured his approval.

Eventually, he caught her around the waist, turned her onto her side, and pulled her close to him, into his arms.

"So what are the rules for this evening?" she whispered, unnerved by the warmth in his brown eyes, the smell and taste and feel of him.

He leaned across and pulled the duvets over them, enclosing them in a warm, safe world full of promise and anticipation. If she lifted her head, she could see the snowflakes whizzing by through the tunnel to the outside world. It really felt as if they were thousands of miles from civilization, just the two of them, closeted in this private world. How had that happened? How had she managed to hook up with such a gorgeous man who really seemed to be into her?

He pulled her closer, moving her leg across him, and nuzzled her neck. "Well the idea was to make love fully clothed, like the Inuit supposedly do." He nibbled her earlobe, and she shivered. "That seems a shame though, when you have such a beautiful body. Why don't we say anything goes—but all clothing has to be removed and all action has to happen beneath the duvet?"

She giggled. "Okay."

"Let's start with our coats." He began to unbutton hers.

Chapter Thirty-Three

It was odd, she thought dreamily as his fingers popped the buttons through the holes, how the scenario somehow mirrored their situation—that although events and time continued to spin in a whorl around them like the snowflakes, they'd somehow managed to find time to explore each other secretly, to develop a relationship outside the office. Okay so it wasn't a relationship as such—he might have met her mother, but this was nothing more than mutual fulfilment during a time of need—but even so it amazed and delighted her that they'd found each other, that, like two comets passing through a solar system, they were briefly sharing the same space until the time came for them to move on.

He reached the bottom of her coat and started to tug it off her shoulders, so she wriggled beneath the duvet, starting to laugh as she got it halfway down her back and then got stuck.

Instead of helping her, however, his eyes gleamed, and he pushed her. She fell back and squealed, unable to move because her hands were pinned behind her.

"You're at my mercy," he said, moving above her. "Mwahaha." His hair fell across dark eyes filled with passion, and he half lay on her, squishing her with his heavy weight.

She couldn't move at all, and she realized that once again he could do whatever he wanted with her. He was the perfect gentleman ninety-five percent of the time, and yet as her eyes met his, she remembered the moment in the limo when she'd been sitting on top of him and he'd changed. At the time, it had been as if he'd flipped a switch and turned on a sexual energy that had flowed between them, following which he'd proceeded to tip her onto the floor and take her like something out of a porn movie.

Deep down, she knew that if she'd protested at any moment, he'd have stopped immediately—she trusted him implicitly, although why she wasn't sure as she hardly knew anything about him. But the thought that she really was at his mercy—that this gorgeous man wanted her and was determined to have her pretty much regardless of anything else—gave her a thrill she'd never experienced before in her life.

She waited for him to kiss her, but he didn't move, studying her face, and she wondered if he was remembering that moment in the limo too, when she'd tried to say that she wanted more—wanted every piece of him, wanted him to hold nothing back. It was more than gratification, although she knew she'd struggle to put it into words. It was about desire, which she was beginning to understand wasn't the same thing as sex at all.

Sex—in itself—was a physical thing, a process of pressing buttons with the aim of achieving an outcome—an orgasm.

But desire was so much more than that. She'd never, ever felt this longing, this absolutely craving for another human being. She hungered for him, ached to have him inside her, to pleasure him, to watch his face crease with the fierce frown of passion that gave her such a thrill. And, judging by his expression, he was feeling the same way—his eyes penetrating, burning into her as something passed between them again—a tremor like an earthquake aftershock, a frisson of excitement.

"Fuck," he said, rubbing a thumb across her cheek. "You're so beautiful."

Her chest heaved and her heart pounded, and when he finally kissed her, plunging his tongue into her mouth as his hand moved up her thigh to cup between her legs, she moaned and arched toward him, shocked and aroused by the sudden heat between them.

Suddenly things turned serious and intense. He pulled off her coat and she unbuttoned his jacket and removed that, and then they started work on the next layer. Although she was desperate to feel his naked body against hers, and clearly, he felt the same, they took their time, making the undressing part of the game, stroking and kissing each part of the other's flesh as it gradually appeared.

She dragged a sweater over his head to find a thinner one underneath and splayed her hands on his chest, stroking up across his ribs and shoulders, impressed by the firmness of his muscles beneath the cotton.

He groaned. "You're driving me crazy." He popped the button at the top of her jeans and tugged them. "I swear, Coco, if I'm not inside you in less than a minute, you're going to be sorry."

"Promises, promises," she panted, helping him push them off.

By now his hair was all ruffled and their faces were pink with the effort of getting undressed and the warmth of the bed beneath the duvet. The impatient look on his face made her giggle, and that made him stop and give her a wry glare.

"You think this is funny?" He leaned over her, supported on strong, muscular arms. "Do I amuse you?" He moved between her legs.

"Yes." She started to unbutton his jeans. "You're a constant source of entertainment for me."

He pushed her hands away and moved down her body, sliding up her sweater so he could kiss down her stomach, making it quiver. "Right, that does it." He kissed her hips and then the sensitive skin of her abdomen above her panties, and then before she could object, pulled them to one side and buried his mouth in her.

She bucked and exclaimed at the feel of his tongue sliding into her folds. "Felix!"

"Lie still," he growled, lifting momentarily to whip off her panties before nestling back between her thighs to continue his ministrations.

"I thought you wanted to be inside me," she panted, closing her eyes as his fingers joined his tongue and slid into her.

"Plenty of time for that later." He rubbed his thumb across her clit before teasing it with his tongue. "You smell too good to pass by on this opportunity."

"Oh jeez…" She lifted her arms to cover her face. He was insane. Did he really enjoy doing this? The deep murmurs of appreciation that rumbled from him occasionally would seem to suggest he did. He didn't appear to be lying there counting the seconds until she came. She bit her lip and forced herself to relax, to allow herself to enjoy it. Who knew if she'd ever have anyone go down on her again in her life? She had to make the most of it whilst it was offered.

So she let her thighs fall open and abandoned herself to his attentions, encouraged by his whispered words of approval. God, he was so good at it. How much practice had he had? How many women had he been with in his lifetime? She surprised herself by feeling a sweep of envy for the nebulous Lindsey, for whom he obviously still felt a deep love and affection. Imagine living with this man, waking up next to him, being able to play with him in bed every single night if she so chose. No, actually she couldn't imagine it. It was so far out of the realms of her experience that she couldn't even begin to comprehend how wonderful it would be.

And now her thoughts were spiraling, her mind that had previously been filled with the taste of wine, the sound of the wind howling outside the door, and the smell of Felix's aftershave as he kissed her, focusing instead on the sensations he was creating down below. Because now he was dipping his fingers inside her to gather her moisture, and then sliding them down right underneath her to her tight entrance, which he proceeded to tease with a finger.

She bit her arm to stop herself crying out as he carried on with his exploration, all the while continuing to tease her clit with his tongue. The sensations were like nothing she'd experienced before, and she couldn't believe he was doing it.

"Felix…" she whispered as her muscles began to tighten, moving a hand down to slide into his hair.

He gave a small murmur of encouragement and probed a little deeper.

The orgasm crept over her like a rising tide, slow and steady, everything tightening before beginning to pulse around his mouth and fingers, exquisite and blissful. She tightened her hand in his hair, crying out with pleasure, calling his name, feeling safe and secure, as if he was guiding her there.

He lifted himself up and moved over her, and before she could stop him, kissed her thoroughly, dipping his tongue into her mouth.

"Yuck," she said when he finally drew back. "Thanks."

He chuckled and lifted her remaining sweater. "Get this off."

She grumbled and drew it over her head, and then he quickly unbuttoned her shirt and whipped that off too. Her bra followed with little more ceremony, and soon she was naked in his arms, acutely conscious that he was still pretty much fully dressed.

"My turn." She started to pull up his sweater.

"No time." He rolled her onto her side away from him, and then she heard the distinct sound of a condom being unwrapped.

"You're eager," she said, feeling drowsy and relaxed, as if she'd had all her bones removed after her climax.

"Honey, you're so wet and swollen down there, if I don't get inside you soon I'll end up embarrassing myself." He moved up close to her back and drew her into his arms, pulling the duvet and the fur blanket over them to keep her warm.

In spite of his words, he still took a while to arouse her again, stroking her breasts and playing with her nipples, kissing her neck and ear and murmuring endearments and compliments that made her sigh as she lay hazy with passion and affection for this kind, hot, sexy man. The fact that he was fully clothed and she was naked only seemed to add to her pleasure—he made everything feel so wicked, and that it was all right to be wicked—that it was part of the pleasure of sex.

How bland it had all been before, she thought as she turned her head to capture his lips briefly. Sex with Michael had been what the word vanilla was invented for—it was okay once or twice, but after a while you craved a dessert with a bit of flavor, with chocolate, cream, biscuits, and liqueur poured all over it. Felix was so... so... *tiramisu*.

He moved his hand down to between her legs and stroked her, then groaned. "That's it. Time's up. You're so fucking wet—I've got to get inside you."

"Charming," she mumbled, unwilling to admit his words turned her on. How did the mechanics of it work in this position? She wasn't sure what to do.

But she didn't have to worry. "Come here." He rolled her almost onto her back, moved her butt on his lap, and hooked her leg across him. Then he pressed the tip of his erection beneath her folds, and slowly slid into her.

She gasped as his long, hard length filled her up, sliding easily into her moistness. "Oh..."

"Yeah," he said vehemently, stroking up her bare thigh and cupping her mound. "Oh yeah."

She lay back and closed her eyes for a moment, just enjoying the new position and how different it felt with him inside her in this way. He moved his hips so he slid in and out of her, and she sighed, stretching like a cat.

"You have such a beautiful body." Beneath the covers, he stroked up from her thighs to her breasts and began to play with them, thrusting all the while.

Conscious of him clothed beneath the duvet, she opened her eyes and smiled shyly. "Thank you."

"I mean it." He propped his head on a hand and surveyed her leisurely, admiring her breasts, stroking down to her hips and back up again. "You're slender but not too thin. Curvy. Fantastic breasts. You have the best figure of any woman I've seen in real life." He rolled her nipple between his fingers.

She didn't know what to say to that compliment. Better than Lindsey? Surely he was just being kind because they were in bed—it was the sort of thing lovers said to each other, even if it wasn't true. But still, it made her glow. He didn't have to say it.

"Thank you," she said again, not surprised to hear her voice breathless with desire. "Quite clearly you're the sexiest man in the universe."

He smiled. "Well, thank you too."

"I mean it." She reached up a hand and touched his hair. "You're so hot. You set me alight."

"I noticed." His voice was filled with humor.

"I love making love with you," she whispered, biting her lip as he dropped his hand back between her legs.

"And I love fucking you."

She gave a little laugh. "Nice. How gentlemanly."

"And you love it." He slid in and out of her.

She looked away, embarrassed. Was it a bad thing, to be so turned on by his shocking statements, by the things he liked to do?

He shifted, and before she could prepare herself, he rolled her onto her front, still inside her, and lay on top of her, pinning her to the bed.

"Still shy?" he teased, nibbling her neck. "Even after what we've done?"

She said nothing, all the air having fled her lungs, turned on more than she could say by his sheer masculinity, his height, his weight, the scrape of his bristles on her soft skin. She'd pay for that tomorrow, but for now it just made her moan and turn her head so he could brush his tongue into her mouth.

He raised his head and thrust his hips forward, burying himself inside her, and she gasped. "Why did you change position?" she asked, shocked once again by his change from gentle, considerate lover to animal in heat.

"Not fast enough." He thrust again. "Why, is that a complaint?"

"N-no." She groaned, aroused once again by the feeling of being at his mercy. "Oh…"

"Is that nice, Coco?" He bit her ear and she squealed. "Tell me."

"Yes, it's nice." Understatement of the year.

"Say, 'Felix, I like being fucked from behind. It turns me on.'" He slid a hand beneath her and rolled her nipple.

She gasped. "No!"

"Say it." He thrust harder.

She moaned, her orgasm hovering but not quite overtaking her. "Felix…"

"Say it."

"I… I like being fucked from behind." Her cheeks burned.

"'It turns me on.'"

"It… it turns me on."

He kissed her cheek and murmured, "You're a perfect woman, you know that? A Madonna out of the bedroom. A whore inside it."

"Felix!"

"It's a compliment."

"It doesn't sound it." Nevertheless, she automatically widened her legs, pushing back, and lifting her hips as he continued to thrust. Perhaps he was right.

"Say it." His breathing sounded harsh in her ear—he wasn't far from coming.

"No."

He kissed down her neck and then sucked hard where it met her shoulder, and she squealed. "You'll give me a hickey!"

"I'm branding you." He lifted her chin and kissed her deeply, demanding, forceful. "You think you're innocent deep down, but you're not. You love it, don't you? Love being naughty—love your limits being pushed."

"No."

"Liar." He was breathing heavily now. "Christ, Coco, the things we could do together, if we had the time."

"There's more?" She panted, things starting to throb and tighten.

He gave a deep laugh, lifting himself up so he could thrust hard and fast. "You have no idea."

She pushed back against him as her climax swept over her, carried away on a wave of lust and longing, and pulsed around him as he finally swelled and came inside her with a triumphant roar. He continued to thrust, and her orgasm seemed to go on forever, until, finally spent, she lay limp and exhausted, in a hazy swirl of physical and emotional sensations that continued to float around and over her like the snowflakes still falling in a flurry outside.

Chapter Thirty-Four

Felix stood in the doorway to Miss Stark's office and leaned against the doorjamb. The office manager had been busy most of the morning—he'd seen her flitting around the workroom, organizing the secretaries, bossing Sam and checking her shorthand, sorting stationery and printers, and having a meeting with finance about stationery budgets, and this was the first time he'd found her in her office.

Had she been avoiding him, or was she genuinely busy? Possibly a bit of both, he thought, watching her frown as she studied a report, underlining occasionally with a pencil. She obviously had a lot to do, but equally, he was sure she'd purposely managed to be the opposite end of the office to wherever he was.

He folded his arms and studied her. Her embarrassment amused and fascinated him. As Miss Stark, she emanated such confidence and calm organization—he couldn't imagine the cool, efficient secretary ever being embarrassed or ruffled. But he knew that beneath the surface lay a completely different person—a warm-hearted, passionate woman who was thoroughly enjoying discovering the delights of sex that he was able to show her, and who had reacted to his encouraging advances with abandonment and pure joy at discovering what she hadn't realized she'd been missing for so long.

She rested the pencil on her lips and nibbled the end. He smiled, surprised by the wave of affection that swept over him. He was rarely short of female company, and he'd been out with several women for a lot longer than he'd been seeing Coco. But she'd touched his heart as no other woman since Lindsey had been able to. Why was that? Yes, she was pretty—beautiful in fact, stunning with her blonde hair, red lips, and curvy figure. She was intelligent, which he liked in a woman—well able to challenge him on all sorts of matters from the law to human rights to the best Disney film. She had a good sense of humor, she was witty and sharp, she worked hard, and she obviously cared deeply for her mother.

But it was more than that. She had an indefinable something—he couldn't put his finger on it, but there was something about her that fascinated him in a similar way to how Lindsey had fascinated him. It wasn't just the way she enjoyed exploring sex so much, or the way she responded so openly.

It was the way she looked at him—the way Lindsey had looked at him. Women often looked at him with interest, eyed him up, flirted with him. But Coco looked at him not just with desire, but with affection, with admiration—not in a place-him-on-a-pedestal kind of way, but with a deep rooted, grown-up, adult appreciation for the person he was.

Shit. His heart nearly stopped. He'd only fucking gone and fallen in love with her.

At that precise moment, she looked up and saw him standing there. He watched her inhale, her eyes widen, her cheeks flush, all within seconds. She stood, flustered for a moment before she gathered her wits and got back into control, and she lifted her chin and gave him her best Miss Stark stare. But it had been there, he was sure—visible briefly like a shooting star—highlighting and reflecting the emotion he felt deep inside but had only just acknowledged.

She felt the same way about him. He was sure of it.

Did she know?

"Hurry up," she said. "I haven't got all day."

He pushed the thought away, filing it to think about later. "Morning. You're one difficult lady to catch."

"Yes, well, I have a busy schedule." She fumbled with some papers on her desk.

He smiled and pushed himself off the wall to walk toward her. "I wanted to ask you a favor?"

"Oh?" She turned startled green eyes up to him.

He grinned. "Not that kind of favor."

She blinked, and for a moment he found himself lost in memories of the night before—the way her hair had curled around his fingers as he'd slid his hand into it to turn her head to kiss her, the feel of her naked beneath him while he'd still been fully clothed, the way she'd looked up at him as he'd thrust inside her, her eyes filled with… what? Lust? Or love?

MR. SENSATIONAL

He blinked back and cleared his throat. "I've finished interviewing the lawyers, and I'd like to speak to Sasha again. I've rung her and told her I'll be visiting her at home today at two. I wondered whether you'd come with me? I think she'd rather have you there."

"Um, yes. Of course. If you think it would help."

"Thank you."

Their eyes met. He held her gaze for a moment, and then she turned to look out of the window. As usual, she'd pulled her hair back off her face into a tight bun, and the starkness of the style accentuated her high cheekbones and her long neck, as well as her flawless pale skin. He knew others thought her cold and haughty, and it thrilled him that he was the only one to know that a deeply passionate creature existed beneath the frosty exterior.

He wanted to leap over the desk and take her in his arms, kiss down that neck to her breasts, rip off her clothes, and make love to her until they both came in a rush of blissful ecstasy.

He didn't, though. He cleared his throat and said, "Okay, so I'll call by after lunch and we'll take a taxi."

"Sure."

He turned and walked out of the room before he did something stupid like getting down on one knee and declaring his feelings. Yes, she looked at him with affection and desire. But how was he to know whether it was purely a physical thing or whether she just thought of him as a vibrator on legs?

*

Felix called in to her office at two o'clock, and they went down to the taxi together. They sat in the back, and he directed the driver to Sasha's house.

Coco sat silently, looking out of the window, but Felix felt her presence with every cell in his body, and he sensed from her rigid posture, the way her chest rose and fell rapidly and the fast pulse in her throat that she was as conscious as he of the tension between them that refused to go.

He ran his gaze up her, from her slender knees just revealed by the short skirt that had risen as she'd sat, to her narrow waist and generous bust, to the strand of blonde hair that had escaped the bun and curled on her cheek. Unable to stop himself, he reached out, picked it up and tucked it behind her ear. She jumped a little at his touch, and then, surprising him, leaned her cheek briefly on his hand before turning once again to look out of the window. It was a tiny, insignificant gesture, but it warmed his heart to think there was even a slight possibility that she felt the same way he did.

The taxi pulled up at Sasha's house on the outskirts of Wellington, and they got out. The house had a pleasant view, situated high on the steep slopes surrounding the city looking down on the harbor, the late-spring sun warm on his face. He asked the driver to wait, certain they weren't going to be that long, judging by Sasha's hostility during their previous meeting.

She answered the door, and to his relief gave a brief smile before standing back to let them in. They walked into a hallway leading to a smallish living room, decorated in shades of cream and brown, as bland as Sasha's personality. There were no CDs on show, no books on the shelves. He'd hoped to garner an idea of her personality from her surroundings, but he was going to be disappointed.

Sasha sat in an armchair, and Felix and Coco took a seat on the sofa opposite her. A cat jumped onto Sasha's lap and settled, and she began to stroke it. She didn't offer them a drink.

"I'd like to start by apologizing for upsetting you during our previous meeting," Felix said, hoping he sounded sincere. "I let my wish to make sure I uncover the truth override my need to be polite, and I apologize for that."

Sasha nodded, but didn't respond the way he'd expected—with a social nicety by saying something like *oh, that's okay, I understand*, or *I'm just glad you're trying to find the truth*. It unsettled him, and he leaned back on the sofa and studied her for a moment, trying to puzzle her out, determined not to let her get the upper hand in the conversation.

He couldn't shake the feeling of dislike he had for her, although he still didn't have any idea why he felt that way. Maybe it was because she seemed so hard, or that she responded with such little humor. He relied on his charm to communicate with women, but she appeared to be immune to it, and that didn't happen very often.

The other problem was that he was struggling to understand her and the way she thought. He could understand why she felt his previous comment about wearing clothes to attract attention had been insulting, especially if she hadn't been trying to attract Dell's attention. But he felt angry at Sasha's indignation that her right to wear whatever she wanted to work was completely irrelevant to the case. Her feminist leanings, while understandable and even commendable, seemed to be obscuring the greater problem here—namely, had she led Dell on or not?

Coco sat quietly next to him, hands folded in her lap. He couldn't help but notice again that although her skirt rode up slightly when she sat, it was a decent length, and she'd buttoned her blouse so no cleavage was on show. He liked her modesty. Did that make him old fashioned and sexist?

"I'd like to clarify a couple of things," he said, trying not to spiral off into thoughts about her when he was trying to concentrate on Sasha. "Firstly, you stated that on the evening in question Peter Dell came into the workroom and asked you specifically if you could work late?"

"What of it?" she said.

"I haven't interviewed the other secretaries formally yet, but one of the partners recalls that he was in the workroom when Mr. Dell entered. He says Mr. Dell asked the office generally if anyone was able to work late, and that you volunteered."

Sasha didn't flinch but looked him calmly in the eye. "It's possible that was the case. I don't really remember."

"It's quite important, Sasha."

"It's hardly the point," she snapped. "What matters is what happened in his office, not how I got there."

Felix held her gaze and refused to look away. The point was, of course, if she'd lied about what Dell had said, what else had she lied about?

Chapter Thirty-Five

Coco shifted awkwardly on the sofa as Felix and Sasha continued their staring match. She could feel Felix's irritation—at both himself and Sasha—rolling off him in waves.

She puzzled over his behavior as Sasha finally dropped her gaze to the cat in her lap and spoke to it softly. He must be used to belligerent witnesses in court all the time—he must have dealt with this sort of situation before. She knew part of the problem was that Sasha hadn't responded to his attempts at being nice, had pretty much thrown them back in his face. But she could also see that deep down, Sasha's attitude angered him, and part of that, Coco was sure, was her fault. It was all interlinked with this issue of attracting the opposite sex, and the confusion in reading signals. Felix was projecting his own frustration with their relationship onto this situation with Sasha, and Coco wasn't sure he was aware of it.

Even though Sasha had dropped her gaze, Felix continued to stare at her, but his hard look softened, and he frowned as if trying to puzzle her out. He wasn't unsympathetic toward her, Coco decided, just confused, and frustrated that the other woman didn't understand his position. Sasha was angry that he wouldn't accept her word as evidence—she couldn't comprehend his need for proof.

His gaze slid across to Coco, and for a moment they studied each other. She'd seen the look on his face when he'd appeared in her office, when she'd suddenly looked up and caught him watching her. He had feelings for her. Clearly, though, he wasn't sure whether she returned them.

She kept her expression carefully blank, not wanting to give him encouragement. Because what would be the point in saying *Yes, Felix, absolutely I do return your feelings—I'm crazy about you and the thought of you returning to Auckland and never seeing you again is going to break my heart?* Why put them both through that? He had a life in Auckland, she had one here, with her mother and her job, and a relationship wasn't going to work, so why voice how she felt? It would be like declaring to a diabetic that she'd baked a wonderful treacle tart.

He moved his gaze back to Sasha. "So you can't remember whether Mr. Dell asked all the secretaries whether they were busy, or whether he asked you specifically?"

"No." Sasha kept her gaze on the cat.

He nodded and thought for a moment. "Something else I'd like to query is related to the document you stated that Mr. Dell asked you to retype."

"Yes."

"You said that the office had already received a typed copy of the call logs relating to the case."

"Yes."

"And that you found it strange that Mr. Dell had asked you to retype it."

"Yes."

He tipped his head. "I asked Miss Stark to find the original file for me, and she couldn't locate it."

Sasha looked up and her gaze met Coco's. Coco's heart sped up, but she forced herself to stay calm. Yes, although they hadn't spoken about it directly, Sasha had obviously hoped that Coco would support her in this case. But Coco wasn't prepared to lie for her.

Sasha's eyes narrowed as she looked back at Felix. "Then someone's deleted it."

Felix frowned. "Deleted it?"

"To frame me." Twin spots of color appeared on Sasha's cheeks. "To make it look as if I'm lying."

Felix took a deep breath and let it out slowly. "Sasha, I find it extremely farfetched to think that someone would go to all that trouble to frame you."

"Really?" She glared at them. "You yourself told me that a man's career is at stake here. As is mine, I have to point out. But don't you think it's at all possible that Peter Dell could stretch to deleting a file to cover himself? I know perfectly well what a negative outcome to this case would mean for him. It could destroy his career, and rightly so. And he would be aware of that. If I'm right, and if he's at fault, do you not think he'd try to cover his tracks?"

Felix ran a hand through his hair, which Coco was beginning to realize meant he was agitated. Sasha unsettled him, and he didn't like it. "Well, those are the two main points I wanted to address with you," he said, moving to the edge of the settee. "Thank you for your time."

Sasha stared at him. Obviously sensing an emotion he didn't like, the cat jumped off her lap. "Is that it?" she said. "You come to my house, throw two accusations at me, basically call me a liar and then just leave?"

Although he barely moved, Coco felt him stiffen. He narrowed his eyes. "Miss De Langen, it is my job to investigate this matter, and you are not helping your case by being so hostile."

Sasha jumped to her feet, her eyes glassy. "This is just so unfair. I've practically been assaulted and just because I got some details wrong, you think I'm a liar."

"That's not the case at all," he said softly, as if calming a rabbit that had been scared by a loud noise, "and you really need to stop treating me like I'm the enemy."

"I know you're only here to prove Peter Dell's innocent," she yelled. "To twist the truth. You're a company man—Mr. McAllister would have told you how important it is to prove Peter didn't do it."

"I'm a lawyer," Felix said steadily. "To be honest, I find it insulting that you would assume I'd do anything other than search for the truth."

Her lip trembled. "I wasn't going to tell you this because I'm a private woman, Mr. Wilkinson, and I don't like everyone knowing about my love life. But do you want to know the reason that I know there's no way I could possibly have led Peter on? Why I wouldn't have been sending out the wrong signals?"

Felix frowned in response.

Sasha bit her lip. "Because I'm gay." Then she burst into tears.

*

Coco sat mutely next to Felix in the taxi as it wove its way through the Wellington afternoon traffic. He hadn't said a word since they'd left Sasha's house, following an awkward five minutes in which Sasha had sobbed, Coco had attempted to comfort her, and Sasha had promptly asked them both to leave.

What was Felix thinking? He sat looking out of the window, his elbow resting on the sill, his fingers touching his lips. His gaze seemed lost in the distance.

Had he been convinced Sasha was lying up until her revelation? Because clearly, she wasn't. Felix must now be convinced that Peter Dell's assurance that Sasha had approached him and declared her affection for him must be wrong.

Had Christopher McAllister told him to make sure that Peter was found innocent? Coco found it hard to believe, but it wasn't beyond the realms of possibility. She liked Christopher, but he hadn't gotten where he was by being a soft touch, and he wouldn't want the company he'd spent years building to crumble over what he might have thought was one stupid mistake by his co-founder. Also, it was entirely possible that Christopher wasn't aware of Peter's continual indiscretions, and that he thought the incident with Sasha was a one-off.

She risked another glance at Felix. He didn't seem like the sort of man who would do what he was told by his superiors and ignore the truth of a case. She couldn't imagine that he ignored the facts in the courtroom just because it would win him a trial.

The taxi pulled up just down from their building, but for a moment Felix sat listlessly, not making a move to get out. A wave of pity swept over her. He was a good man who'd been unravelled by the strange, socially awkward Sasha, who'd accused him of being sexist, something he would obviously never normally consider himself at all.

She reached across and took his hand. "Would you like to go grab a coffee?"

He looked across at her then, surprise lighting his features, and a smile curved a corner of his mouth. "Sure."

He paid the driver, getting a receipt for expenses, and they exited the taxi and walked across to *Bella's*. They took a seat, ordered a latte each in a mug, and then sat looking at each other.

Coco studied his calm brown eyes, wondering what he was thinking. He must be spectacular in court, she thought. He had the sort of personality that would win juries over with the least amount of effort. Plus he looked hot as sin in his slate-gray suit, white shirt, and silvery-gray tie with a faint red stripe. His dark hair looked just the right amount of ruffled, and he wore an expensive-looking tie pin and cufflinks. He exuded taste, style, and sex.

"What made you want to be a lawyer?" she asked, trying not to think about sex.

He looked down and played with the sugar container for a few seconds before looking back up at her. He seemed embarrassed.

"I... ah... was a miscreant in my youth," he said.

She laughed. "You?"

His lips twisted wryly. "I wasn't always this perfect."

"Really?" She smiled.

He played with the sugar again and sighed. "When I was at school, I got in with the wrong crowd. My older brother, Matt, was the perfect student, and my younger brother, Toby, was the cool one. I didn't know where I fitted. I rebelled and bunked lessons, played up in class. Most of the boys I was mates with were the same as me, restless, typical teenagers, looking for fun and fed up with school. But a couple who were friends of friends were nasty pieces of work."

He sat back as the waitress delivered their coffees, then took a sip from the mug before he continued. "One evening I had a cold and didn't feel like going out, so the guys went out without me. They were messing around on the school grounds. An old guy and his dog passed them, and the boys started taunting him. They threw things at the dog, and one of the objects hit the old guy. He walked over and gave them a mouthful. The rest of them would have run off, but one of the nastier boys stood up to him and started pushing him around."

Coco stared, horrified. "Oh jeez."

"It gets worse. They beat him badly. And the worst thing was that afterward, he went to the police, but he couldn't identify the boy who beat him, and the others covered for him. A bunch of the kids were taken to court, but the main guy was the son of one of the board governors, and he paid for an expensive lawyer who got them all off. I changed after that. I couldn't bear to be near those kids. I threw myself into my schoolwork and turned things around. I hated that lawyer, for defending those kids who he knew must be guilty. I was determined to be the opposite—to fight for the innocent. And I've been fighting ever since."

Chapter Thirty-Six

Coco smiled. "That explains a lot," she said. He shrugged. She stirred her coffee and took a sip. "So you've never defended someone in court you're sure is guilty?"

"I'm a family lawyer, not a defense lawyer."

"Don't be picky—you know what I'm saying. You stand up in court and defend your clients. Are they ever guilty?"

He took a long breath and let it out slowly. "The defense lawyer doesn't make a case. The prosecutor makes cases. The role of a defense lawyer is to sow doubt."

"That doesn't answer my question."

He shifted in his seat. "If defense lawyers only defend people they think are innocent, then they're substituting their own judgment for that of the judge and jury."

"That still doesn't answer my question."

"Coco..."

"A yes or no will suffice." She didn't want to make him squirm, but suddenly it was important for her to know.

He leaned forward. "Ideally, the answer would be that yes, I have defended someone I knew to be guilty. Like I said, the defense lawyer shouldn't make decisions of guilt or innocence, but rather assist the judge and jury in making that determination. However, you're asking what does a lawyer do when asked to defend, say, a rapist who has already committed an offence in the past and who is almost certainly guilty? Or especially who admits his guilt to his lawyer? The law demands he have a defense, but it must be down to each individual lawyer to say whether he or she can stand up in court and defend that man, knowing him to be guilty."

Coco took his hand. "And what would your decision be?"

He looked into his mug. "I couldn't do it."

Suddenly she understood—he was ashamed of his answer. In spite of what had happened in his youth, he wanted to be professional— the sort of lawyer who believed that the job was separate from the powers of light and dark, the kind who fought for their client, even if the client privately admitted he or she was guilty. But poor kindhearted Felix was too ethical, too honorable to do that. He really was a defender of the innocent, a knight in shining armor, whose principles and integrity meant he had to believe in the person standing before him, who threw his heart into every case, and that was why he was having such trouble with this one.

He was an optimist and a romantic, and Coco loved him for it.

Shit. Loved him?

Felix raised his eyes and looked into hers. She was too shocked at her revelation to do anything but stare at him.

She couldn't possibly love him. She'd known him less than a week. It didn't make sense. She wasn't in love, she was in lust. They'd purposely settled on a physical relationship because they didn't have the time for an emotional one. Sure, they'd been attracted to each other from the beginning, but he was in Wellington temporarily, and he obviously wouldn't want anything more than a brief fling.

He looked at her with tender affection, a smile gradually spreading over his face as she continued to study him. His hand was warm beneath hers, and his eyes were warm.

"Meet me again tonight," he said.

She released a slow breath. "I can't. Frances is visiting her daughter and I don't have anyone to look after Mum."

"Then tomorrow." His eyes twinkled. "I'll work on exotic fantasy number four."

I shouldn't. I mustn't.

"Okay." Jeez, she was weak.

He reached across the table, slipped a hand behind her head, and leaned forward, pulling her toward him. Their lips met briefly in a sweet kiss before they parted to sit back in their seats.

"What was that for?" she asked, amused.

His fingers stroked hers where they lay next to their coffee mugs. "I can't stop thinking about you. I miss you when I'm not near you."

She caught her breath. "Felix…"

"I know." He looked down at her left hand, his fingers stroking hers. He brushed lightly over her empty ring finger, lingering for a moment. Or was it her imagination?

"We have to be careful," she said softly.

"I know—it's so difficult working together."

That wasn't what she'd meant, but she decided not to correct him. "Exactly. Especially with the nature of the case. I can't imagine what Dell would say if he knew about us."

Felix shifted in his seat. "I know."

"Or Sasha, for that matter."

His wry look told her he knew exactly what she meant. "I did not expect her little revelation," he said, withdrawing his hand to lift the mug and take a mouthful of his coffee.

"Me neither." She sat back, relieved and disappointed at the same time at the turn of the conversation. "I guess it simplifies things for you, though?"

"Maybe." His face went carefully blank, and he looked out of the window.

She puzzled over that. Surely it was an open and shut case now? How could Peter possibly be in the right if he'd declared Sasha had been the one who'd made the move on him, when in fact she was gay? Coco couldn't believe that Sasha was the one at fault. It just didn't make sense.

She wanted to ask him what he thought about the case, but that wasn't fair, not when she was a witness. Still, she wished she could talk to him about it. It would be interesting to see what he really thought of Peter Dell and the whole situation.

"So what's your next step?" she asked.

"I need to talk to the other secretaries. Establish whether they picked up anything strange about Sasha's behavior, and of course whether Dell has ever acted inappropriately to them as well. I'd like you there, if possible—I think a woman needs to be present during the interviews."

"Yes, of course."

He cleared his throat. "I need to interview you, too."

She'd expected that. "I know."

"I'm sorry."

"It's all right—of course you have to. I'm the office manager."

Clearly, though, it made him uneasy. He played with the sugar container again. "I may have to ask some... searching questions. It may make you feel awkward. But I want you to know it's purely professional."

"I understand."

He raised his gaze to hers then and looked pained. "I don't want to upset you."

"Felix, it's okay. I don't have anything to hide." Guilt swept over her. Only a secret that would put the record straight and solve the entire case for him once and for all. But she was going to pretend that had never happened. It didn't matter anyway—Dell was hardly innocent, and he'd sign his own death warrant by the end of Felix's investigation. She was sure of that.

"What?" he said, obviously picking up on her unease.

"Nothing."

He frowned. "Is something bothering you about Dell?"

She hesitated for a moment, wishing she could confide in him. She'd never told anybody about what had happened to her when she was seventeen, not her mother, not a counsellor or doctor, certainly not Michael. She'd pretended she was a virgin when she first slept with Michael, and he'd believed her.

But she couldn't confide in Felix, because she knew he wouldn't understand why she'd given in to Peter, nor why she'd kept it to herself. He'd see it as a weakness, and she didn't want him to think she was weak.

She shrugged. "The whole case makes me uneasy. Peter's my boss—he represents the firm I've worked at for ten years. It's very unsettling."

"I understand." He picked up her hand again. "You know you can tell me anything, right?"

He knew she was hiding something. She reminded herself that he was a skilled lawyer. They often had a strange sixth sense regarding whether a witness was telling the truth, and something she'd said—or done—had made him suspicious. But she had to remember that even though they were sleeping together, and they'd done the most intimate things a man and woman could do with each other, she didn't know him. Her gut instinct told her she could trust him, but she couldn't be a hundred percent certain he wasn't trying to use her.

"I'm not," he said.

She blinked. "Pardon?"

"Using you for information."

It so mirrored what she was thinking that her jaw dropped.

"I wouldn't do that," he said. Was that hurt flickering in his eyes?

She looked into her mug. "I didn't mean to imply you were. It's just... I don't really know you. I hardly know anything about you."

He sighed. "I know."

"I want to trust you, especially after what we've shared." She could feel her cheeks reddening, and looked up to see the beginnings of a smile curving his lips. "But we've gone about this all wrong, working together and having a relationship. It's not surprising we're both wary."

"I guess." He reached out and took her hand again. "I wish it had happened differently. I wish we could have met without the shadow of McAllister Dell hanging over us."

"Yeah." But it was pointless to discuss it, wasn't it? She couldn't unravel the past, wave a wand, and make the case disappear, turn back the years to before she turned seventeen, before she met Peter and he met Lindsey, and make her and Felix each other's first love. Life didn't happen like that. She just had to play the hand she'd been dealt and live with the consequences of the decisions she'd made.

She sat back, suddenly depressed about the whole situation. Why couldn't things have been different?

"Okay, so we'll say Friday for your interview," he said.

She shrugged. "Sure."

"I have something else to ask you." His gaze softened and took on a mischievous look.

"Oh?"

"Friday is actually my birthday."

"Oh!" She smiled.

"Yeah. I had a call this morning from a good friend of mine, Jean."

Coco's heart missed a beat. A female friend?

"He's coming to Wellington on Friday," Felix continued.

Now she was confused. "Sorry, he?"

Felix stared, then grinned. "Ah. That's G-e-n-e, not J-e-a-n."

"Oh." Relief swept over her. "I see."

"Yeah, he gets that all the time. Anyway, he'll be here Friday with his girlfriend, and he's organized for my brother, Toby, and his wife to be here, and also you remember me saying I was friends with Faith Hillman and Rusty?"

"The Seven Sexy Sins couple?"

"Yes—they're going to be here too. We're going to meet up for dinner and..." A smile curved his lips. "I wondered whether you'd like to come along?"

She frowned. "Do they know about me?"

He looked shifty. "Maybe."

"How on earth have you described me?"

"Blonde," he said, and grinned.

She glared at him. "You know what I mean. How have you described our...?" She tried to think of a word and failed.

"I haven't." He smiled. "I said there's a girl I might bring along."

"And now they're curious," she said, reading between the lines.

"Sort of."

She couldn't squash the little thrill that rose in her at the thought that he wanted her to meet his friends and family. It probably wasn't sensible, but she might as well make the most of his time in Wellington until he had to go. "Okay, I'll come."

"Good." He ran a hand through his hair. He'd been nervous about asking her. *Aw.*

"We'd better get back," she said to cover her shyness.

"I suppose." He finished off his coffee, and they stood and left.

They walked across to the building. He hesitated outside, and she turned to face him.

"Thanks," he said, although for what she wasn't sure. For not resenting the fact that he had to interview her? Or for agreeing to go out with him?

"You're welcome."

"I'm looking forward to tomorrow night." His warm brown eyes caressed her, the sudden, hungry desire in them taking her breath away.

"You only had me last night," she scolded, bold under his hot gaze.

"It wasn't enough."

They stared at each other for a moment. Longing and regret, desire and wistfulness for more twisted inside her so that for a moment she could barely swallow.

Without another word, she turned and walked into the building.

Chapter Thirty-Seven

Felix spent the rest of Wednesday and most of Thursday interviewing the secretarial staff. The majority of the time, Coco sat with him and Rob, introducing the secretaries to Felix when they came in, putting them at ease and taking notes as the interviews progressed.

Felix began by informing them that although their statements would be kept within the circle of partners at the firm, he could not guarantee to keep them confidential if they contained information important to the case. He asked whether they were aware of the situation between Sasha and Peter Dell—had they been in the office when it happened or had they already gone home? He asked what Sasha's behavior had been like the few days after—had she seemed upset, stressed, or angry? Had she talked to any of them about what had happened? He questioned them about Sasha's conduct in general—what did they think of her as a person, did they like her? What did they know about her social life? And then he asked them about Dell—did the senior partner flirt with them? Had he ever made advances—acceptable or unacceptable—toward them? Did they believe Sasha's claim was true?

Time and again, the answers came back the same. All but one of the secretaries had gone home by the time the incident was alleged to have occurred on the day in question. Sasha's behavior had not really changed following the incident—she was always sullen and kept herself to herself, and she'd been much the same afterward, perhaps a little moodier. None of Sasha's colleagues knew anything of note about her. They knew she lived just out of town, that she was single, that she had a cat. Not one mentioned she was gay, and Felix didn't ask, feeling it wasn't his place to break her confidence. None of them really liked her, although they couldn't put a finger on why—just that she refused to join in, even though they asked her out with them, and that she made no effort to be friends, choosing to eat her lunch in solitude, her head stuck in a book and discouraging any attempt at conversation.

The one secretary who'd stayed late the night of the alleged incident stated that she caught a glimpse of Sasha in the elevator. The secretary had been walking toward her and asked Sasha to hold the doors, but Sasha had let them shut, even though she'd clearly seen and heard the other secretary. Sasha had been crying, the secretary said, and her cheeks had been red, but that was all she could remember.

Their answers had been frustratingly unhelpful, and left him as much in the dark about Sasha as when he started.

His questions regarding Dell, however, proved more entertaining. Two of the fifteen secretaries he interviewed admitted to having had an affair with Dell in the past. And Felix was sure at least another two had as well, although they were too nervous to say so, perhaps for fear of losing their jobs. Most of the other secretaries knew of at least one person who Dell had had an affair with.

The two who'd admitted it had similar stories. Dell had flirted with them, flattered them, persisted with his attentions until—certain he was crazy about them—they gave in and slept with him. The affairs lasted several weeks before Dell lost interest and moved on. Both women had looked hurt by his callous disregard of them, but they explained that because they'd entered into the relationship willingly, they felt there was nothing they could do. He was a philandering pig, one said, and there was no cure for that.

By the end of the interviews on Thursday, Felix felt no closer to finding an answer than he had the moment he arrived. Dell was clearly a womanizer who saw nothing wrong in having affairs with the women he worked with. But to be fair to the guy, if Sasha was removed from the equation, there was nothing legally wrong with his behavior. Certainly, all the other women he'd seduced appeared to have welcomed his advances, and there'd been no question of rape so far. Although he would probably have used his position of authority to impress women, it didn't sound as if he'd used it to blackmail them into affairs by threatening their jobs if they didn't—again, discounting Sasha's accusations.

No, the reason Felix disliked Dell was based not on legal but on moral objections. The man had cheated numerous times on the woman he'd promised to love, "forsaking all others". That, together with his apparent assumption that the secretarial staff were there for his personal entertainment, revolted Felix and made him want to punch Dell's teeth down his throat. But equally, if Dell asked the women out and the women said yes knowing perfectly well he was married and had had other affairs, who was Felix to cast Dell as the bad guy in this case? And, most importantly, just because Dell had slept with God knew how many other women, that didn't necessarily mean he'd made unwanted advances to Sasha. Perhaps she had been the one to initiate it, and he'd turned her down because it was the chase that turned him on and she'd been too pushy. Hell hath no fury, and all that.

After the final secretary left, Rob went out to get a coffee, and Felix rose and stood by the window, looking down at the harbor with his hands behind his back, conscious of Coco watching him. He felt uneasy about the whole case, finding the women's stories a little too close to his own situation for his liking. After all, wasn't that what he and Coco were doing? They'd found each other mutually attractive and had come together for some hot sex. They both knew it could only be temporary, and even though he liked to think they'd talked a lot more than Dell and his conquests, they didn't really know much about each other at all. Could he be a hundred percent certain that she hadn't slept with half the men in the office? He was sure that wasn't the case, but he couldn't be certain. She'd jumped into bed with him pretty quickly, after all.

She'd been very quiet during the interviews, ramrod straight in her chair, her posture almost disapproving, and for the first time he wondered whether maybe she'd had an affair with Dell. He couldn't understand it, but the senior partner obviously held a strange fascination for women. Had she succumbed to his advances at all?

Something touched his arm, and he looked around to see Coco standing beside him, looking down at the harbor. She said nothing, and for a moment they both just watched the seagulls floating above the waves as if suspended on wires, the tips of the choppy sea lined with white.

"You're agitated," she said. "What's the matter?"

He looked across at her. "What makes you say that?"

"You keep running your hand through your hair. You only do that when you're upset or nervous about something."

He gave a wry smile at that. "Oh really?"

She turned to face him. "Are you thinking that what we're doing is the same as what Dell did with those secretaries?"

He couldn't stop his eyebrows rising and his eyes widening with surprise. "How did you know that?"

"It's written all over your face and in your body language. What we are doing is not the same as what Dell did with those women." Her voice was vehement, her eyes hard. She didn't want it to be the same. That didn't mean it wasn't.

Then he met her gaze, saw the anxiety deep in her eyes, and affection swept over him. She was thinking the same and had the same fear—that he was just using her, that he saw her as an object, and had no feelings for her at all.

How could he explain to her that was not the case? That he was starting to panic because he *did* have feelings for her, strong feelings, and that wasn't good news when he had to return to Auckland after the weekend?

He stared into her eyes, wishing he could voice his emotions, but knowing to do so would be pointless and make it harder when he eventually had to leave. They had to pretend this was just fun, otherwise they were going to dig themselves deeper into this hole and make it completely impossible for themselves to climb out without getting badly hurt.

Still, he needed to show her how he felt. After casting a quick glance at the door to make sure Rob hadn't returned, he leaned forward and touched his lips to hers in a brief but sweet kiss.

When he pulled back, the hardness had vanished from her eyes, and her whole countenance had softened.

"I'm sorry," she whispered, clutching the clipboard she was holding to her chest like a shield. "This whole case has gotten to me."

"Me too," he admitted.

"I know what we're doing has complicated matters, and I'm sorry for that. I don't like the thought of making things more difficult for you."

He couldn't deny her statement because it was true, but still, he didn't want her to think that he wished they hadn't slept together.

"I don't know," he said. "It's clarifying things for me as well, in a strange way. I've always considered myself an advocate for equality between the sexes and I supposed I believed women needed my help and support, but that in itself is patronizing in a way. In the past, I would have assumed those women that Dell had an affair with had been coerced into it somehow, but the experiences you've shared with me have shown me that sometimes there are other factors at play, and that women like sex and are happy to indulge in a purely sexual relationship as well as men. I don't know that I really believed that up until now."

She looked down at the harbor. "I think that's true. But I would imagine—although obviously I can't speak for everyone—that for women sex is still mostly about feeling desirable, about being wanted. We all love to be loved, after all."

She looked back up, her green eyes glittering beneath her glasses.

He glanced up at the clock. It was five past five.

He smiled. "Time to clock off."

Her eyes widened. "Oh."

He could hear Rob's footsteps approaching. "I'll pick you up at six." He leaned closer and whispered in her ear, "Wear a skirt."

Chapter Thirty-Eight

Coco hovered by the living room window, waiting for the taxi, and nibbled her fingernails. What did Felix have planned for tonight? She had no idea, and couldn't remember what fantasies she'd mentioned to him the night they'd first visited the bar. Wear a skirt, he'd said—why was that? Easy access? Her heart pounded at the thought. What was he going to do to her?

"Where are you going?" Eleanor wheeled herself into the living room.

Coco turned, took a deep breath, and let it out slowly. "I'm not sure. He likes to surprise me." And that was the understatement of the year.

Eleanor smiled. "He seems like such a nice young man. He obviously cares about you if he goes to all this trouble to arrange these evenings out for you."

Coco looked back out of the window. It had been such a strange conversation she'd had with him in the office, after he'd finished interviewing the secretaries. It had been a stressful day, for her at any rate, sitting there and listening to the women who'd admitted having an affair with Peter Dell. She'd curled up inside with shame at her sex, only to then grow angry with herself, because wasn't she doing exactly the same thing with Felix?

But she wasn't going to think about it tonight. She'd left Veronica Stark at the office, and had deliberately taken the time to dress as Coco, donning a calf-length, flowing, summery blue skirt and a pretty blue blouse, and she wore her hair down, the sides plaited and joined at the back like a medieval princess. She knew he liked her hair—he liked to thread his hands through it, and she'd caught him curling it around his fingers after they'd made love, admiring the color. She wanted to please him—she wanted him to look at her with that light in his eyes that made her heart beat faster. It wasn't just about sex.

A taxi drew up outside, and she turned, kissed her mother on the cheek, shouted goodbye to Frances who was making tea in the kitchen, and opened the door just as Felix rang the bell.

"Hey," she said, stepping out and closing the door behind her.

"Hey." He ran his gaze down her, then slowly back up. And there it was—that light in his eyes, and her breath caught in her throat. "You look fantastic," he murmured, and leaned forward to press his lips against hers.

"You too." It was the truth—he wore a pair of Levi Mechanic 501s, a white T-shirt, and a casual black jacket, and he looked good enough to eat. Ooh, there's an idea…

He smiled and took her hand. "Ready?"

She nodded and followed him along the path to the taxi. "Where are we going?"

"It's a secret." He grinned at her and opened the door so she could get in, then went around the other side and climbed in beside her. The taxi set off, so he'd obviously already instructed the driver where to go.

She nodded toward the backpack that sat on the floor by his feet. "What's in that?"

He tapped the side of his nose, and she rolled her eyes. He laughed. "You'll find out soon enough."

The taxi threaded through the city, and she felt a wave of satisfaction at the thought of being with this man, enjoying his company, with the evening stretching out before them, hopefully ending in some good sex. "It's a nice evening," she said, looking out of the window up at the sky. "I think summer is on its way."

"Yes," he said with some relief. "We might have been in trouble if it had been raining." Refusing to elaborate, he started talking about a review he'd read on the movie they'd seen at the Empire, and she had to content herself with enjoying the feeling of anticipation at what lay ahead.

Before long the taxi pulled up. To Coco's surprise, they were outside the entrance to the Wellington Cable Car. Her eyebrows rose. "Where are we going—to the Botanic Gardens?"

Felix paid the driver and got out, and she followed him, taking his hand as he offered it. He nodded happily and gestured to the bag on his back. "I've packed a picnic. I thought we could find a nice private spot in the gardens somewhere."

"A picnic?" Warmth filled her. "Oh, what a nice idea."

They went into the building and Felix bought the tickets, and before long they were in a cable car climbing the hills of Wellington.

"I haven't done this for years," Coco said.

"I've never been on it," Felix said, taking her hand. "I haven't been to Wellington much at all really—when I was younger we tended to go to Auckland if we wanted to go shopping or to a show or something."

He went on to tell her a bit about his childhood, and Coco listened, conscious of the warmth of his arm pressed against hers and the fact that a couple of the other younger women in the cable car were casting him admiring glances. *He's with me*, she wanted to yell exultantly. She still couldn't believe out of all the women in the office, he'd chosen her.

But then she was thinking they had a choice in the matter, wasn't she? That he'd cast his eye around looking for a woman to dally with, and thought her a likely candidate. But it hadn't been like that. He'd told her he never had office affairs, which meant their meeting and connection had been something on a chemical, instinctive level—something it was impossible to fight, which explained why it felt so… right.

Or was she just being romantic and impractical? It would be easy to think they were just driven by hormones, but they also had brains, and they should have been sensible enough to react against their basic drives.

Then Felix smiled at her, leaned forward, and kissed her on the cheek, and she felt her cheeks flush and looked down, unable to stop a swell of happiness flowing through her. How could she fight this? She didn't want to feel emotional about what she had with him—she wanted to keep it purely physical. But however much she wanted to, she couldn't fight her feelings. She was falling in love with him, and it might be too quick, and it might be the most stupid thing she could ever have done in her life, but she was powerless to stop it.

The cable car arrived at their stop, and they got out and headed along the path to the Botanic Gardens. It was a beautiful evening, warm and slightly sultry, heavy with the promise of summer to come, and they held hands, fingers linked, and walked slowly along the meandering paths, through the native forest, the conifers, the duck ponds, the begonias and roses, the statues and other pieces of artwork that lined the route. It was quiet and peaceful, the warm sunlight filtering through the leaves of the trees and casting yellow bands across the paths, and fantails and tui birds flitted between the bushes, calling out to them as they passed.

They walked for a while, talking about this and that, and Coco thought how comfortable she felt in his company, how pleasant he was to be with. Knowledgeable and well-educated, he had an opinion on every subject under the sun, but he was happy to listen to her talk too, and she found him fascinating, entranced by his deep voice, his infectious chuckle, and the way he looked at her with an endearing mixture of affection and desire.

Her heart beat faster every time she wondered if he had an ulterior motive for planning the picnic. Hadn't she mentioned that one of her fantasies was having sex outdoors? Surely he wasn't expecting them to do it in the Botanic Gardens?

She tried not to think about it, but it was difficult when she kept smelling his aftershave, when every time he laughed, it sent a shiver down her spine. And when he put his arm around her, she became acutely aware of his height and strength and remembered how it felt to have him making love to her, sliding inside her.

By the time, he drew to a halt and slid the backpack off, she was in a sexual daze and had to take deep breaths to calm herself down while he undid the bag and drew out a blanket.

"This should do," he said, looking around. They were in a secluded corner of a rose garden, far from the busy center. A waist-high wall ran around one side of the garden, covered with climbing creeper, backed by tall conifers. They'd already walked through the Lady Norwood Rose Garden, but this secluded area had small rose bushes planted in circular mounds among the carefully tended lawn, and the garden was filled with their scent. The garden was at just the right angle for the sun to fill it with evening warmth.

"It's beautiful." She helped him spread out the blanket and sat, and he sat facing her, cross-legged, and began to pull boxes out of the bag.

He'd brought freshly made chicken-salad rolls, small savory pastries, a large tub of strawberries, and a bottle of champagne with two plastic flutes and two plates.

"You have been busy." She smiled, warmed right through at the effort he'd put into it.

"Nothing's too much trouble for you." He smiled back and gestured for her to start opening the boxes while he popped the champagne.

She opened the boxes and placed a roll on each of the plates. "What a lovely idea."

"A bit odd midweek I know, but we have to make the most of our time." He finished taking off the foil, undid the metal cage, and popped the cork before pouring them out a glass.

Coco said nothing, saddened at the thought that this had to come to an end. What a cruel twist of fate that they lived at opposite ends of the country.

He reached out and cupped her face, brushed her cheek with his thumb, then leaned forward and touched his lips to hers. Then he pulled back and carried on talking as if nothing had happened, but she knew he'd caught the sadness that had passed over her, and the kiss had been an apology for mentioning the temporary nature of their relationship. Somehow, she knew he felt the same, and that comforted her. Yes, their situation sucked. But it sucked for both of them, and that made it easier.

Chapter Thirty-Nine

They talked for ages, lying there in the sun, feeding each other strawberries, and sipping the champagne as the shadows lengthened and bees buzzed lazily from rose to rose. Coco grew slowly more relaxed as the alcohol threading through her veins, the warm evening, and Felix's presence brought about a hazy sense of contentment.

At one point, she lay back on the blanket, and Felix stretched out beside her, brushing her lips with the strawberries and then licking off the sweet juice until she giggled and sighed, opening her mouth to him so he could dip his tongue inside. She raised her hand and slipped it into his hair, threading her fingers through the short, dark strands, and murmured her approval as he ran his tongue along her bottom lip and then nibbled it.

She'd never grown aroused so slowly and languorously, and she waited for him to start undoing her blouse or run a hand up her skirt, at that moment willing to let him do whatever he wanted.

But after a while he pulled back, turning his gaze up to the setting sun and giving a silent sigh before saying, "I suppose we should be going. I don't want you to get cold."

She frowned and sat up as he began to pack away the boxes and put them in the bag. She waited for him to look at her, but he continued to busy himself with packing, and then he stood, obviously waiting for her to rise so he could fold up the blanket.

She got to her feet slowly and caught his hand. "Felix?"

He turned to her, but busied himself with removing a speck of grass from her shoulder. "Mmm?"

She lifted his chin so his gaze met hers. "What's the matter?"

He smiled, although it didn't reach his eyes. "Nothing."

She stroked his cheeks, his five o'clock shadow scraping against her thumbs. "I thought you were going to make one of my exotic fantasies come true," she said mischievously.

He studied her for a moment, then dropped the bag and put his arms around her. He pulled her into his embrace and kissed the top of her head. "I had thought maybe we could find somewhere, but now we're here..." His voice was husky. "It seems seedy, and I don't want that for you. You deserve more than a quick screw."

She buried her nose in his T-shirt, inhaling his scent, feeling the hopelessness and desire that ran through her veins mirrored in him. His arms tightened around her, and she pressed herself against his hard form, hungry and aching for him. She lifted her chin, searching for his lips, and when his kiss came, it was brutal and desperate, consuming her with a dark desire.

She moved backward into the shadows of the trees, bringing him with her, until she felt the wall against her butt. Her hands clenched in his hair, holding him firmly as her tongue searched for his, and she deepened the kiss. He pressed against her, and she felt his erection through his jeans as he ground it against her mound, arousing her through their clothing.

"I want you," she whispered against his mouth, not caring they were outside and could be seen at any moment if someone rounded the corner. She couldn't wait until they got back home. He filled her senses, and she felt that if she didn't have him inside her in minutes, she was going to implode. Was that the alcohol? Or just her pheromones talking? Either way, she wasn't willing to wait.

"I want you too." His hands found her breasts, and he groaned as he found her braless. He weighed her breasts in his palms and brushed his thumbs across her nipples, and she moaned, hooking her leg around him to try to pull him closer.

To her surprise, he tore himself away and extracted the blanket from the bag, folded it over the top of the wall behind her, and then placed his hands under her butt and lifted her up. She wrapped her legs around him and pulled him close again, heart pounding at the thought that they were really going to have sex here, in public, shrouded in shadow, but still visible if someone were to look closely.

He kissed her again as he unbuttoned her blouse, and she arched her back and pushed her breasts into his hands, closing her eyes as he lowered his head and his mouth found her swollen nipples. He sucked, hard, and she gave a soft cry, clenching inside at the exquisite sensations rippling through her.

He swapped to the other nipple, then back again, and before long she felt like a supernova, pulsing with light and energy, about to explode at any second. "I want you in me," she whispered furiously, and he stood to kiss her again, fumbling in his pocket and producing a condom.

"Are you sure?" he murmured, even as he unbuttoned his fly.

"Yes," she said, unable to believe the word was leaving her mouth. How slutty must she look, sitting there with her blouse open and her breasts visible to all, pulling up her skirt and laughing as he realized she wasn't wearing any panties, either. But she didn't care, and her lack of concern filled her with a strange thrill, and exultation that at last, for once in her life, she was living, really living, young and free from care of anything except pleasuring this glorious man before her, and receiving pleasure in turn.

He slid his fingers down into her, his lips hovering over hers as his fingers slipped easily through her folds, proving to her she was already aroused and ready for him. He explored her for a moment, but she was too hyped up and excited about the thought of having him here, in the garden, to put up with extended foreplay. She pushed his hand away, took the condom from his other fingers and extracted it from the packaging, then pulled him close. His erection strained toward her through his boxers, and she pushed the elastic down and released him, letting out a slow, approving breath at the sight of him so eager and ready for her.

"I'll do it," she whispered as he reached for the condom, and he nodded. She placed it carefully on the tip and rolled it down, taking her time, noting that he closed his eyes, obviously enjoying the feel of her hands on him.

When she'd done, he paused to kiss her again. His lips covered hers, and his tongue swept into her mouth as he pushed his hips forward to slide into her.

Coco gasped at the sensation of being filled, feeling herself stretch to accommodate him. He pulled out and moved forward again, and again, until she'd accepted all of him, filled to the brim with his thick, hard length. His arms came around her, holding her safely, and he lifted his head so he could look into her eyes, his own fiercely hot with desire. It was the first time they'd made love like this, face to face, and it felt intimate and sensual, emotional as well as physical.

She tipped her head back, swimming with sensation. "Oh... that feels fantastic."

He planted kisses along her neck and up to her ear, then along to her mouth again, beginning to move regularly with slow, leisurely thrusts. "I know," he murmured, mirroring the movement of his hips with thrusts of his tongue into her mouth.

She moaned and abandoned herself to him, knowing she was flooded with moisture, her orgasm already hovering in the wings. Her bare nipples brushed against his cotton T-shirt, the material teasing her sensitive skin. She widened her legs so he could plunge deeper into her, sighing as he obeyed and pumped harder, his hips meeting hers with a smack each time he thrust.

She didn't hear the voices at first, only becoming aware that something was wrong when he stiffened and stopped moving, raising his head to look at her. Startled, she went to say something, but he lifted a hand and put his finger to his lips, then gestured behind her.

Glancing over her shoulder, she saw movement on the other side of the trees. Half a dozen people were having a tour of the rose gardens, and they'd stopped to admire one of the bushes that grew on the other side of the path that ran past the wall.

Coco's eyes met Felix's, wide with alarm. She put her hands on his chest to push him away, but to her surprise his face lit with amusement, and he shook his head.

Still inside her, he lowered his lips to her neck and kissed up to her ear.

She wriggled, trying not to groan at the feel of him inside her. His arms tightened around her and he moved his hips again, and she suddenly realized he intended to continue to make love to her with people standing only six feet away, albeit with a wall and trees between them.

She could hear their voices clearly, one man—who presumably worked at the gardens—detailing the names of the roses visible in that area, and others asking questions about the care and maintenance of the flowers. Were they not going to move on?

"I love this one," said a woman clearly, "do you know the origins of the name?"

The guide answered, and Coco closed her eyes, panic mixing with excitement at the thought that they could be discovered at any moment. If any one of them turned around, they'd be able to see through the trees, although how much of them was visible in the shadows she wasn't sure.

Felix nibbled her earlobe, and she gasped, stifling it hurriedly. He gave a silent chuckle, one arm around her waist holding her tightly as he increased the depth of his thrusts. His other hand came up to hold her breast, and he squeezed her nipple, prompting her to arch her back and bite her lip to avoid crying out with pleasure.

"...and the third earl of Buckingham had already been married once, but his second wife was Lady Elizabeth Darnley," the guide droned on.

Coco's muscles tingled with anticipation, and she had to stop herself exclaiming. Oh dear God, she was going to come, with all those people just feet away. She looked up at Felix and shook her head with alarm, but his eyes were like fire and his thrusts were deepening, and she realized he wasn't far from coming himself. He looked so sexy, his dark hair ruffled where she'd tightened her fingers in it, and excitement shot through her again at the thought of what they were doing, at the thought of those people turning around and seeing them having sex, seeing Felix fucking her.

He covered her mouth with his and then with one hand caught hold of the collar of her blouse and yanked it down her back. She squealed, her cry muffled by his mouth, aware there would be no hiding now—if anyone came upon them she was quite obviously topless, her nipples engorged with the blood that was speeding around her body. Felix dropped his head and sucked one nipple to a tight peak, then the other, and she clenched inside, unable to do anything but give in to his ministrations.

Her orgasm swept over her, and again he covered her mouth with his. She gave a muffled moan as she came, her muscles squeezing him, burning exquisitely. He held her tightly as he continued to thrust hard, finding his own pleasure and swelling inside her as his climax took hold. They stilled, locked in blissful satisfaction, frozen in mutual gratification. Their fingers clasped, their breaths exchanged, and their bodies pulsed and tightened into and around and inside one another.

And then finally, eventually, they relaxed, breathing heavily, and looking into one another's eyes.

"I think there's a fantail in the trees," someone said on the other side. "I can hear it fluttering around."

"There's a lot of wildlife here," said the guide, moving along the path. "If you look closely you'll see squirrels and possums and all kinds of birds..." His voice faded away.

Felix's lips curved. Coco gave him a mock glare.

"That was wicked," she murmured as he withdrew and disposed of the condom.

He buttoned up his pants, and she pulled her blouse on and did it up. Then he put his arms around her and pulled her close again.

He kissed the top of her head. "I'm sorry."

"Don't be. It was fun."

He hugged her. "I'm crazy about you. You know that, right?"

Yeah, she thought, *I know that. And I'm crazy about you too.*

Oh dear.

Chapter Forty

Felix thumbed listlessly through the pages of transcription that Coco had typed up from her shorthand notes, detailing the interviews of the secretaries he'd carried out over the past few days. Along with this, he had his own notes from the interviews with the partners, plus sheaves of scribbles he'd made as he worked his way through the case in the spider diagrams he used to brainstorm.

He tried to concentrate, but struggled to get his brain to work.

The truth was that he was nervous.

He'd spent all morning reading the notes and making more on his iPad, checking a few details with Rob, and trying to come to some sort of decision on the case, but he still had one more interview to carry out—the one he'd been putting off all week, and the one that he wanted to do even less now.

He looked at his watch. Miss Stark was coming to his office at two p.m. after her lunch break. He'd asked her whether she wanted anyone in with her apart from him and Rob, but she'd declined in the cool, calm, collected way she had, looking at him over the top of her glasses with no sign of the passion she'd exhibited the night before.

He put down his iPad and stood to look out of the window. He had to stop thinking about Coco and focus on Miss Stark. She was able to separate her two personalities with ease, so he should be able to as well.

But it was difficult, because that morning when he'd walked into her office, even though she'd scraped back her hair and buttoned her shirt up to her chin, he saw in his mind's eye the moment he'd tugged her blouse down her back to expose her breasts, and the way she'd responded not by yelling blue murder and pushing him away, but by opening up to him and encouraging him to thrust harder. How could he forget Coco, even though she'd clothed that persona in the cold, shrewd façade of Miss Stark? The two were one and the same, and although she might not accept that, he could no longer separate them, and he loved them both.

He rested his forehead on the cool glass and closed his eyes.

What the fuck was he going to do? How could he have gotten himself into this situation? He'd been in the office precisely a week. How had he fallen for her so quickly?

He thought of Lindsey, wondering whether the usual guilt would sweep away his feelings for Coco. But he'd already noticed that Lindsey had not featured in his thoughts much over the past week. And even that hadn't made him feel guilty, like he usually felt whenever he realized he hadn't thought about her for a length of time.

He looked down at the dark blue sea of the harbor, but he didn't really see the waves. He was done mourning. The realization took his breath away. It had taken nearly seven years, and he'd never forget Lindsey or cease to miss her, but for the first time he felt he was ready to move on. Even in the short time he'd known her, Coco had filled the hollow within him that had been left when Lindsey's death ripped out his heart.

He'd been lucky enough to meet another woman of his dreams, and yet on Monday he was due to return to Auckland and never see her again.

What was he going to do about it?

"Felix?"

He turned to see Coco standing in front of his desk. She'd caught her bottom lip between her teeth and her hands twisted the pen she was holding. In spite of her calm appearance, she was nervous too, which didn't help his agitation. If it wasn't for Rob, he could have completed the interview informally, but Rob had been present at the interviews for all the secretaries and had arranged the time for Coco to visit himself, so it would look weird if he suddenly declared he didn't need to see her.

"Hi," he said.

"Hi."

They studied each other for a moment. She looked stunning, chic and elegant in a dark gray jacket and skirt with a pink blouse that reflected the blush in her cheeks. He was not going to think about ripping that blouse off.

He tried to think of what to say, but his mind emptied. There was too much to say, that was the problem. The day before, they'd walked from the gardens down the long path back to town, arms around one another, talking all the way, but they'd carefully avoided the topic they really needed to discuss—how they felt about each other, and what they were going to do. He needed time alone to sit and think about things, but he had to get this case sorted first because it was muddying the waters, and his lawyer's instinct told him there was something swimming in the depths that he wasn't aware of yet, that would illuminate the case when it eventually surfaced.

He wondered whether to mention the night before, tell her again that he'd enjoyed himself, but at that moment Rob appeared behind her, so he kept his words to himself.

"Right, all ready?" Rob gestured to the chairs and Felix picked up his pad and joined them as they sat.

"Thanks for coming," he said to Coco, trying not to think about the double meaning behind the words. *She's Miss Stark. Concentrate, for God's sake. This is serious.*

Coco just nodded and pushed her glasses farther up her nose, although she continued to look at him over the top of them. Her green eyes appraised him, and he had to tear his gaze away from their mesmerizing stare.

He looked down at his pad and took a moment to gather his wits. It was time to don his professional hat.

He cleared his throat. "I'm sure you can expect the type of questions I'll be asking you, Miss Stark, as you've been present during the interviews of all the other secretaries. I apologize for having to put you through the process as well, but as Sasha's direct superior, your input is obviously required and valued."

"Of course." They were the epitome of politeness and professionalism. Her expression had gone carefully blank and she'd stopped fidgeting. He had no idea what she was thinking.

He scrolled down his pad. "I refer you back to the night in question, Monday, the fifth of December. Sasha claims the incident occurred at around six o'clock. Were you still in the building at that time?"

She nodded. "My hours are nine until five thirty, but I'm often here earlier in the morning and later in the evening. That evening I was reorganizing the secretarial roster for the week because we'd had two girls ring in sick and another on holiday."

"Were you there when Peter Dell entered the work room and asked for a secretary to help with his case?"

She nodded again. "Yes. I'd just printed a draft spreadsheet and I was waiting by the printer to pick it up."

"So you saw Dell enter the office?"

"Yes."

"What did he say? Can you remember?"

She hesitated. "Not his exact words..." She met his gaze and then looked at her hands.

She didn't want to tell the truth. Interesting. "A summary then," he suggested.

"He asked the three or four girls who were still there whether any of them would mind staying a little longer to help him out." She didn't look up.

He glanced at Rob, who raised his eyebrows. So Sasha had lied. And at the time, Coco hadn't corrected her. And even more interesting, she appeared to be disappointed that Dell hadn't asked Sasha directly. What did that mean? She wanted Dell to be guilty? Why?

His brain working furiously, Felix kept outwardly calm and tapped a few words on the pad before continuing. "Did any of the other girls volunteer?"

"No. Only Sasha."

"What happened then?"

"He started explaining what he wanted her to do. I only listened with half an ear—I didn't think it was important, you see. This kind of thing happens a lot."

"So it wasn't unusual for a partner to request someone work late?"

"Not at all."

"And it wasn't unusual for Sasha to volunteer?"

Again, she hesitated. "Actually, it did cross my mind that it was odd. In my experience, there are two sorts of secretaries. Those who are in at twenty to nine, making coffee so they're sitting behind their desk at nine, ready to start work, and who often stay twenty or thirty minutes past five to finish off a document. And then there are those girls who come in at a minute to nine and leave at a minute past five—and that's if they work overtime. Sasha has always been the second sort."

"So it registered as strange for her to volunteer to stay late?"

"Yes. I suppose so." Again, the blank, almost resentful stare. She wanted to defend Sasha. But she couldn't bring herself to lie.

He shifted uncomfortably, not liking where this was going. "So what happened then?"

"I took my printed spreadsheet back into my office."

He nodded and jotted a few things down. "Okay. So did you speak to Sasha after she finished the document?"

"Yes. She put her head around the door and told me she was going to drop it into Peter's office before she left. I packed up and walked out of the office. His door was closed, but I didn't think anything of it. I assumed she'd left and he was working on his case. I left the building and went home."

Felix sat back in his seat tiredly. He was no closer to deciding whether Peter was at fault, and now he had a headache. "Can you remember what Sasha's behavior was like the next day?"

Coco shrugged. "She didn't seem much different at first. She was always fairly quiet and kept herself to herself. She sat at her desk with her earphones in and concentrated on her work. It wasn't until about halfway through the day that I got a phone call from the head of HR who said she'd just been into his office and filed a complaint against Peter."

"How did you feel about that?"

She stared at him. He could see his question had thrown her. "How did I feel about it?"

"Yes."

"What's that got to do with it?"

Her defensiveness told him how she felt, and he knew his initial instinct that there was something she wasn't telling him about Dell was right. Had she had an affair with Dell? Jealousy surged through him, hot and fierce, shocking him with its intensity. "I'm curious," he said, meeting her gaze, challenging her.

She continued to stare at him, then eventually lowered her eyes. The human equivalent of a dog rolling over and showing its underbelly. "I was glad," she said. She raised her eyes again and they were cool and defensive. "Happy now?"

Chapter Forty-One

Coco saw the frown crease Felix's brow and cursed herself for her honesty. Why couldn't she just lie and say she didn't feel anything at all? But she'd always been a terrible liar, and part of the problem was that deep inside she wanted to confess what had happened all those years ago, for Sasha's sake—because she could see Felix struggled to believe the young secretary—and for her own. She wanted Peter punished for what he'd done to her.

But she couldn't bring herself to say the words.

Felix glared at her, his iPad lying forgotten in his lap. "Did you have an affair with Peter Dell?"

Rob Drake, who'd been sitting quietly up until this point taking notes, looked up, glancing across at Felix and then over to her with curiosity.

Coco kept her cool. "No." Well that was true anyway. One quick fuck was hardly an affair.

Felix didn't say anything, and she could see he didn't believe her, but he couldn't outright call her a liar. Her heart sank. He thought she'd had a thing for Peter. How wrong could he be?

"So why were you glad when you heard that Sasha had filed a complaint against him?" Felix pressed.

She shrugged. "I don't like the man. I don't like his attitude toward women. I knew he'd had office affairs—that he used women and then cast them aside when he'd done with them." She couldn't stop bitterness creeping into her voice.

Felix stared at her, then looked out of the window. Was he thinking she was referring to him—that she thought he was doing exactly the same thing? Or did he think that's what happened between her and Peter—that they had an affair and he dumped her, and she was bitter about it? Either way it sucked, and she couldn't ask him because Rob was still sitting there quietly, chewing his pen as he observed them.

MR. SENSATIONAL

Felix ran a hand through his hair. Agitated, then. But he looked calm. Was he going to press her in spite of Rob's presence? But he didn't, he changed tack. "You say 'I knew he'd had office affairs'. How many were you aware of?"

"Seven or eight definitely, over the ten years I've been here. And I suspect there's been many more."

His eyebrows rose. "And nobody's ever complained about him before?"

She hesitated then, and looked down at her hands, examining her fingernails. How could she explain to him the sort of man Peter Dell was? She puzzled for a minute, then decided she had to just come out with it and be honest.

She sat back in her chair and looked at Felix, suddenly tired and wishing it was all over. She'd known this would be difficult, and she'd suspected it would be the death knell for their relationship. It was Felix's birthday and they were supposed to be going out to dinner with his friends that evening, but would he still want her to go after this?

"You have to understand what kind of man Peter is," she said, all resistance gone. "On the surface, he's funny and charming. When he talks to you, he makes you think you're the most important person in the world. He knows all the tricks—eye contact, asking you questions about yourself, all the body language to prove he's interested—and he uses it to its utmost. Practically every woman he comes into contact with falls for him."

Including her, she thought miserably. She'd been bowled over by his sweet talking, made to think she was special. And she'd been too young to see through his act, the fact that he was only playing a part, wearing the charm like a costume.

"Do you think he does it consciously?" Rob spoke for the first time. "Even if they say they don't, most people use their 'charm' to interact with the opposite sex." He looked at Felix. "Including me and you."

The look on Felix's face made a giggle issue from her lips before she could stop it. He sent her a wry glance before turning back to Rob. "That's bullshit."

"No, it's not." Rob leaned forward, eager to prove his point. "It's perfectly natural—it's how we communicate. I know Sasha got upset by your intimation that she was dressing to attract attention from the opposite sex, but the truth is that although we dress for ourselves because we want to feel good, we do dress for other people too—it's human nature. Everyone loves a compliment. And the truth is that men and women flirt with one another. It can be very subtle, or it can be overt, but we all do it."

"I don't agree," said Felix. "I'm always very careful not to flirt." He flicked a glance at Coco, as if to say apart from with you.

"It depends on your definition of flirt," said Rob. "I don't mean it has to be double entendre and personal comments all the time. But we use our charm to get women to warm to us. That's flirting."

"No, it's not." Felix glared at him. "That's just communicating."

Rob looked over at Coco. "What do you think?"

"Well, I tend to think of flirting as overtly sexual, comments that are more intimate, personal references, that sort of thing. But I think you have a point. It's in our genes to communicate in this way. We all know that if we want someone to do a job, the best way is to give them a compliment, ask with a smile, and if it's a really big ask, maybe finish with a touch on their arm or something." She smiled as they both raised his eyebrows. "You thought Miss Stark never utilized those techniques? Of course she does. Is it flirting? I wouldn't call it that because it's not meant to bring about a specific outcome. But after watching Peter and seeing how he interacts with others, I agree that many people do use their charm." She shrugged. "That's why Sasha finds it so difficult to communicate with others—she has no natural charm, no way to get people to warm to her."

She fell quiet, and so did Felix for the moment. She met his gaze. His anger seemed to have evaporated, and like her he seemed tired and a little defeated. This case had certainly got to him.

"Do you think Peter Dell made inappropriate sexual advances to Sasha De Langen?" he asked.

Surprise rippled through her. It was an un-lawyerly question to ask, because her answer would provide no evidence, and opinions should really count for nothing. But she wasn't going to pass up on this opportunity to voice her feelings about the senior partner.

"Yes," she said. "I do." After all, Sasha had told them herself she was gay. Why on earth would she have made advances to Peter if that was the case? It was time the man got his comeuppance for all the women he'd used and abused over the years.

Felix nodded. He glanced at Rob and smiled. "Okay, let's call it a day. I think we're done."

The three of them rose.

Rob glanced at them both. "I'm just going to get myself a coffee. Then we'll do a summary, eh, Felix?"

"Sure."

Rob left the room.

Coco breathed out a long sigh and met Felix's gaze. At least he no longer seemed angry with her. "You think Rob knows about us?"

"I think he suspects."

"Will he say anything?"

Felix shrugged as if to say *don't know, don't care*. She got the feeling he was thoroughly fed up with this case. He was probably desperate to return to his own branch.

She bit her lip, not wanting to think about that now. Instead, she reached into her folder and, casting a quick glance at the door, extracted a small, flat package and handed it to him. "Happy birthday."

He took the package and his eyes met hers. A smile spread slowly across his face. "I thought you'd forgotten."

"Of course not. We're going out for a birthday meal later, aren't we?" There, she'd told him she still wanted to see him. What would he say in return?

Something like relief crossed his face. "Yes. I'm meeting Gene's at five-thirty, then we'll come around to you."

"Okay." She nodded at the parcel. "Aren't you going to open it?"

He smiled and tore the paper off to reveal the circular disk—a coaster with the words *Lawyers do it in their briefs*.

He grinned. "I love it."

"I'm sorry it's not an expensive piece of tom, but…"

He laughed. "Since when have you used 'tomfoolery' for jewelry?"

"All the time," she said airily, then grinned. "I looked up some Cockney slang. Honestly, most of it's so convoluted I had trouble understanding."

"That's kind of the point." For the first time since she'd walked into his office, his eyes took on the look of lazy desire she was beginning to know and love. "By the way, not connected to Cockney but still connected to language, did you know that the French word for a kept woman is a 'Cocotte'?"

She gave him an indignant look. "Charming."

"I thought you should know."

They smiled at each other, and her heart rate sped up a little.

He put the coaster on the table and slid his hands into his pants pockets. "I'm sorry," he said, taking her by surprise.

"What for?"

He gestured around the room. "Having to do that."

"It's okay. It had to be done."

He looked down at the floor. "Did you tell the truth?"

He meant about Peter, she was sure. He wanted to know if she'd meant it when she'd denied having an affair with him.

"Yes." She had to force herself to meet his gaze when he looked up.

He nodded, took a deep breath, and let it out. "Okay. See you just after six then?"

"Sure." She walked to the door just as Rob came back in.

"Thank you, Miss Stark," Rob said.

She nodded and left the room, relieved it was over.

*

For the first time in several years, she left the office at exactly five o'clock. Suddenly she missed Amy, who would have been gleeful at seeing Miss Stark exiting the building at such an early hour. Perhaps it might have helped to talk things over with her, although of course Amy knew nothing about what had happened when Coco was seventeen.

She walked home slowly, thinking about Sasha. She'd criticized Sasha for finding it difficult to connect with people, but wasn't she exactly the same herself? She had hardly any friends, only Amy. No social life to speak of. That was her own choice, of course, born out of her wish to look after her mother.

For the first time, however, she thought she could understand her mother's anger at Coco's refusal to let her go. Would she want her own daughter, if she were ever to have one, to have a similar life? Of course she wouldn't. The thought was horrifying, and Coco's breath caught in her throat at the realization of the guilt her mother must be feeling.

But she pushed the horror away, refusing to accept it. Their situation couldn't be any other way—she couldn't let her mother go into a home, just couldn't. Her father's plea to her rang in her ears.

And besides, she was never going to have a daughter, or a son for that matter, so the whole topic was irrelevant.

A sweep of sorrow engulfed her, so powerful and so sudden she had to bite her lip so she didn't cry out. She stopped walking, the pedestrians still striding past, cars whizzing by on the road, but in her mind the Earth seemed to have ceased turning.

She'd never have children. She knew it instinctively. This thing with Felix was fleeting, like the seasons, and once he'd gone, that would be it.

For a brief—a very brief—moment, she let herself imagine what would happen if he got her pregnant. Would it be a boy or girl? With her blonde hair, or his dark locks and warm brown eyes? She imagined herself holding the wrapped bundle to her breast while he looked down at them, tenderness in his eyes. A hunger consumed her that she'd never experienced before, and she wrapped her arms around herself defensively, unaccustomed to feeling broody.

And then it passed and she was left with an underlying sadness. That life wasn't for her. If she told Felix she was pregnant he'd probably have a coronary before getting on a plane and flying as far away as possible. Oh, no doubt he'd do the right thing and pay his child support, but he wouldn't want to be tied down, to be a father.

She shoved her hands in the pockets of her coat and carried on walking, refusing to think about it anymore. She was going out on a date and she had to get ready, and that was as far as she'd let herself think.

Chapter Forty-Two

Felix was waiting in the bar where he'd arranged to meet Gene at five-thirty. Gene walked in, scanned the room, saw him, and walked over.

"Gene!" Felix said. "My old China, good to see you."

Gene shook his hand and raised an eyebrow. "Sorry?"

Felix grinned. "China plate. Mate."

Gene rolled his eyes, and then the two men laughed and bear hugged.

They'd been friends for a few years, since Gene had left the Army and returned to Auckland, and Felix had come home from England. Not quite as tall as Felix at six-one, Gene still had the build he'd developed in the forces, slender and muscular, even though Felix knew that physical exercise wasn't as easy as it had once been for his friend. An Afghanistan bomb resulting in a bad leg wound had put paid to Gene's career as a soldier. His new role as head of his own large security firm appeared by its nature to be more sedentary, but Felix knew Gene got bored sitting behind a desk and often took jobs on himself, which obviously kept him fit enough.

"Happy birthday," Gene said. "Old man."

"I'm younger than you," Felix pointed out. Gene would be thirty-one in February.

"True. Don't worry, the big three-oh's not as bad as they say. Kind of like Y2K—it's all hype."

Felix grinned and clapped him on the shoulder, and they both ordered a drink. "You look good. Busy?"

"Surprisingly so." Gene leaned on the bar and ran a hand through his short, dark hair, just a shade too long to be a buzz cut. "Seems like there's always a call for security. We're branching out into online stuff now too. Physical and internet security, you know?"

"Great idea." Felix smiled as the barkeeper passed him the glass of Mac's Gold and he took a long swig. "Moving with the times?"

"You have to, don't you? Or things move past you." Gene took his Steinlager and paid the barkeeper, then said, "Cheers."

"Cheers." Felix took another draught, sighed, and smiled at his friend. "It's good to see you—it's been a while."

"I know." Gene leaned on the bar. "Too long."

"Where's Mel?" Felix glanced at the doorway, half-expecting Gene's girlfriend to walk through. "She coming later?"

Gene looked into his glass. "We, ah, broke up."

Felix sighed. "Shit."

"Yeah."

"You or her?"

"Kinda joint. More her." He shrugged and took a swig of the lager. "Can't say I blame her. My heart wasn't in it."

Felix frowned. "Your heart's never in it."

"Takes one to know one, mate."

Felix gave in. He could hardly talk, he thought—at least, if he didn't bring Coco into the equation. "Yeah, I suppose so."

Gene took another swallow of lager and wiped his top lip. "So, tell me about Coco."

Felix studied his glass. "Tallish. Slim. Blonde. Beautiful. Sexy. Smart." He thought he'd better stop there before he started turning Shakespearean, and concentrated on drinking his lager.

"I see." Gene's eyes gleamed. "Why's this one different?"

"I don't remember saying she was."

Gene smirked. "Yeah. Whatever."

Felix put down his glass and played with the beermat. "I'm only here temporarily. I'm back to Auckland Monday night. It's only a thing."

"It's more than a thing."

"It's a thing, a brief thing."

"Dude, seriously. You didn't stop talking about her over the phone. I haven't heard you talk like this about anyone but Lindsey."

Felix closed his eyes. If even Gene was picking up on it, he knew he was in trouble.

Gene finished off his drink. "Come on. I want to meet her. Surely she can't be all that. I'll note down all her faults and give you a list later, and you can meditate on it over the weekend."

Felix opened his eyes and laughed. "Yeah, all right." He finished off his own drink. Gene was right. She wasn't perfect—no girl was perfect. He just needed to focus on all the problems between them rather than the good things and everything would be fine.

They caught a taxi to Coco's house, and both of them got out to knock on her door. Felix ran a hand through his hair as he waited. The afternoon had been unpleasant. He'd worried about upsetting her, and the insinuation that she'd had an affair with Dell had unsettled him. At least they'd parted on good terms, and he loved that she'd been thoughtful enough to buy him a present. But half of him wished he hadn't invited her out this evening. He'd find it difficult to relax, he was sure, and he always enjoyed going out with his brother and friends.

The moment she opened the door, however, all his worries fled. She looked stunning, dressed in a short white summery dress that showed off her beautiful legs, and she'd done something to her hair so it fell down her back in golden waves. She smiled hesitantly, and his heart swelled. How could he have thought the evening would be better without her?

"Hey," he said, leaning forward to kiss her on the cheek, breathing in her light, flowery perfume as he did so.

"Hey." She lowered her lashes, her cheeks turning a becoming rosy pink. "Happy birthday, again."

"Thanks." He turned to Gene, whose eyes looked about to fall out of his head. "This is Gene. G-e-n-e."

She laughed and held out a hand. "Hello, G-e-n-e. Pleased to meet you."

"Likewise." Gene shook her hand. Then, as she turned her back to them to shout goodbye to her mother and Frances and close the door, he looked across at Felix and mouthed *Fuck!*

Felix smothered a grin and smiled at her as she turned back. "Ready?"

"Sure." She looked nervous but excited, and he held her hand as they walked back to the taxi.

They talked for the five minutes it took to get to the restaurant, Felix holding her hand all the while, and he couldn't help glancing down at their hands occasionally, at her fingers linked with his. There was no doubt in his mind that he'd lied to Gene—for him, this was much more than a fling. Yes, he hadn't known her for long, and thinking about it was pointless because he was returning to Auckland on Monday, but he couldn't change how he felt. No other girl he'd dated since Lindsey had made him feel this way. He thought about her all the time when they were apart. He only had to see her and he lit up like a Christmas tree. On the surface, he talked to her and Gene and laughed and joked with them both, but inside he was thinking, *what am I going to do when it's time to leave? How can I bear to never see her again?*

They pulled up outside the restaurant and got out, paid the taxi, and went inside. Gene had booked a family restaurant, as both Rusty and Toby had young children. The place buzzed with noise and laughter, the air filled with the smell of chicken, fries, and ice cream.

The waitress directed them through to a table at the back next to a children's play area, and Felix grinned as he saw his brother and his wife, and Faith and Rusty, sitting waiting for them.

Everyone stood and came over to give him a hug and say happy birthday. He introduced his brother to Coco first. Slightly taller than himself, built—as Felix always told everyone—like a brick shit house, and with a thatch of dark curly hair, Toby Wilkinson was a couple of years younger, and in spite of his newly married status, still retained some of his boyish mentality.

"Felix! You old fart." Toby clapped his brother on the back.

"Charming." His wife, Esther, came forward to give Felix an apologetic smile before laughing and kissing him on the cheek. "Good to see you."

"You too." Felix smiled at her warmly. Her four-month bump was clearly visible, and the two of them glowed with shared happiness. "How are you feeling?"

"Better now the sickness has gone." She pulled a face. "Faith passed on some good home remedies though, which helped."

"I'm an expert in vomit now," Faith said cheerfully, wrapping one arm around Felix and planting a kiss on his cheek. Average height and slender with long brown hair, Faith was a sweetheart who Felix had grown to be very fond of over the years.

He laughed and placed a gentle kiss on the head of the baby in her other arm. The tiny girl snuffled and squirmed, and Faith smiled and said to her, "Pippa, it's Uncle Felix. Look! He's come to see you!" The baby sneezed, and they all laughed.

"How's parenthood?" Felix asked, liking that the baby smelled of powder and shampoo rather than the more unpleasant smells he'd always associated with kids.

"Great." Rusty held out a hand and they shook. "If you don't mind only having two hours sleep at night and feeling like a zombie half the time."

"Don't listen to him," Faith scolded. "He loves it really." She turned to the woman waiting shyly at Felix's side and smiled. "You must be Coco. It's lovely to meet you—Felix has told me so much about you. I'm Faith."

"Oh," Coco said, and blushed as they shook hands. "Pleased to meet you."

Felix shot Faith a wry glare, knowing perfectly well what a matchmaker she was, and introduced Coco to everyone else while Gene also kissed and shook hands. Then, the welcomes over, they started taking their places at the table.

But he'd forgotten one person.

"Uncle Felix!"

Felix turned and grinned as the tiny three-year-old boy came running out of the children's play area to launch himself at Felix's knees. "Charlie boy!" He swung the toddler up into his arms. "Crikey, look how big you've grown. You're almost as tall as me!"

Charlie beamed and planted a wet kiss on Felix's cheek before enveloping him in a fierce hug. "Daddy said it's your birthday."

"It is. I'm thirty."

"You're an old man," Charlie said, and everyone laughed.

"Charlie," Esther scolded. "That's not very polite."

"True, though." Toby grinned.

"You're not far behind," Felix reminded him, seating himself at the table with Charlie on his lap. "So what's for dinner then?"

"Chicken nuggets!" Charlie said with delight.

"Chicken nuggets it is." Felix gave him a squeeze before putting him down so the boy could run off again to the tiny slide and ball pit in the play area. He'd grown incredibly fond of the boy since Toby had met up again with Esther the previous February and brought her up to the Northland. They'd had an affair several years before and parted, only for Esther to fall pregnant afterward. It had been a bumpy ride for both of them, but it had had a happy ending.

How strange the way things went. Felix had wondered not so long ago whether Toby would ever settle down, but here he was, happily married with another one on the way. It gave him hope that one day he might also find happiness.

His glance slid across to find Coco watching him. They exchanged a small smile, but he could read the sadness in her eyes that he was sure was reflected in his own. No doubt marriage and family lay in the future for both of them. But almost certainly, it wasn't with each other.

Chapter Forty-Three

Coco had been terribly nervous about meeting Felix's family and friends, but in the end she had a great time. They ate chicken wings and fries and corn-on-the-cob dripping with butter, and drank pitchers of beer and shared ice creams piled high with chocolate sauce and marshmallows. She didn't say much, spending her time listening to their banter and laughing at their jokes, but she got out so little that it was fun to be sociable for once.

And it was nice to be amongst people her own age who weren't giggly girls talking about nothing but fashion and celebrities and who they were going to date that night, but instead couples with children who included her in their chat as if she and Felix had been going out for years and were any minute going to join them in the happy realms of matrimonial bliss.

What a shame that could never be the case.

Still, she tried to put her sadness to one side for Felix's sake, and make his birthday a happy one. Certainly, he seemed to be enjoying himself. He talked business and politics with Gene, a dark-eyed, serious man who'd obviously been wary of the girl his best mate had talked about, but had warmed to her almost immediately. Felix had murmured to her that Gene had just broken up with his girlfriend, and Coco wondered why that had happened when he was gorgeous, clever, and athletic in spite of his obvious limp. Like Felix, he dressed well, his jeans, shirt, and jacket all named brands, an expensive watch on his wrist. He obviously had money. For goodness' sake, what more could a girl want?

But then those things didn't guarantee a happy relationship, did they? She could see from his quiet manner and his sometimes cynical comments that he was dubious he'd discover for himself the sort of happiness the other couples at the table had found. That was obviously behind his concern for Felix, too, and she caught Gene watching her curiously from time to time as if he was trying to work out her relationship with Felix.

MR. SENSATIONAL

It was nice to watch Felix interact with the others at the table, and she learned more about him over the space of an hour and a half than she had in most of the time she'd spent with him so far. He had a natural, teasing relationship with his younger brother, Toby, who was very like him to look at, big, charismatic and with a natural sexiness that appealed to her, although he had none of Felix's attention to style and wore an old T-shirt and slightly ripped jeans with scuffed trainers, and his hair was all over the place. But he clearly adored his wife, and spent most of the evening touching her hand or leaning forward to whisper in her ear and make her giggle.

Felix and Rusty were clearly old friends too, and their relationship was more traditional bloke versus bloke, less intimate, and more piss-taking and verbal banter. Coco had read Faith's blog and knew a little about Rusty, and now she'd met him in the flesh she could see completely why Faith had fallen so hard for him. Six-foot, slender, and muscular, with reddish-brown hair, he also had a natural, innate sexiness, although at that moment he looked tired, presumably from his disturbed nights. His wry wit and the way he watched Faith when he thought she wasn't looking told Coco that he was probably a handful in bed, corroborated by the stories she'd read about him.

The women she was less sure about. After the meal, Esther stood to join Charlie in the play area as he begged her to watch him come down the slide on his own, and Faith rose with the baby and said, "Want to come, Coco?" Coco hesitated, suddenly nervous about being alone with these women who seemed so confident in themselves and with their men. But she didn't want to be impolite, so she nodded and got up, giving Felix a quick parting smile, noticing the way he held her hand until she walked away from him.

The three of them entered the tiny play area, and Esther sat on one of the big beanbags to watch Charlie carefully climb the steps. He gave her a running commentary as he came down the other side and then repeated the process. Faith joined her, collapsing tiredly onto a beanbag beside her, the baby lying with her cheek resting on Faith's shoulder, fast asleep.

Coco lowered herself as gracefully as she could onto another beanbag. "You can tell I'm not a mother," she said wryly. "You can't go into these places in such a short skirt."

"I seriously cannot remember the last time I wore a skirt," Esther complained. "It's so much easier to wear pants, but I do worry I've forgotten how to be feminine."

Faith flapped a hand. "That's rubbish. At least you always wear makeup and jewelry."

"I've only started recently. Charlie liked to pull my earrings out when he was a baby. I didn't wear anything but studs for three years."

The girls all laughed. "It's certainly not easy," Faith said. "But it's worth it."

"Yeah," Esther said, watching Charlie and stroking her bump contentedly.

Coco said nothing, feeling an uncharacteristic pang of envy. She'd never envied mothers before and had always felt a sense of relief whenever she saw tired women with squalling kids, glad she didn't have to compromise her peaceful life for another person. But being with these friends and their children made her realize what she was missing, and just like earlier she felt a hunger for marriage and motherhood she'd never experienced before.

She looked up to see Faith watching her with bright, curious eyes. "So…" the brown-haired girl said with a touch of mischievousness. "Felix, eh?"

Coco said nothing, her lips twisting and her cheeks growing warm as the two girls grinned.

"I never thought I'd see the day," Esther said, stretching out her legs and tipping her head at Coco.

"What day?"

"That Felix fell in love."

Coco's eyes widened. The two girls started laughing.

"Don't tell me you're shocked," Faith teased. "It's written all over his face."

"I…" The truth was, Coco *was* shocked. She'd known he had feelings for her, but love… "We've only been dating a week."

Both girls shrugged, said at the same time, "So?" and then laughed.

Coco watched Charlie come headfirst down the slide after watching an older boy attempt it, excited to try something different, only to fly off the end, land flat on his face, and burst into tears. Esther opened her arms as he ran over to her and let him climb onto her lap, completely unbothered by his tears. "Silly boy," she said, tightening her arms around him and kissing his hair. "You're just tired, aren't you?" She rested her cheek on his head and smiled at Coco. "I'm so pleased for you. Felix is lovely. Like a slightly classier Toby." She grinned.

Coco shook her head, flustered. "Sorry, but you've got it wrong. He goes back to Auckland Monday. We're not… I mean, we're just having a… um… fling, I guess. It's not serious."

Faith and Esther exchanged a glance. "Sure," Faith said. She smiled and leaned forward conspiratorially to change the subject. "So what about Gene, then? Who can we fix him up with?"

Glad that Faith had picked up that she didn't want to talk about her relationship with Felix, Coco let them talk about his best mate, but her brain worked furiously as they chatted.

Felix loved her? Was that true? Surely it couldn't be. Not that it mattered even if he did. Although, if he did love her, was there a possibility they could work something out?

"I need a pee," Faith suddenly announced out of the blue. She squirmed in the beanbag, trying to get up, then gave in and sighed. She glanced at Coco. "I don't suppose you'd hold Pippa for a minute while I go? I'd get Rusty but he's practically asleep at the table, poor fellow."

The last time Coco had held a baby had been when one of the secretaries brought one into the offices a year ago. She'd been all fingers and thumbs, and had been glad to hand it on to one of the other women who'd been eager to have a cuddle. But it felt impolite to say no, so she said, "Sure," and leaned over as Faith passed her the baby girl.

"Thank God," Faith said, struggling to her feet. "My pelvic floor's completely gone to pot since giving birth."

"Tell me about it." Esther gestured to her jeans. "One cough and I'm in serious trouble."

Coco watched Faith go, and then turned her attention to the tiny bundle in her arms. The girl was dressed in an adorable white all-in-one with tiny pink rabbits on it, and she was wrapped in what was obviously a handmade shawl. She stirred and waved a small hand in the air for a moment before relaxing back into sleep.

"Nice like that, aren't they?" Esther said. "It's great when you can give them back if they start screeching."

"She's beautiful." Coco inspected the miniature nose and rosebud mouth that pursed and moved as if sucking, and the curling lashes that lay on her whiter-than-white cheek. "Just perfect."

"You should see Rusty with her," Esther said. "You'd never have thought a guy like that would be good with babies, but he does everything."

"Is Toby like that?" Coco asked.

Esther smiled. "He's great with Charlie—they're like a lion and his cub, all rough and tumble, you know? God knows how he'll be with a baby though. He's all fingers and thumbs usually so it's going to be fun watching him with something so tiny." The baby gave a loud burp, and the women laughed. Esther rolled her eyes. "So, do you want one now?"

Coco looked at the baby and let herself imagine for a moment that it was her and Felix's daughter lying in her arms, and to her shock a wave of emotion rolled over her, bringing tears to her eyes and making her breath catch in her throat.

"Oh crap." Esther sat up hurriedly and leaned across to rub her arm. "I'm so sorry, I didn't mean to upset you."

Embarrassed, Coco sniffed and shook her head. "It's okay, I'm all right. It's just… I don't think this is going to happen for me, you know?"

Esther's forehead crinkled with concern. "You don't think you and Felix have a future?"

"I can't see how we can make it work."

Esther smiled. "I thought the same with his brother. I lived on a different island from him, for God's sake. But it worked out. Sometimes you have to trust in love."

I'd like to, Coco thought. But even though the girls had teased her that he was in love with her, how was she to know if it was the truth? And even if it was, she had her mother and he had his job in Auckland—how could they ever make that work?

Chapter Forty-Four

Felix glanced at Coco, and the breath caught in his throat as he saw her with the baby cradled in her arms. Esther was leaning forward, frowning, and he got the impression she was concerned because Coco was upset. As he watched, Coco rubbed her nose and said something that made Esther laugh and lean back on the beanbag, Charlie cradled in her lap. Coco looked back down at the baby, and he watched as she placed a kiss on Pippa's dark hair.

He'd never thought about having kids before. Not because he didn't want any particularly—he was content to think it might happen in the future, but ideally other things needed to come first, like a wife and mortgage, although to be fair it hadn't happened that way for Toby. But the thought of having a child, of picturing himself holding a baby, had never entered his head.

Sometimes it had crossed his mind that it would be nice if one day he could have a son at his side, when he was fishing maybe, and he'd picture himself teaching the boy how to tie on the hook and load a worm. Or when he was playing rugby, he'd imagine showing the lad how to throw and catch, and the best way to pass the ball. But a baby? The thought had filled him with horror. Babies were noisy and smelly and interrupted your sleep. They stopped you going out and ruined your sex life. He'd never found the thought appealing.

But watching Coco sitting there, singing to the little bundle in her arms, for the first time in his life he had a surge of paternal desire, an urge to take her, plant his seed in her, watch her swell with his baby, and be at her side as she brought that child into the world. It was so strong it made him dizzy, and so unexpected that if he'd been standing, he was sure he'd have fallen over.

Someone said something, and he blinked and looked across at his friends. Gene's eyebrows had risen half an inch. Rusty was smirking even though his eyes were half-closed. Toby was grinning outright, and as Felix focused on him, he sang, "Felix and Coco, sitting in a tree, K-I-S-S-I—"

"Fuck off," Felix said, throwing them a glare as they all started laughing.

Toby sat back in his chair, fingers linked, and studied him, eyes gleaming. "Jeez, bro', you've got it bad."

Felix finished off his beer and poured himself another from the half-full pitcher on the table. "Just because you're saddled with a ball and chain, you needn't take it out on the rest of us."

"Yep," Toby said cheerfully. "Hitched and saddled."

"That was supposed to be a sarcastic comment."

"Don't care. I like being married. I can have sex whenever I want and I don't have to wear a fucking condom."

Rusty heaved a sigh. "I used to. When I had the energy."

They all laughed. Toby grinned at Felix and Gene. "Aren't you two tempted?"

"Nope," Gene said.

Felix opened his mouth, then shut it again. Against his will, his gaze slid across to Coco. Faith had returned and taken the baby, and Coco now stretched out her legs, bare to mid-thigh, long and tanned. At the top, he knew they paled to a strip of white which led to a beautiful soft patch of skin.

He leaned forward and rested his forehead on the table, and they all burst out laughing.

He banged it a few times, then sat up and stared at the ceiling. "I don't know what I'm going to do."

"Ask her to move to Auckland," Rusty suggested.

"She looks after her mother, who's got Multiple Sclerosis."

They all thought about that for a while.

"You could move to Wellington," Toby said.

Felix hesitated. Toby had moved to Christchurch to be with Esther, so he didn't consider it a difficult proposition. But then Toby hadn't had a career. Or rather the one he did have, carpentry, he could do anywhere.

You can be a lawyer anywhere too, asshole, Felix's brain whispered, and he cursed himself and let out a heavy sigh.

The problem was that he loved working at the Auckland office, and he heartily disliked the Wellington branch. He disliked the building, the décor, and most of the people in it, which was a bit of a drawback.

No, that wasn't strictly true. He did dislike the décor, but on the whole the people were okay. He disliked Peter Dell and his sidekick with a passion though. He would never be able to work with them, even if there was a possibility that Dell would welcome him into the branch, which was unlikely.

He could try to get a position at another law firm, but he liked McAllister Dell. He'd worked hard to gain a reputation there, he liked working for Christopher McAllister, and if he moved firms now it would take him several more years to make partner, whereas he was sure Christopher was going to put him forward to the board early the following year.

He couldn't see a way out. It would take a huge sacrifice in the career in which he'd worked a good portion of his life, for this woman he'd only known for a week. Didn't that sound crazy when he said it out loud—or, rather, when he voiced it in his head?

He looked at Gene, who'd steadfastly avoided any attempt from previous girlfriends to tie him down. "Come on, mate, back me up. It's just a fling. There's no need to start talking about forever and ever amen, eh?"

Gene shrugged. "Marriage isn't for everyone. Personally, I can't imagine wanting to tie myself to one person for the rest of my life. That doesn't mean it won't happen—just that I haven't yet met anyone that's made me think about commitment to that extent." He smiled. "But I have to admit, I haven't seen you this happy since, well, forever really."

"Since Lindsey," said Toby.

Felix rolled his eyes. "Next you'll all be getting out the choc-chip ice cream and making me watch Bridget Jones."

"Classic avoidance," said Toby. "Done it all my life so I recognize it in others now. If she's the one, you've got to go for it."

"It's not that easy." Felix gripped the handle of his glass. "I've only known her a week, for Christ's sake. We've slept together precisely four times. How am I supposed to make a life decision based on that?"

"Four times?" Toby said. "Is that all?"

Felix threw him an exasperated look. "Give me a break. I have been working."

"Even so. You're slacking. You're supposed to be in your prime."

"It's quality, not quantity. I've made up for it in content."

Toby's eyebrows rose. "Content?"

"It's a fantasy thing, there was an igloo and..." His voice faded away at the look on their faces. "Never mind."

"You fucked in an igloo?"

"Inappropriate, Toby," Rusty said.

"I'm interested." Toby leaned forward. "Didn't you worry your dick would get frostbite?"

Felix gave in. "It wasn't a real igloo. There were boxes and a white sheet... Look, that's not the point. It was about sexual fantasies."

The guys started laughing. Rusty grinned. "You know Faith's going to want a list for her magazine column."

Felix closed his eyes. "I've had too much to drink. Please don't say anything to her." He knew what Faith was like. She was always looking for ideas for her blog, and once she got wind of someone having fun in the bedroom, she demanded details.

"It's not exactly a long-term commitment," Gene agreed.

"I've been out with other girls for months," Felix pursued stubbornly. "I can't change my whole life after one week."

Their smiles faded. "It's a tough call," Gene said. "I guess she'll be the one that got away."

Felix watched Coco get to her feet and help Faith up with the baby. *The one that got away.* Gene was right. It was easy for Toby to get all romantic and talk about moving across the country, but he'd had a child with Esther—that had made the decision a lot easier. Felix liked Coco, and it was possible that if they'd lived close enough to continue seeing each other, the relationship might have grown into something. But their circumstances meant that was impossible. And he had to stop fantasizing about happy ever afters, accept this was just a fling, and deal with it.

The girls came back to the table, Charlie now dozing on Esther's shoulder. "Jeez, he's getting heavy," she said. She looked at the wet patch on her top. "And he dribbles in his sleep, just like his father."

Toby grinned and kissed her on the cheek, and she giggled. Felix smiled. It was good to see his brother so happy. He didn't resent him for the way his life had turned out. He did envy him a little, though.

The waitress came up, and they decided to order a quick coffee before they all left and returned to their hotel rooms for the night. I'm getting old, Felix thought, looking at his watch and seeing it was only half past seven.

"I need to feed Pippa," Faith said. "Um, does anyone mind if I do it at the table? I'll happily go into the ladies' if you'd rather."

Everyone said of course not, that she was fine where she was, and they all politely averted their gazes and carried on talking while she slipped a hand up her top to unbutton the maternity bra and nestled the baby close to her. Truthfully, Felix would never have known she was nursing if she hadn't told them.

It was, of course, not the done thing to stare at your mate's wife's breasts, but Felix found his gaze drawn to Faith as she sat there only half-listening to the conversation, enveloped in her own little world with the baby, curled up against Rusty who had his arm around her, and who murmured something in her ear that made her smile before he placed a kiss on his daughter's head.

Felix felt a deep hollowness inside, born out of envy and a rising sadness that for him this moment of marital and parental bliss seemed further away than ever. Part of him felt cross at himself at that—the thought of having children hadn't even entered his head before he came to Wellington—why was he suddenly all glassy-eyed and broody?

But then he glanced at Coco to see her watching him, and he knew why. He caught her gaze and held it, seeing within her eyes the same emotions passing through him. She felt the same way, although she knew she couldn't voice her feelings, because what was the point? She gave a small smile, and he returned it, and it was as if at that moment they knew—it would never work out. It just wasn't meant to be.

They all had their coffees and then it was time to go. Everyone hugged Felix and wished him happy birthday, and they parted at the door, promising to see each other again soon. Rusty and Faith walked off in one direction, Toby and Esther in another with Toby carrying Charlie.

Felix turned to Coco. "Want to join us for a drink?"

She shook her head. "I'd better not. Frances needs to get back tonight—her daughter's had a few contractions and she wants to go around there this evening."

"Of course. I'll call you a taxi." He rang from his mobile, and they hung around for the few minutes it took to turn up.

"Nice to have met you," Coco said to Gene with a smile.

"It was my pleasure." He kissed her on the cheek.

"I hope you had a happy birthday," she said to Felix.

Gene politely walked along the road a little to look in a shop window, and Felix turned and took her hands in his.

He looked into her eyes, and suddenly it didn't matter that he couldn't think what to say because she gave a little shake of her head and smiled.

Still, he couldn't leave it like that. "Can I see you tomorrow?" he asked, knowing he shouldn't, but unable to stop himself.

"It depends on Frances," she said. "But yes, I'd like to."

"I think we have time for one more fantasy," he teased.

"Hurrah!"

He chuckled, then drew her into his arms. "Thanks for a lovely evening."

She wrapped her arms around his waist and rested her cheek on his chest. "And thank you for asking me. It was nice to meet your friends and family."

It was nice to have you as a part of that group, even if it was only fleeting. He thought the words but didn't voice them, just lifted her chin and kissed her. She returned it eagerly, melting against him, and he gave himself over to the taste of her, the softness of her lips beneath his. Only when the taxi pulled up did he move back and release her.

"I'll call you tomorrow," he said.

"Sure." She gave Gene a parting wave and got in.

Gene walked up to him and they both watched the taxi pull away. Gene cleared his throat. "All right?"

Felix grunted. "If I'm not Brahms within thirty minutes, I'll be very surprised."

"Brahms?"

Felix sighed. "And Liszt. Pissed, Gene. It's not rocket science."

Gene clapped him on the back. "I thought as much. Whiskies all round. Come on, mate." He led him off to the nearest bar, where Felix proceeded to lose himself in alcohol, and wax lyrical about Coco for the rest of the evening.

Chapter Forty-Five

To Coco's relief, when she got in Frances informed her that her daughter's contractions had only been Braxton Hicks, and she wasn't yet in labor. Coco stifled her irritation at the thought that she could have spent longer with Felix and concentrated on the fact that it probably meant she'd be all right to go out with him the next day.

Unfortunately, however, at ten in the morning Frances rang. "She's had the baby!" she announced triumphantly. "Her waters broke around midnight, and the baby was born at eight o'clock."

"Congratulations," Coco said, feeling like a heel because she felt like yelling down the phone how incredibly selfish the new mother had been not to be able to hold on for another few days. "You're a grandma!"

"I know!" Frances sound blissfully happy. "Sweetie, I'm so sorry but I won't be able to come around tonight."

"Of course not. Don't even think about it. You concentrate on your grandson and have a lovely time." She passed the phone over to Eleanor so her mother could congratulate her too, then went into the kitchen.

She poured water in the kettle, put it on, then walked into the garden and rang Felix on her mobile.

"Hello?" His deep voice sent a shiver running through her. Just the one word, and she was already turned on.

"It's me."

"Hey." He sounded pleased. "I was just thinking about you."

She squashed the thrill of pleasure his words gave her. "Look, I'm really sorry but Frances's daughter has had the baby. She can't come around tonight."

He fell silent for a moment, then said, "Honey, I'm sorry."

Not half as sorry as me, she thought bitterly. "It's me who should be sorry. I should have thought about it and got a nurse organized."

"It's okay."

"It's not." Tears pricked her eyes. "It's fucking awful."

She heard him take a deep breath and release it slowly. "It's not the end of the world," he said, and she thought he she could hear a smile in his voice. "Look, would you like me to get a takeaway or something and bring it around? We could play cards with your mum, or watch a DVD or something."

Coco closed her eyes and her fingers tightened on the phone. She couldn't bear his kindness. And she wouldn't be able to bear her mother sitting there looking all smug every time she glanced over at Felix, expecting them to announce any minute that they were eloping or something.

"No," she said hoarsely, "I've got stuff to do."

"Okay," he said easily, "I should probably work on the case anyway. Perhaps Frances may be free tomorrow."

"I doubt it." A tear ran down her cheek. "I think we should just accept we're done, Felix."

He went silent for a moment. Then he said, "Don't say that."

"Why? It's pointless. We're only delaying the inevitable. One more shag—yes it would be fun but really, why put ourselves through it?"

"Because I want to spend time with you."

She gave an exasperated sigh. "Felix…"

"Let me speak to Eleanor."

"For God's sake, what for?"

"I want to talk to her."

Irritation washed over her. "No, don't be stupid."

"Coco." His voice was sharp. "I'll only be a minute. Put her on."

"She's on the phone."

"No, I'm not." Her mother's voice sounded from behind her, and Coco turned to see that she'd wheeled herself into the kitchen. Eleanor held her hand out calmly. "Let me talk to him."

Coco stood there, rigid with rage, but couldn't think how to get out of the situation other than by hanging up on him, so she just handed the phone over mutely.

Eleanor took it and held it up to her ear. "Hello, Felix." She listened as he spoke for a while, then smiled. "That's fine, of course. No, it's the other one, on Bank Street. No, I don't think it will be a problem, they're very flexible. Yes, I'll tell her. Of course." She smiled again. "I appreciate it. Thanks, Felix." She flipped the phone shut.

Coco glared at her. "What was that about?"

"Felix is arranging for a nurse to look after me tomorrow so he can take you out. He'll pick you up at six, and he wants you to stay the night." She grinned mischievously.

Coco was too upset by now though to take the news of them both organizing her life for her well. "How dare he?" She gritted her teeth and held her hand out for her phone. "I'll ring him and cancel it."

Eleanor pulled her blouse open and tucked the phone into her bra. "No you won't."

"Mum!" Coco was aghast. "Don't be so childish, give it back."

"No, darling, you only have one life. You're bloody well going to make the most of it even if I have to force you out that door."

"I won't go!" Coco snapped. "I'll put on my pajamas and stay in bed until he's gone."

Eleanor looked exasperated. "Now who's being childish?"

Abruptly, all Coco's anger faded and instead she covered her mouth with a hand as emotion welled. "I don't want this. You don't know everything, Mum."

"I know you have feelings for this boy."

Coco felt a brief sweep of amusement at the thought of what Felix's face would look like if he heard himself called boy, and then she felt even more upset. "Yes, I do have feelings for him. But don't you see? It just makes it worse. He's going Monday."

"Even more reason to spend time with him, then, while he's here."

She sat and put her head in her hands. Unbidden, tears rolled down her cheeks, a culmination of all the emotion that had built up over the last week, plus the frustration she felt constantly at her mother's pressure to be more sociable.

Eleanor sighed and wheeled the chair forward to put a comforting hand on her daughter's shoulder. "Please don't cry. Falling in love can make you feel wretched, I know, but ultimately it's got to be a good thing."

"I don't want to be in love," Coco said through her sobs. "I can't be. I've only known him a week."

Eleanor blew a raspberry. "Like that matters. I fell in love with your father the moment he walked into the room."

Thinking of her father only made Coco sob more.

"What's wrong?" Eleanor murmured, patting her knee. "Please don't cry. I don't like to see you like this."

Coco put her face in her hands. "I wish you wouldn't keep talking about going into a home," she wailed. "It upsets me so. I love you so much."

"I know." Eleanor's voice was husky. "But, honey, I think the main problem is that you're frightened about being alone—about going out into the big wide world on your own. I know you never felt you could talk to me about it, but Michael obviously screwed you up inside, and ever since you broke up with him you've withdrawn from, well, everything, and I hate to see you separating yourself off from the world. You deserve everything—a husband, a home, children. I'd like to be a grandmother, you know. You can't get those things all the time you're looking after me. And because you're too frightened to do it yourself, I'm going to have to make the break for you."

"Don't leave me," Coco sobbed.

Eleanor removed Coco's hand from her face and pressed the back of it against her cheek. "Darling, I don't know whether Felix is the one you're supposed to be with. But he makes you so happy—it's written all over your face. Love doesn't come to us handed on a plate—we have to work for it sometimes, and it's hard and it hurts, but it's worth it in the end, and perhaps the hard work makes it more worthwhile. So anyway, what I mean is, go out with him tomorrow. Have a fun time. Stay the night. And keep an open mind as to the future. Please. For me."

Tears trickled through the fingers of Coco's other hand. "Don't be so reasonable. Please, I can't bear it."

Eleanor kissed her. "Don't worry too much about everything right now. Concentrate on tomorrow and on having a nice time with that young man. And hopefully everything else will fall into place."

*

Coco couldn't possibly see how everything was going to work out right, and part of her was still angry that Felix had gone over her head and organized care for her mother without asking. But ultimately it meant she could have a final date with him, and in the end, she gave in and admitted to herself that she couldn't pass up on the chance to see him one last time.

So when he knocked on the door at six o'clock Sunday evening, she was ready and waiting, and opened it with a mixture of pleasure and exasperation at his mischievous, slightly rueful grin.

MR. SENSATIONAL

"Hey," he said. "Are you going to swing a baseball bat at my head?"

She laughed at that and kissed him on the cheek. "No, you're safe. I've calmed down now." She stepped out and closed the door.

"The nurse came then?" He took her hand and led her over to the taxi.

"Yes. And Felix, I'm still a bit angry that you went over my head, but I understand why you did it, and I'm grateful that you bothered."

He pulled her to him and kissed her. "I only want to get in your panties one last time."

"Yeah, I know." She smiled and kissed him back. She'd determined she was going to put everything else behind her and enjoy this evening, and obviously he thought the same way.

The taxi took them to his hotel, and he led her inside and through the foyer to the bar. "I thought it might be nice to have a drink first," he said.

"First?"

He grinned and ordered himself a brandy, the grin broadening when she asked for the same, and they sat for a while in the peace of the bar and chatted while they drank their spirits, then ordered another round and drank that too.

Coco finished off the glass and stretched, enjoying the feel of the alcohol making its way around her body, releasing all the tension from her muscles. "Are you trying to get me drunk?"

Felix finished his, then stood and took her hand, leading her out of the bar and along to the elevators. "Maybe." He kissed her. "Just trying to relax you."

"Another scenario?" she teased, her heart beginning to speed up at the knowledge that he'd planned something else.

"Absolutely." The doors opened and he led her into the lift and pressed the button. "And for this one there are a few rules."

"Oh?" She swallowed nervously.

He turned to her as the doors closed and stroked her cheek with his hand. "First, you have to trust me, okay?"

She blinked, wondering what had prompted that instruction. "Um, okay."

"I mean it. This will only work if you put your trust in the fact that I would never hurt you or do anything to embarrass you or make you uncomfortable. Whatever happens, I do because I want you to enjoy yourself, and to help you explore your sexuality. Okay?" His eyes had turned molten, scorching with heat.

Her knees went weak and her mouth went dry. "Okay."

"Secondly…" He put his hand in his pocket and pulled something out. It was a black silk scarf. Her heart hammered. "I'm going to tie this around your eyes. And, whatever happens, you mustn't remove it, understand?"

Dear God, what was he going to do to her?

"Promise?" he said.

"I promise." Her voice was a little more than a whisper. "What… what are we doing?"

He kissed her nose. "You remember your final fantasy?"

She struggled to remember, and then the memory hit her with full force. She stared at him. "You mean…the sex club?"

A naughty light filled his eyes.

Her mouth fell open. She'd talked about a room that could be hired out for parties, and described her fantasy of being tied to a bed while a group of men got to use her any way they wanted. Jesus. She'd not been serious. *Please God, tell me he didn't think I was serious.*

The elevator pinged, and the doors opened. Felix walked forward, taking her with him, and she walked in a daze to his room at the end. Could she hear music behind the door?

The corridor was empty, and he turned to her and held up the scarf.

"Remember," he murmured, looking into her eyes, "trust me." And then he tied the scarf around her eyes, opened the door and led her forward.

Chapter Forty-Six

Coco stopped inside the doorway, her heart pounding. Behind her, she heard Felix close the door and then felt his presence at her back. He rested his hands on her upper arms and waited.

Her senses spun with light and noise, and she struggled to comprehend where she was. Felix had said he'd arranged a room in a club for her, and that was exactly what it felt like. Behind the blindfold, she could just see flashes of colored light against the darkness like laser lights dancing across the room. The music was loud but not deafeningly so—probably because he didn't want to disturb his neighbours, although the fact that they had the end room with the kitchen and bedrooms between them and next door would make it more difficult for anyone to hear.

The room was also filled with people. As she entered, a loud cheer went up and everyone clapped. She shrank back into Felix's chest, and he chuckled and kissed her ear. "They're pleased to see you," he murmured into her ear, sounding amused. "Don't worry, they're all good friends of mine. Just nice guys looking for a good time."

A good time with her? Had he taken her at her word when she said she wanted to be taken by a room full of men? She'd been talking fantasy, not reality. She couldn't really have sex with more than one man, in front of all the others. What was he thinking?

She shook her head. "Felix, I can't do this."

Half-expecting him to immediately open the door and take her out, apologizing profusely for misunderstanding, she stiffened when he chuckled again and locked his arms around her. "Trust me," was all he said. He placed a kiss on her shoulder and waited again.

Chest heaving, head spinning, she forced herself to think of everything he'd done for her since she'd met him—all the fantasies he'd gone to such time and effort to organize for her. He'd been so kind and caring every time they'd been out together. He'd gotten jealous when he thought she'd slept with Peter Dell—she'd seen it in his eyes. He wouldn't want her being taken by a room full of men—

he would never do that to her. *Trust me*, he'd said, and she had to do that. She had to place herself in his hands and understand what he was trying to do for her here.

He wanted to fulfil her fantasy, but that didn't mean he'd arranged twenty guys to come to his room. She listened to the voices that rose and fell, the cheers, the clink of glasses, the wolf whistles. It must be a recording. He wanted her to feel as if she were in a room full of men, to throw herself into the fantasy. But she had to trust that he had her best interests at heart.

He kissed slowly up her neck to her ear and then nibbled the lobe. "Ready?"

She moistened her lips, deciding to go along with it for a while until she could work out whether they were truly alone. She nodded.

He kissed her hair. "Good girl." He moved her forward to stand in the center of the room. Then he left her side.

Coco stood there, trying not to panic, reassuring herself that there weren't twenty or so sex-craved men in the room waiting to take her in front of their friends, but it was difficult. It felt like there were twenty men there—the room was warm as if packed with bodies, and the voices were very convincing. The brandy she'd drunk earlier had dulled her brain a little too, and having her eyes covered meant the rest of her senses reached out to try and make sense of her surroundings. Her skin prickled, and against her will, her nipples tightened at the thought that maybe there were people there, waiting for her. Maybe these men were expecting to have sex with her. She was going to have group sex, in public. Oh dear God.

She was just about to panic when once again she felt a presence at her back and Felix took her arms again. He kissed her shoulder. "They want to check out the goods before they buy. I'm going to undress you now. Okay?"

She breathed rapidly, about to refuse. She couldn't go through with this.

Then Felix's fingers slipped around her face and he turned her head so he could kiss her. His warm lips moved across hers, his tongue stroking her lips before brushing into her mouth. In the room, a cheer went up, and her heart pounded in response. If that was a recording, how had he organized a cheer right at that moment?

His hand brushed her arm, something cool resting on her skin. A small rectangular object. It felt like… a remote control.

He removed it and lifted his head. "Ready?"

He'd tried to show her how he was making this work. To put her at her ease. There were just the two of them here. But she had to believe there were others to make the fantasy work.

Moistening her lips again, heart thudding from his kiss as well as the cheers, she nodded. "Okay."

From behind, he unbuttoned her jacket, then slid it down her arms. The group cheered.

Felix then slid down the zipper on the back of her skirt. He held it in place for a moment, saying, "Ready, guys?" before letting it fall to the ground. A huge cheer went up with wolf whistles all around.

Coco's mouth had gone dry. Felix ran his hands across the lace of her panties to the top of her thighs, where a strip of skin lay exposed above the top of her thigh-high stockings. "Nice," he murmured, pressing against her back. His erection fit snugly between the cheeks of her bottom, hard as stone. His fingers danced tantalizingly across her skin, sending tingles across her stomach, making her nipples harden again.

His hands now began to undo the buttons of her blouse. *It's just me and him*, she told herself hurriedly, but it was so difficult to believe when the warm room felt cramped with bodies. He popped the buttons through the holes leisurely. When he reached the bottom, he slid the material slowly off her shoulders, and it slipped down her arms to the floor.

Everyone cheered. Coco automatically crossed her arms over her breasts, heart thundering. Felix trailed the tips of his fingers down the back of her arms, then up the front to her shoulders. "You look beautiful," he murmured. "I think they agree too, don't you?"

She leaned back against him, feeling safe in the circle of his arms. He kissed her shoulders, up her neck, trailed his tongue around her ear. "I want you," he whispered. "I'm going to let some of my friends play with you for a bit, and then I'm going to take you in front of all them because you're mine, understand?"

She shivered, entranced by the possessiveness in his voice. "Yes," she said, wishing she could see him, knowing his eyes would be hot with desire.

"But first I'm going to take off your bra. They deserve to see how pretty your breasts are."

She felt his fingers at her back, unhooking the catch. The elastic gave, and she tightened her arms across her breasts as he slid the straps off her shoulders.

"Now, now," he teased. "You agreed to do as you were told. Drop your arms."

She swallowed, still fearful the room really was full of strangers, nervous about stripping naked in front of other men.

He gripped her upper arms and put gentle pressure on them. "Do. As. You're. Told." His voice sounded amused, as well as firm.

Trust me. She focused on the words he'd whispered earlier and dropped her arms. He slid the bra down them and it fell to the floor. Then, before she could cross her arms over her breasts again, he caught her hands behind her back. To her surprise, she felt him tie them with another scarf.

A huge cheer went up, and Coco stood there frozen, blood racing through her body, naked except for her tiny lace panties, her hands fixed behind her back. Felix moved away. Her chest heaved with her rapid breaths and she could feel her nipples tightening under his silent stare, but she forced herself to remain still. *This is just a game*, she told herself. And she had to play her part in it too.

After a few moments, her skin prickled—he was standing in front of her. He came forward and she felt his hands on her breasts.

"You're so fucking beautiful," he said, his voice husky. The men roared in response. "Are you enjoying this?" he asked, rubbing his thumbs across her nipples.

Coco sucked her bottom lip, unable to confess how aroused she was at that moment. The thought of performing in front of an audience was a fantasy she'd had for years, and she couldn't believe she was actually carrying it out, with Felix, possibly the most gorgeous man alive.

"I think you are." He moved closer to her, and then his lips brushed hers. "I think the thought of being fucked in front of all these men—by these men—is turning you on."

"Oh God..." She shook a little, although whether from desire or nervousness she wasn't sure. "Felix..."

He kissed her, sliding his hand to cup the back of her head like he usually did, plunging his tongue into her mouth, and taking possession of it until she was gasping for breath, a dull throbbing beginning between her thighs.

He lifted his head, and his lips hovered over hers. "They have a list of requests," he murmured. "First of all… They want to see you perform oral sex."

She licked her lips. "Oh."

"Every man's dream. Are you up for that?"

Moisture was now dampening her panties. "Oh God, yes."

He laughed at that. "You're sure? You're happy to go down on me in front of all these men?"

Michael had enjoyed oral sex, and because of that he had refused to let her do it very often, seeing something wrong in the pleasure it gave them both. How twisted his mind had been, she thought now. Why was sexual pleasure such a bad thing? Felix had proved to her that the human body was something beautiful to be enjoyed, and for that if nothing else she was glad she'd met him.

She nodded, the thought of taking him in her mouth making her knees go wobbly. "Yes," she whispered. "Yes, please."

"Okay." His voice had gone husky again. She was turning him on.

He moved her a few steps to one side, and she felt the softness of a duvet on the floor. He'd placed it there so she had something soft to kneel on. That made her soften inside. He was so sweet.

"Kneel down," he instructed. He helped her to do so, as she still had her hands tied behind her back. The whistles in the room grew louder, the cheers echoing, and her heart thumped. What if there really were men in the room, about to watch her go down on Felix? She licked her lips, hot desire and excitement coursing through her veins. Well, she was going to give them a bloody good show, that's what.

Felix stood in front of her, planting his feet either side of her kneeling form.

"Ready?" he said.

She nodded, breathless with excitement.

She could just hear the sound of his zipper sliding down above the cheers in the room.

Chapter Forty-Seven

Coco waited obediently, moistening her lips in anticipation of what was to come. She smelled him first—the warm, musky, sexy scent of hot male, and then the tip of his erection brushed across her lips. She inhaled, opening her mouth to take him inside, conscious of her audience watching eagerly.

He'd showered—she could smell the fresh scent of manly body wash, and he tasted clean. She ran her tongue around the head, then underneath, exploring him, tracing the ridges and dips, the veins and sensitive skin. Felix shivered, hardening even further, if that were possible, and she knew he was enjoying observing her carrying out this act. She wished she could see him, but there was also something intensely erotic about touching and being touched in the dark. Her other senses came sharply into focus until he seemed everywhere, and all she could think about was him.

She ran her tongue back over the head of his erection and tasted the moisture on the tip, listening to his answering groan with satisfaction. A burning desire to pleasure him rose inside her—she wanted to feel his body's urges take over his gentleness, to feel him thrust in her mouth, to taste his warm, silky fluid. She wanted to be the cause of his undoing.

Covering the tip with her mouth, she took him inside and sucked.

He inhaled, his breath whistling through his teeth, and she murmured her approval and ran her tongue over the head. For a while she experimented with her tongue and lips, finding out what he liked, what made him exclaim and swell in her mouth. Pretty much everything, was the answer, although when she moved her head forward and took him deeper inside, his answering curse and the way he threaded his hand through her hair told her she'd found his weak spot.

He held her head and pushed forward gently, then pulled back and removed himself from her mouth. "Okay?" he said softly.

Coco tipped her head up, ran her tongue around her lips and said, "More." The crowd cheered.

He swore again, but did as she bid, accompanying the dips of her head with subtle thrusts of his hips, careful not to push too far. But it wasn't enough. She wanted him deeper, needed to drive him wild.

She pulled back and said, "Stand still and watch." He stopped moving, and she took him into her mouth again. But this time she moved forward, sliding her lips down his shaft, showing him what was comfortable, where she wanted him, deep inside, touching the back of her throat. Then she pulled back. "You do it," she said, her voice husky even to her own ears.

He hesitated, then tightened his fingers in her hair and pushed forward, burying himself in her mouth. She gave a low moan and tipped back her head, welcoming him in, and he grunted and did it again, thrusting forward, still gentle, but deeper than before.

Coco's head spun with dizzy pleasure, his rising lack of control making the blood race around her body. Her body felt damp with her own wetness, and where she knelt, legs together, she could squeeze her thighs and feel an answering tremor between her legs. *I could come like this*, she thought hazily, the whole erotic situation arousing her in a way she'd never have imagined. The crowd seemed to have gotten louder—was that Felix? How had he done that, the remote again? And the chants of the men and their encouraging cheers were driving her crazy. She couldn't believe she was doing this, kneeling there practically naked with Felix thrusting in her mouth for all to see. But she was past embarrassment, past everything except the dark desire clawing its way up inside her.

Felix's thrusts were becoming jerkier, harder, and she sensed he wasn't far from coming. His hand tightened in her hair. She moaned again, and he cursed, holding her head and pushing deeper into her throat. Saliva coated her lips and ran down her chin, but she didn't care—all she could think about was making him come.

"Fuck," he said vehemently. "Move away now if you don't want me to come in your mouth, honey."

But instead she leaned forward and took him deep as she could, and with a triumphant, hoarse roar he gave into his climax, filling her mouth with hot, salty fluid as the room echoed with the cheers and hoots of the watching men.

Coco clenched her thighs as her own orgasm swept over her. It was a tremendous feeling, everything pulsing between her legs as she swallowed him down, and part of her wanted it to go on forever, this moment of bringing him fulfilment, of joining with him in sensual bliss.

But gradually the pleasurable ripples died away, and he withdrew gently from her mouth. She heard the sound of him rearranging his clothing and doing up the zipper, and then he was helping her to her feet.

He brushed her lips and cheeks, wiping away any moisture. And then he kissed her, soft, tender kisses as he wrapped his arms around her and held her tightly. Did he not mind tasting himself? Clearly not, she thought as his tongue played with hers. Typical Felix. She had a feeling the word disgusting wasn't in his vocabulary.

"Thank you," he murmured when he eventually raised his head.

"Oh, you are more than welcome." Her knees felt a little wobbly. "I may have to sit down."

He chuckled. "I hope you don't think the evening's over."

"Um…"

"The guys have had enough of watching. They want to take their turn now." More cheers.

What did he mean by that? She puzzled over his words as he led her a few steps forward. Surely he didn't mean…

"Stop there," he said. She did so, still shaking a little from the intensity of her orgasm. Next she felt his hands on her hips, tugging down her panties. He peeled them down her legs, and held her steady while she stepped out of them, and then he stood facing her again. He reached behind her and untied her hands. "There's a mattress behind you. Climb onto it."

She knelt and moved forward onto the mattress.

"Turn on your back."

She lay down on her back, feeling exposed in her nakedness. Felix took her hands and raised them, tying them somewhere above her head. Then he looped silky material around her left ankle. He tied that off to her left, and then he did the same to her right.

Coco lay there, legs open for all to see. She could draw up her knees a little so her feet were flat on the bed, but she couldn't get her legs together. She was defenseless and vulnerable, completely at the mercy of whoever was in the room.

She nearly came again at the thought.

Her heart pounded at the yells and whistles. By now she was certain she and Felix were alone, but with her eyes still covered it was easy to pretend she was surrounded by hungry, testosterone-filled males who were all determined to have a piece of her before the night was out.

The mattress dipped, and Felix stretched out beside her. He kissed her stomach, then up her ribcage to her breasts. His tongue circled her nipples lazily before he finally kissed up to her mouth. "Okay, honey?" he asked, sounding amused again. His chest brushed against hers—he'd undressed.

"Um, yes." Her heart rate sped up again at the anticipation of what he had planned.

"Are you comfortable?"

"As comfortable as you can be with your private parts on show for all and sundry."

He kissed her ear. "You look fucking amazing." He kissed her mouth leisurely, dipping his tongue inside, nibbling her lips. "You realize I could do absolutely anything to you like this and you'd be powerless to stop me?"

She nearly fainted with pleasure. "Felix…"

He chuckled and ran his tongue around her ear. "Are you ready to service these fine young men who are waiting to enjoy you?" A chorus of cheers greeted his words. The intoxicating music threaded through her veins, along with the alcohol, sending her into a spiral of pleasure.

She felt breathless with nerves and excitement. "Oh God…"

"If you want us to stop, we'll stop." He kissed her. "But I promise you won't want us to."

She moistened her lips. "Okay."

"I'll be here," he said. "I won't leave your side." He shifted slightly. "Here's the guy who begged me to be first in the queue. His name's Tom."

Coco said nothing, breathing heavily, uncertain what to expect.

"His cock's not too big," Felix said, sounding amused. "But it ain't what you do, it's the way that you do it, right?"

"I guess," she said faintly.

"Get ready. Here he comes, pardon the pun."

She tensed, flinched as something brushed her thighs, then almost sagged with relief as he ran an object lightly between her legs. A vibrator. Of *course* he wouldn't want her to have sex with other men. This was all about her imagination. He'd done it all for her, and all he wanted was for her to enjoy it and throw herself into the fantasy.

"He's lubed himself up," Felix said, "but I'm not sure he needs it, judging by how turned on you are." Tom pressed his tip into her folds.

"How rude," she said breathlessly. "Can you blame me after what we've been doing?"

"Hey, it wasn't a complaint. I'm flattered. We all are." His lips touched her nipple at the same moment that Tom moved forward.

Coco moaned and arched against him, welcoming the stranger's erection deep inside her. He felt different from Felix, not as big, but firm and cool. She caught her bottom lip between her teeth as he thrust slowly while Felix teased her nipple, nibbling and sucking alternatively.

"Oh…" She shivered at the thought of the two men having her, a complete stranger fucking her while Felix watched. "Oh, that's good…"

Felix murmured his approval and kissed her while Tom increased his thrusts, sliding easily in and out of her moistened skin. "I don't think he's going to last long," Felix murmured with a chuckle, "and I can't say I blame him. You're sexy enough to make a man come without being touched."

Tom jerked once, twice, and pushed deep within her as he came, then withdrew, making her give a long moan of longing as the orgasm she'd hoped for slipped away from her.

"Patience," Felix scolded. "There are plenty more guys here waiting to take their turn with you. Are you ready for the next one?"

Chapter Forty-Eight

Coco nodded, long since having lost any sense of dignity or reservation. She wanted Felix inside her, wanted to pleasure him again, but knew he was enjoying himself, and she was happy enough to go along with it for the time being.

"This is Liam," Felix said. "He's a bit taller than Tom, with a slightly bigger cock."

Coco bit her lip as Liam moved between her legs and, without any further ado, pushed straight into her. She gasped and jerked instinctively, but the ties around her hands forced her back down and she could only lie there, clenching around him as he waited for her to adjust.

"Liam's great," Felix said huskily in her ear. "Not only is he bigger, but he has this fascinating special ability..."

She jumped as the hard erection inside her started buzzing. "Jeez!"

Felix chuckled. "What a shame all men don't have the same skill, eh?"

She groaned as the vibrations spread through her, arousing her wet and swollen skin. "Oh God..."

"Let the sensations take you, baby." He started to pay attention to her nipples again as Liam gave long, slow thrusts.

Coco did as he told her and gave herself over to the sensations threading through her. It felt amazing, and she quivered with erotic pleasure as Liam continued to move, sliding against her ultra-sensitive skin with such ease she knew she must be incredibly wet.

Her orgasm hovered, but just as before, Felix sighed and said, "Sorry, honey, looks like he can't last the distance either," and Liam shuddered and came inside her, stilling for a final moment before withdrawing and leaving her empty.

She let out her breath in a rush, aching and desperate for fulfilment. "Now you?" she asked hopefully.

But Felix wasn't finished yet. "Sorry. There's one more guy who wants his turn with you."

She lay with thudding heart, waiting to see what he'd come up with this time.

"This guy's big," he said, moving closer to her. "Taller than me. Huge guy. He's undressing now, and… fuck me. His cock's huge."

Her heart pounded and she licked her lips. "Felix…"

"I'm not sure you can take all of him," he said, voice husky again. He was getting turned on. "Are you sure you want to try?"

She strained against her ties, nervous and excited at the same time. "I don't know…"

"His name's Carl. He wants to get inside you." He kissed her cheek. "He can see you open and glistening, ready for him. He's desperate to slide into you." He kissed her mouth, deep and hungry, and she moaned, dissolving into nothing except nerve endings and sensitive skin and sensation.

"Okay," she whispered when he finally raised his head.

"Good girl." He kissed her again, claiming her mouth as Carl pressed into her.

She murmured as the tip slid between her folds. She could feel already the size of his erection, bigger than Felix. She couldn't take it, surely. This was too much.

He pushed forward, slowly, one or two inches, stretching her and waiting for her to accommodate. Jeez, he was big. She couldn't do it.

She moaned against Felix's mouth, half-protesting.

Felix lifted his head. "Okay?" he murmured.

"I don't know," she said breathlessly, not sure.

"Want me to stop?"

Against her will, her internal muscles tightened around the tip of the man inside her, and she groaned. The feeling was unbelievably erotic. God help her, but she didn't want him to stop. "No. But… slowly," she whispered.

"Of course. Just relax." Felix planted small kisses around her mouth. "I promise you, you'll enjoy it." He lifted his head to watch her as Carl continued to slide forward.

She moaned and arched her back, and he stopped. Felix kissed her again, waiting for her to adjust, and gradually she relaxed back into the mattress.

Then Carl pushed forward again, sliding easily into her moistness, burying his huge, thick erection inside her until he'd pushed in right to the hilt.

She gasped, shocked at the size of him, feeling him all the way up. Everything clenched around him, and she moaned again, overwhelmed at feeling so stretched.

"Okay, baby?" Felix murmured.

She moistened her lips. "Yes."

"Good. Relax." Felix kissed down her throat to her breasts, and she did her best to obey and accommodate the man inside her. Gradually, as Felix licked and sucked her nipples and she grew used to the feeling of being so tight, her muscles loosened, softening around the huge erection. As she relaxed, so he slid deeper in, until she felt him press right to the top. The sensation of being so full was amazing.

Felix raised his head and observed her as Carl pulled out, teased her entrance a few times, then slid in again. She moaned and arched again, full to the brim, desperate for him, wanting more.

"You're fucking amazing," Felix growled, kissing down her throat, sucking hungrily at her skin. "I'm going to watch him fuck you now, are you ready?"

"Yes, God, yes, please…"

He dropped his mouth to her breast, and she exclaimed as he sucked hard on her nipple, while Carl began to move inside her, stretching her and then withdrawing time and time again. She couldn't do anything but let him have his way, completely at his mercy. He filled her repeatedly, and she moaned again and again, unable to believe she was being so soundly screwed.

Her orgasm began to build, driven by the sensations of the man who plunged deeper each time until she felt so full she was going to burst at the seams.

The climax swept over her suddenly, and her body stiffened, making her squeal out loud as her muscles contracted around the man inside her. She'd never had an orgasm like it, and the pulses went on and on, waves of pleasure rolling over her until eventually they died down and she lay back, throbbing and exhausted.

Carl slid out of her, and she moaned at the sensation, disappointed at the feeling of emptiness. Felix leaned on her, covering her face with kisses.

"Was that nice?" he murmured.

"Yes…" She couldn't say anything else, too exhausted and sated to form a coherent thought.

"Good." He kissed her for a while, then moved down to her breasts and teased her nipples. She lay limply, letting him do whatever he wanted. She was spent—she'd never be able to come again. Part of her was disappointed—she'd wanted him inside her. But she could hardly complain. He'd just given her an orgasm the like of which she'd never known existed. And two in one night was more than enough.

But Felix appeared to have other ideas. He played with her nipples for a while, then kissed down her stomach, and then he shifted and lay between her legs. Before she could protest, he buried his mouth in her. She complained, squirming, embarrassed that she must be soaking wet and swollen, but he held her tightly around the legs and forced her to lie still, and in the end, all she could do was let him kiss her.

And unbelievably, once again pleasurable sensations began to spiral within her. Surely not… She couldn't come again, could she? But he teased her with his tongue, flicking her clit and plunging his tongue inside her, and soon she was panting, writhing against him, desperate for release once more.

Felix lifted himself up and moved on top of her. There was a brief rustle of paper, and then he lowered himself down.

She stopped him with a murmur of protest just before he entered her. "Felix…"

He kissed her. "What, sweetheart?"

"Can you take the blindfold off?"

He hesitated. Then he lifted off her. She felt his fingers at her ankles, loosening the ties, then at her wrists, releasing her. He moved back on top of her before finally sliding the blindfold off her eyes.

She blinked. He was looking into her eyes, his brown ones filled with such affection and desire that it made her want to cry.

She turned her head and glanced around the room. As she'd suspected, they were alone, and as she watched, Felix flicked a button on the remote lying on the bed and the voices and cheers of the men faded, leaving only the music, and it was just the two of them.

She met his eyes again. "That was amazing."

"Was?" He kissed her. "I haven't done anything yet."

She scored her nails down his back, enjoying his answering shiver. "You know what I mean. Thank you for… everything."

"You're very welcome." He moved his hips and she felt him push into her folds. She lifted her hips, and he slid inside her.

"Oh…" She stretched out beneath him, filled with contentment at the feel of him all the way up.

"Hopefully you're not disappointed after Carl." He chuckled and kissed her.

She returned the kiss dreamily. "Not at all." This was what she wanted. This man had taken the time to bring her fantasy to life in a way only he could have done.

She couldn't believe he was going on Monday. This would probably be the last time they would make love. The thought hit her like a sledgehammer, making her heart thump behind her ribs. She swallowed and ran her hands up his muscular arms, down his back to his waist, then felt the muscles in his butt bunching as he moved inside her. How was she going to let him go?

He thrust leisurely. "God, you feel fantastic." He kissed her, continuing to move, sliding out and then thrusting in all the way to fill her up. "You're so wet and swollen. It feels fucking awesome."

She'd given up scolding him for embarrassing her. Instead she met him thrust for thrust, moving her hips to welcome him deeper, once again sensation overtaking her until all her concentration seemed centered on the nerve endings between her legs and on the tips of her breasts. This was heaven, absolute heaven, and she couldn't believe she was going to have to let him go. She couldn't see herself ever sleeping with another guy. No man would match up to him, ever.

For a while he made love to her tenderly, taking the time to make sure her arousal grew with his. But gradually his movements became firmer as his body began to take over, instinct replacing his natural urge to stay gentle. She welcomed it, though, recognizing the approach of his climax and loving the way he became driven more by instinct and need and desire.

It was the first time they'd made love in the missionary position, but this was nothing like how it had been with Michael, with him either closing his eyes to shut her out or looking over her shoulder, concentrating on his body and almost ignoring the person underneath. Felix pushed himself up on his strong arms, kneeling beneath her, and she melted at the mixture of hot desire and tenderness in his eyes. He fixed his gaze on hers, dropping his head occasionally to capture her lips with a heated kiss, and she felt overwhelmed by him, as if this was her whole world, and he was everything, everywhere.

She widened her legs and let him take her hard and fast as he wanted, and as he finally came, she tightened on him, an orgasm claiming her for the third time that evening, and they clenched around each other, locked in blissful sensations, like a marble carving of two lovers in the heat of passion.

Chapter Forty-Nine

"At what point," Felix said, drawing on Coco's stomach and thinking how soft and creamy her skin was, "did you realize we were alone?"

She rolled her head to look at him lazily. "When you took the blindfold off."

He stared at her, shocked, only understanding when she started giggling that she was joking. "Tease."

"Serves you right." She stretched and yawned. "I have to admit, I wasn't a hundred percent sure. But it was that which was so exciting, I suppose. The knowing and not knowing at the same time."

He kissed her cheek. "I'm glad you enjoyed yourself."

"That's the understatement of the year." She grinned.

"I suppose two orgasms in one night isn't the worst thing in the world."

She met his gaze and a wry smile twisted her lips. "Um, well, three actually."

He raised his eyebrows. "Three? When?"

"While you were in my mouth." She looked down. Pink stained her cheeks.

No wonder she'd been so wet when he started using the vibrators on her. He gave a small shake of his head and trailed his fingers down her body. "You're a complete sex kitten, you know that?"

She giggled again. "I like being called that."

"It's true. You're quite a hussy actually."

Her eyes widened and she gave him a playful smack. "Am not!"

"Says the woman who wasn't a hundred percent sure that she wasn't being fucked in front of a room full of men."

"Felix!"

He laughed and pulled her into his arms. "We should really move into the bedroom, but I'm so comfortable..." He'd drawn the quilt she'd knelt on over them, pulled some cushions off the couch, and turned off the music, and they were curled up now in the semi-darkness, lit only by the lights of the city through the open curtains.

"Let's stay here." She snuggled up to him.

"Okay."

She rested her head on his shoulder, and he enjoyed the feel of her pressed against him, the silkiness of her hair where it flowed over his shoulder. He tangled his fingers in it and lifted it to his nose, inhaling the smell of coconut from her shampoo.

"I'm so glad we met up again." She kissed his chest. "I've thought about you all day."

"Me too," he said honestly.

"What have you been up to?"

He hesitated, not wanting to bring work into the room, but not wanting to lie to her either. "The case."

"Oh. Have you come to a decision?"

He had, but he didn't want to talk about it. "Almost."

She lifted up, put a hand on his chest, then rested her chin on it. They lay quietly for a moment. He said nothing, but he could feel her brain working as she debated whether to tell him something. Then she raised her head. "I have a confession to make."

He studied her, suddenly uneasy. "Oh?"

"Yes." She pushed herself up to a sitting position, her arms around her knees, still wrapped in the duvet. "I should have told you ages ago, but, well, I've never told anybody." She examined her fingernails.

He sat up with her, his stomach churning. "Coco, I don't know that this is the place…"

"I want to tell you." She met his eyes, her green ones shining. "I want to get it off my chest—to tell someone."

He said nothing, not wanting to hear what she had to say. But she'd already started talking, and there was nothing he could do to stop her.

"When I was seventeen," she said huskily, "I started work at McAllister Dell. I liked the job—I was really pleased to get it fresh out of college. The main reason—and I haven't told you this before—but my father was a gambler. He died and left us terribly in debt."

Felix stared at her. "I didn't know."

"I didn't want you to know. The last time I saw him, he cried and begged for forgiveness. Made me promise to look after Mum. It was only after he'd died that I found out how much he owed. I've spent the last ten years paying it back."

Cold slithered down inside him. Suddenly it all made sense—her struggle to make ends meet, the tiny house she lived in, her guilt at letting someone else look after her mother. She must love and hate her father at the same time, he thought. No wonder she was so screwed up where men were concerned.

"Anyway," she continued, oblivious to his thoughts, "I was thrilled to get the job. As you know, it pays a lot better than, say, working as a secretary in a school, even though I was just a typist, in the general typing pool. But after six months I'd earned a reputation for being quick and accurate, and I was often called upon by the partners for special jobs. Well, one evening Peter Dell asked me to come into his office to work on a particularly urgent file."

"Coco..." He didn't want to hear details of her affair with Dell. The thought of her having sex with anyone else made him feel sick.

She carried on as if he hadn't spoken. "He sat next to me on the sofa and we talked about the file for a few minutes, and then he started talking more generally. He was funny, charming. He told me he'd liked me from the moment I started work at the firm, that he found me attractive, that he wanted me. I was a virgin, remember, fresh from Catholic school—I had no idea what was going on."

"Coco..."

She waved a hand, in full flow, seemingly unable, or unwilling, to stop herself. "It wasn't rape—I have to make that clear. I didn't try to stop him. But he seduced me, Felix. I was flattered at the attention, scared and excited to finally find out what all the fuss was about..." She ran a hand through her hair. He'd never felt so in love—or so fucking mad—as he did at that moment.

"He flattered me, made me think he was crazy about me. Like I was the love of his life, you know? But in the end, it wasn't that great. Now I know what it can be like—" and she gave him a brief smile, not seeming to realize how angry he was, "—I can see what I was to him—just a quick fuck. And it was quick. He didn't pay any attention to my needs at all. He took his pleasure and then pulled my skirt down and started talking about the case as if nothing had happened."

Felix was certain he was going to throw up. He got to his feet and went into the kitchen to pour himself a glass of water. Coco followed him, the duvet wrapped around her, so caught up in her memories that she didn't see his distress.

"I got upset, and he talked to me like I was eight years old. Told me I was a good girl and patted my knee. I swear if he'd had a bag of sweets under his desk, he'd have given me a lolly. He told me because I'd been so good, he'd speak to Mrs. Ingram and get me a promotion. Which meant more money. I wasn't stupid—I knew what had happened and that I should go straight to Christopher McAllister and tell him, or to Mrs. Ingram at least. But I knew it was possible they wouldn't believe me, and that I could lose my job over it. And I needed that money desperately. So I said nothing. And I've kept it a secret ever since."

She studied him, her green eyes pleading for him to understand. "I know I should have told you earlier, and I'm sorry I couldn't. But I think you should know, now that you have to make a decision."

He went to drink from his glass of water, but his throat had a lump in it, and he put the glass down, untouched. His chest heaved. "Why now?" He glared at her. "Why tell me now?"

Her eyes grew cool. "So you could use the information to make an informed decision."

He put his hands on his hips. "You can't throw that at me at the eleventh hour, straight after we've had sex, and expect me to just add that into the evidence."

She blinked, startled by his words. "Why not?"

"Because it's not fair, Coco."

"To whom?"

Irritation rose in him at her inability to understand. "To Dell."

Her eyes flared with anger. "Fuck Peter Dell."

"Well, it sounds like you've already done that."

The words were out before he could stop them. She turned without another word, walked over to her clothes, and started pulling them on.

"Coco…" He ran a hand through his hair. "Don't go."

She pulled on her panties and skirt, stuffed her bra in her purse and yanked on her blouse. He caught her arm. "Coco, please…"

She tore it free and turned on him. Tears sparkled in her eyes. "I've never told anyone that," she bit. "It's personal and private. But

I told you because you were the one person who could finally help me give that bastard the outcome he deserves. And you won't do anything because it's not fucking *fair*?" Her voice rose to a shout at the end.

"Don't be so bloody black and white." He huffed with exasperation as she walked to the door and opened it. "Come back, for God's sake!"

She walked out without another word and strode down the corridor. He walked after her and caught her arm. "Coco!"

She turned and gasped at the sight of him. "Felix! Get some clothes on, for crying out loud."

He'd forgotten he was naked. "All right, but wait for me, will you?" He let her arm go to turn to the door, but she continued walking, and he cursed under his breath. He went back to his room and pushed the handle—but the door had locked.

"Fuck!" He yelled and kicked the door, then stood there, hands on hips again, as the elevator doors closed and Coco vanished.

At the same time, the doors of the elevator next to hers opened and an elderly couple walked out and down the corridor toward him. He covered himself with his hands and gave them a bright smile as they stopped and stared. "Good evening," he said in as calm a voice as he could manage, trying to pretend he wasn't standing there with his arse on show. "I don't suppose I could ask you a favor and get you to call the front desk for me?"

Chapter Fifty

Coco sat in the chair with her notepad perched on her knee, her back ramrod straight, her heart pounding. The boardroom was almost full. For this final meeting at which Felix was to present his verdict, nearly all the Wellington partners were present, including Christopher McAllister and Peter Dell. Rob Drake was the only non-partner present, along with herself.

Coco hadn't wanted to be there, but Christopher had asked her to take minutes, and even though she'd protested she was busy and another secretary could just as easily take her place, he'd insisted that because of the sensitive nature of the case he wanted the office manager there, and she couldn't think of a good reason to refuse.

Sasha wasn't there. The results would be revealed to her once Felix had announced his findings and the board had discussed the relevant course of action, depending on whether he found Dell innocent, or whether he thought Sasha had lied.

Coco fidgeted with her pencil. After she'd walked out of the hotel, she'd caught a taxi home, half expecting Felix to be right behind her, but it had been almost half an hour before he'd finally rung. She'd answered curtly, yelled accusations down the phone, and their brief conversation had ended abruptly when she hung up and threw the phone across the room.

He hadn't called back.

She couldn't blame him, really.

She'd hardly slept a wink all night. Her brain went around in circles, thinking that maybe it was all for the best they'd ended on a sour note, because at least she wouldn't be lying there for months picturing his smile and remembering how wonderful he'd been, but that had just made her picture his smile and remember how wonderful he'd been, and then she'd burst into tears and sobbed into her pillow.

She'd woken with red, puffy eyes and had spent half an hour trying to cover the dark rings with foundation before admitting defeat. And now she had to sit through this damned hearing. She couldn't wait until the day was over, the case was done and dusted, and he'd finally flown back to Auckland.

The thought made her want to lie on the floor and scream like a two-year-old who'd been told she couldn't have a chocolate bar.

The door opened, and she glanced up briefly as Felix entered. Damn, but the man looked good. He wore a suit she hadn't seen him in before, charcoal grey, with a crisp white shirt that looked fresh out of the packet, a blue and grey silk tie, and a blue handkerchief sticking out of his top pocket. His cufflinks matched his tiepin, and his dark hair was neat with just the right amount of fashionable ruffle at the front. He looked sharp enough to cut yourself on, sexy enough to eat, and she could have burst into tears there and then.

She didn't, though. She swallowed and concentrated on her pad, recording the names of everyone present as he took his seat next to her. His aftershave wafted across, and she couldn't stop herself breathing it in, her senses stirring at the memory of the way it had filled her nostrils when he'd made love to her, along with the feel of his hands on her skin, his lips on hers.

She closed her eyes briefly. *Focus, Veronica.* Today, she'd left Coco at home. She was all Miss Stark in this meeting, and she had to remember that.

Felix placed his iPad on the table, but he didn't turn it on. He nodded to the two senior partners, but he didn't sit.

He didn't look at her, either.

"Thank you all for coming," he said. He didn't seem nervous, and she remembered that he did this for a living, standing up in front of strangers and discussing facts and findings all the time. He slid his left hand into his pocket, but as usual he gestured with his right, the single signet ring on his third finger glinting in the electric light. She remembered that hand sliding up her thigh, the ring bright against her pale skin, and shivered.

"I might as well get straight to the point as you're all busy men," he said. Was it her imagination, or had he slightly emphasized the word men? The one woman partner was still on holiday. "I've spoken to all of you here individually, and I've also interviewed a good portion of the rest of the staff of the Wellington branch, including all the secretaries who worked with Miss De Langen. I've also spoken to Miss De Langen, in the presence of Mr. Drake and Miss Stark."

His deep voice stroked over her nerve endings, and her heart rate increased at the memory of him whispering highly erotic things in her ear. Then she blinked as the memory vanished, and only the smart, aloof lawyer remained, formal and professional.

He hesitated and straightened the iPad on the desk. "This hasn't been an easy task." He glanced over at Christopher, who sat with one elbow on the arm of the chair, his hand covering his mouth, masking any emotion he might be feeling. "And I suspect you knew that would be the case. Why you decided to appoint me, I have no idea. I thought you liked me." Laughter rippled around the room. Felix smiled wryly and cleared his throat. He didn't run his hand through his hair, but he did straighten his jacket and brush at an imaginary speck of dust. Perhaps he *was* nervous, then. Just trying not to show it.

As he smoothed down his tie, however, she saw that his gaze was fixed on the table, and realized the gestures were automatic, reflecting the fact that he was working through what to say next. He continued, "It became clear to me on entering the Wellington branch that the office has one foot firmly in the past. This is reflected in the ratio of male to female partners, as well as in the office's high expense accounts, company cars, and considerably large overheads."

"We didn't ask you to give us a report on the whole branch," Jack Lawson snapped.

"I know," Felix said smoothly, "and I'm telling you this not because it's my personal opinion that it needs dragging into the twenty-first century—although that is my opinion—but because it has a direct bearing on the case. The fact that all but one of the partners is male, and all but one of those is aged over fifty, has given the office an extremely 'old school' atmosphere, even down to the décor. Secretaries are seen as little more than human typewriters, there for the partners to use as they wish, and I'm afraid that view has also spilled over on a personal level where Mr. Dell is concerned."

Intakes of breath sounded from around the table. Coco looked up, startled by his direct words. Peter glared at Felix, but Felix returned his gaze calmly, unperturbed. "Mr. Dell, I have no doubt whatsoever that your behavior with regard to sexual relationships within this office has been far from exemplary. Two secretaries admitted to having had a sexual relationship with you, and several more intimated the same, although clearly they were nervous about admitting it. Other people have stated they know of seven or eight relationships that you've carried out with other staff members. I understand that all of these women were willing to have a relationship with you, but that you initiated the first contact each time, and that you ended the liaison on each occasion. These relationships were conducted mainly outside of the office, usually at weekends, often during trips away from the city."

Coco finished writing and glanced around the room again. The majority of the partners were either frowning or looking startled, clearly unaware of Peter's behavior. However, Jack Lawson and a couple of others stared stonily at the table. They knew, she thought. Had they known about what had happened to her? Had Peter boasted about it to them at the time?

Felix looked at his iPad and straightened it again. "I also have it on good authority that, some time ago, you seduced a very young secretary in your office."

Coco's heart nearly bounced out of her chest and along the table. Her pencil slipped on the paper, and she had to bite her lip to stop herself from exclaiming out loud. She glanced up, straight into the eyes of Rob Drake. He looked startled, and then his eyes filled with pity as he obviously recognized in her expression the confirmation that Felix was indeed talking about her. Coco dropped her gaze again, hoping she didn't pass out. What else was Felix going to say?

"The young lady was seventeen," he continued, "just out of secretarial school. She'd never had a sexual partner, and was innocent where men were concerned. There is no suggestion of rape, but it seems clear to me that the idea to sleep together was yours, and you used your age and your position of authority to charm and seduce this young woman into doing something that she later regretted."

Coco felt sick. Her chest heaved, and she didn't dare look up in case Peter was glaring at her. Her hand shook slightly on the paper, and she gripped the pencil harder to try to stop it.

"After the incident," Felix continued, "as an incentive to keep quiet, you also offered her promotion, which she took because she needed the money. I personally believe she now regrets not speaking up at the time. I wish she had done so because this kind of behavior by men should not be seen to be acceptable. However, I understand her reasons for keeping silent, and I applaud her courage in finally coming forward and confessing what happened."

Tears came into Coco's eyes and she swallowed down the lump in her throat. Glancing up quickly, she saw several pairs of eyes on her, including Christopher's, and knew it was obvious that she was the secretary who Felix was talking about. Their expressions held sympathy and pity, and she lowered her gaze again, feeling a strange weight lift off her chest at the thought that it was finally out in the open.

Felix cleared his throat. "As I said, your behavior toward women at this firm has been far from exemplary. However, the purpose of this investigation was to discover the truth behind the claim made by Miss De Langen that you made unwanted sexual advances toward her in the office. And after much thought, I've come to the conclusion that you are innocent of this allegation."

Chapter Fifty-One

Felix was unable to avoid a dramatic pause at the end of his findings. He was, after all, a performer, and it came naturally to him to play up to the audience, especially when he'd led them down a particular path, and they were expecting a different outcome.

Part of his pause, however, was due to the sweep of relief he felt at finally having come to a decision. He'd wrangled with himself all weekend—especially after Coco's little confession—his personal dislike of Dell and the man's frankly disgusting behavior toward women vying with his natural urge to do things right and proper.

Plus, of course, he knew that in finding Dell innocent, he'd destroyed any future chance of a relationship with Coco. She sat next to him, stiff-backed and oozing resentment, anger rolling off her in waves. She'd made her confession to him hoping it would help him conclude that Dell was guilty. No matter what evidence he put forward to the contrary, she would see it as a betrayal of her confidence, and she would take it personally, believing that firstly he didn't care about her enough to give her the punishment she felt Dell deserved for what he'd done to her, and secondly that Felix had been coerced by Christopher and the other partners to find Dell innocent. She was smart, but Dell had done a lot of damage with that one brief seduction, and she was too emotionally invested to put her feelings aside and look at the case dispassionately.

Felix had gone through all this in the night, having slept hardly at all, wanting to put his better self aside and throw the book at Dell for what he'd done to her, for what he'd done to all these women. He despised the man and wanted him to suffer, but even in spite of the fact that Felix knew he'd fallen in love with Coco and he could quite easily have beaten Dell to a pulp for seducing her, he couldn't go against his belief that the truth was more important than anything else, even more so than his own happiness.

Still, that hadn't stopped him sowing the seeds of Dell's gross misbehavior to the other partners. He certainly wasn't going to let the man get away with it, and he was hanging onto the hope that now it had come to light, the partners would deal with the man appropriately and bring about some small form of justice.

But for now, he had to concentrate on the matter at hand, and he shut out the thought of the only woman he'd loved since Lindsey died—and drew his professionalism around him like a cloak, focusing instead on the man sitting opposite him, who looked as surprised as everyone else at his announcement.

"There are several reasons that I believe Miss De Langen's accusations to be false," he continued. "Firstly, several other secretaries—as well as Miss Stark—corroborated Mr. Dell's claim that he did not approach Sasha directly that evening to ask for help, but merely put the request to the whole room. Miss De Langen then said she couldn't remember exactly what had happened, but the fact that she changed her story suggested to me it was possible there were other areas where she wasn't telling the truth.

"Another piece of evidence she used as proof for Mr. Dell's guilt was that he asked her to retype a file that had already been sent to him in a suitable format for use at court. She claimed Mr. Dell had deleted this file—however, unknown to Mr. Dell, I asked the firm's IT expert to run an analysis of his machine and found no evidence that he had deleted any such file, and no evidence that he had received an email containing such a file in the first place."

Dell looked both indignant and relieved, and Felix hid a smile.

He smoothed down his tie, thinking about the final point. He'd wondered whether to raise the last issue, unwilling to spread rumors about Sasha's private life, but he sincerely believed she had lied to him and that Dell had not made unwanted advances to her. And even though Dell's behavior repulsed him, it didn't warrant a woman spreading lies about him and maybe even ruining his career, and therefore she hadn't earned the right to ask him to keep what she'd told him a secret.

"The last point, the one that has given me most concern, is that Miss De Langen told Miss Stark and me when we visited her at her house that the reason she couldn't possibly have been the one to initiate the contact with Mr. Dell was because she is gay."

There was a general gasp around the table. Dell just gave a humorless snort.

"I've struggled with this," Felix continued, "because of course it's something that's very difficult to disprove. Sasha doesn't appear to have any friends at the firm, and nobody has heard her talk about any partner, male or female. But my instincts tell me she is lying. Two other secretaries have said they've watched her talk to Mr. Dell and, whilst they agree she doesn't particularly dress to attract attention, they said her manner has been mildly flirtatious, and if they were pushed they would say they thought she was attracted to him. Another secretary also saw Sasha in town with a man, her arm through his. We can't be sure it was her partner—it might have been a member of her family. It does, however, give me reasonable doubt.

"Therefore, it is my conclusion that Mr. Dell did not make sexual advances to Miss De Langen. The most he was probably guilty of was perhaps flirting with her and making her think she stood a chance, especially considering his track record with women at the firm." He was unable to keep the sarcasm out of his voice, and he was relieved to see Christopher's mouth lift in a brief smile. "But that in itself isn't a crime, and I don't believe Mr. Dell was sexually interested in Sasha. I believe that she made advances to him, and he refused her, and the embarrassment and anger at being scorned prompted her to create a false charge against him."

Peter Dell blew out a long, slow breath. The other partners began murmuring amongst themselves. Christopher McAllister said, "So what recourse would you suggest for the way forward, Felix?"

"I would suggest that Miss De Langen be given an official warning and given the option of moving to another department or branch, or resigning."

"And for Mr. Dell?"

Felix met Christopher's eyes. He still couldn't read anything in them. Was Christopher annoyed at his findings, or relieved? "In this particular case, I don't believe Mr. Dell has done anything wrong. However, his past behavior proves to me that his attitude toward the women in this firm needs to be addressed." Should he stop there? Christopher's eyes gleamed, and Felix decided to take the chance. "To be honest, I believe the Wellington branch to be failing in projecting the image that McAllister Dell as a whole should present to the public if it wishes to stay one of the most successful New Zealand law businesses: that of a forward-thinking, modern law firm that puts the needs of its customers first, and I believe Mr. Dell's leadership at the branch is probably the main influence behind this stagnation."

The three partners who had obviously been aware of Dell's relationships with the secretaries glared at him, but the others looked interested, and Felix thought they were probably well aware of the failure of the branch to meet its overheads. "What would you suggest to rectify this?" asked one of the slightly younger men.

"A radical overhaul," Felix said. "Either a redecoration of the offices or a move to a new building. A slash in the expense accounts. A complete renovation of the secretarial system to keep things as digital as possible. And someone at the helm who's prepared to accept that women form half of the population and therefore should represent as near that percentage as possible at the higher levels." A couple of the partners nodded, and he let out the breath he hadn't realized he'd been holding.

"Do you have anyone in mind to carry out these renovations?" Jack's voice dripped with sarcasm, as if he expected Felix to put himself forward for the role.

Felix nodded. "I believe Rob Drake would make an excellent partner and business manager for the firm." Rob looked startled. "He's astute and forward thinking, flexible and motivated. I also think Miss Stark would be an excellent choice to carry out the move to digital." It wasn't false praise, nor an attempt to get back into her good books—he was aware that bird had long since flown. But it was the truth. She was smart and not averse to technology, and he knew instinctively she'd enjoy taking on the task.

Christopher nodded. "Thank you, Felix. If I may now ask everyone who isn't a partner to leave the room, we'll discuss the situation and let you know our thoughts."

Felix picked up his iPad and headed for the door. He held it open for Rob, and then for Coco, who walked past without looking up at him.

He closed the door behind him. "Coco, wait." She ignored him and walked off. He strode past Rob to her and caught her arm. "Please."

She stopped and turned to him, eyes blazing, twin spots of scarlet on her cheekbones. "Let me go."

He released her arm. "Don't be angry with me."

"I don't believe you," she snapped. "He deserved to be punished, and you've practically said I and all the women he treated like shit deserved it."

He caught her arm again and maneuvered her into the smaller boardroom next door, casting an apologetic glance at Rob, who just nodded and closed the door behind them. She ripped her arm away, but to his relief she remained in the room, even though her eyes blazed.

"That's bullshit," he said. "Nobody thinks that at all."

"You don't know that." Now she looked upset and close to tears. "They all know you were talking about me, and now they think I asked for it—either that or I'm weak because I didn't complain. You've undermined the reputation I spent years building up."

"Coco, for God's sake." Please don't let that be true. "One or two of them might be sympathetic to Dell but the majority had no idea what was going on, I could tell by their faces."

She looked into his eyes, hurt glimmering in their depths. "I really thought you had feelings for me."

"I do. You know I do. But this wasn't about us. I couldn't find Dell guilty just because I was in love with his office manager and I felt sorry for her."

She stared at him, and he realized it was the first time he'd said he loved her.

Then she shook her head as if dismissing the point. "Of *course* it was about us. You knew about all his other conquests and what he'd done to me. It was the perfect opportunity to make him pay, but obviously your feelings weren't strong enough to give you the courage to go through with it."

Irritation rose inside him. "That's unfair. Sasha lied, Coco. Whatever Dell has done in the past, I couldn't let her get away with such an untruth. And when it comes down to it, Dell hasn't done anything legally wrong. Morally—yes. He's an adulterer, and he obviously uses his position of authority to charm women into sleeping with him. But that's not a crime, sweetheart. I understand your resentment toward him because I feel the same, but I can't punish a man just because I dislike him."

She bit her lip. Her shoulders slumped. She understood. She wasn't stupid, and she knew he couldn't have gone against his conscience. That wasn't what this was about. This was about the fact that he was leaving, and neither of them wanted to end it, but they couldn't see a way out.

"Forget it," she said tiredly. "It's too late to do anything about it now. It's done and dusted." She gave him a brief, sad smile. "I had a good time with you, and I'm sorry it had to end this way. I wish you all the best for the future—I'm sure you'll be a big star. Mr. Sensational." Her lips twisted.

He stared at her, his stomach knotted. *I love you.* He wanted to say the words, but what was the point in delaying the inevitable?

Their eyes met, and he had a flash of memory, of her naked in his arms in the heat of passion, so passionate, so different from the cold woman standing before him now. And then Coco was gone and only Miss Stark remained, stiff, unyielding, and hard.

She turned and walked out of the door, and he didn't bother to stop her.

Chapter Fifty-Two

Coco sat on the bench overlooking the harbor and tipped her face up to the sun. There were only two days until Christmas, and the weather had warmed significantly over the past week. She wore a thin orange sundress and sandals, and although her hair wasn't in its usual bun, she'd still looped it up with a clip, finding the weather too hot to wear it loose around her neck.

It was still relatively early on Friday morning, not even ten o'clock, but usually she would have been at work several hours by now, already dealing with phone calls and customers and sorting out disputes amongst employees. For the past few days, however, since the hearing, she'd been on vacation, unable to summon the energy or the enthusiasm to return to work.

She'd have to go back eventually—she couldn't afford not to work. But she'd needed time to process the events of the previous weeks, and Christopher McAllister had somehow recognized this and granted her a week's holiday.

She'd thought she'd take the time to think things through, to purposefully process the sequence of events and their outcome, but in the end, she'd just spent the time *being*, drinking coffee and walking, her mind filled with memories of her time with Felix, her heart filled with sadness that he'd gone and the knowledge that she'd probably never see him again.

Eleanor hadn't mentioned moving out again since he left, and Coco was relieved, knowing that her mother saw her unhappiness and recognized that she couldn't deal with that problem at the moment.

Amy had returned from her holiday, heard about all the drama of the previous week at work, demanded to know what had been going on, and then had to deal with a sobbing Coco as it all came spilling out—what had happened when she was seventeen, the time she'd spent with Felix and how she felt about him, and what had happened after the hearing in the boardroom.

Christopher and the other partners had agreed with Felix's suggestion that Sasha be offered a position in another department, but she'd handed in her resignation immediately and left the same day, and they'd let her go without working her notice, glad to see the back of her.

What to do with Peter Dell and the Wellington branch had proved a trickier problem. On the surface, Peter had been exonerated, and therefore the reputation of the company was safe. However, Rob Drake rang her at home on the Monday evening to say that Christopher had announced that at the end of a decent period of time—maybe three months—he expected Peter to announce he was taking early retirement, and someone else would take over as head of the Wellington office.

The victory had tasted sour in Coco's mouth. She was glad he'd finally got his comeuppance, but it was a weak triumph—his transgressions would be swept under the carpet, and he was a rich enough man to be able to live a life of luxury until the day he died.

"I suppose the problem is that he didn't actually do anything legally wrong," Amy had said to her. "Many men wouldn't turn down sex if it was handed to them on a plate, and it sounds like everyone who had an affair with him went willingly."

Coco had had no reply to that. Amy's comment had stung, because she knew it could relate to her relationship with Felix, too. She'd handed herself on a plate to a young, virile, single male—of course he was going to say yes! No doubt he'd seen her claim of being sexually inexperienced as a challenge. What a boost to his ego to teach her the ways of love. Yes, he'd said he'd fallen in love with her, and she knew it was unfair to blame him for not finding Dell guilty just to please her, but she didn't know whether she could believe him. If he'd loved her, wouldn't he have found a way for them to be together?

Then she'd cried again, because she knew it was wrong to blame him for what had happened between them. He'd flown back to Auckland the afternoon after he delivered his findings, clearly unwilling to stay there once the deed was done. His career was in Auckland and her mother was in Wellington, and nobody could be blamed for that. It was unfortunate, as well as magical, the way they'd felt about each other after such a brief time, and all she could do was treasure those memories and be glad that she'd experienced real love, even though it had been so brief.

She closed her eyes and let the sun warm her lids. She'd cried so much over the past few days, she hadn't thought there were any tears left, but they still threatened to fall.

The bench she was sitting on creaked as someone sat beside her, and she cursed under her breath. The quay was practically empty and there were a dozen benches along the path—couldn't the person have picked somewhere else to sit?

She opened her eyes to see whether an impatient glare would send the person on their way, and then stared.

It was Felix, sitting there with one arm hooked over the back of the seat, watching her.

Her heart banged against her ribs, and she couldn't stop the sharp intake of breath and the "Oh!" of surprise spilling from her lips.

His warm brown eyes surveyed her. "Hey."

She scrambled to gather her wits and sat up straighter, blinking against the bright sunlight. "Hey."

For a moment, his gaze moved across her with a gentle caress that took her breath away, and then he looked out to sea, watching the gannets diving into the waves to emerge with fish in their beaks.

She supposed she should be angry, or resentful, or feel something negative at the thought that she'd been trying to move on and now he'd upset the applecart of her emotions once again, but all she could summon was a flood of relief and pleasure at the sight of him. He looked young and hot in his Levis and an open-necked white shirt, his dark hair more ruffled than usual, as if he'd spent a while running his hands through it. The thought that maybe he was more nervous than he looked at seeing her again gave her courage to ask, "What are you doing here?"

"Looking for you." His gaze came back to her. He still didn't smile.

"How did you know I was here?"

"I went to your house. Your mum said you'd been walking a lot lately." Emotion flickered in his eyes, but it was gone before she could catch it.

They sat silently for a while. It was as if there was so much to say, they didn't know where to start. Coco watched the waves, then risked a glimpse back at him. He continued to look at her, thoughtful and serious, and she could tell by the way he moved a hand down his shirt from button to button as if checking they were all done up that he was on autopilot, thinking about what to say.

In the end, however, all he said was, "Nice to be out in the old currant bun, eh?"

"I'm guessing you mean the sun." She smiled wryly. "Enough of the small talk. Felix, for God's sake. Spit it out."

That made the corner of his mouth quirk up. "Yes, Miss Stark."

She laughed and looked down at the floor. "Miss Stark's gone for good, I'm afraid. Somehow half the staff knows my nickname's Coco, and I think the partners look at me quite differently now they see me as a real person and not as the Dragon."

His smile faded. "I'm sorry for any part I've played in that."

She shrugged. "It wasn't your fault. You were right. We were all stuck in the Stone Age there. Something had to change."

"Yeah," he said. "About that."

She looked up at him. "What?"

"I have a proposition for you."

Coco's eyes widened and her heart pounded.

That made Felix grin. "Actually I wasn't referring to that kind of proposition—yet. It's about McAllister Dell."

She blinked and struggled to concentrate, her head spinning at his use of the word yet. "What do you mean?"

He sighed and looked out to sea again. "I flew home on Monday. I was like a bear with a sore head for the rest of the day, and the whole of Tuesday and Wednesday. By Thursday afternoon, I finally admitted why to myself." His gaze came back to her. "I missed you."

She held her breath. "Oh."

He studied her mouth for a moment, making her moisten her lips nervously, and then he watched the waves again. "While I was in Wellington, I kept telling myself it was ridiculous to jack in my whole career for a girl I'd only known for a week. Obviously, I was infatuated—I had a teenage-style crush. It was the only explanation. I couldn't possibly be in love after such a short time."

Her heart pounded, but she made herself sit still and listen.

"And I realized," he continued, "that even if it was only an infatuation, that didn't mean it wouldn't or couldn't develop into something more." He looked back at her again, and this time turned on the bench to face her, his face intense with his need to make her understand. "I haven't felt this way about anyone else since Lindsey. I loved her, and I thought I'd never feel that way about a girl ever again, but when I look at you…" He reached out a hand and brushed the back of his fingers against her cheek. "It feels as if something's moving beneath my feet, as if tectonic plates are shifting."

"The earth moved for me too," she said breathlessly, then cursed herself for sounding glib.

But he just smiled. "I know. And that made me decide—I had to do something, to give us a chance. I had to make a gesture to show you how serious I was about you—to show you that I thought we could work. So I went in to see Christopher, and I handed in my resignation."

Coco stared at him in horror. "Felix, no!"

He held up a hand. "Hold on. I was fully prepared to leave there and then, but he made me sit down. We talked for ages. I ended up telling him everything, about Lindsey, about you… And he understood. Coco, he knew all about Peter. I don't think he knew about the two of you, but he certainly knew what Peter was like. That was why he asked me to investigate him. He wanted Peter to be found guilty."

His lips twisted in a wry smile. "He didn't bank on the fact that I'd find him innocent. He'd assumed Dell had sexually harassed Sasha and that I'd come to that conclusion. I think I made things more difficult by deciding he hadn't done it. But the outcome was that the rest of the board decided to force him to take early retirement, and even though Peter kind of gets away with it, at least it means the company saves face."

She nodded. "I understand."

"But he had an offer for me. Coco, he wants me to move to Wellington. Four older partners are also taking early retirement, including Jack Lawson. The board have agreed to make Rob Drake and me partners, and they want us to co-manage the Wellington branch and drag its sorry arse into the twenty-first century. We're to have a budget to redecorate it however we see fit. And they want you to help us digitalize everything and make it into a proper modern office."

She stared at him, her head spinning. "Jesus."

"I know. He's going to speak to you about it when you return to work."

She shook her head, amazed at the turn of events. "What do you think?"

"I'm flattered, of course. It would be an exciting challenge." He leaned forward and took her hand. "But that's why I'm here. I said I had to talk to you first."

Her mouth had gone dry, and she swallowed several times, trying to concentrate on what he'd said. But her mind just kept coming back to the fact that he'd said he was moving to Wellington. "What do you need to talk to me about?"

A look of impatient amusement crossed his face. "Honey, Wellington is your home. You practically run the branch as it is on your own. I'm not going to march into the city and just take over. You've got to want it too."

Was he asking her permission to take the job? Was that all?

"That's not all," he said as if reading her mind. He bent his head and kissed her fingers. "I like my job. I'm happy at Auckland. My making partner isn't reliant on moving here. The new job would be fun, but, sweetheart, that wouldn't be why I'd move here. Part of the reason Christopher offered me the job was because you're here. I'd move here to be with you."

"With me?" She blinked stupidly. "At work?"

"Coco…" He sighed. Then, as if deciding words weren't going to work, he pulled her into his arms and lowered his lips to hers.

She warmed from the top of her head to the tips of her toes as his lips moved across hers tenderly, then more passionately as she responded, and when her mouth opened and his tongue brushed against her own, the heat kindled between them as quickly as if they'd never been apart. By the time they pulled apart, they were both breathing heavily.

"We've known each other such a small amount of time," he said, looking deeply into her eyes. "And I know it's probably premature and stupid, but I don't care, I'm going to say it anyway. I love you, and I want to get to know you. I'm willing to do it properly if you'd rather. Go out on dates, get to know one another slowly, make sure we're certain before we take it further."

He dropped his hand and ferreted around in the pocket of his Levis. And extracted a small navy blue velvet box. He opened it to show a huge sparkling diamond solitaire. "I don't know what your answer's going to be. I wouldn't be surprised if you told me to fuck off, although after that kiss I'm beginning to think that won't be your answer. But I'd like more. I'd like to move in with you. I'd like to get a place together so we can share the same bed and wake up every morning together, because I can't bear to be apart from you again."

He spoke more quickly now, as if he had to get the words out before he forgot what he was going to say. "I'd like to get somewhere with an annex, a separate apartment, for your mother, and then we could pay for her to be cared for full time, so you could call in whenever you wanted but also have the freedom to come and go as you pleased because I think she'd like that, but if you'd rather she lived with us, I don't mind." He kissed her fingers. "I'd like to marry you, to have children with you, to be with you forever. But I'm afraid to ask in case you say no, because I know it's ridiculous to ask you so early, so all I shall say right now is that I'd like you to wear my ring and be mine, and think about it. Would you do that for me?" He took the ring out of the box and held it out to her.

Coco stared at it. The diamond glittered in the sunlight.

He waited for a moment. Then, slowly, his hand dropped into his lap. "Yeah," he said. "I guess that was a bit overpowering."

Her brain, which had ground to a halt, suddenly clicked into gear, and she gasped. "Felix!" She caught his hand and brought it back up in front of her. "Oh my God, you are kidding me?"

His eyes lit up. "You like it?"

"Oh my God, oh my God, oh my God."

He laughed and slid it onto her finger. "If it's too big we can get it resized."

"It's perfect." She held it up and watched it sparkle.

"No, no, no." He pulled her into his arms. "Please don't cry. This is supposed to be a happy moment."

"I am happy." Tears poured down her face. "I know it's stupid too and that I can't possibly love you, but I do, I do, and I want to be with you too."

He lifted her chin and kissed her lips. "I want to curl up with you at night and wake up with you. I want to be able to explore our exotic fantasies every day."

"Every day?"

"Twice a day. Three times a day." He kissed her again. "I want to stand in the aisle next to you in a whistle and tell everyone—"

"A whistle?"

"And flute. A suit, honey. And tell everyone I love you and that I'm going to look after you for the rest of my life."

"Don't," she sobbed. "I can't bear it."

He kissed her mouth, her cheeks, her eyelids. "Do you think we can work together? Could you bear to put up with me all day as well as all evening?"

"I could."

"You'll be sick of the sight of me within a week."

"Felix…" She threw her arms around his neck. He was there, he was really there—she wasn't dreaming—and he wanted her, he loved her. She buried her face in his neck and breathed in the smell that was all him, of manly aftershave, coffee and muffins and warm, hunky man. "I love you."

"I love you too." And he held her tightly, while the currant bun beamed down on them until their skin was as warm as their hearts.

The Four Seasons

Book 1: Seducing Summer
Book 2: Tempting Autumn
Book 3: Bewitching Winter
Book 4: Persuading Spring

Find out what happens next in Gene's story – Seducing Summer. Available from most major retailers.

Excerpt – Prologue – Five years ago

"Whose stupid idea was this?" Neve grumbled.

Callie Summer glanced to her right and chuckled at the sight of her friend tugging up the bodice of her bridesmaid's dress. "Will you stop fidgeting? You've got a ton of tit tape on—it's not going to fall down."

"One sneeze," Neve stated, "and I swear my boobs will pop out."

"Along with the best man's eyes," Bridget said.

Neve snorted, and the rest of the bridesmaids laughed. The best man, Rhett, appeared to have the hots for Neve. They'd been teasing her all morning that he'd make a move on her by the end of the day.

"I understand why men can't take their eyes off us. I think we look fantastic," Rowan said.

Callie had to agree. When Rowan's twin sister had first told the four of them that she wanted them to be bridesmaids at her wedding, they'd all been super excited, as none of them had been a bridesmaid before. Then Willow had revealed that the wedding was to take place in Matamata, at one of the sets from the movie *The Lord of the Rings*.

"Please don't say you want us to dress up as hobbits," Bridget had begged.

"No, silly." Willow had rolled her eyes. "I thought you could be the four seasons, with gorgeous, flowing Elven dresses."

"There are six seasons in the Elven year," Liam, the groom-to-be, had pointed out.

Willow had thumped him. "We're not making a Tolkien documentary. I just want them to look beautiful."

"I'd rather be an orc than wear a bridesmaid's gown," Neve had grumbled. "Can't I have a pantsuit?"

But Willow had asked her sister to design their dresses, and as they stood together waiting for the photographer, Callie thought that even Neve couldn't deny what a marvelous job Rowan had done. All four gowns were the same style—simple and strapless with a tight bodice and a full-length satin skirt—but they differed in their color and in the pattern on the flowing layers of tulle.

With the surname Summer, Callie's choice of season had been obvious. She had a dress of sunshine yellow, and the tulle of her skirt bore a gold-and-orange pattern that looked great with her pale, English-rose complexion.

Between the four of them, they'd decided that Rowan should be autumn because the foliage of the tree after which she'd been named turned red at that time of year. A rich gold-and-red tulle covered her russet gown, complementing her brown hair.

"My name's Latin for snow," Neve had suggested. So she'd become winter, with a pale blue dress covered in a shimmering white tulle flecked with blue to make sure she looked different from the bride.

That left spring for Bridget, and as her nickname was Birdie they thought the season fitted her rather well. Tiny pink and purple flowers covered the tulle over her pastel pink dress.

Together, the four gowns made them look like a row of flowers, and Willow had cried when she'd first seen them all together at the rehearsal. Rowan had made her dress, too—a flowing white gown based on Galadriel's, with thousands of beads and glittering thread. She'd also made all their underwear—beautiful lacy, strapless bras and matching panties—and it was when Callie had stood in front of her mirror and admired the garments that she'd had a revelation.

"I've had an idea I want to talk to you all about," she said as they watched the photographer taking the final shots of the bride and groom. "I think we should go into business together."

The other three looked at her with raised eyebrows. "Doing what?" Neve asked. "Running a circus?"

"No, silly. The Four Seasons Lingerie Shop."

They all stared at her.

"What?" Bridget said.

"After we finish university, we should open a lingerie shop. Rowan can design the clothing, I'll manage the business side of things, Birdie—you can run the shop, and Neve can be in charge of promotion. She can hold naughty lingerie and sex toy parties and spread the word."

"I like it," Neve stated while the other two burst out laughing.

"You're serious." Rowan's smile faded when Callie didn't join in.

"Perfectly. Don't you think it would be fun? Between us, we have all the skills we'd need. We get on really well, and I'm sure we'd work well together, too. It would be fantastic. I can just see us all in five years' time—rich, successful businesswomen, happily married, babies on the way… It'll be great."

Rowan smiled, Bridget looked thoughtful, and Neve rolled her eyes, but Callie could see she'd sown the seeds.

She turned her gaze back to Willow and her new husband. The photographer had finished their shots and beckoned to the bridesmaids and best man to join them, so they all walked forward to surround the bride and groom. Callie watched Rhett bend his head and whisper something in Neve's ear. She shook her head, but a smile played on her lips.

Callie's stomach bubbled with excitement and hope. She knew the lingerie shop would be successful. With Rowan's artistic talent and the combined fashion and business knowledge the rest of them were amassing from their university degrees, they'd make it work through sheer effort and determination.

All the girls were warm-hearted and sincere, and Callie knew it wouldn't be long before some decent guys snapped them up. Bridget had her eye on one of the ushers, Callie herself had plans to chat up the hot guy in charge of the catering, and even Rowan—with all her hang-ups—was casting sidelong glances at one of Liam's cousins.

Five years, she thought as the photographer gestured for them all to move closer together. It would be five years, maximum, before their business was super successful, and they'd all settled down with roses around the door and babies in their arms. *Just wait and see.*

MR. SENSATIONAL

Chapter One – Present Day

Callie sat at her desk, her chin in her hands, and read the email that had just popped up on her computer screen. It was from Willow, thanking Callie for the anniversary card she'd sent the previous week.

"I can't believe Liam and I have been married five years," the email read. "Where does the time go? And yes, baby's due on February 29th—typical! The poor thing will only have a birthday every four years. Hey, I know my baby shower is going to be the day before Valentine's Day, but I really hope you can come."

Yeah, Callie thought, she'd go. It wasn't as if she had anything better to do.

She pushed her chair away and walked over to stand at the window of her office, looking down at the bustling city center of Wellington, capital of New Zealand. Many of the shop windows were decorated with red hearts and Valentine's Day gifts, and the usually quiet boutique chocolate shop across the pedestrianized high street had a queue out the door.

Love was in the air. Allegedly, anyway. Callie had yet to see any evidence of the fat baby archer and his bow.

So much for her predictions on the day of Willow's wedding. She couldn't have been more wrong if she'd tried. She sighed as she contemplated not just her own disastrous love life, but also the failed relationships of her three friends. Maybe she'd jinxed them with her prophecies.

Neve's brief fling with Rhett had ended abruptly—Callie had never discovered why, and since then Neve had moved from one relationship to another without any sign of them being serious. Rowan had proven useless with men, having no clue as to what made them tick, and had yet to stay with any guy for more than a few months. Bridget's on-off relationship with her boyfriend seemed more off than on lately. None of them appeared close to settling down and having families.

Callie's own love life also seemed doomed. After a couple of failed relationships, she'd eventually moved in with Jamie, and she'd thought things were going well right up until the moment she'd walked in on him in bed with his secretary.

Her eyes stung, and she swallowed hard. She'd done her crying over Jamie Verne—over any man, in fact.

She lifted her chin. Not every prophecy she'd made had been wrong. The Four Seasons lingerie shop in Wellington had not only come to fruition, it had been hugely successful. They'd leased a shop toward the busy end of Cuba Street, and although it hadn't been cheap, it had proved to be a worthwhile investment, especially as it came with a couple of rooms above, from which Callie was able to run the business. As well as selling well-known brands of lingerie and swimwear, they distributed Rowan's own brand that specialized in lingerie for "real women," built on the belief that all women liked to wear pretty undergarments, no matter what their shape or size.

And now she was about to embark on the next phase of the business. Today was Thursday, and on Monday she was setting off for a countrywide tour of high street clothing shops to promote Rowan's Four Seasons brand of lingerie with the hope that a large proportion of the shops would agree to stock it. It was an ambitious move that could propel their brand from small scale to nationally recognized, and might even mean expansion to Australia and beyond.

She had far too much on her plate to even think about romance. She should have been thanking her lucky stars that Jamie had shown his true colors before she'd done anything really stupid like gotten married or—horror of horrors—fallen pregnant. Now she could concentrate on the business, which was what she was best at, when it came down to it. Finding love would stay at the bottom of her to-do list, where it belonged.

Checking her watch, she realized that several minutes had gone by since she'd buzzed Neve to send in the next interviewee. Becky, her heavily pregnant PA, had unfortunately had to start her maternity leave early when her blood pressure had shot up, and Neve was sitting in for a day or two until the temp agency came up with a replacement.

Callie turned and, to her surprise, saw someone waiting in the doorway.

She'd expected a middle-aged woman with graying hair, glasses on a lanyard, frumpy clothes, and possibly a hairy lip.

This person was neither middle-aged nor frumpy. He was about six-foot-two with short brown hair, and wearing what looked like a tailored charcoal three-piece suit with a sparkling white shirt and a stylish sky-blue tie. He stood with his hands behind his back, his head tipped a little to the side as he surveyed her, suggesting he'd been there for a while.

He was also the most gorgeous guy she'd seen in... well, possibly ever, if you liked your men hard and rather dangerous. He looked as if he could complete a million-dollar business deal for a piece of land, build a shelter on it with his bare hands, and drag a woman to it by her hair. Callie hadn't thought that kind of guy appealed to her, but she had to admit that if she'd ordered herself a late Christmas present, or an early Valentine's Day present, or indeed any kind of present, this was the kind of parcel she would have hoped for. All he needed was a bow tied around... somewhere interesting.

"Oh," she said, confused, and flustered at his steady gaze. "Can I help you?"

"I'm here for the interview."

She stared at him. Part of her was aware that her jaw was sagging, but her brain couldn't process the information he'd just given her.

He raised a hand to scratch his cheek. "Ma'am? Is there a problem?"

Ma'am. That one word melted her a little inside.

She looked at the name she'd scribbled on her notepad. "I understood that the next candidate was called Jean Bond." She looked back up, confused. "As in Simmons, Harlow. Miss Brodie—the Prime of."

"It's G-e-n-e," he clarified. "As in Hackman, Wilder. Kelly—who sings in the rain." He brushed a hand down himself, drawing her attention to his suit again and the undoubtedly male physique that lay beneath it. "I'm a guy, in case you hadn't noticed."

As it happened, Callie *had* noticed. And that was where the problem lay.

*

Available at most major retailers.

About The Author

Serenity Woods is a USA Today bestselling author. She lives in the sub-tropical Northland of New Zealand with her wonderful husband and gorgeous teenage son. She writes hot and sultry contemporary romances with a happy ever after, and would much rather immerse herself in reading or writing romance than do the dusting and ironing, which is why it's not a great idea to pop round if you have any allergies.

She is the author of over fifty romance novels. You can check them all out on her website.

Website: http://www.serenitywoodsromance.com
Facebook: http://www.facebook.com/serenitywoodsromance
Twitter: https://twitter.com/Serenity_Woods

Printed in Great Britain
by Amazon